❦ DULL MARGARET ❧

꙾

FANTAGRAPHICS BOOKS INC. 7563 Lake City Way NE Seattle, Washington, 98115
www.fantagraphics.com

Editor and Associate Publisher: Eric Reynolds • Book Design: Keeli McCarthy
Production: Paul Baresh • Publisher: Gary Groth

ISBN 978-1-68396-098-0 Library of Congress Control Number: 2017956972
First printing: June 2018. Printed in China

꙾

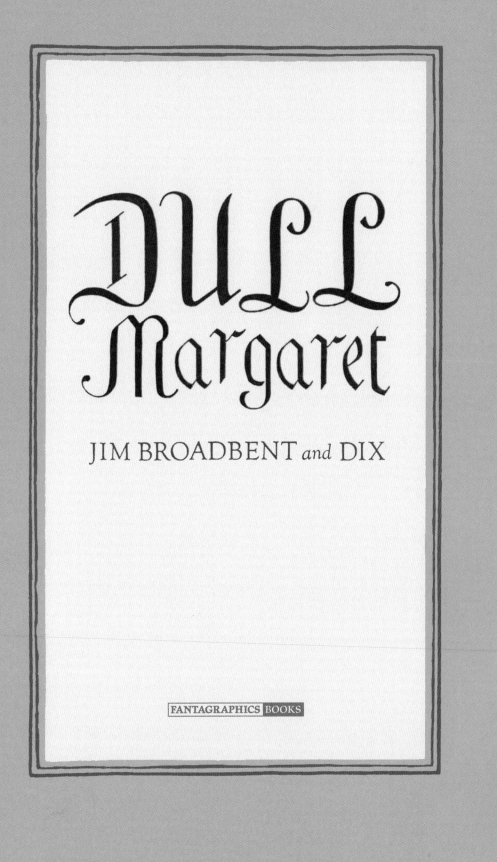

DULL Margaret

JIM BROADBENT and DIX

FANTAGRAPHICS BOOKS

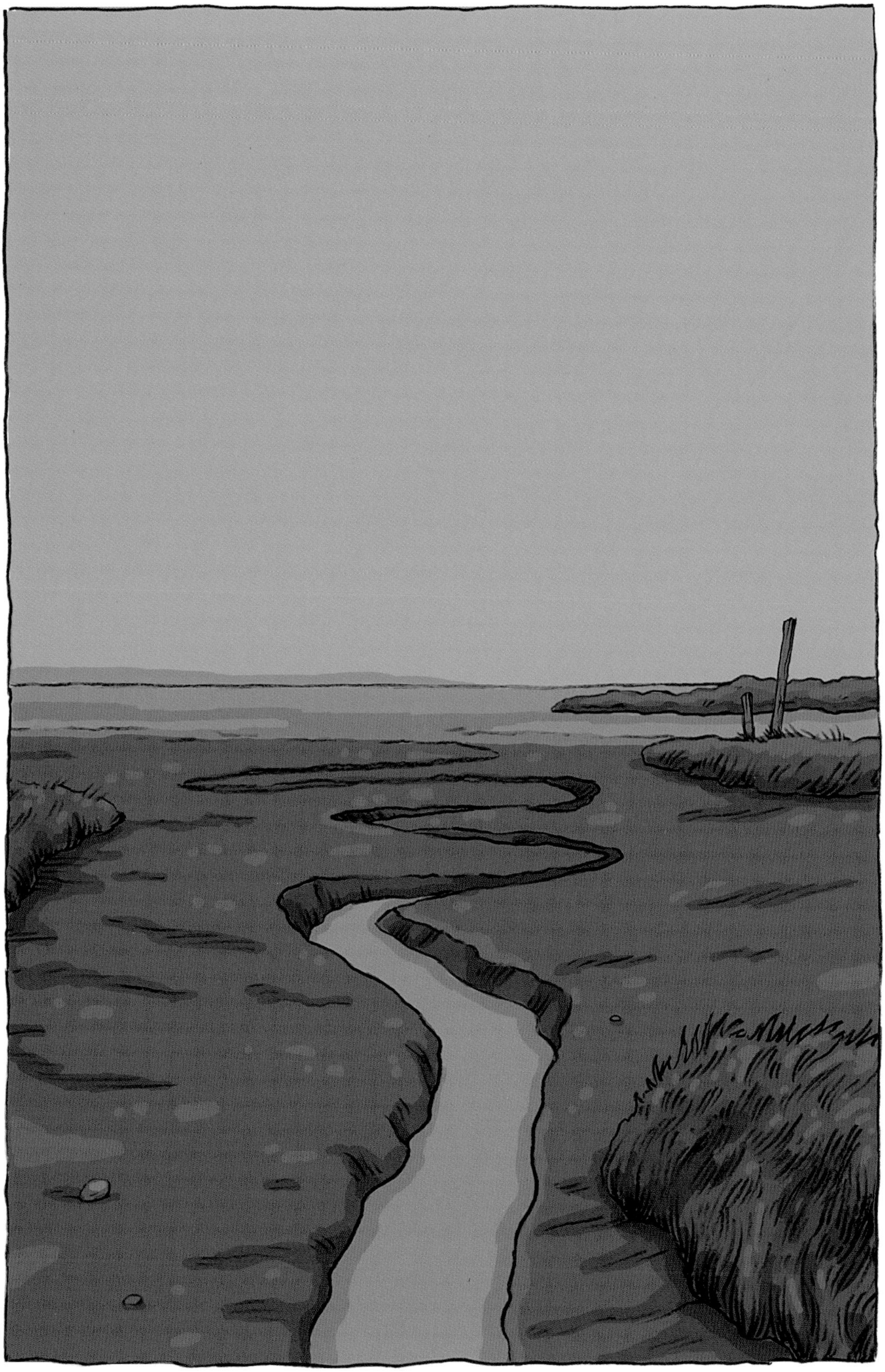

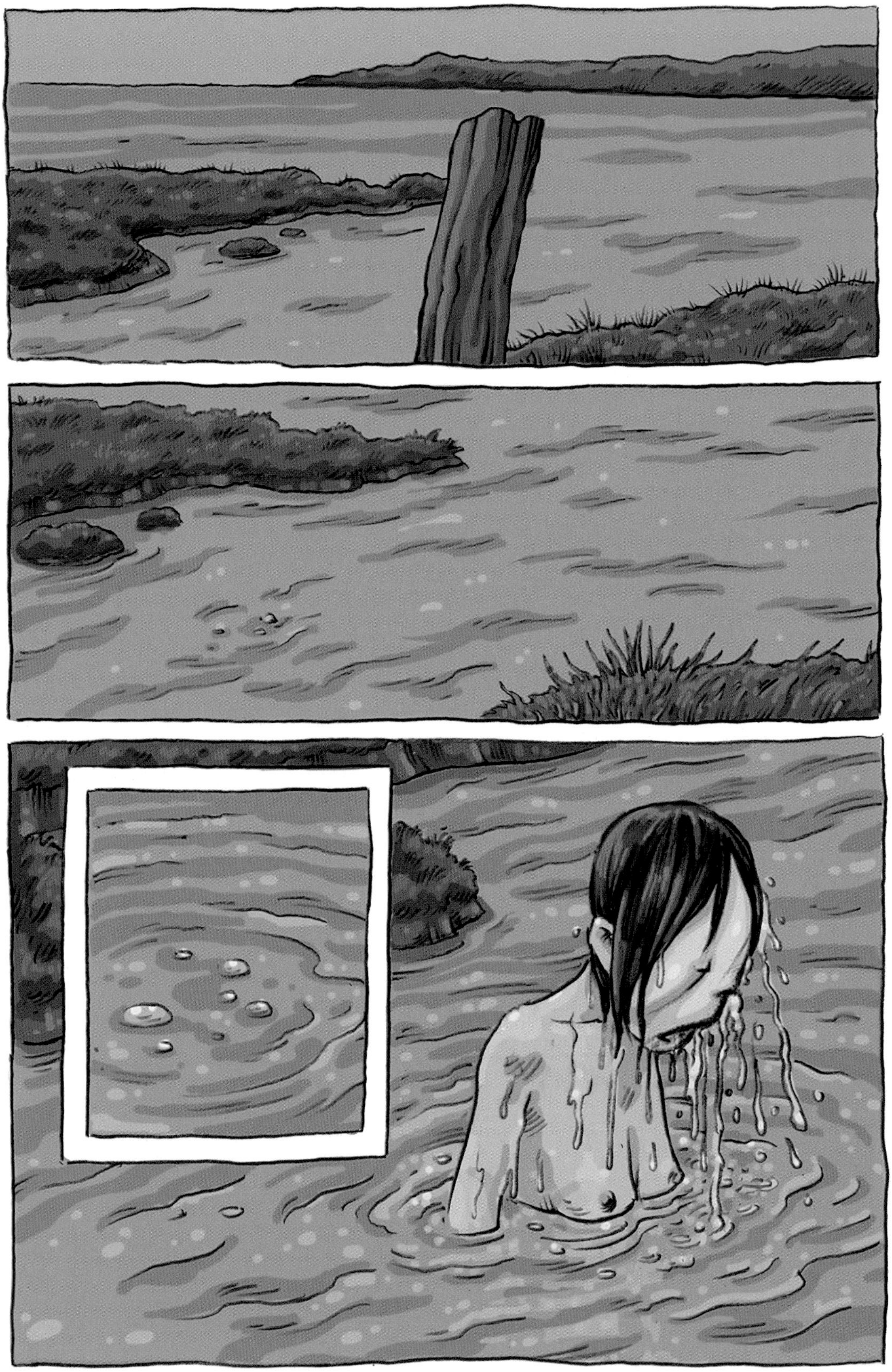

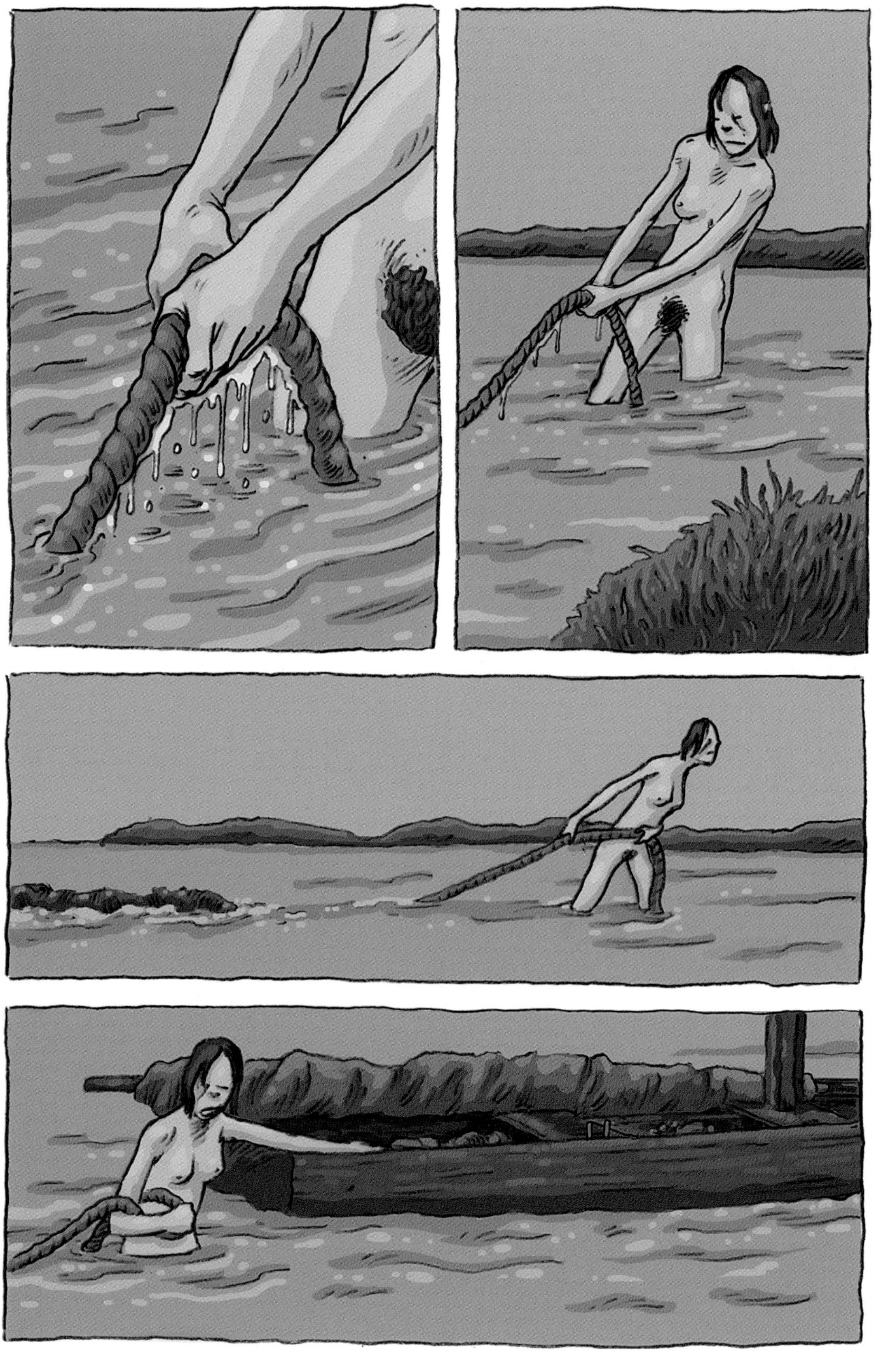

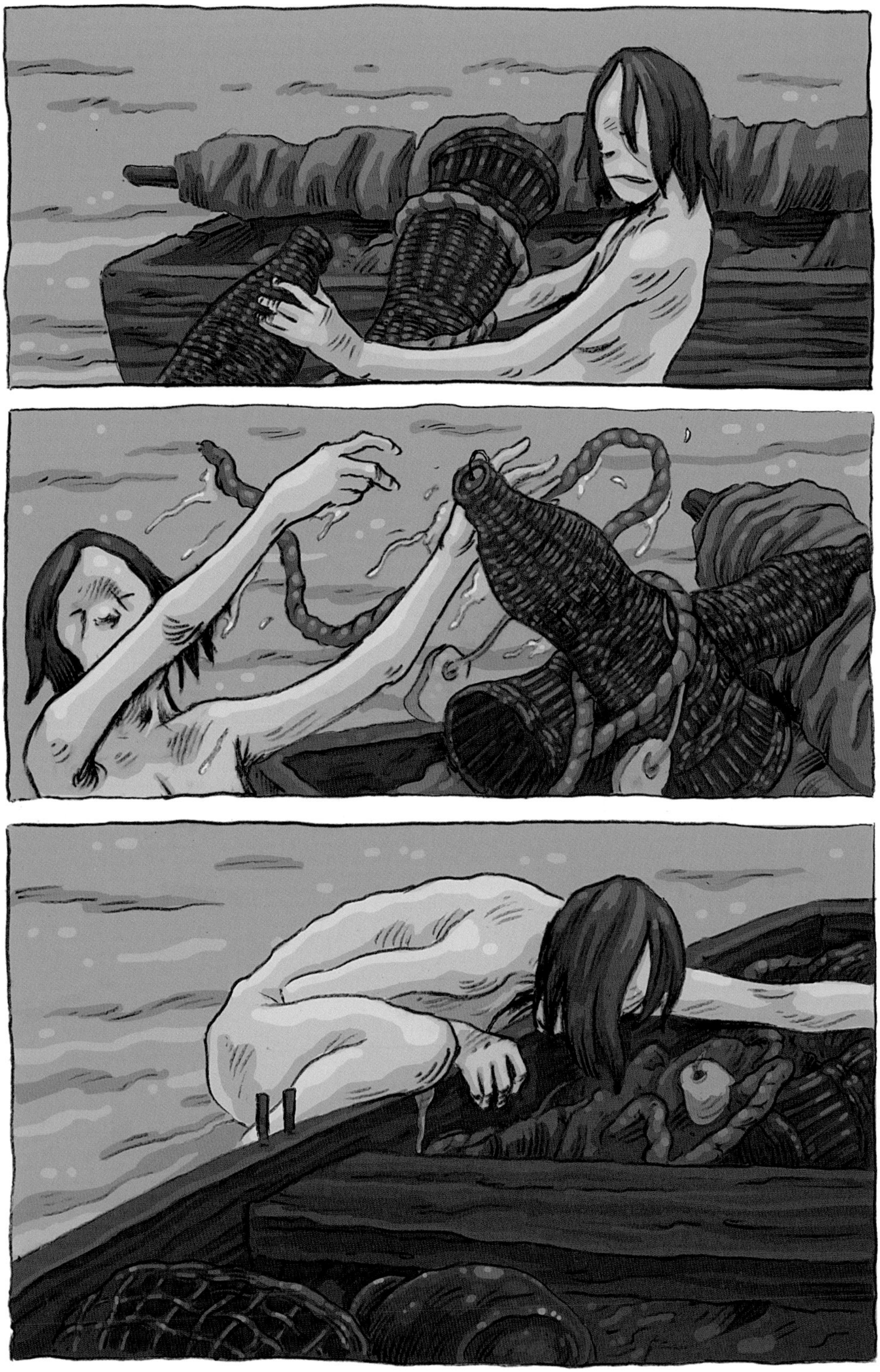

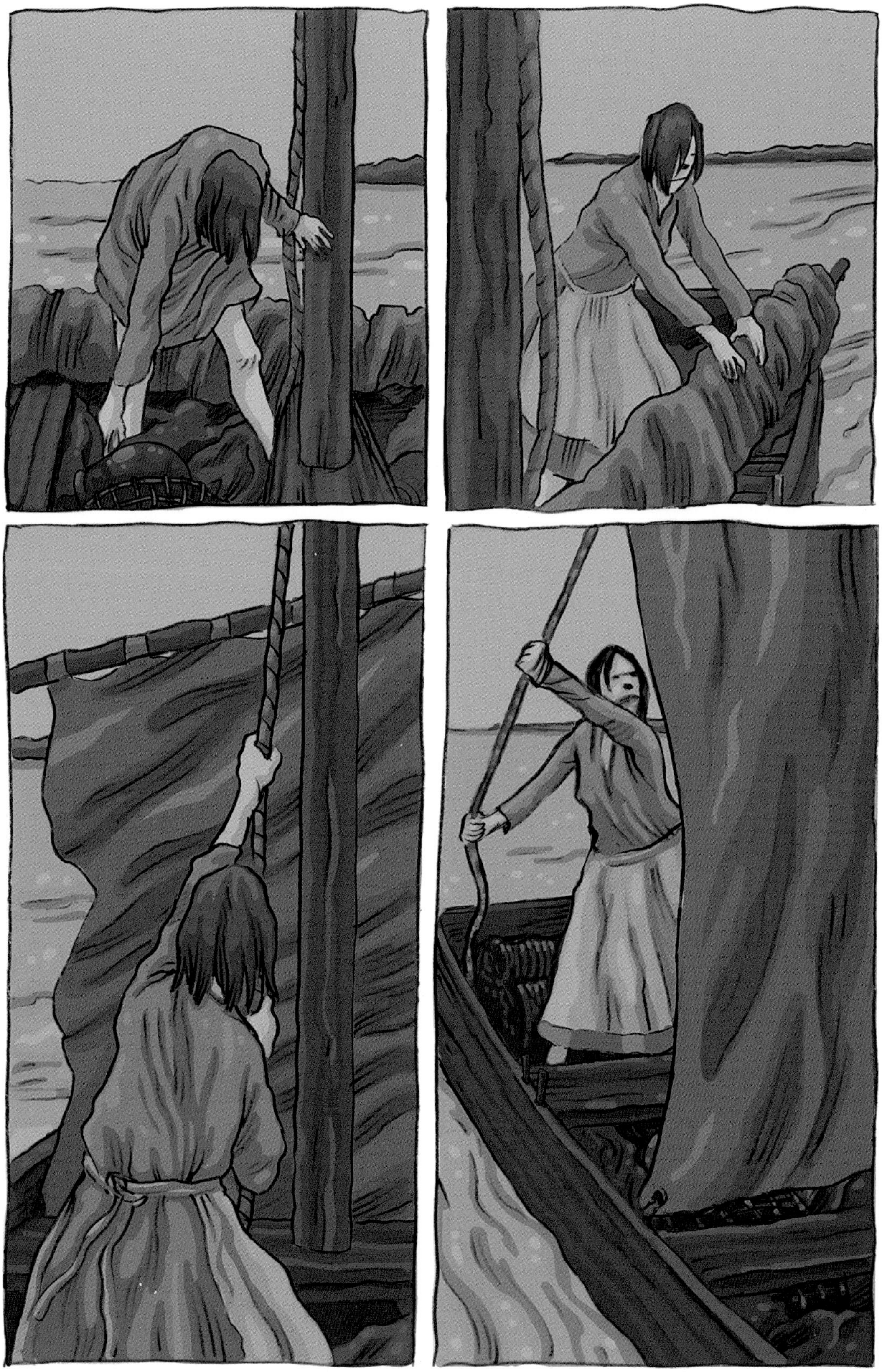

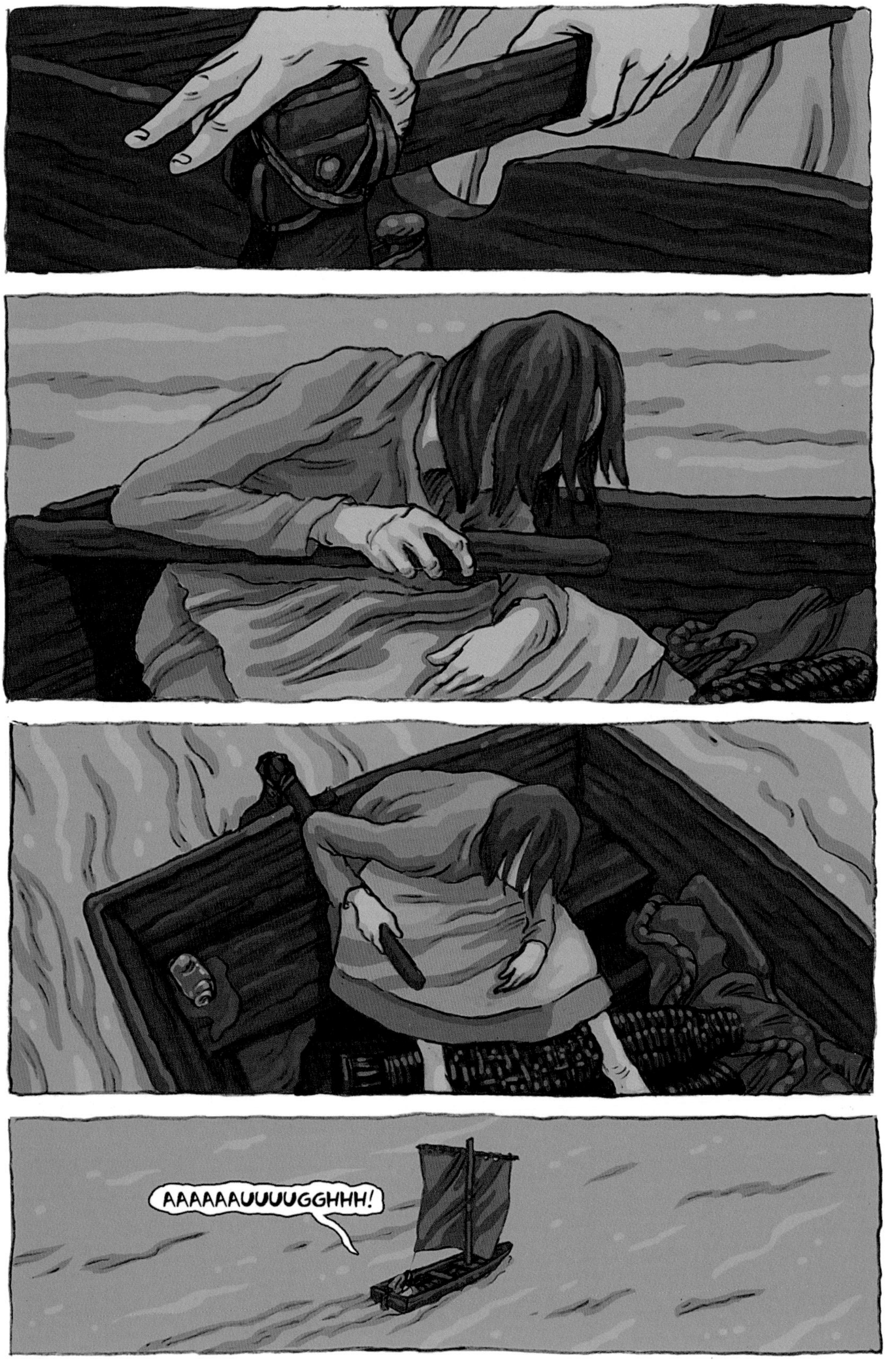
AAAAAAUUUUGGHHH!

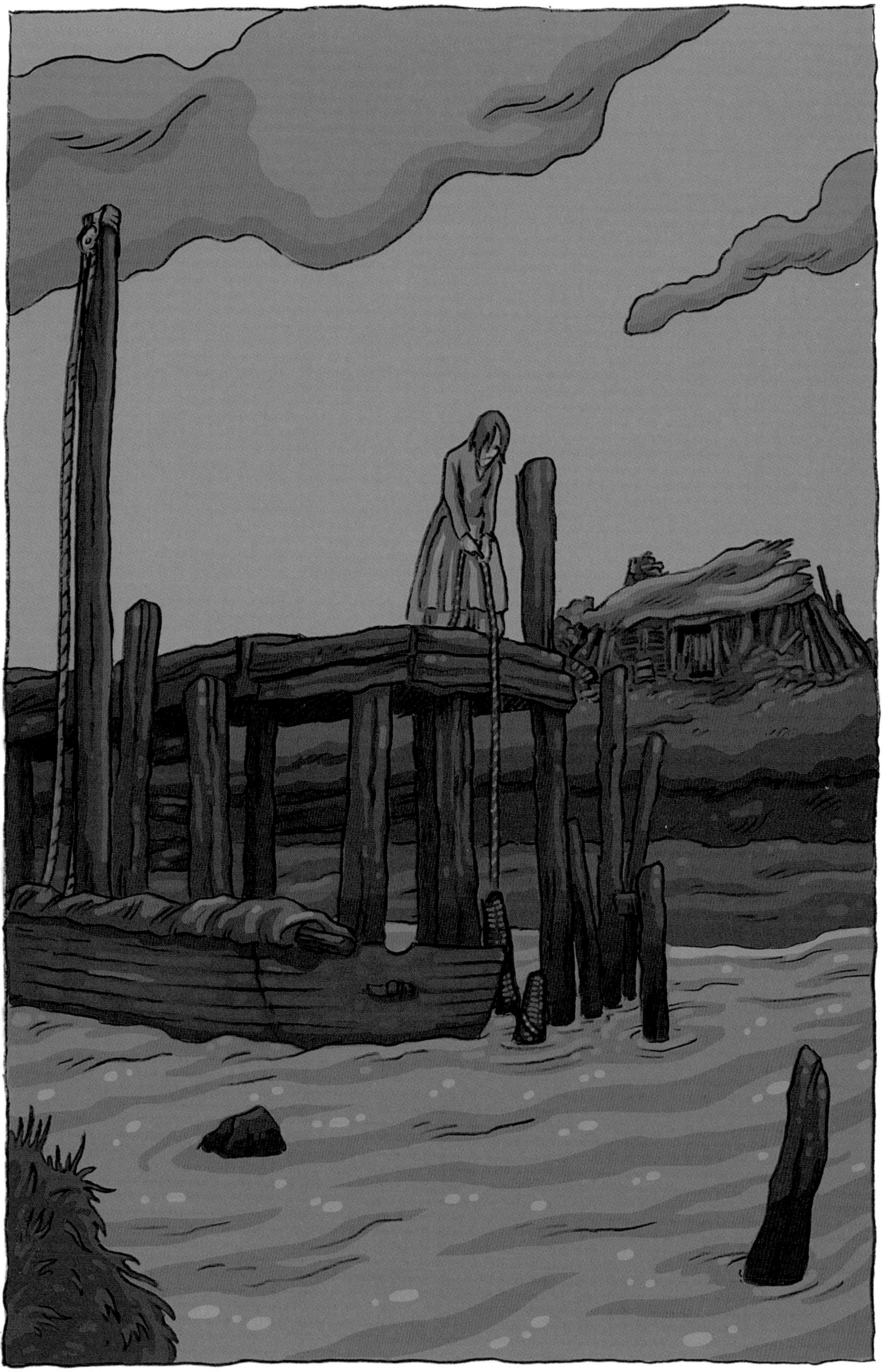

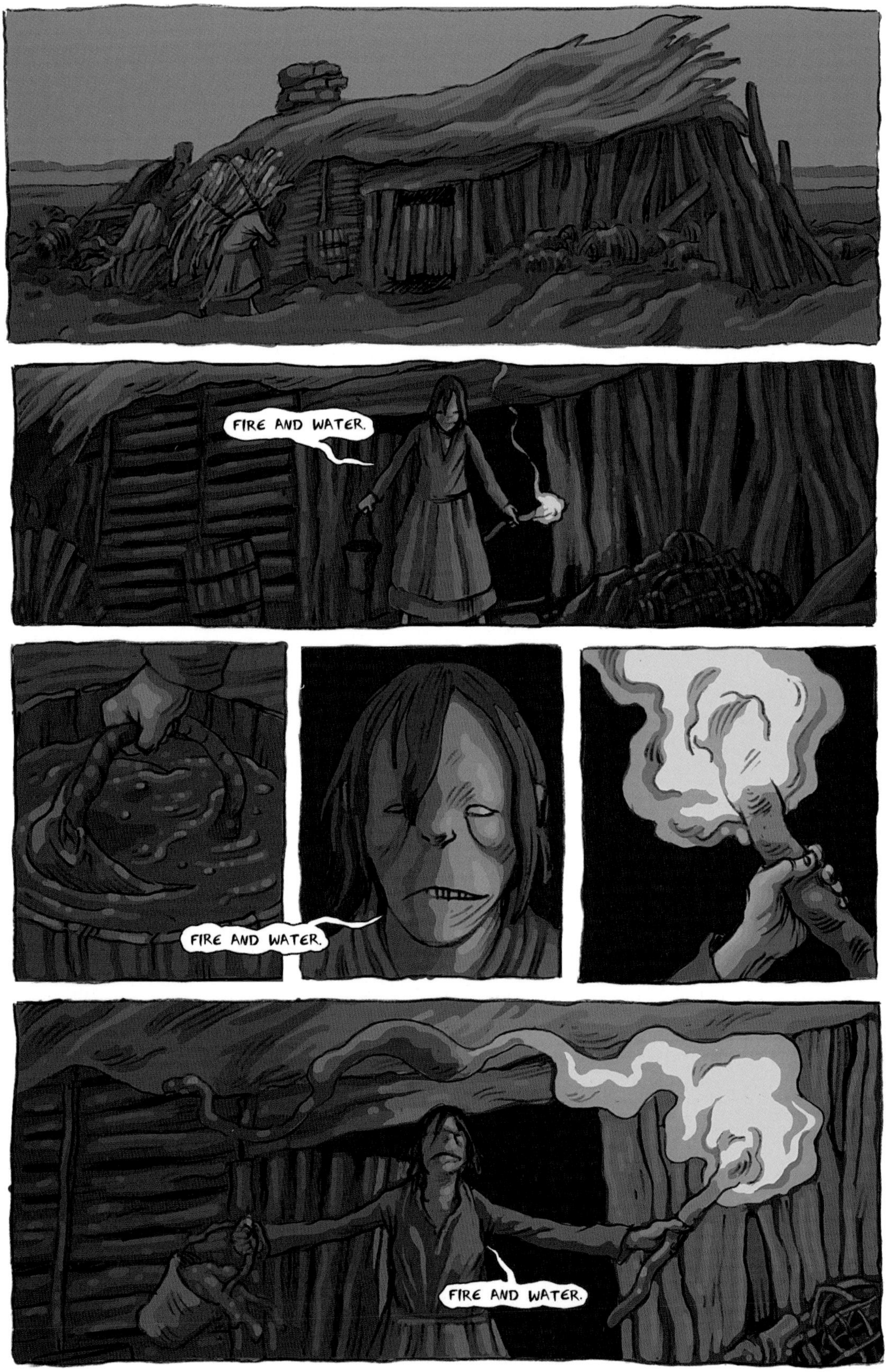
FIRE AND WATER.
FIRE AND WATER.
FIRE AND WATER.

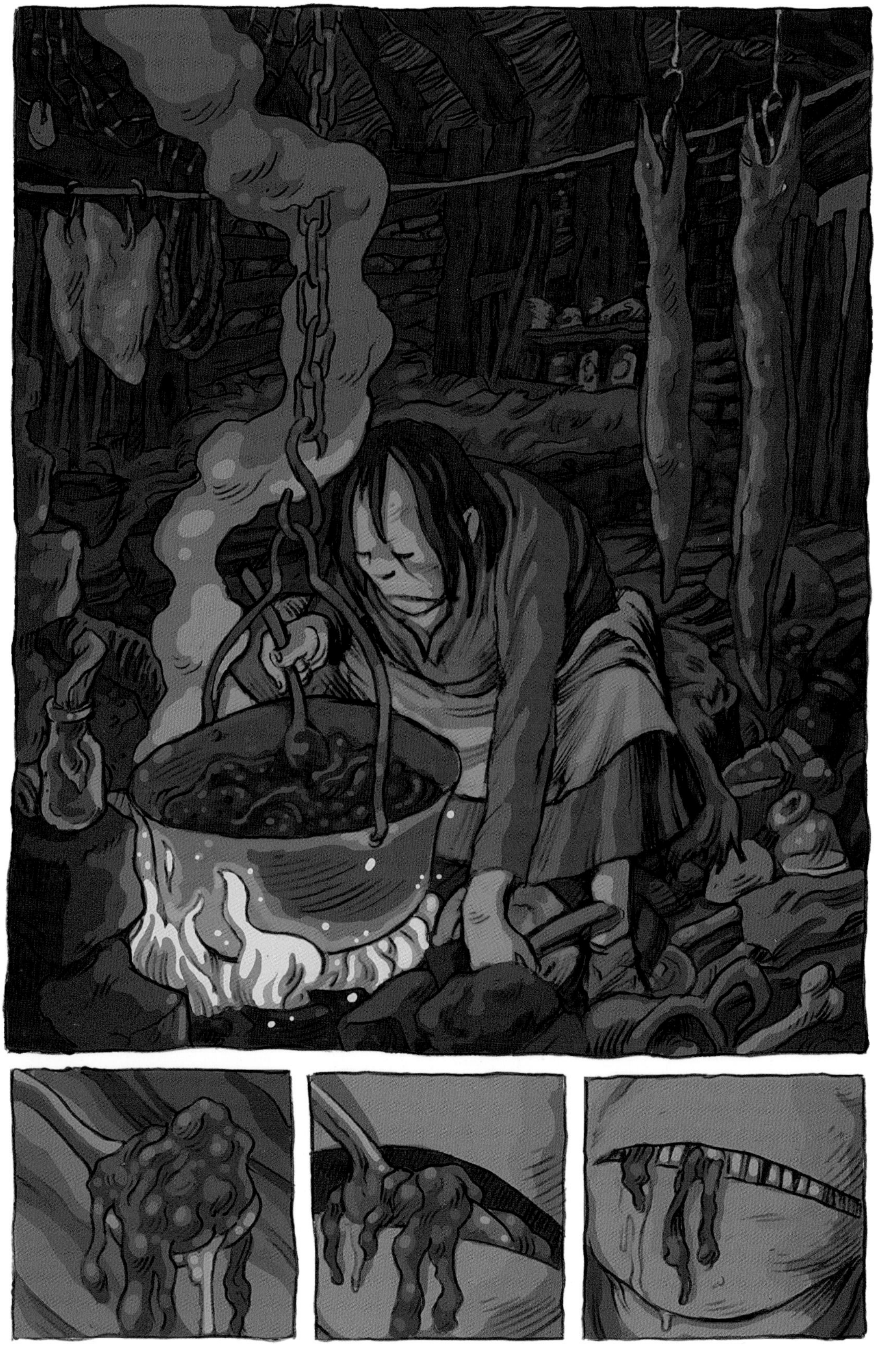

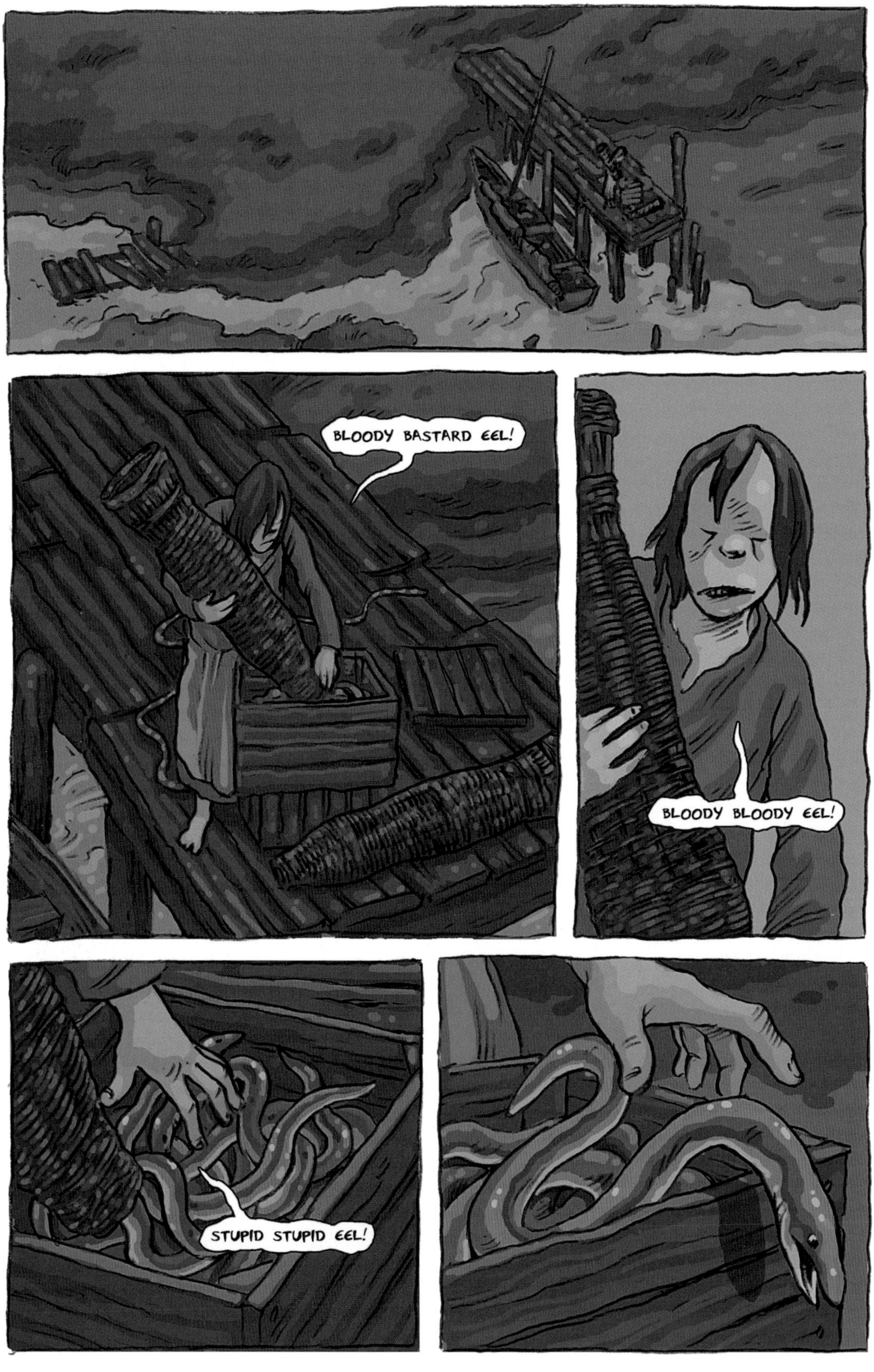
BLOODY BASTARD EEL!
BLOODY BLOODY EEL!
STUPID STUPID EEL!

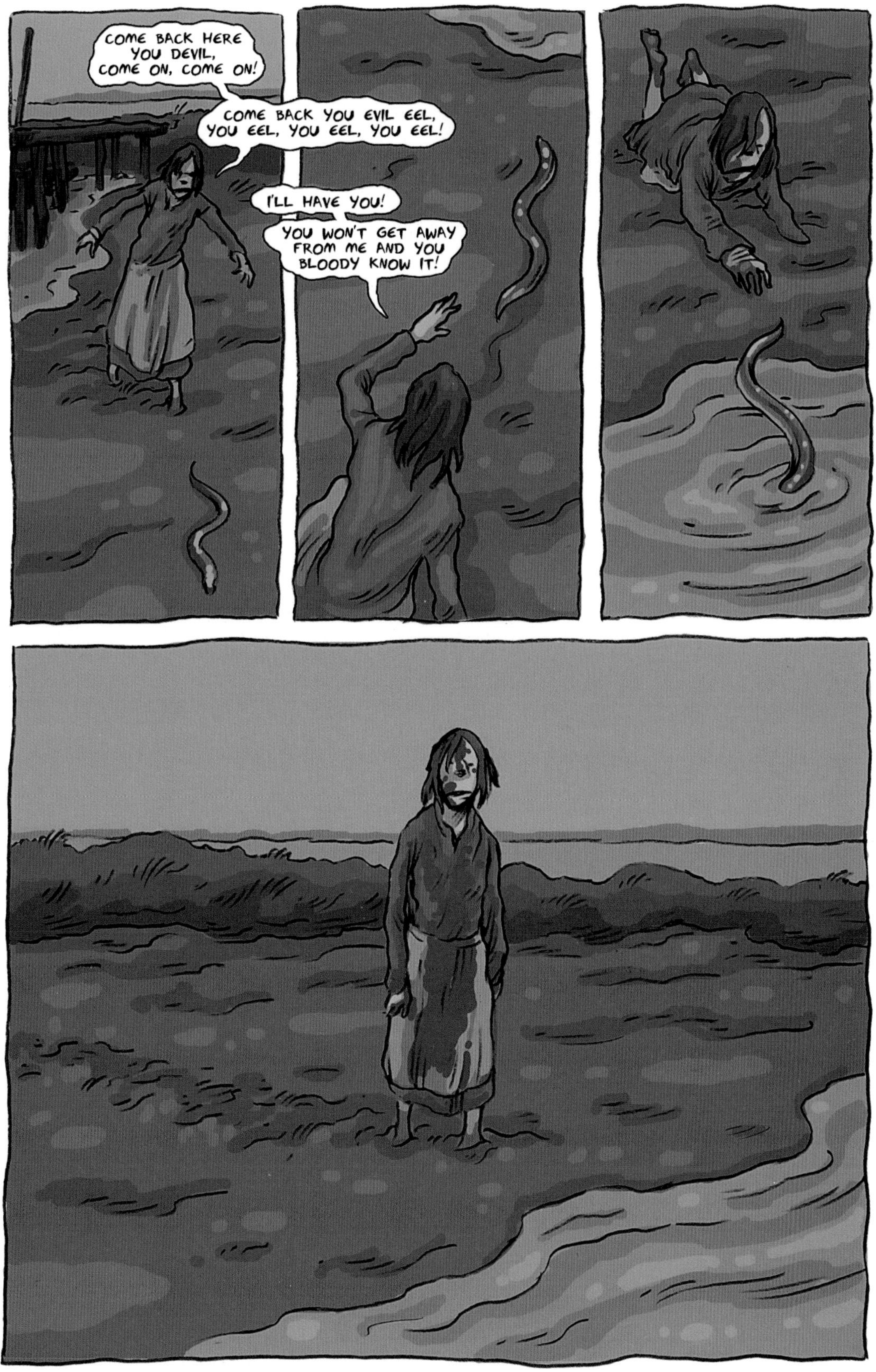
COME BACK HERE YOU DEVIL, COME ON, COME ON!
COME BACK YOU EVIL EEL, YOU EEL, YOU EEL, YOU EEL!
I'LL HAVE YOU!
YOU WON'T GET AWAY FROM ME AND YOU BLOODY KNOW IT!

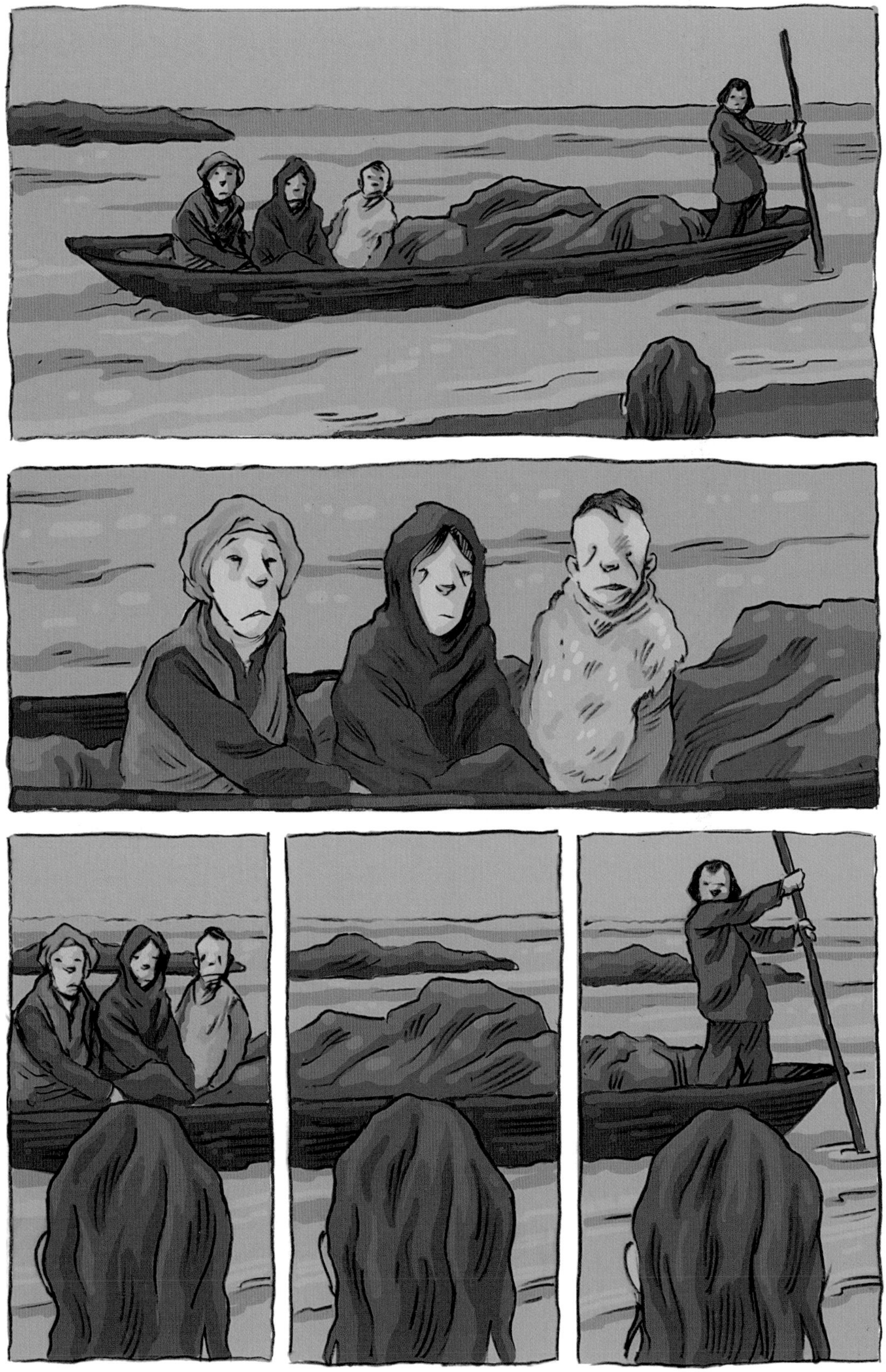

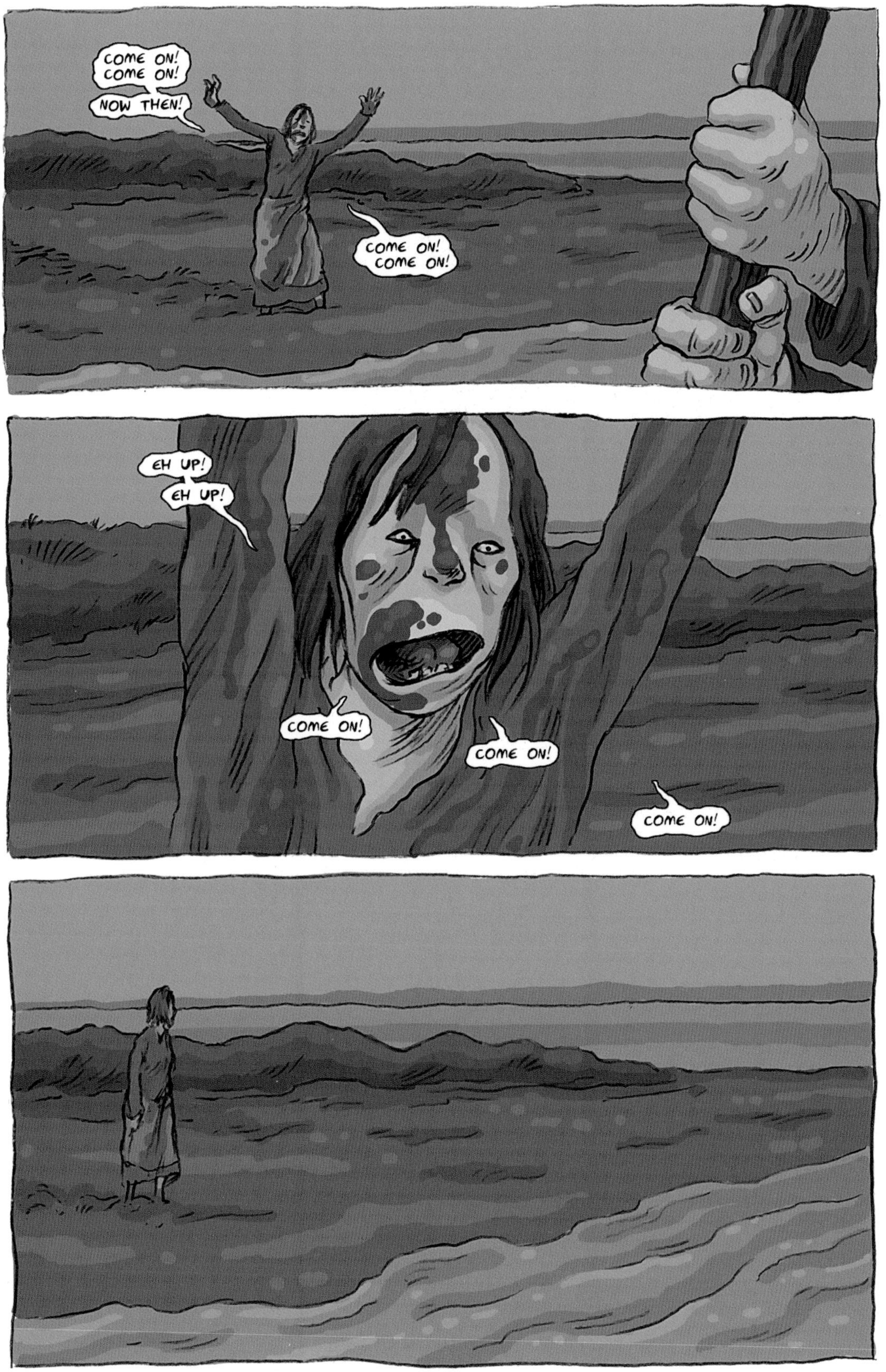
COME ON! COME ON!
NOW THEN!
COME ON! COME ON!
EH UP!
EH UP!
COME ON!
COME ON!
COME ON!

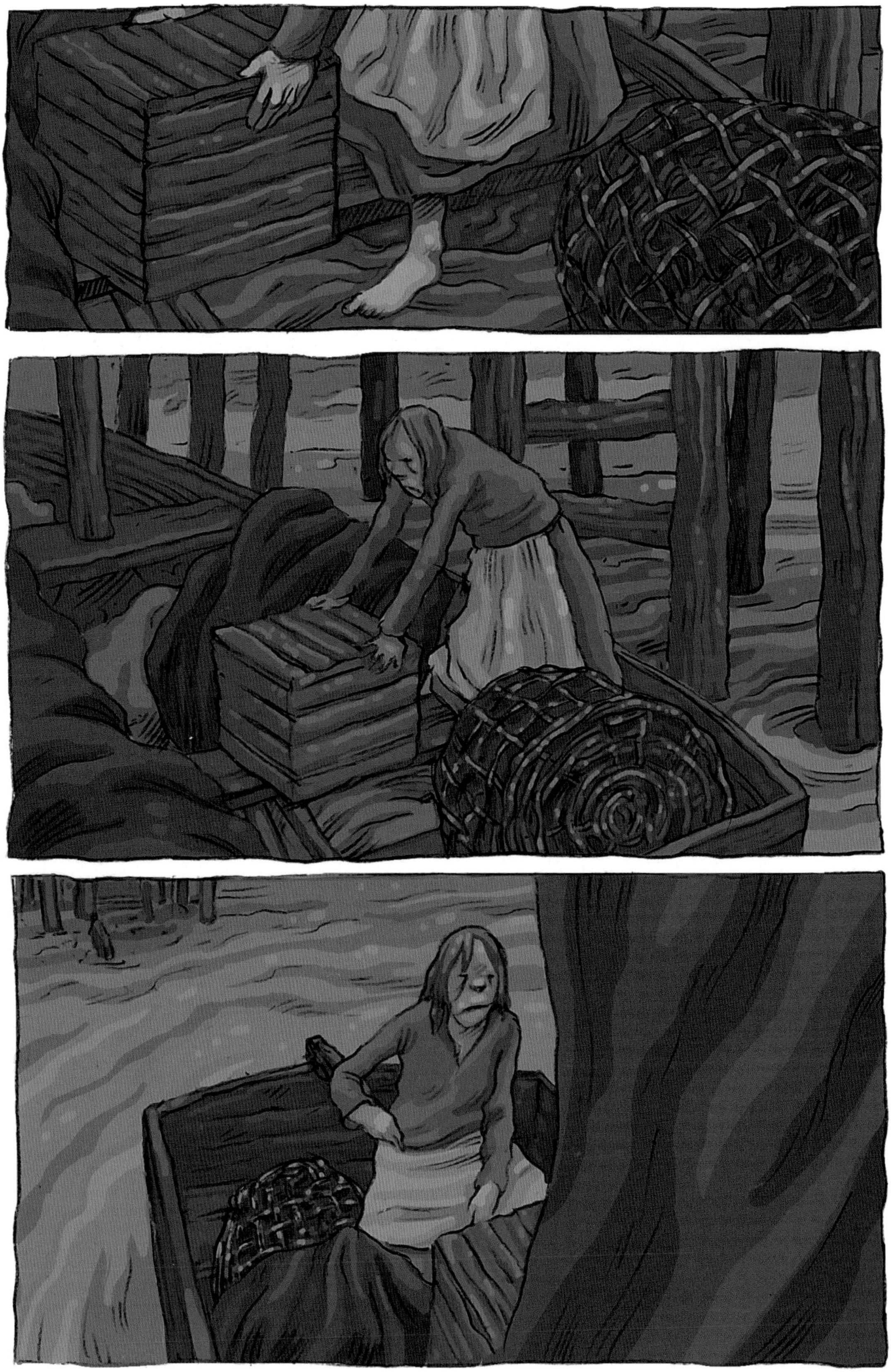

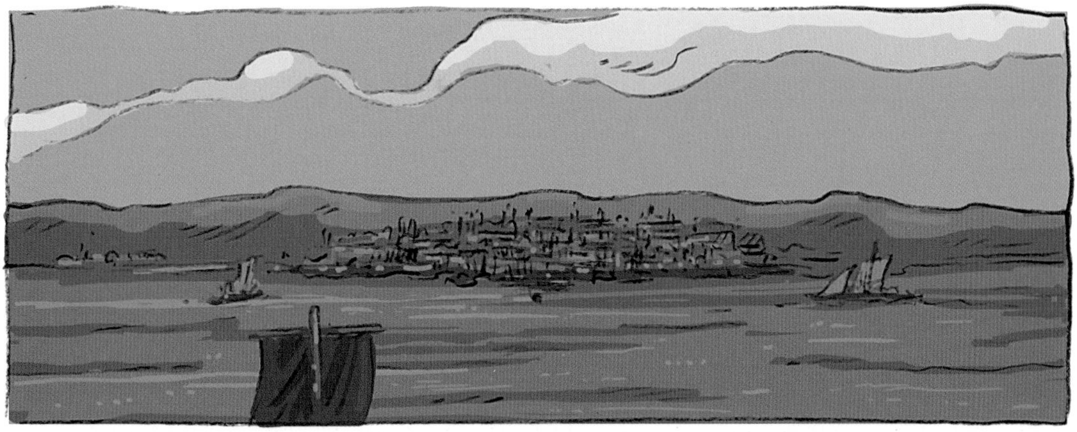

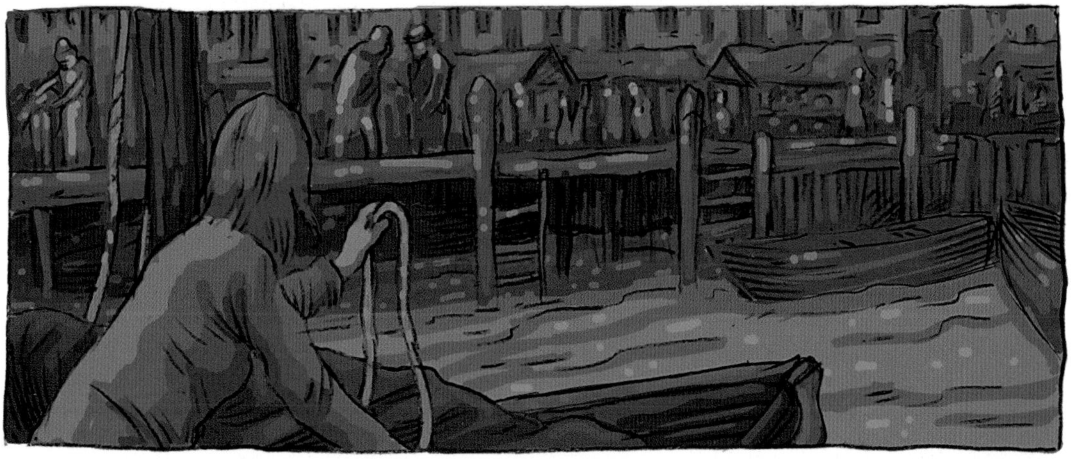

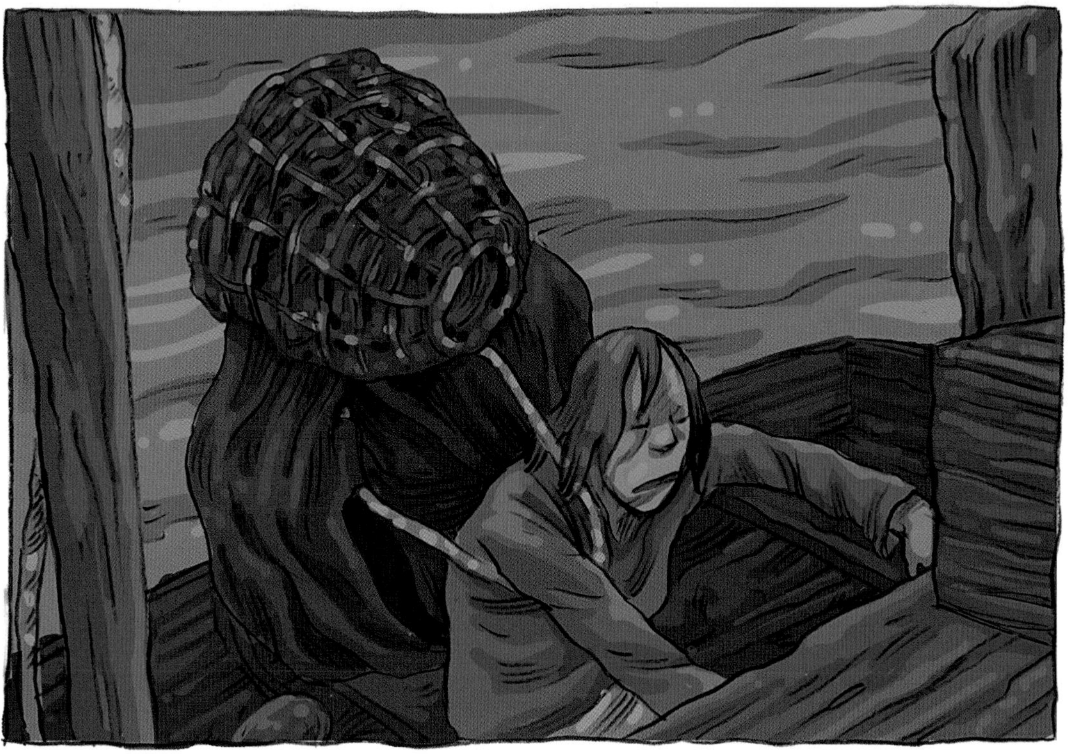

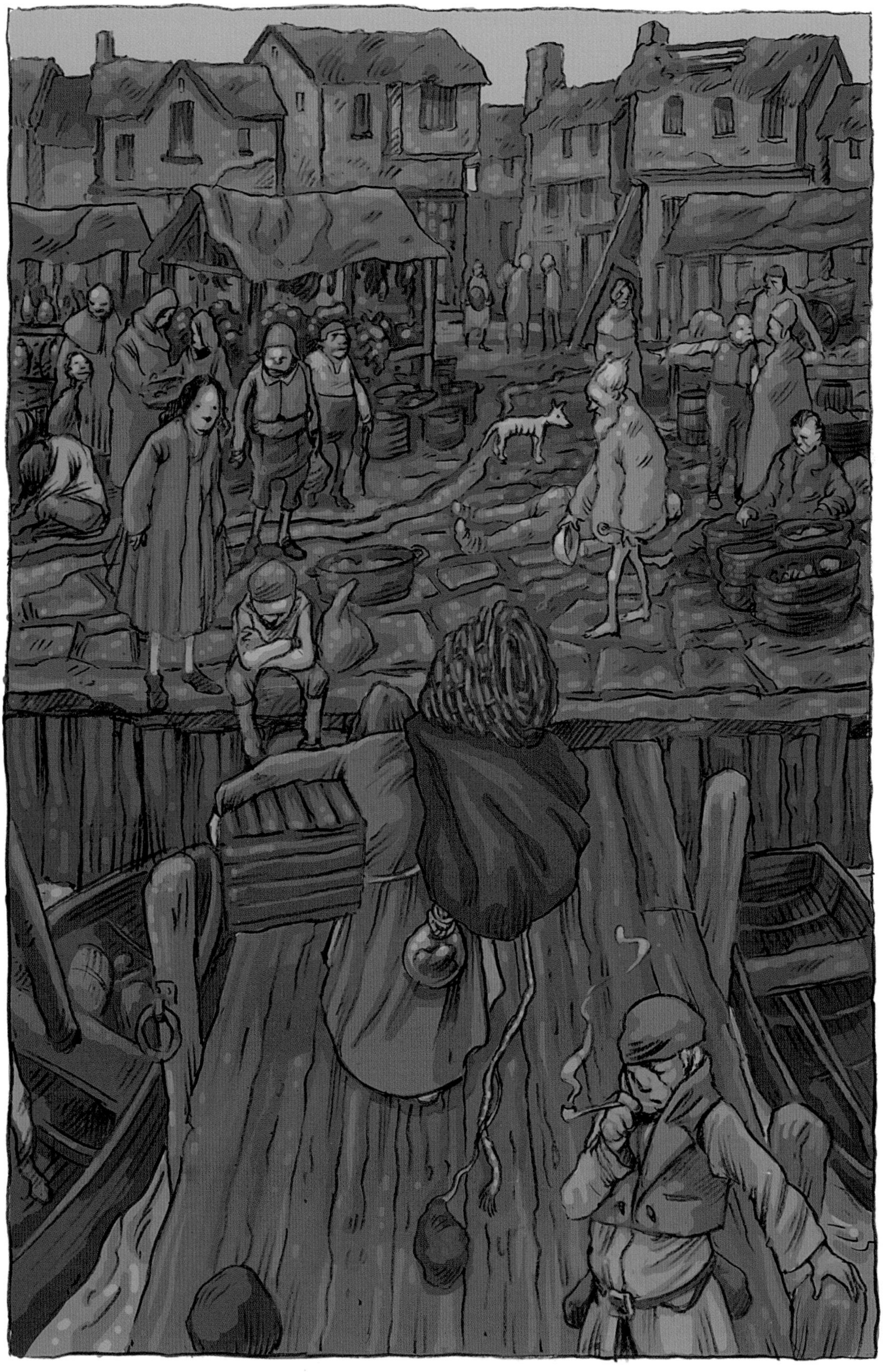

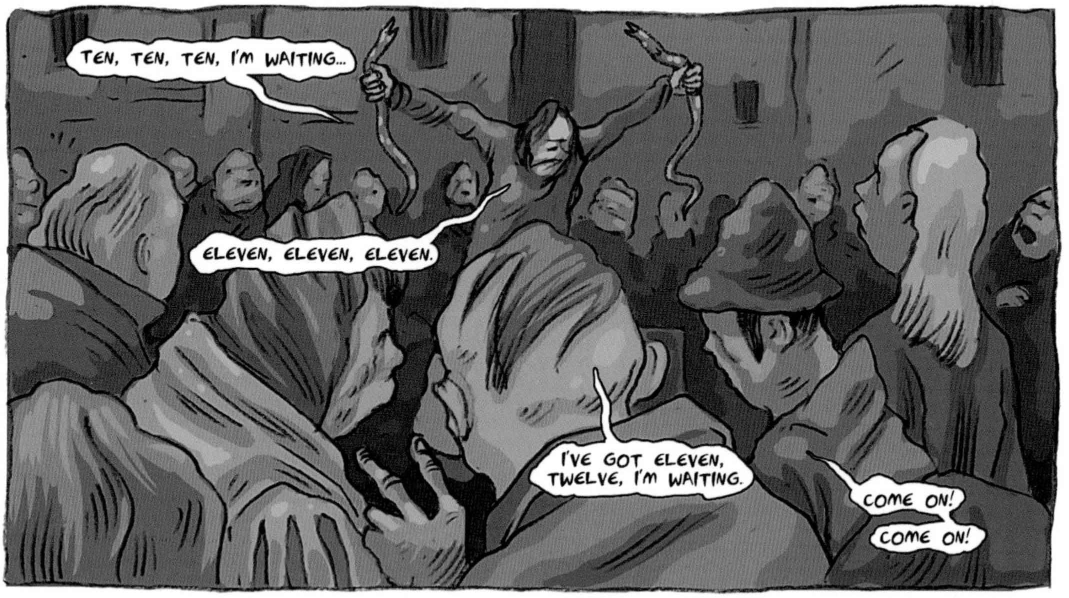
TEN, TEN, TEN, I'M WAITING...
ELEVEN, ELEVEN, ELEVEN.
I'VE GOT ELEVEN, TWELVE, I'M WAITING.
COME ON!
COME ON!

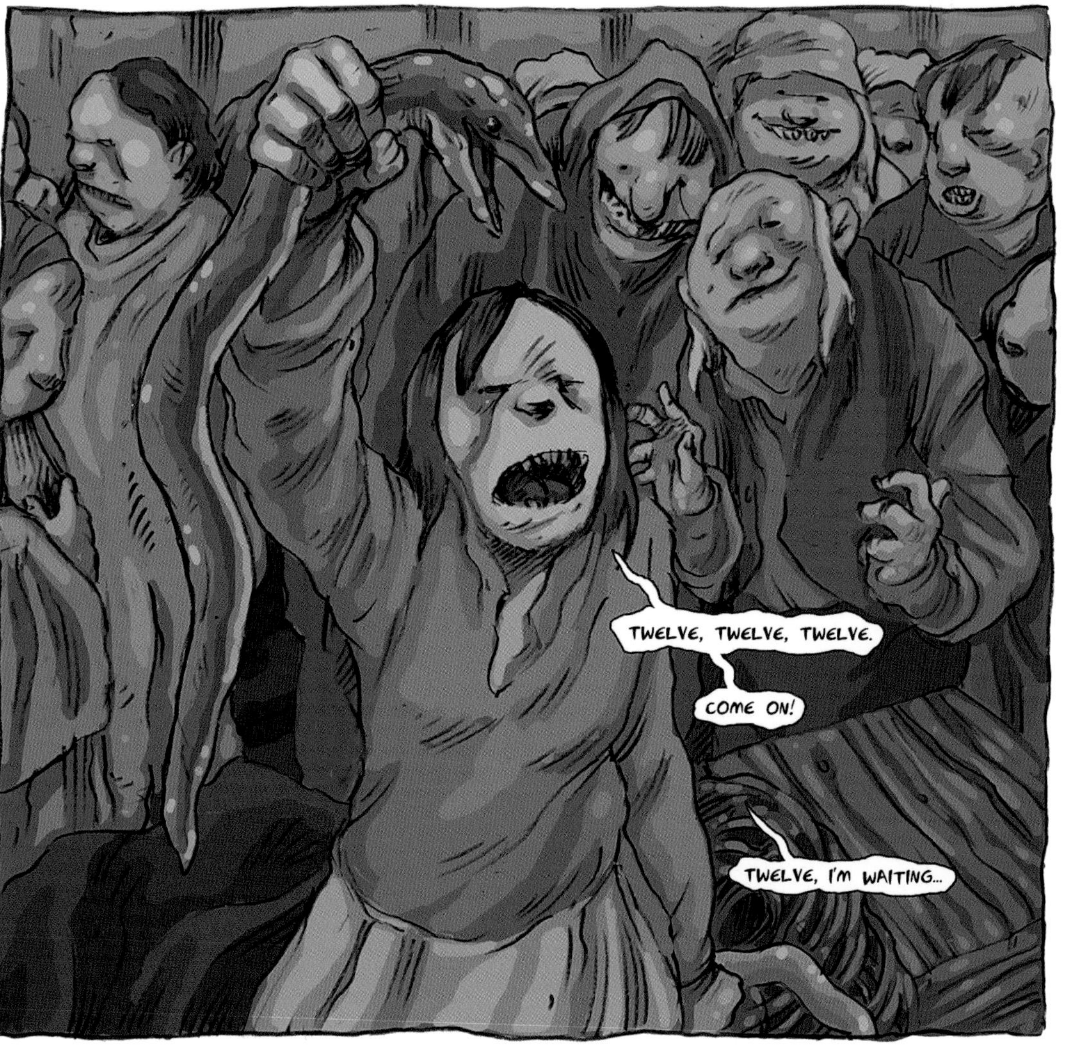
TWELVE, TWELVE, TWELVE.
COME ON!
TWELVE, I'M WAITING...

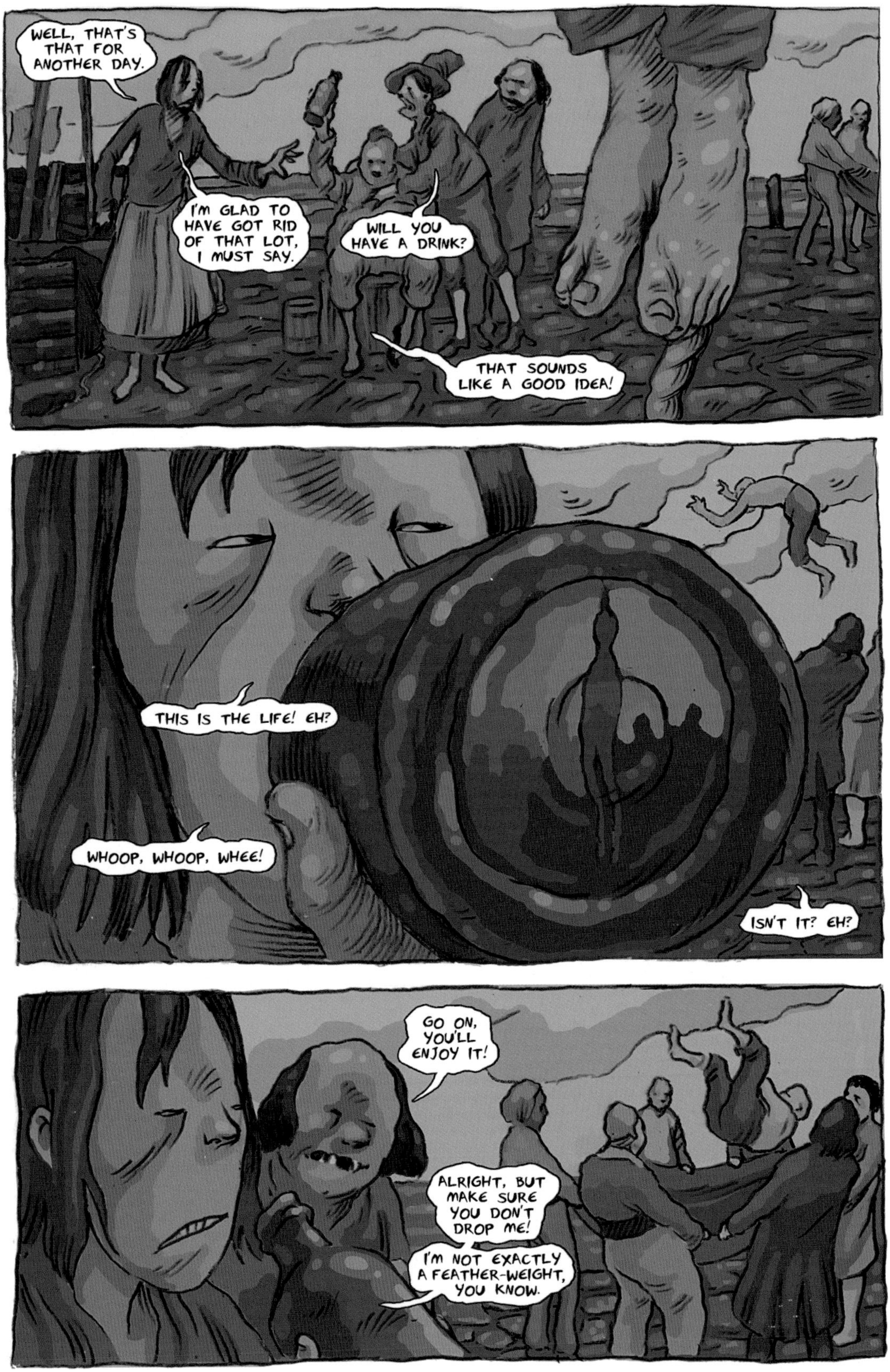
WELL, THAT'S THAT FOR ANOTHER DAY.
I'M GLAD TO HAVE GOT RID OF THAT LOT, I MUST SAY.
WILL YOU HAVE A DRINK?
THAT SOUNDS LIKE A GOOD IDEA!
THIS IS THE LIFE! EH?
WHOOP, WHOOP, WHEE!
ISN'T IT? EH?
GO ON, YOU'LL ENJOY IT!
ALRIGHT, BUT MAKE SURE YOU DON'T DROP ME!
I'M NOT EXACTLY A FEATHER-WEIGHT, YOU KNOW.

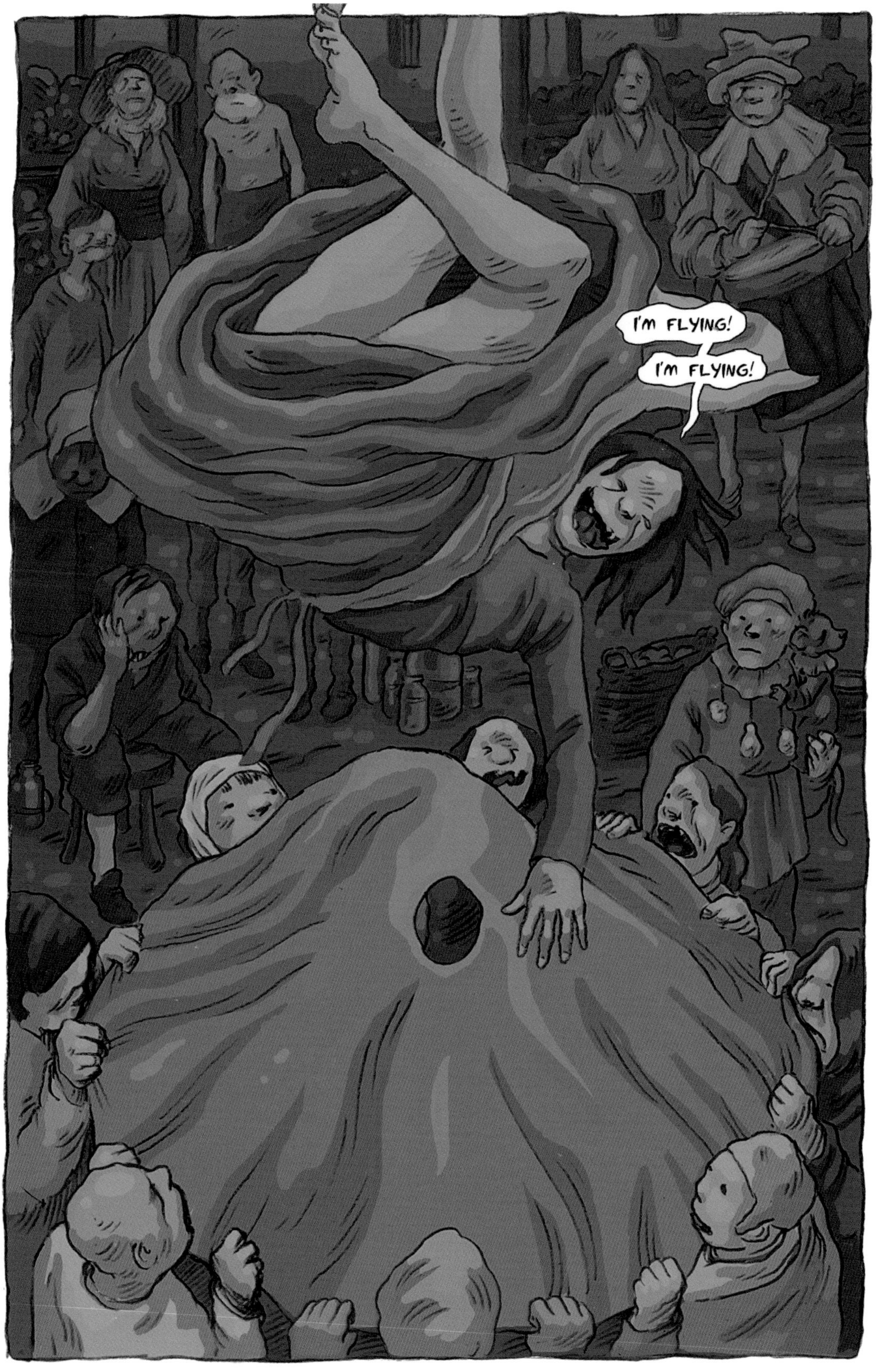
I'M FLYING!
I'M FLYING!

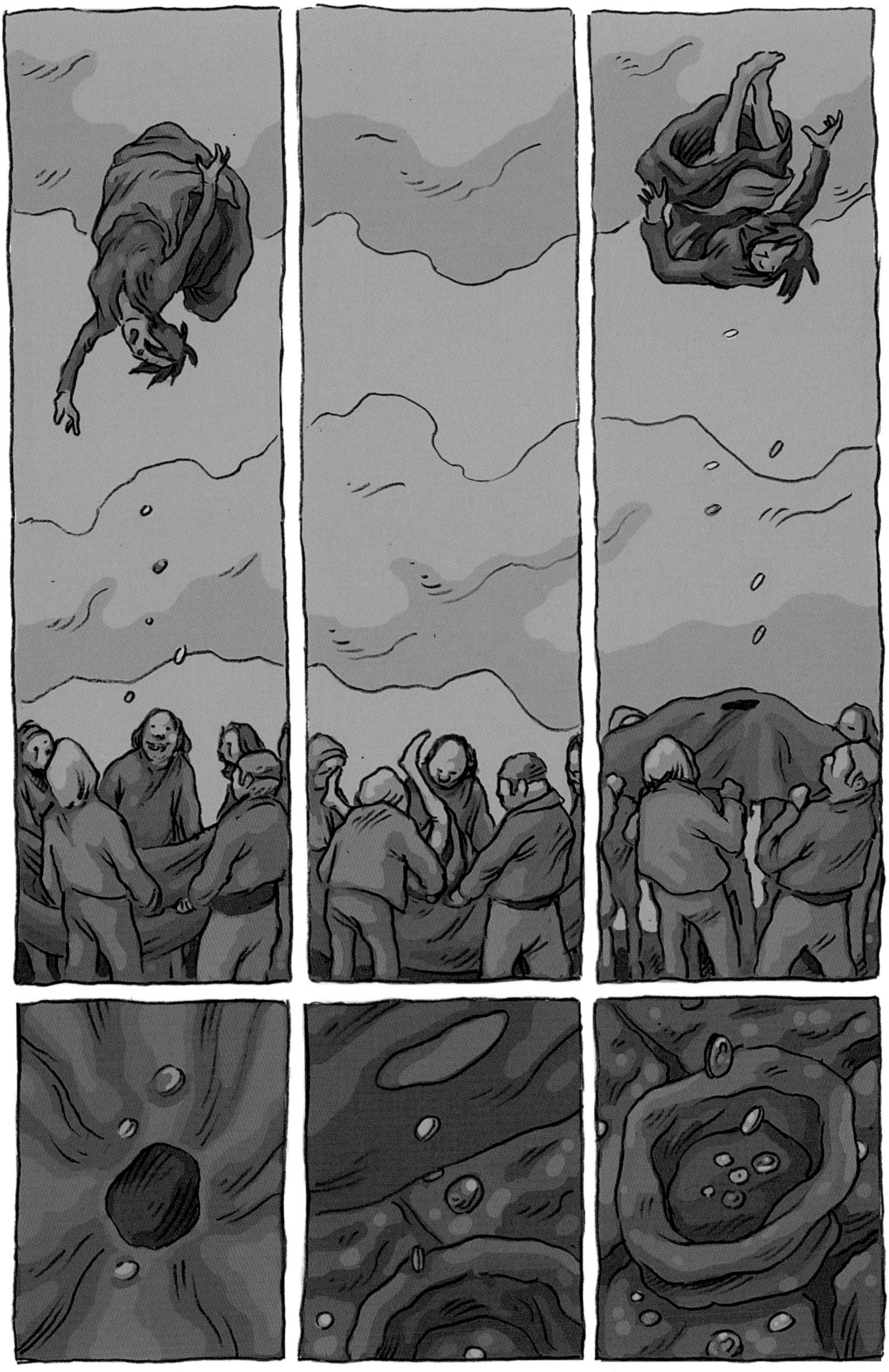

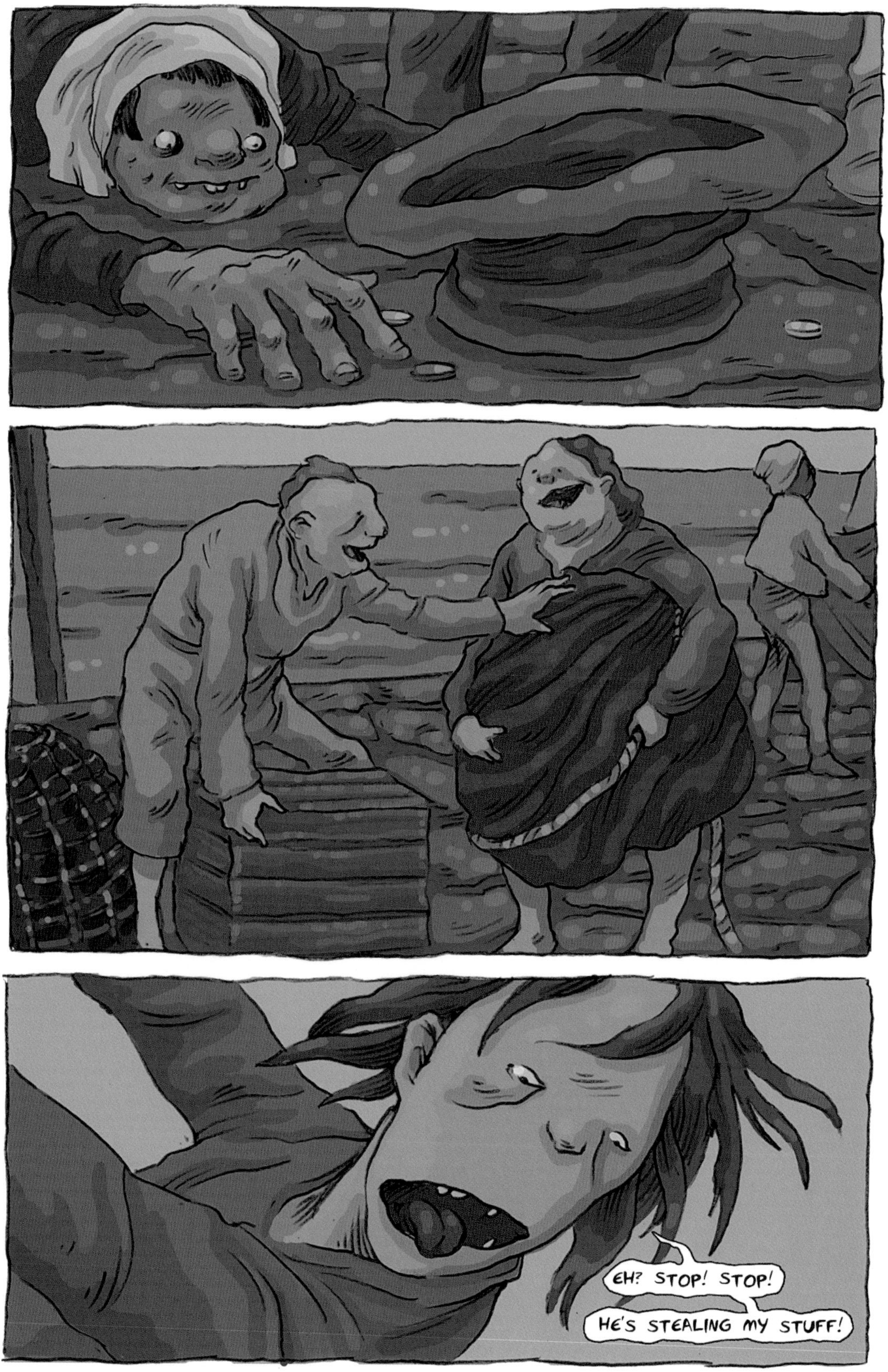
EH? STOP! STOP!
HE'S STEALING MY STUFF!

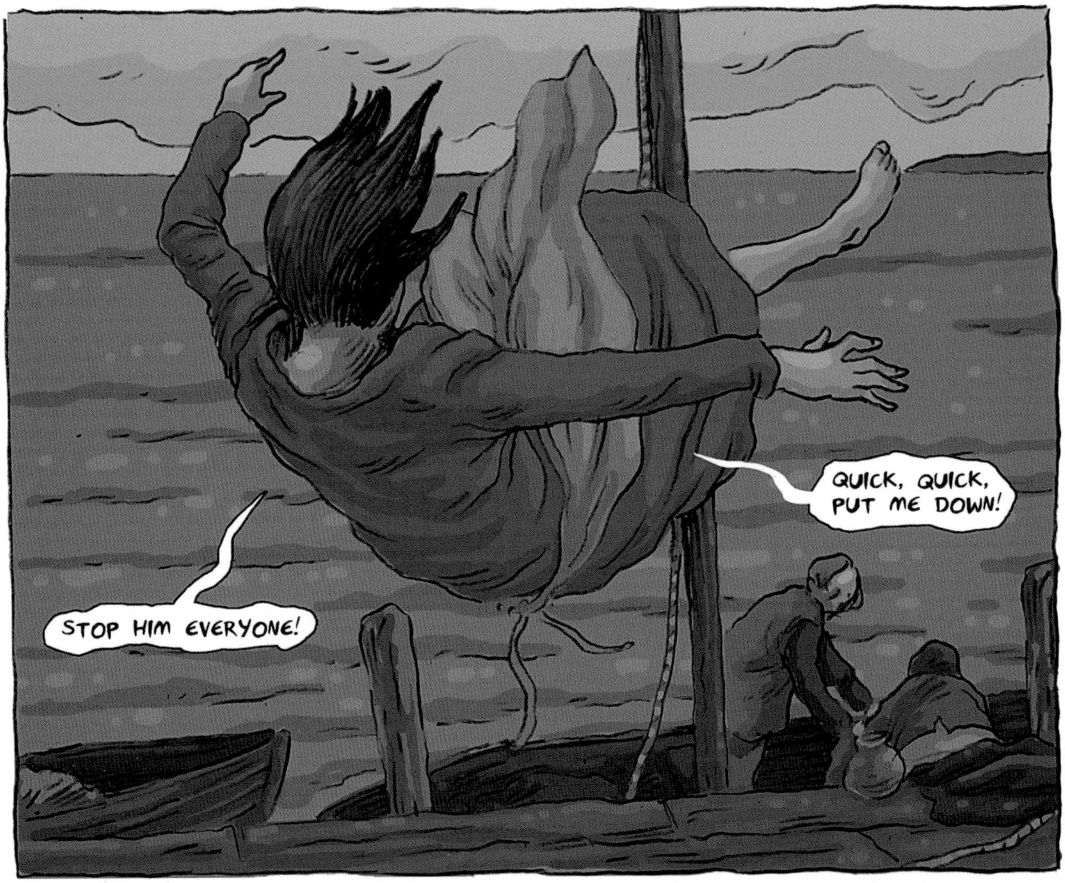
STOP HIM EVERYONE!
QUICK, QUICK, PUT ME DOWN!

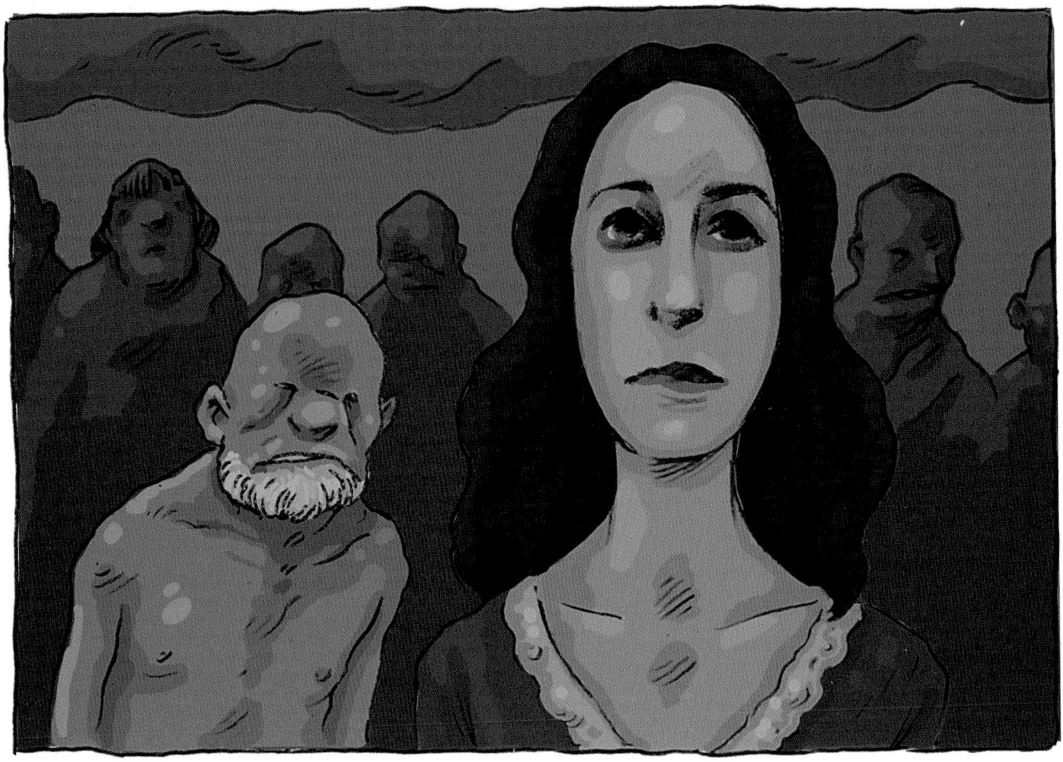

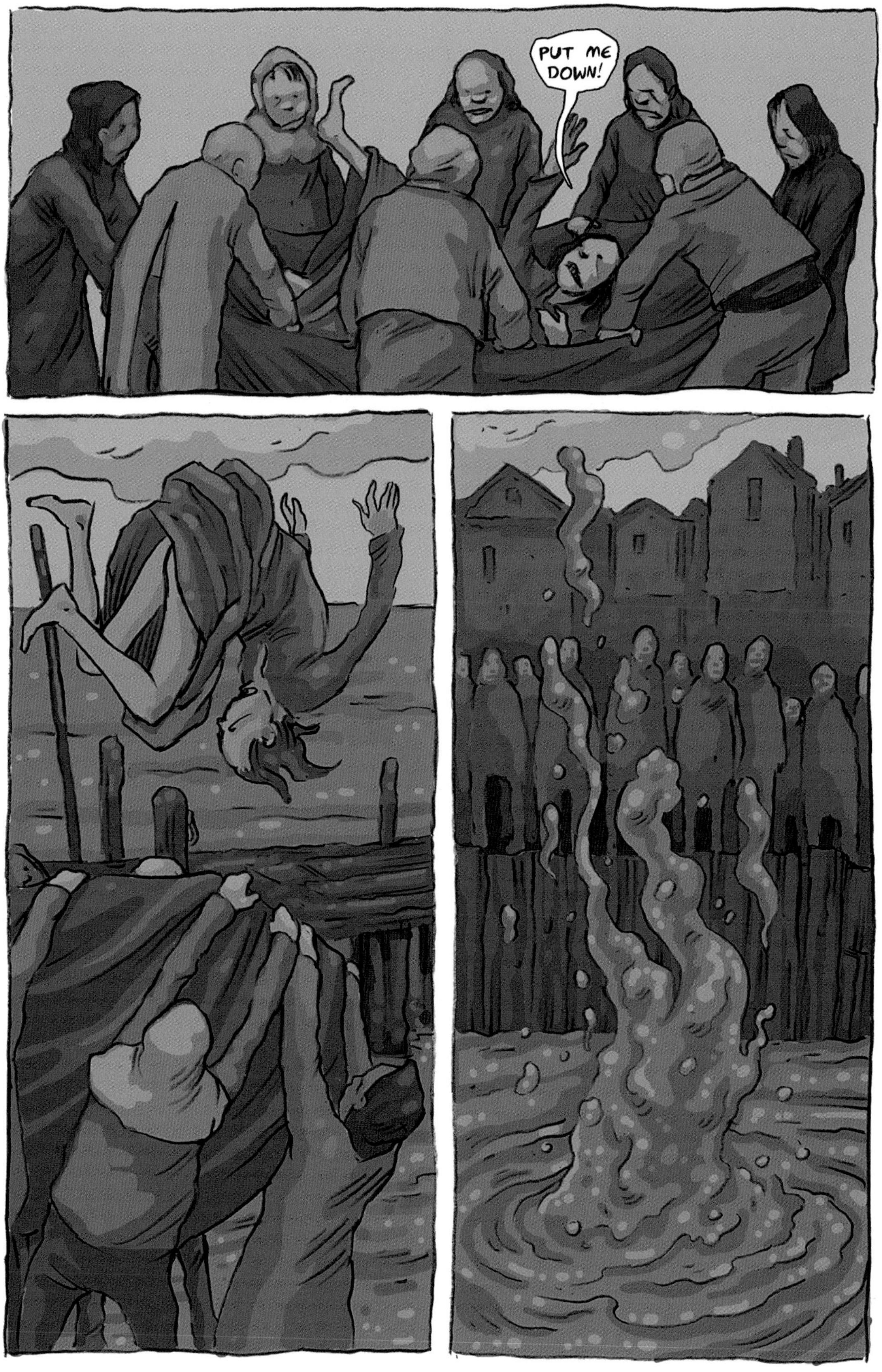
PUT ME DOWN!

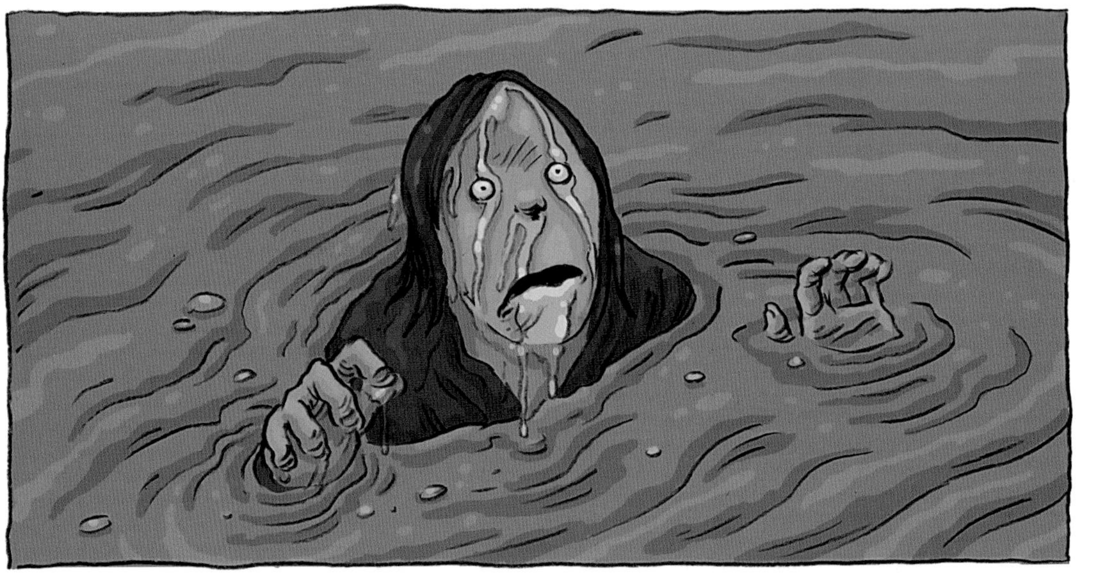

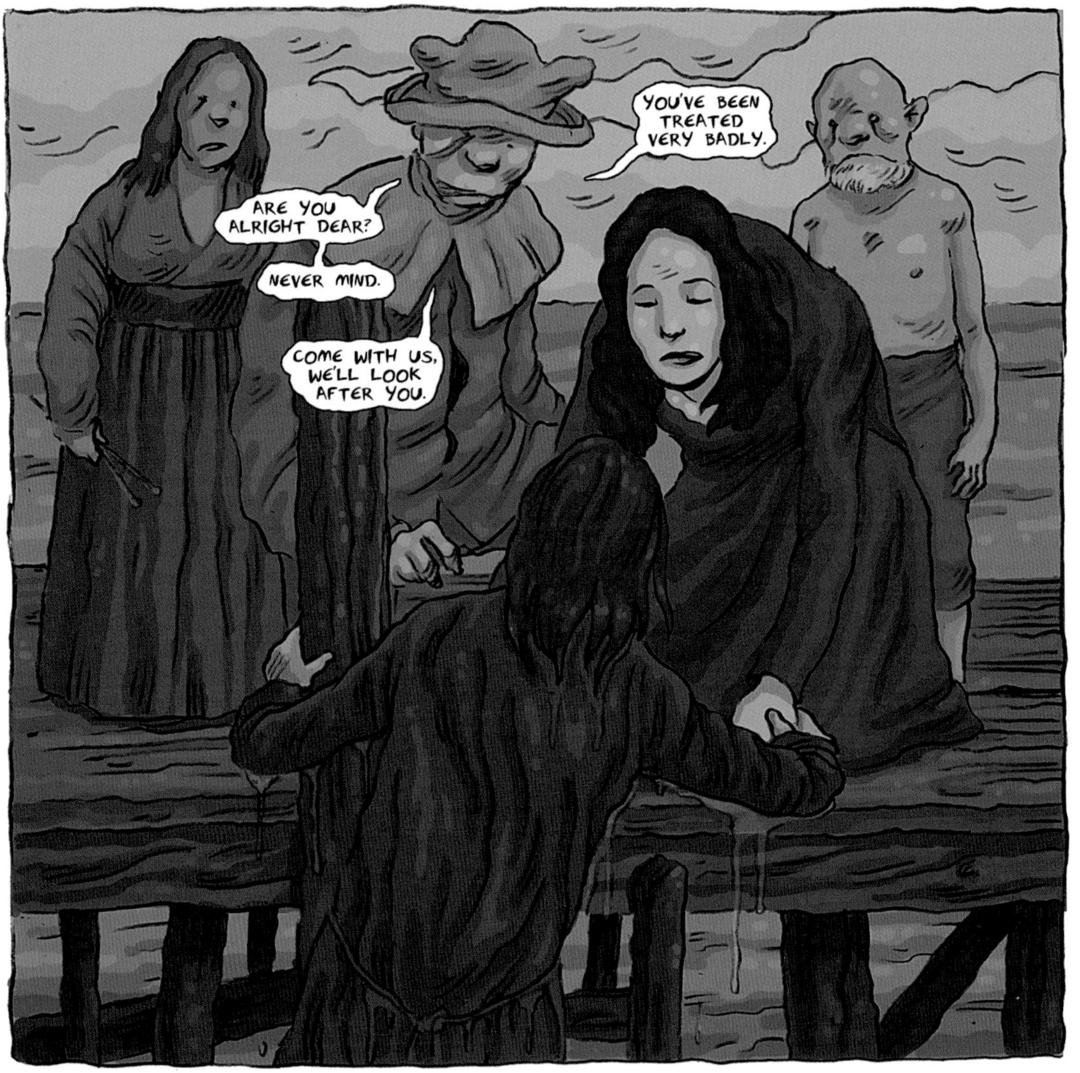
ARE YOU ALRIGHT DEAR?
NEVER MIND.
COME WITH US, WE'LL LOOK AFTER YOU.
YOU'VE BEEN TREATED VERY BADLY.

GET OFF, GET OFF, DON'T TOUCH ME, YOU PIGS!
YOU'RE ALL HORRID BASTARD PIGS!
GET OFF, GET OUT, GO AWAY!
BASTARD PIG BASTARDS!

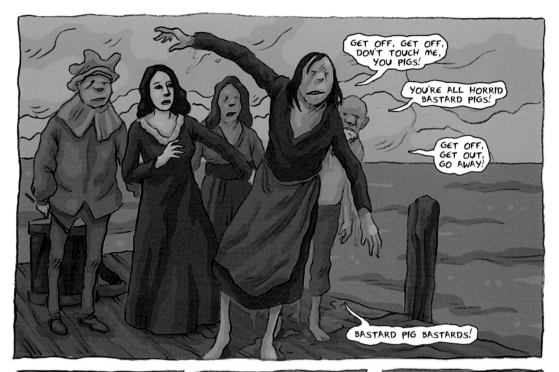

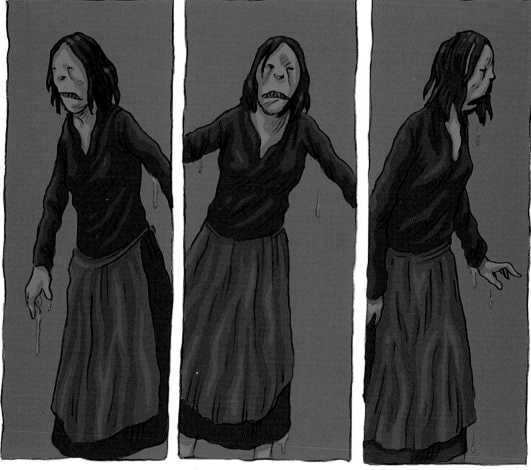

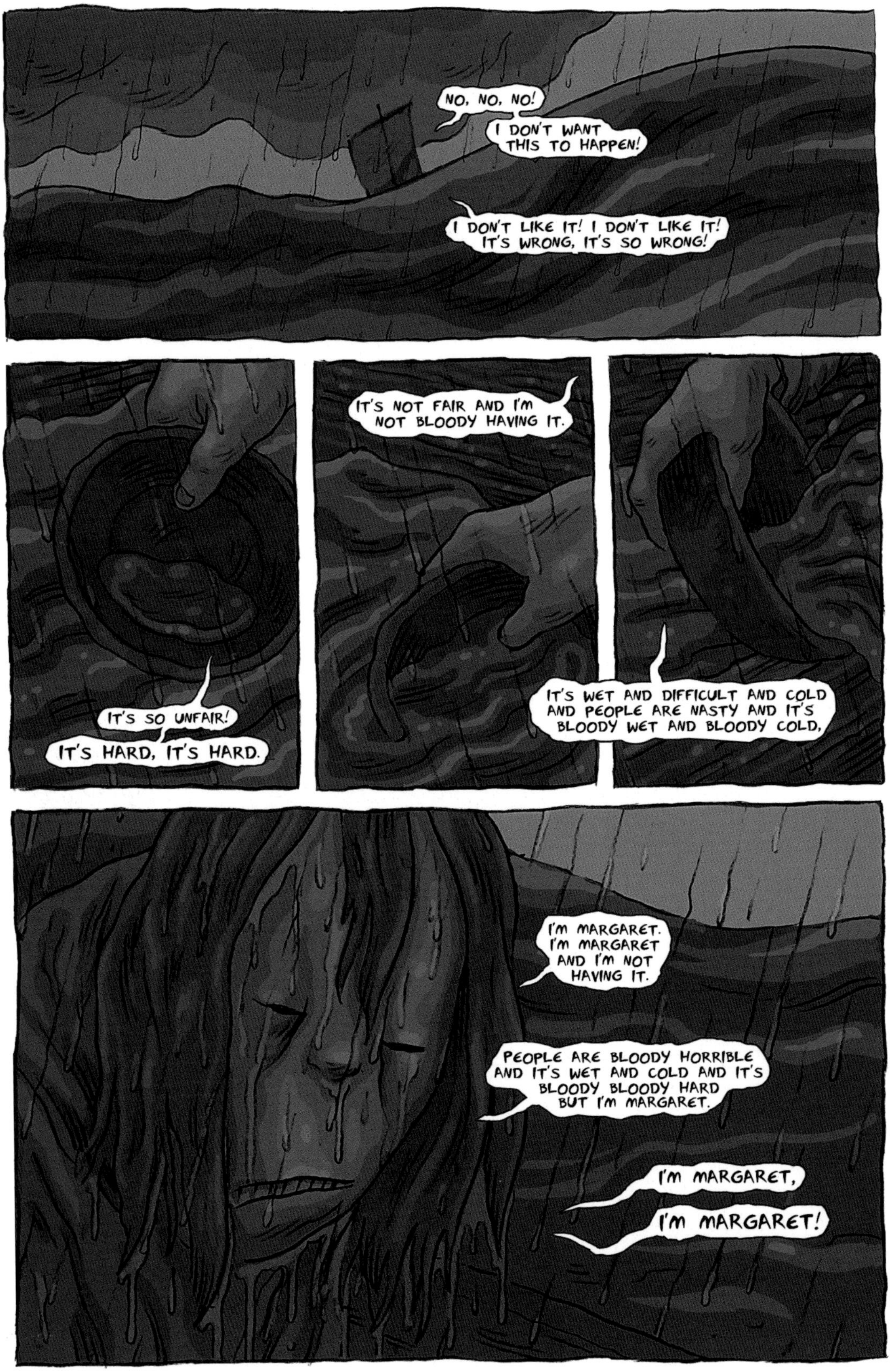
NO, NO, NO!
I DON'T WANT THIS TO HAPPEN!
I DON'T LIKE IT! I DON'T LIKE IT! IT'S WRONG, IT'S SO WRONG!
IT'S SO UNFAIR!
IT'S HARD, IT'S HARD.
IT'S NOT FAIR AND I'M NOT BLOODY HAVING IT.
IT'S WET AND DIFFICULT AND COLD AND PEOPLE ARE NASTY AND IT'S BLOODY WET AND BLOODY COLD,
I'M MARGARET. I'M MARGARET AND I'M NOT HAVING IT.
PEOPLE ARE BLOODY HORRIBLE AND IT'S WET AND COLD AND IT'S BLOODY BLOODY HARD BUT I'M MARGARET.
I'M MARGARET,
I'M MARGARET!

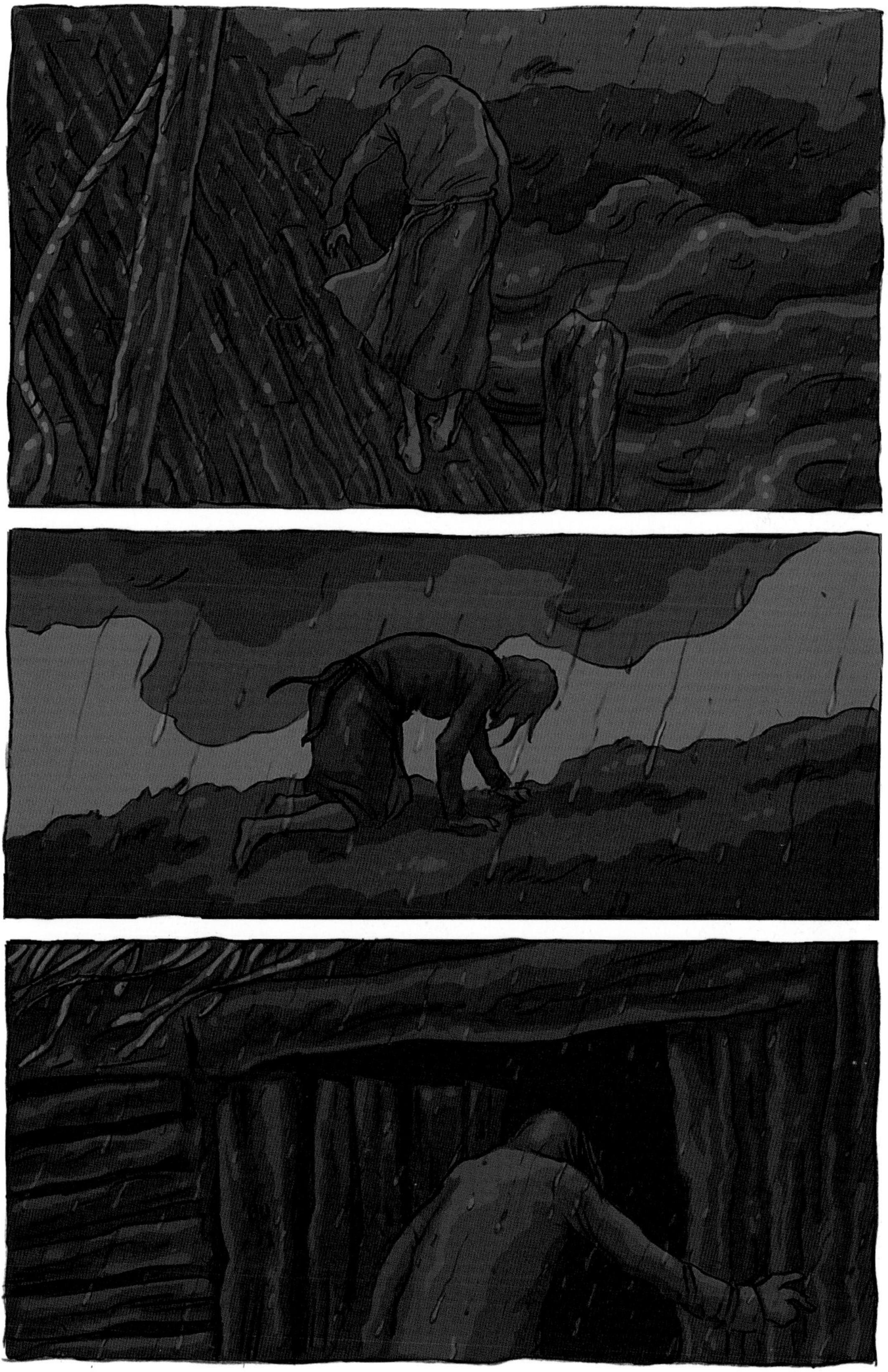

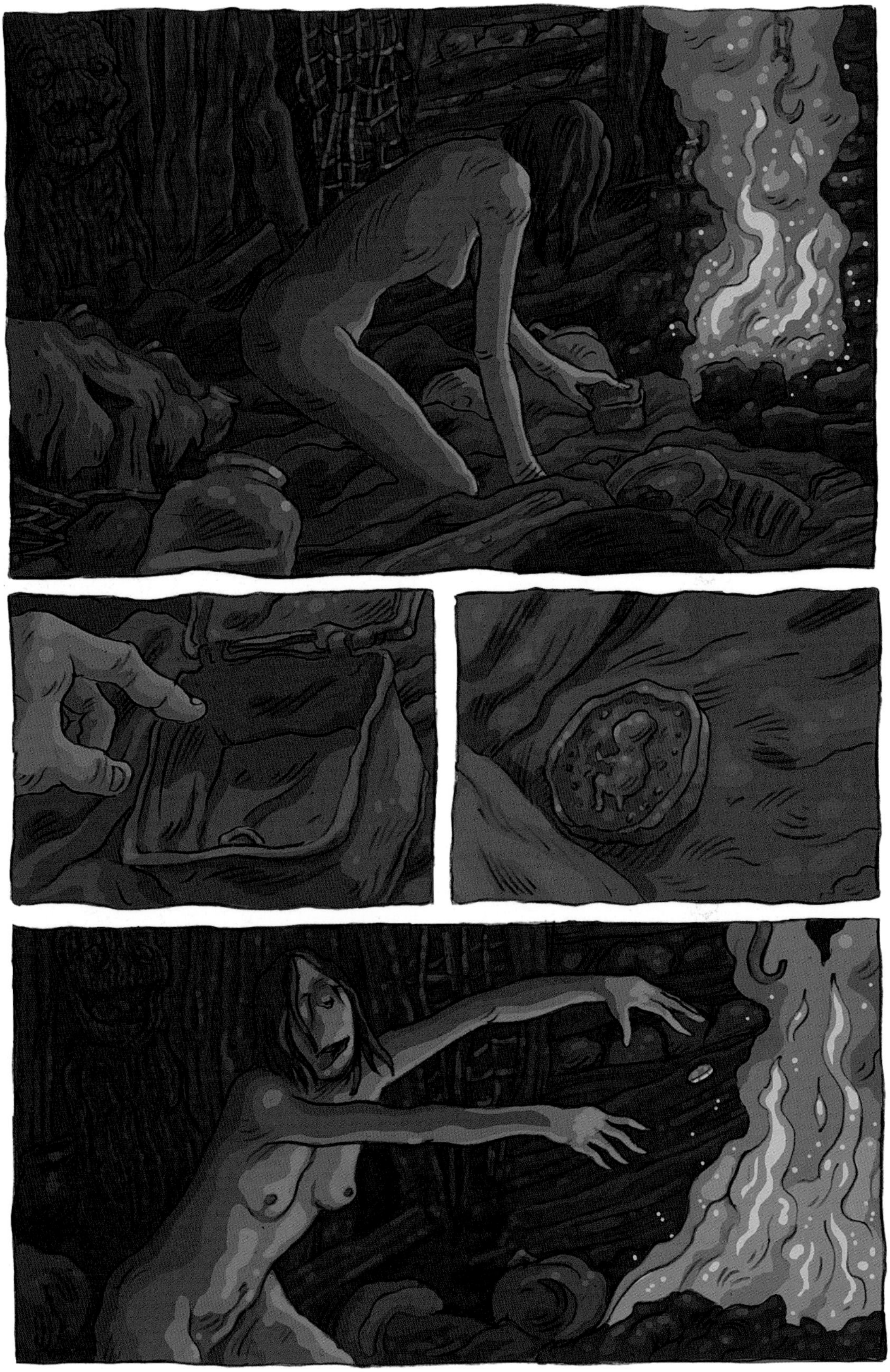

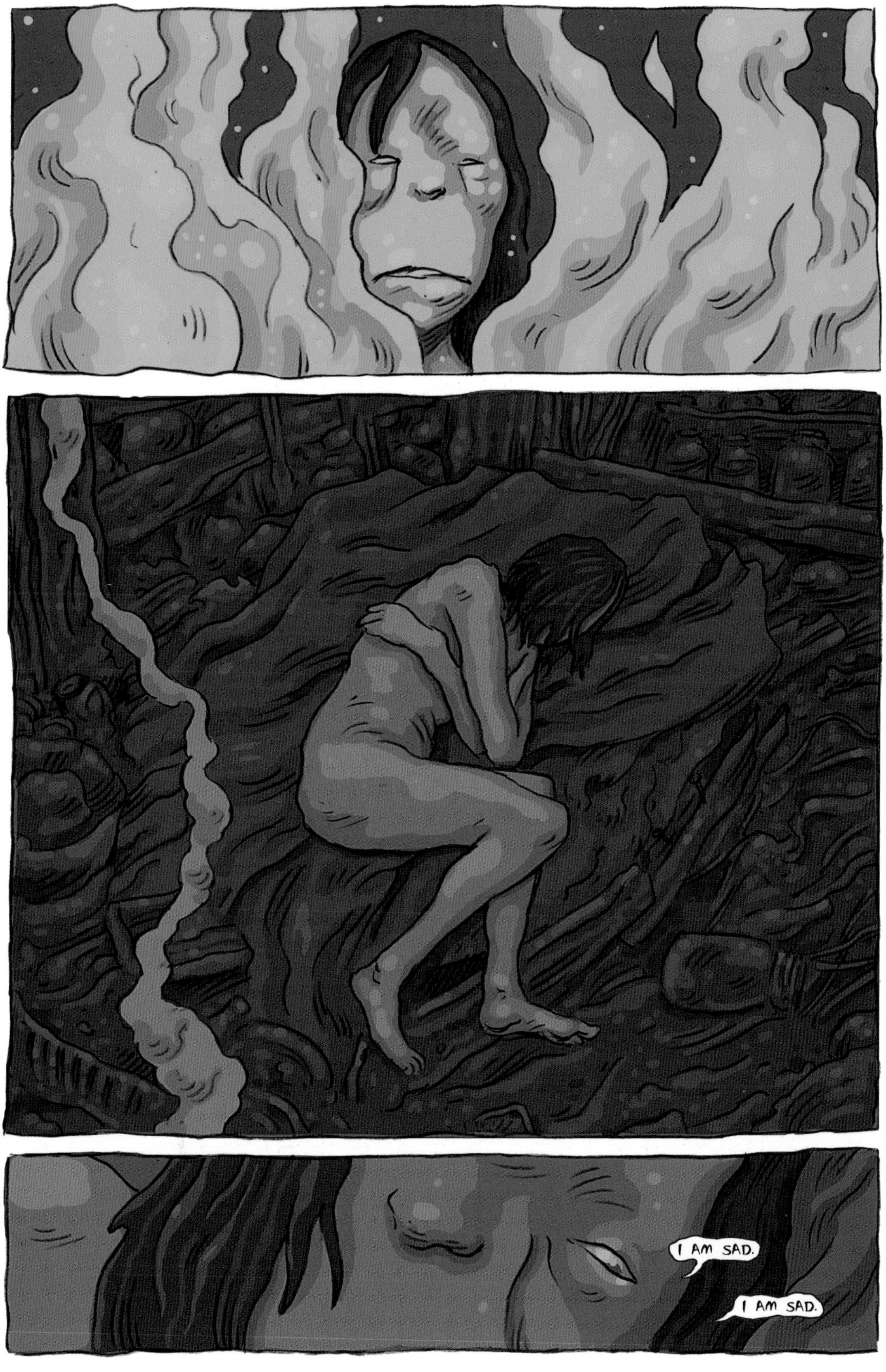
I AM SAD.
I AM SAD.

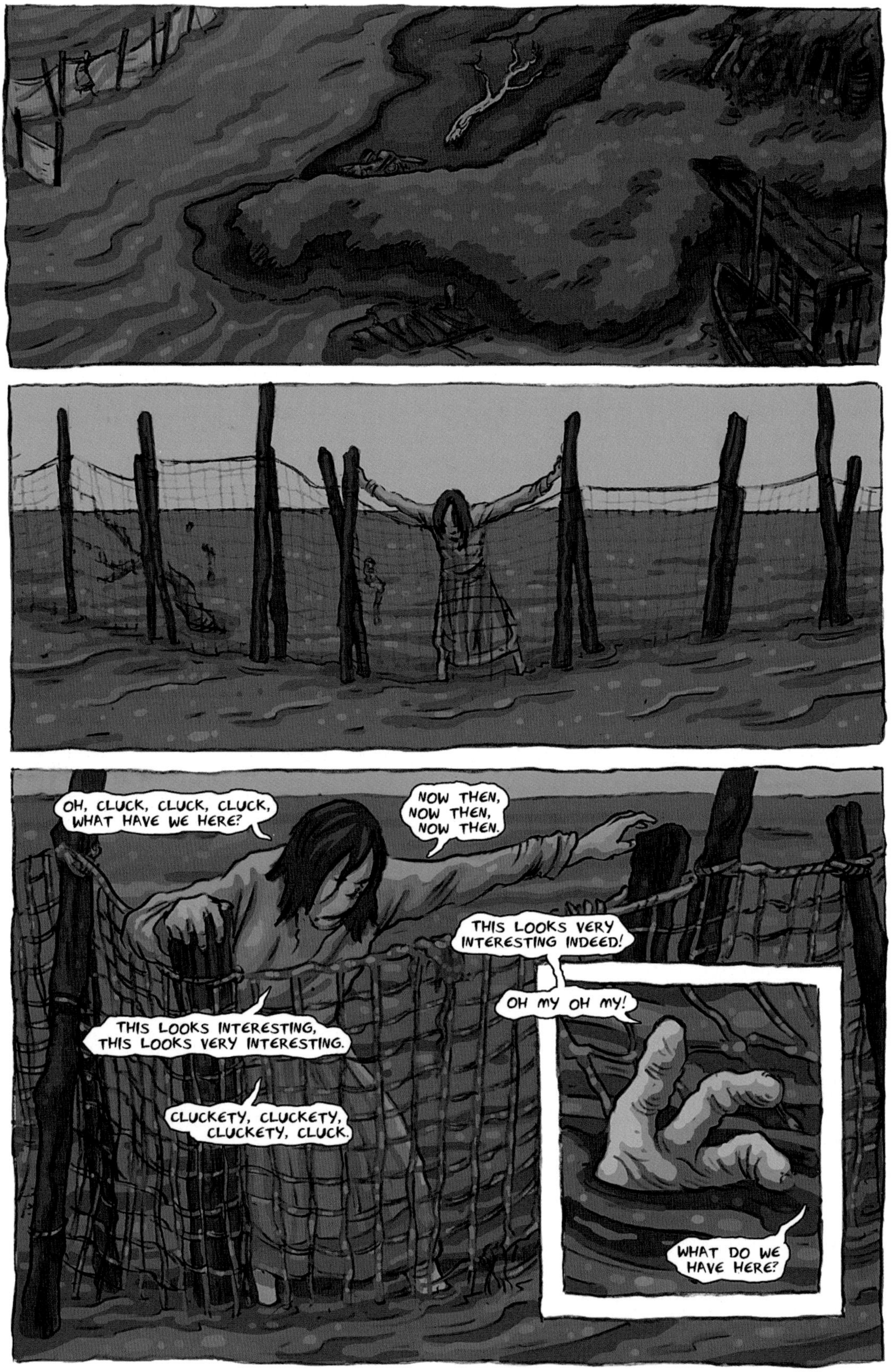
OH, CLUCK, CLUCK, CLUCK, WHAT HAVE WE HERE?
NOW THEN, NOW THEN, NOW THEN.
THIS LOOKS INTERESTING, THIS LOOKS VERY INTERESTING.
CLUCKETY, CLUCKETY, CLUCKETY, CLUCK.
THIS LOOKS VERY INTERESTING INDEED!
OH MY OH MY!
WHAT DO WE HAVE HERE?

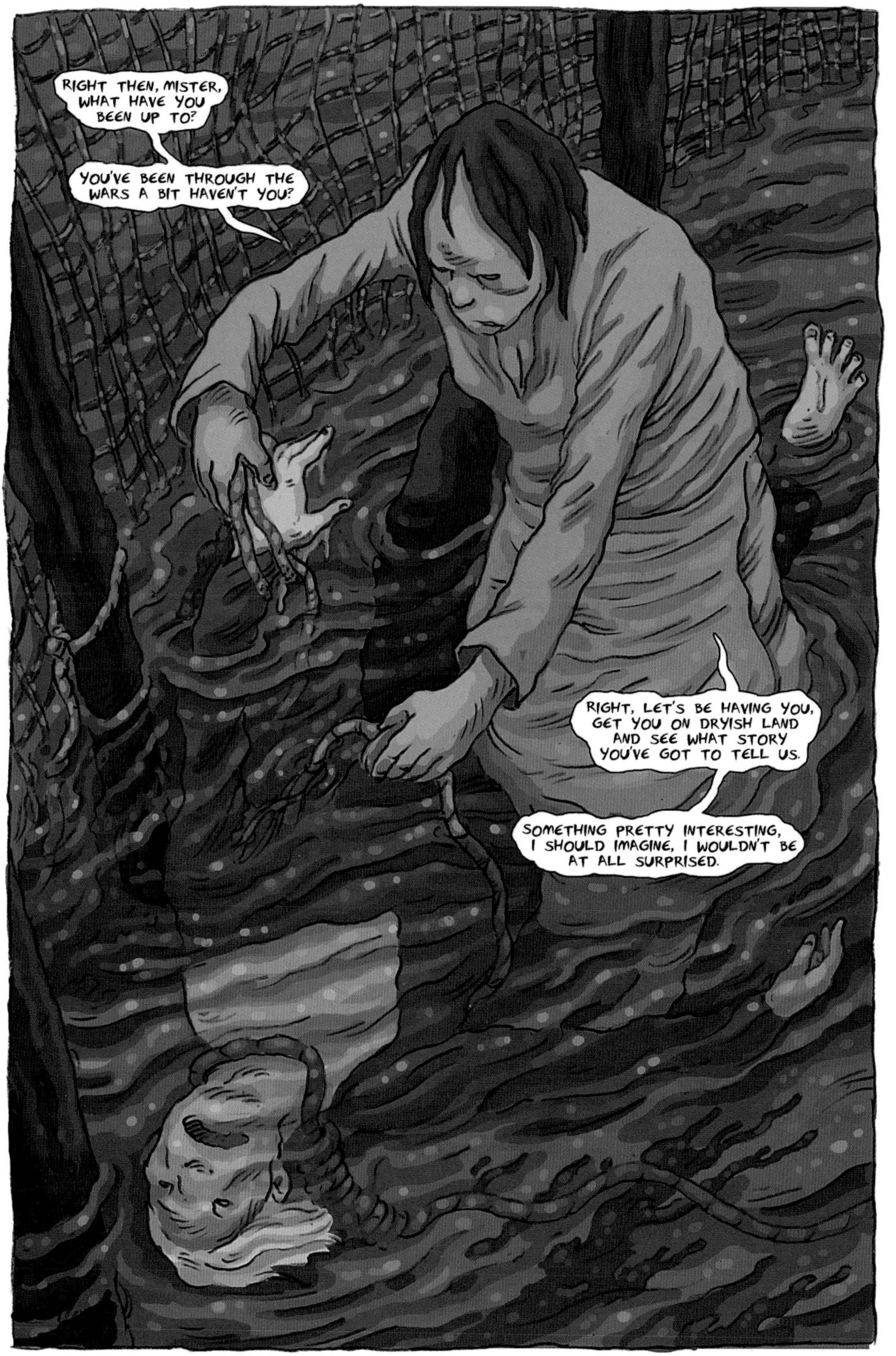
RIGHT THEN, MISTER, WHAT HAVE YOU BEEN UP TO?
YOU'VE BEEN THROUGH THE WARS A BIT HAVEN'T YOU?
RIGHT, LET'S BE HAVING YOU, GET YOU ON DRYISH LAND AND SEE WHAT STORY YOU'VE GOT TO TELL US.
SOMETHING PRETTY INTERESTING, I SHOULD IMAGINE, I WOULDN'T BE AT ALL SURPRISED.

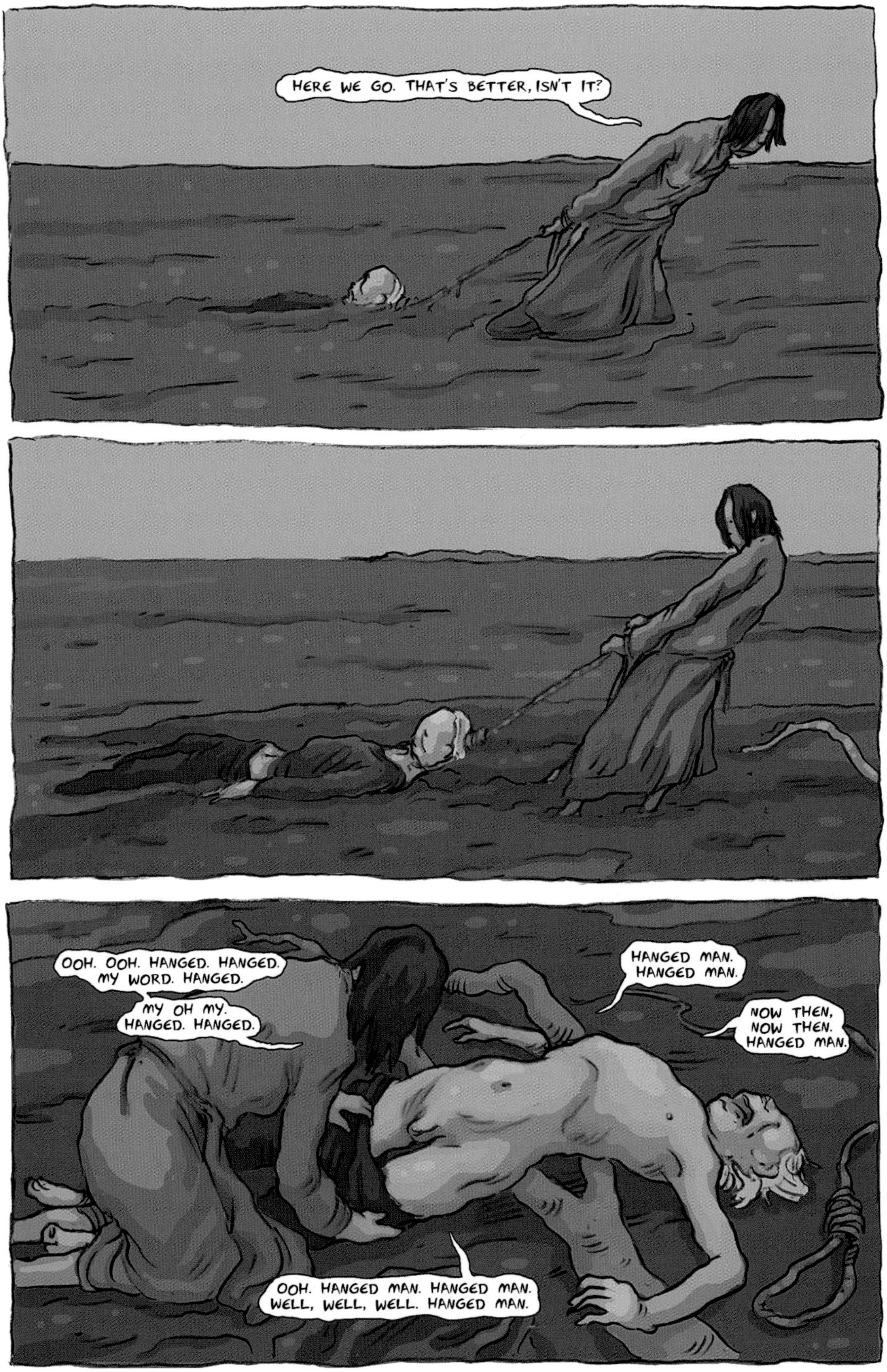
HERE WE GO. THAT'S BETTER, ISN'T IT?
OOH. OOH. HANGED. HANGED. MY WORD. HANGED.
MY OH MY. HANGED. HANGED.
HANGED MAN. HANGED MAN.
NOW THEN, NOW THEN. HANGED MAN.
OOH. HANGED MAN. HANGED MAN. WELL, WELL, WELL. HANGED MAN.

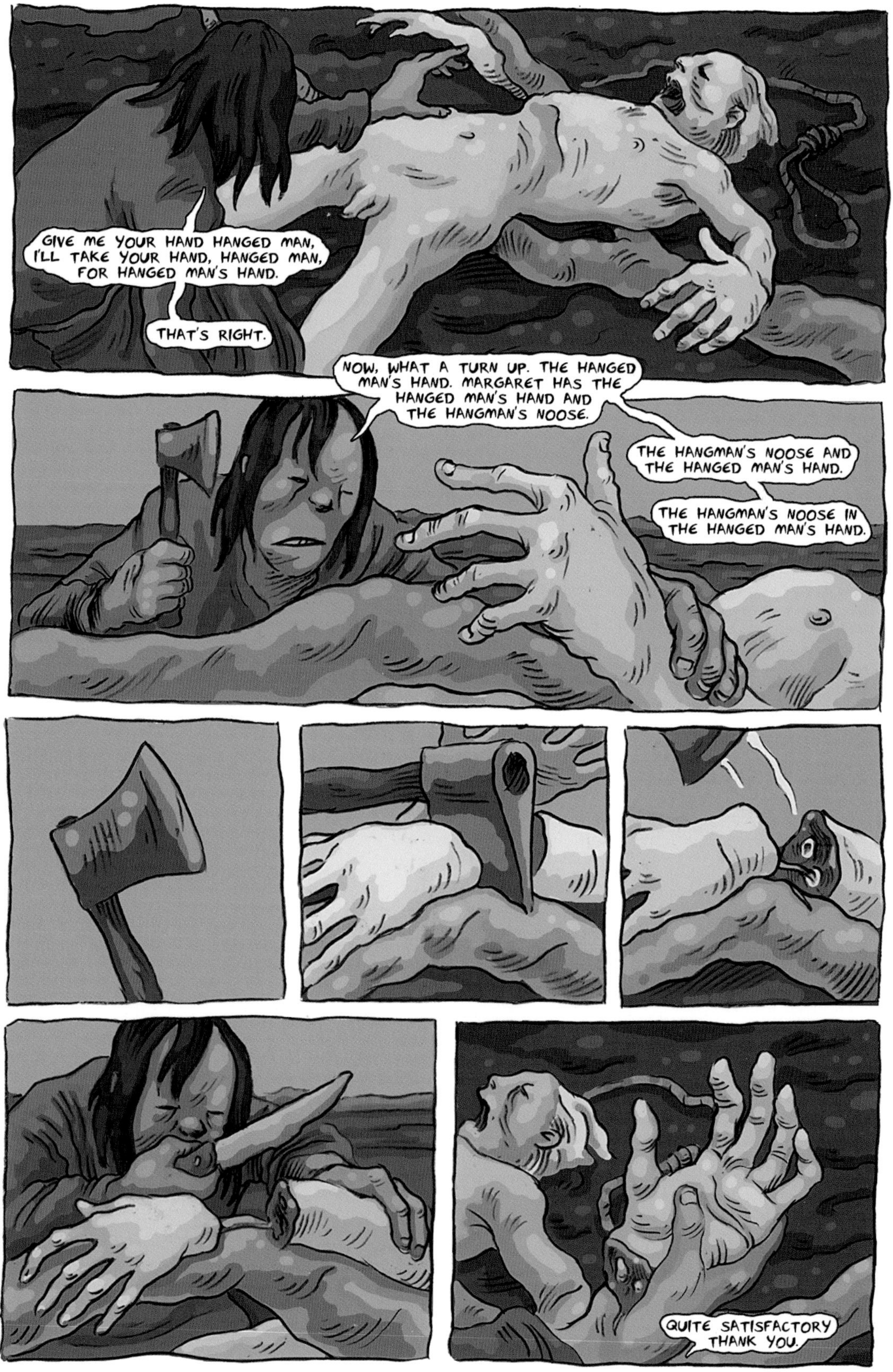
GIVE ME YOUR HAND HANGED MAN, I'LL TAKE YOUR HAND, HANGED MAN, FOR HANGED MAN'S HAND.
THAT'S RIGHT.
NOW, WHAT A TURN UP. THE HANGED MAN'S HAND. MARGARET HAS THE HANGED MAN'S HAND AND THE HANGMAN'S NOOSE.
THE HANGMAN'S NOOSE AND THE HANGED MAN'S HAND.
THE HANGMAN'S NOOSE IN THE HANGED MAN'S HAND.
QUITE SATISFACTORY THANK YOU.

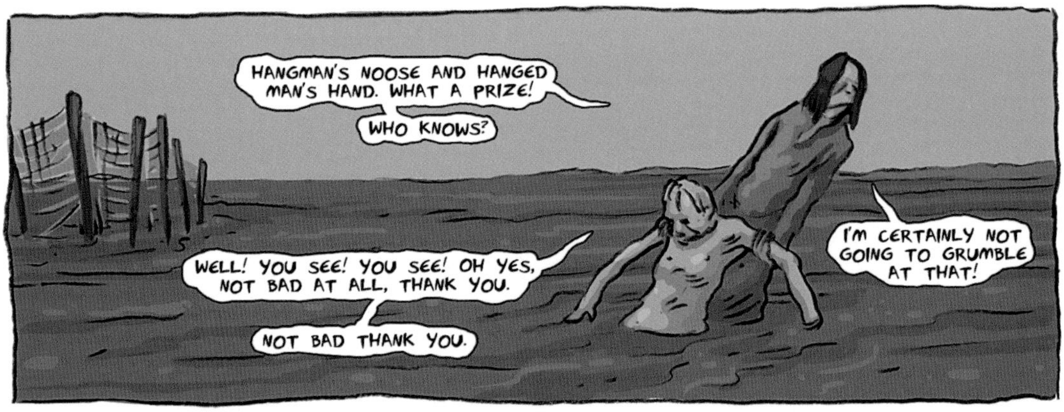
HANGMAN'S NOOSE AND HANGED MAN'S HAND. WHAT A PRIZE!
WHO KNOWS?
WELL! YOU SEE! YOU SEE! OH YES, NOT BAD AT ALL, THANK YOU.
NOT BAD THANK YOU.
I'M CERTAINLY NOT GOING TO GRUMBLE AT THAT!

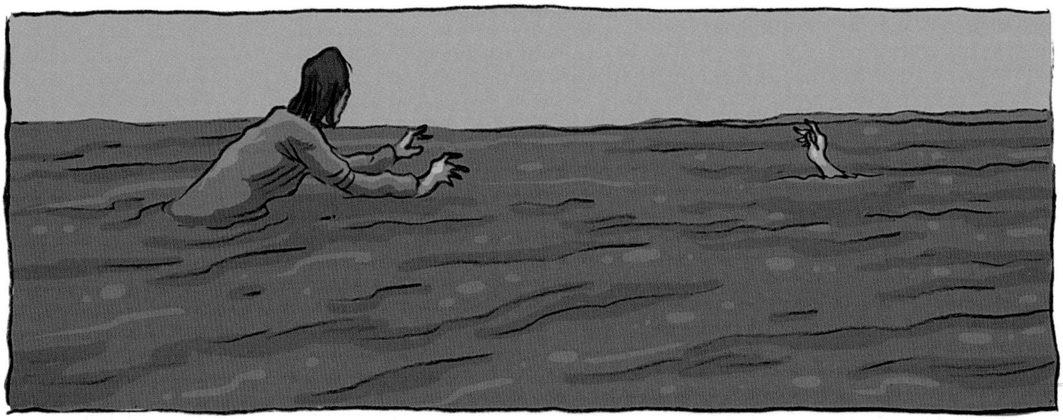

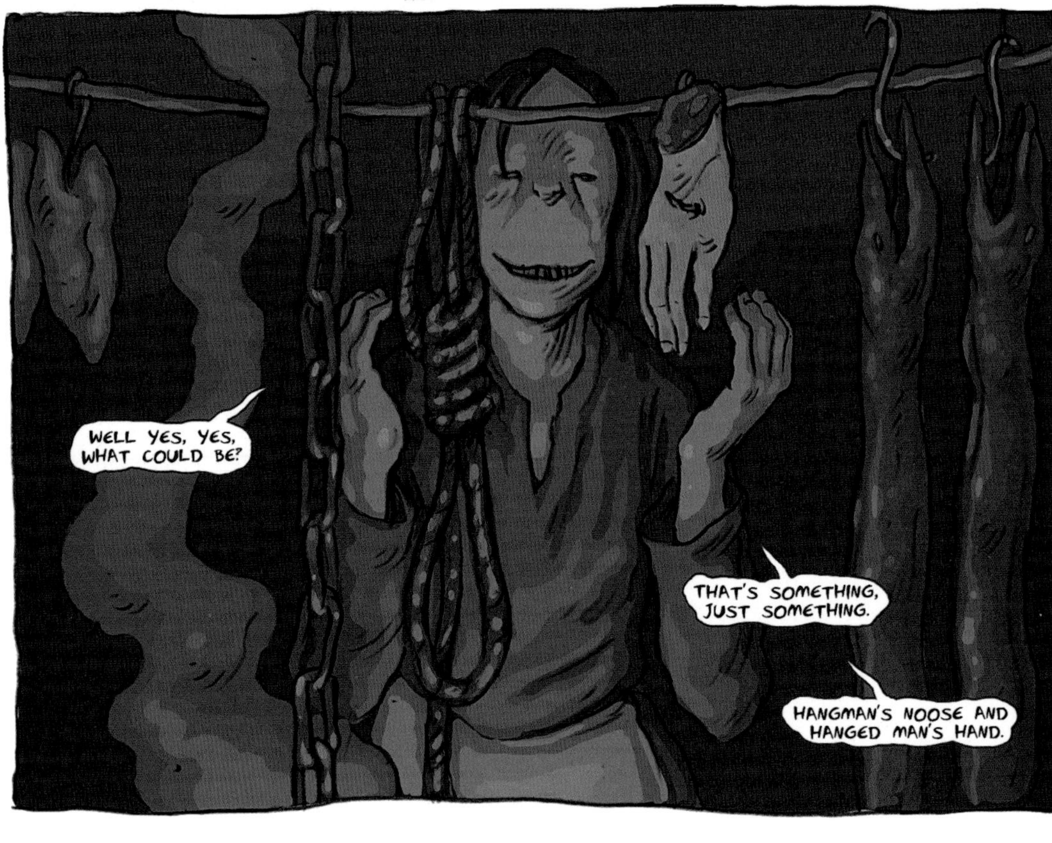
WELL YES, YES, WHAT COULD BE?
THAT'S SOMETHING, JUST SOMETHING.
HANGMAN'S NOOSE AND HANGED MAN'S HAND.

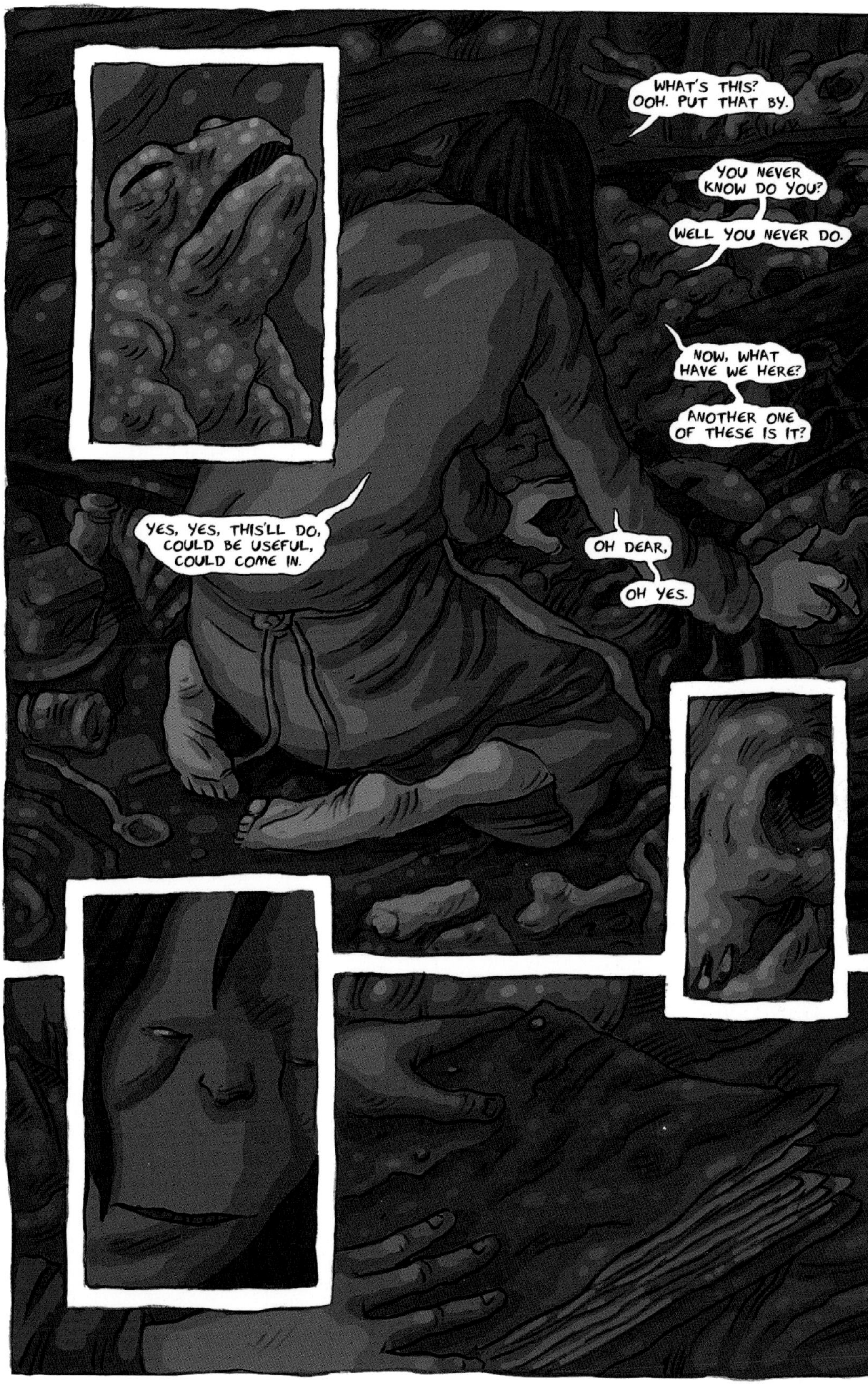
WHAT'S THIS? OOH. PUT THAT BY.
YOU NEVER KNOW DO YOU?
WELL YOU NEVER DO.
NOW, WHAT HAVE WE HERE?
ANOTHER ONE OF THESE IS IT?
YES, YES, THIS'LL DO, COULD BE USEFUL, COULD COME IN.
OH DEAR,
OH YES.

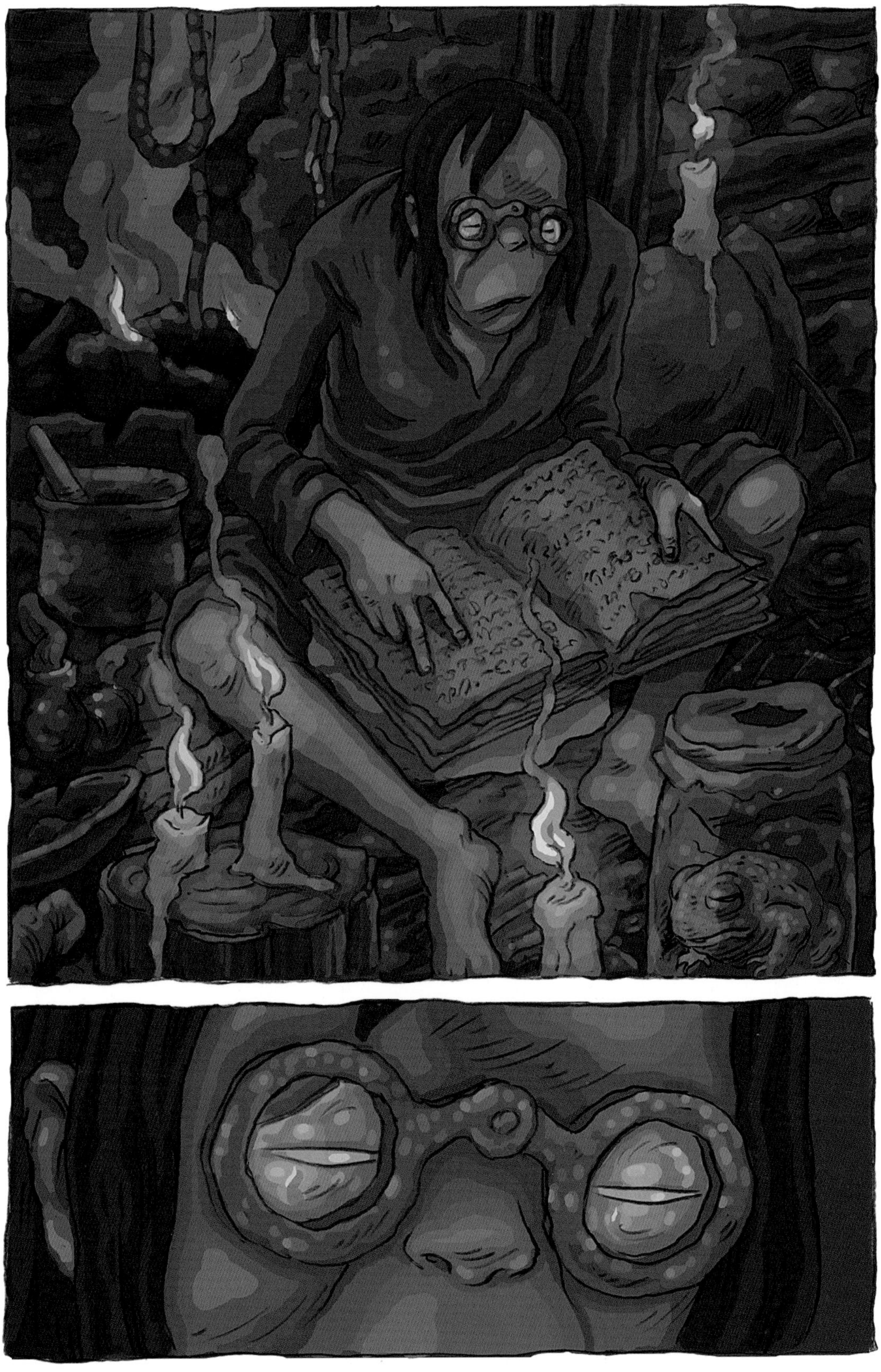

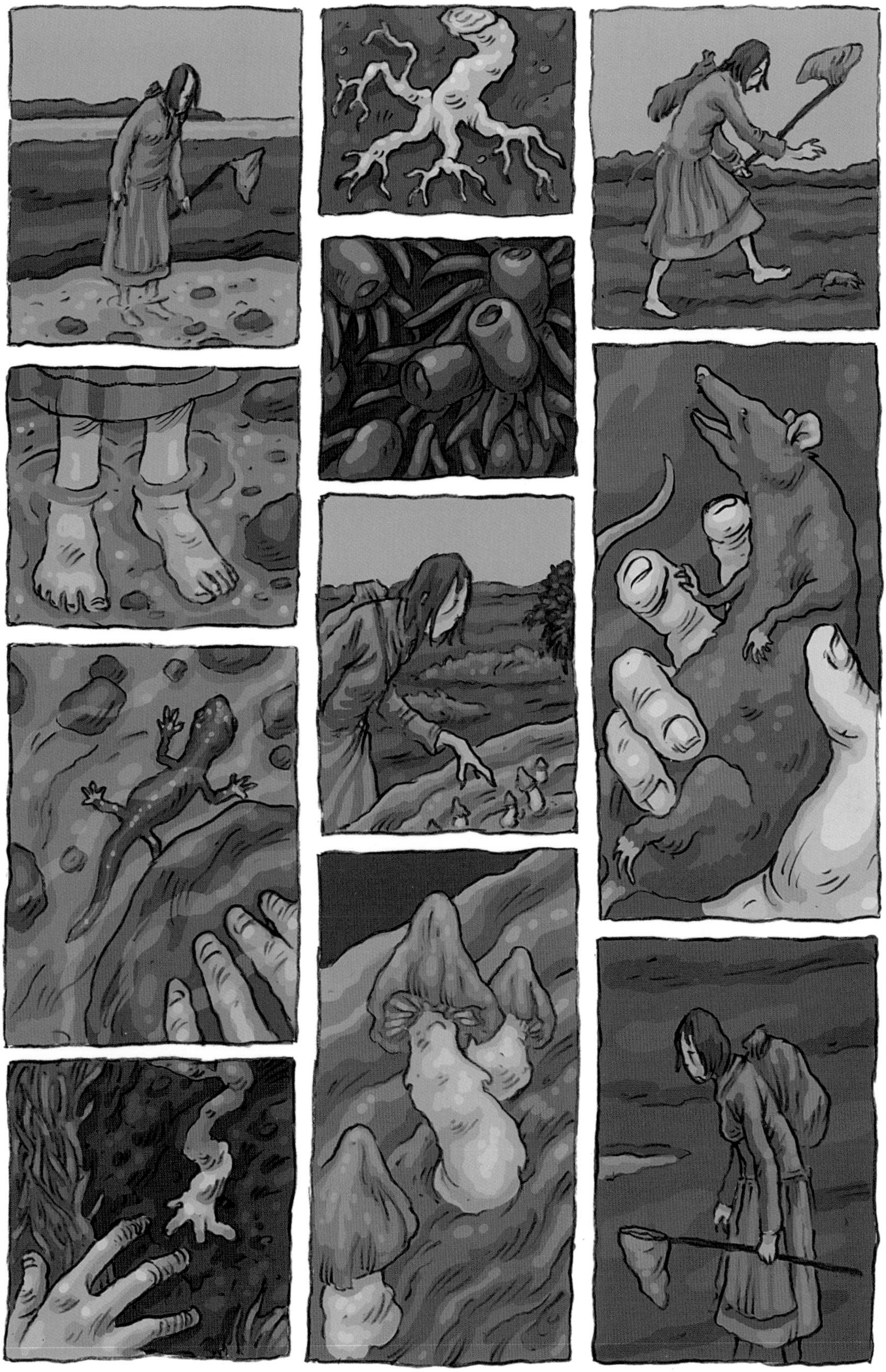

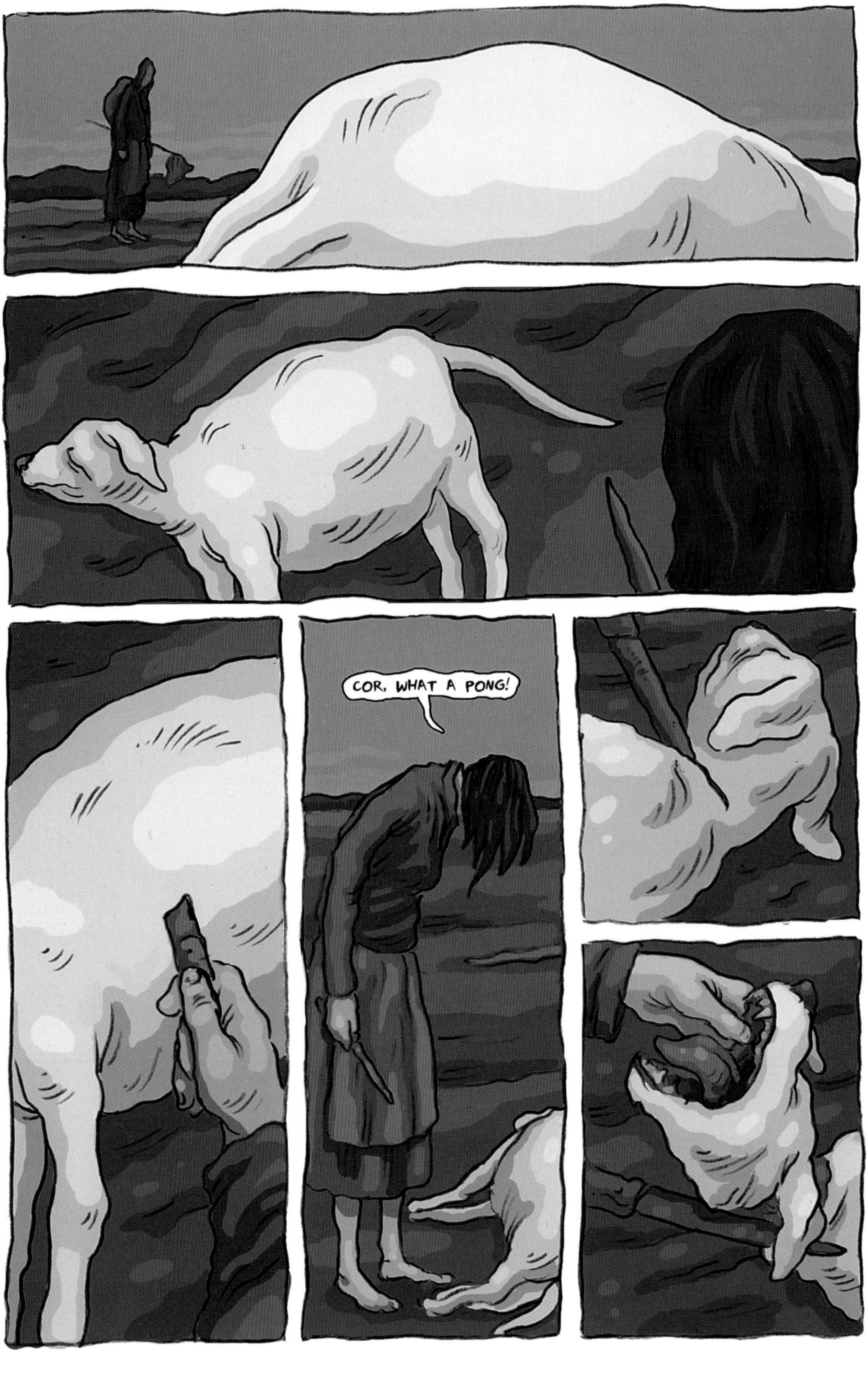
COR, WHAT A PONG!

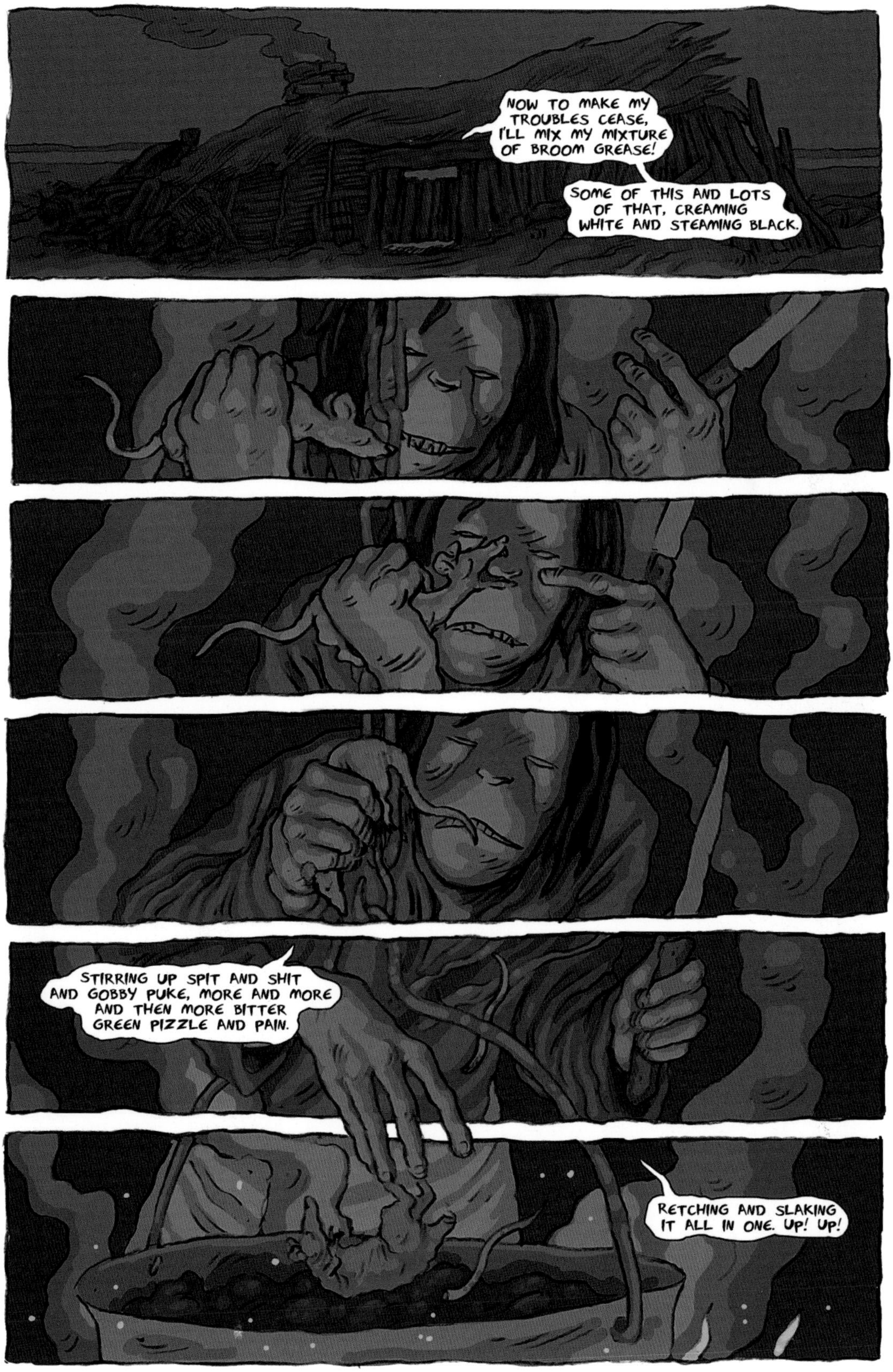
NOW TO MAKE MY TROUBLES CEASE, I'LL MIX MY MIXTURE OF BROOM GREASE!
SOME OF THIS AND LOTS OF THAT, CREAMING WHITE AND STEAMING BLACK.
STIRRING UP SPIT AND SHIT AND GOBBY PUKE, MORE AND MORE AND THEN MORE BITTER GREEN PIZZLE AND PAIN.
RETCHING AND SLAKING IT ALL IN ONE. UP! UP!

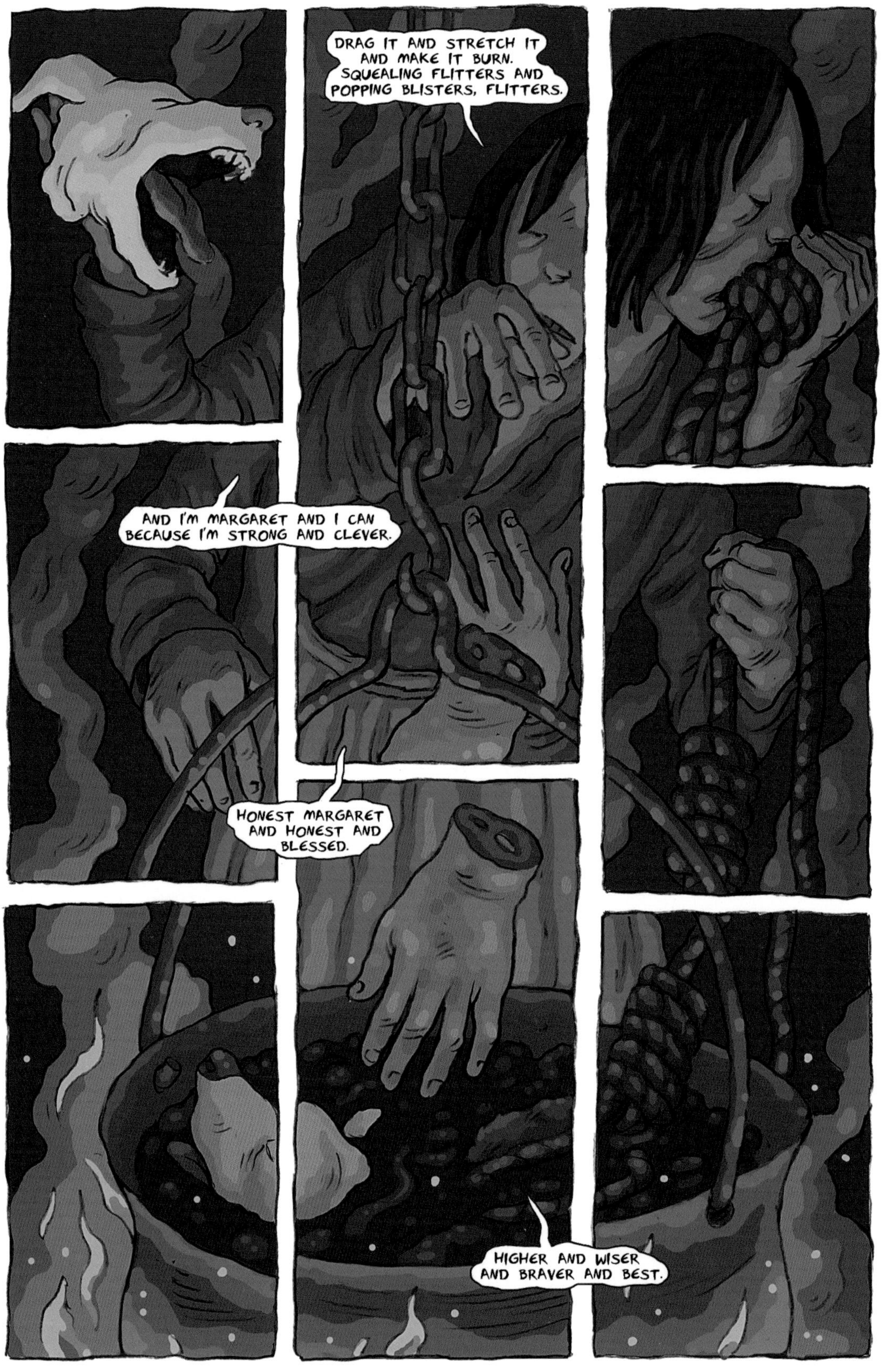
DRAG IT AND STRETCH IT AND MAKE IT BURN. SQUEALING FLITTERS AND POPPING BLISTERS, FLITTERS.
AND I'M MARGARET AND I CAN BECAUSE I'M STRONG AND CLEVER.
HONEST MARGARET AND HONEST AND BLESSED.
HIGHER AND WISER AND BRAVER AND BEST.

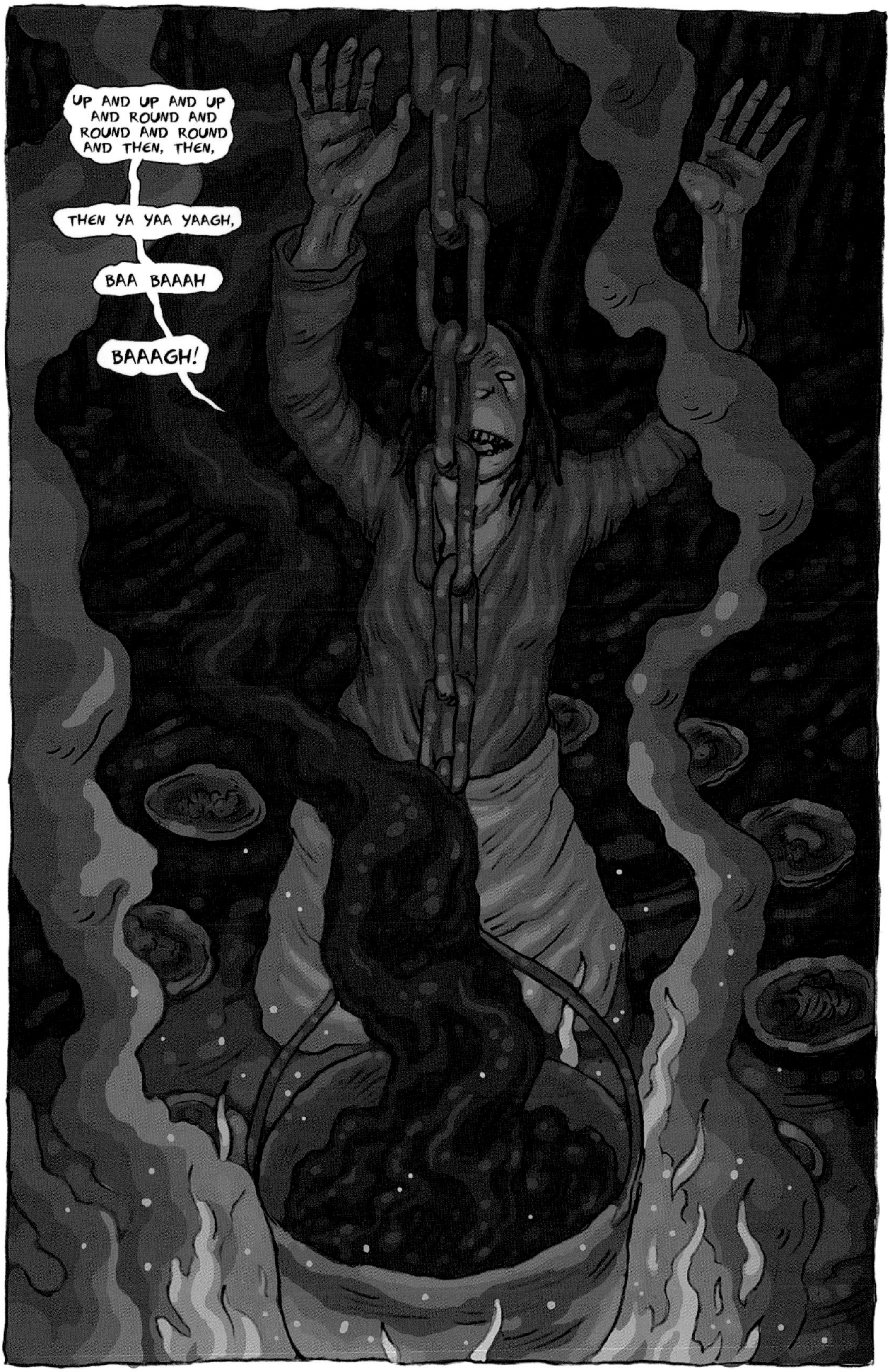
UP AND UP AND UP AND ROUND AND ROUND AND ROUND AND THEN, THEN,
THEN YA YAA YAAGH,
BAA BAAAH
BAAAGH!

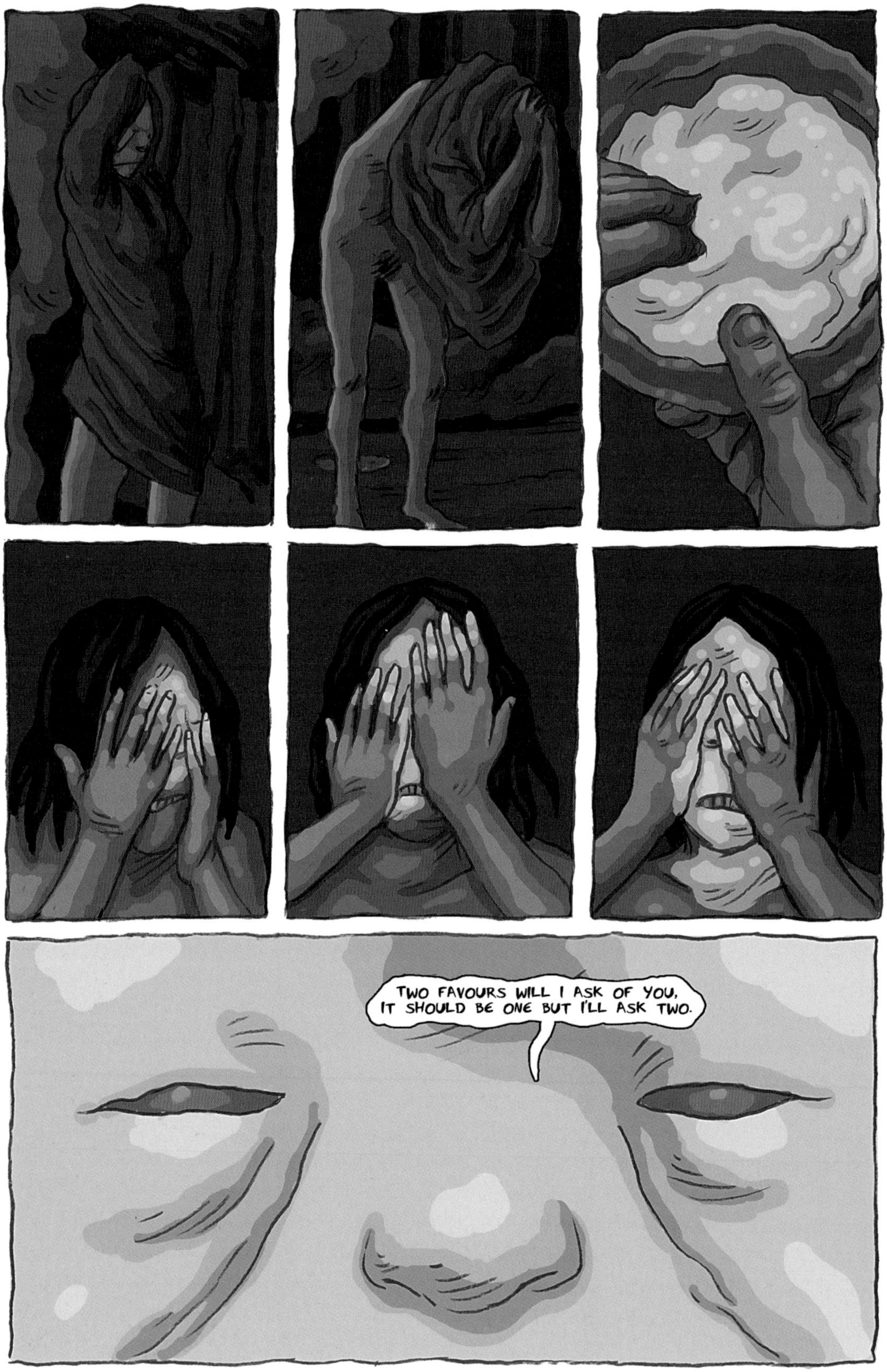
TWO FAVOURS WILL I ASK OF YOU,
IT SHOULD BE ONE BUT I'LL ASK TWO.

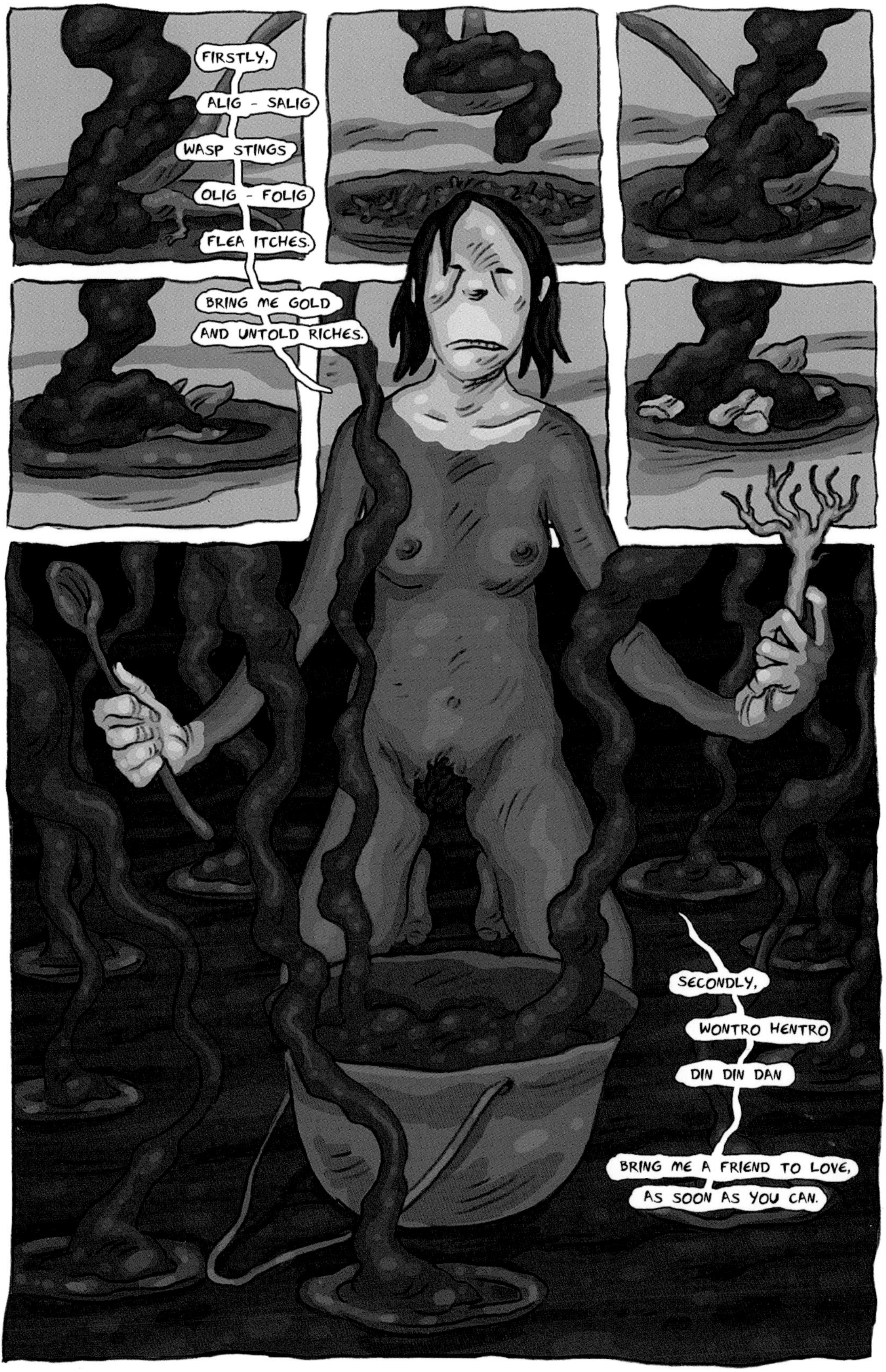
FIRSTLY,
ALIG - SALIG
WASP STINGS
OLIG - FOLIG
FLEA ITCHES.
BRING ME GOLD
AND UNTOLD RICHES.
SECONDLY,
WONTRO HENTRO
DIN DIN DAN
BRING ME A FRIEND TO LOVE,
AS SOON AS YOU CAN.

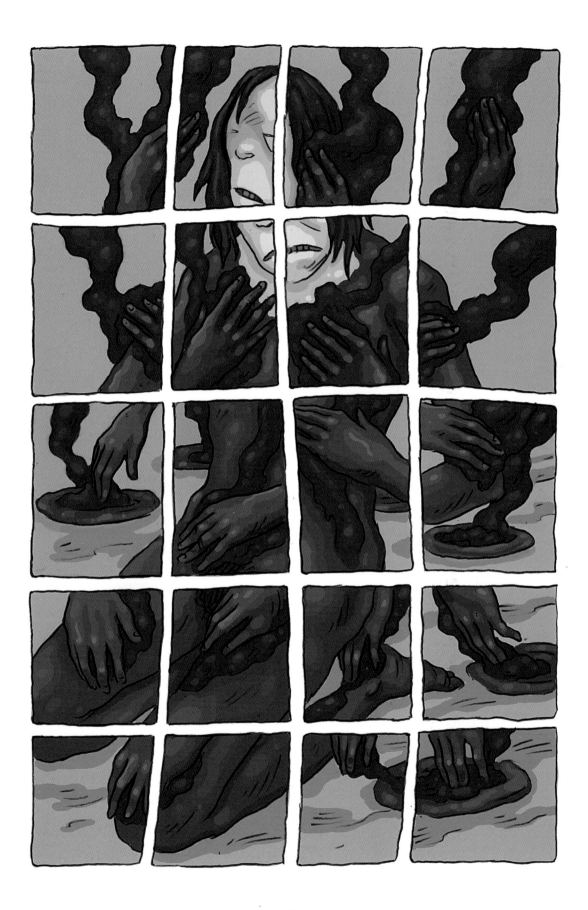

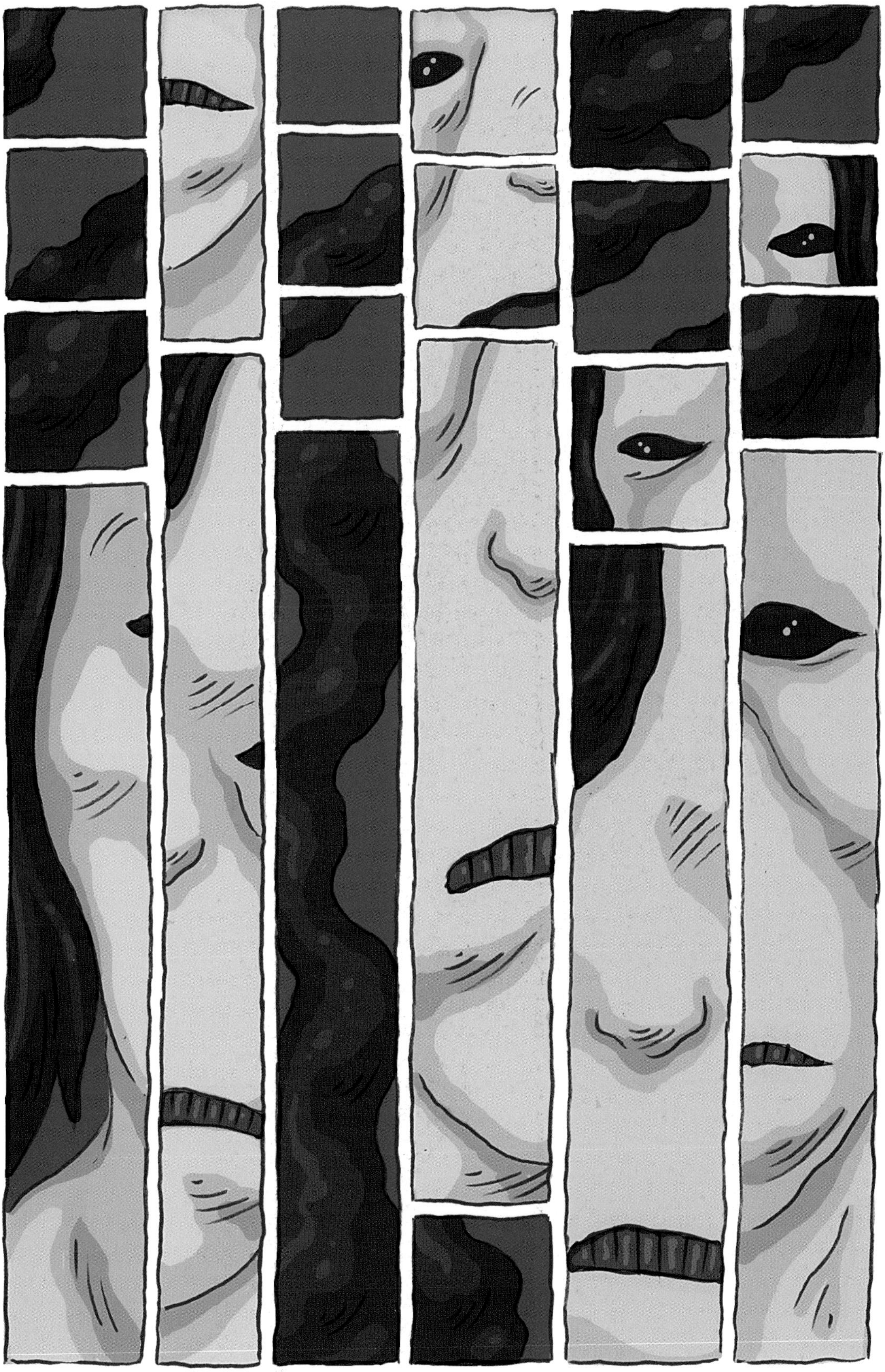

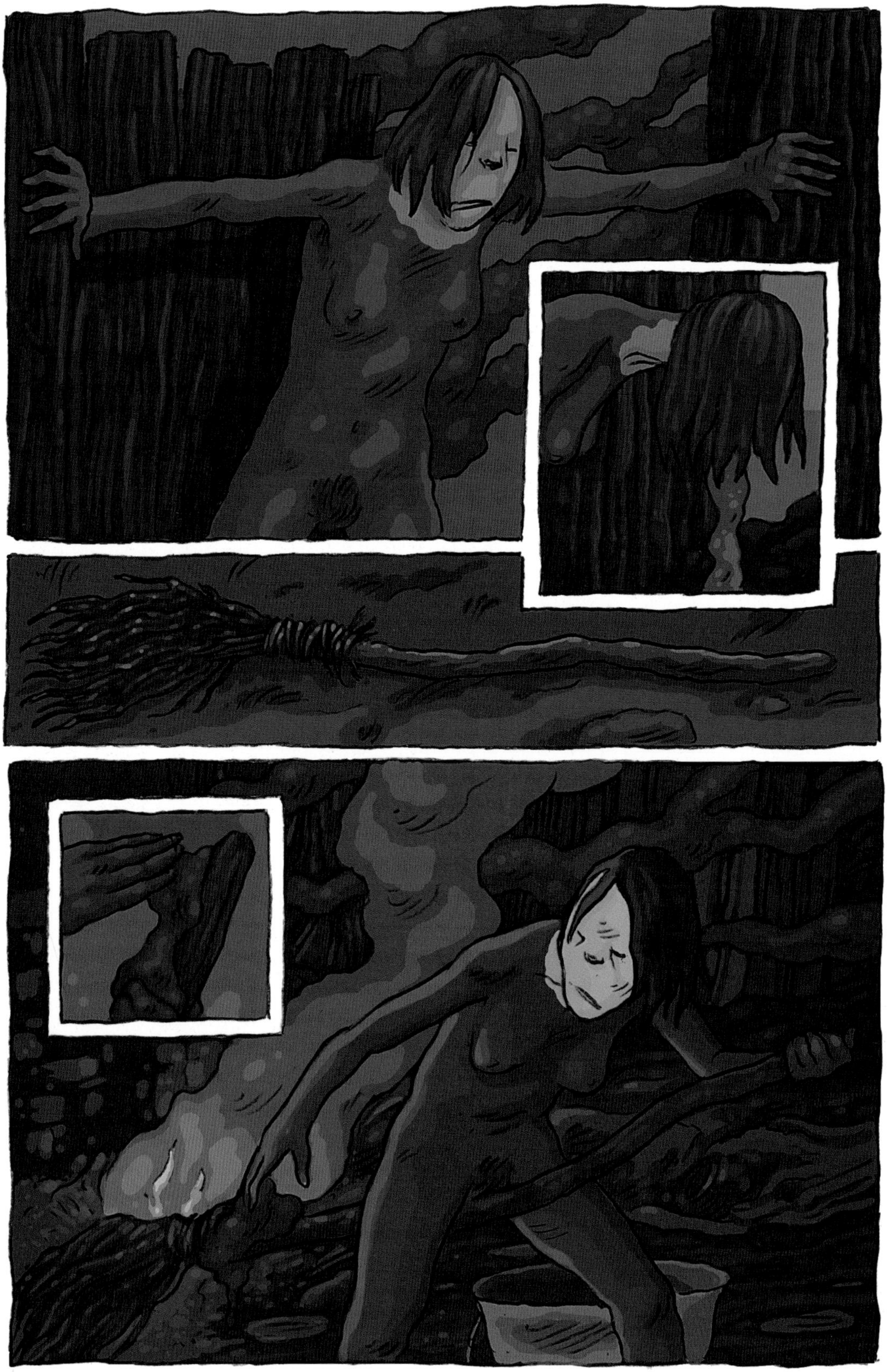

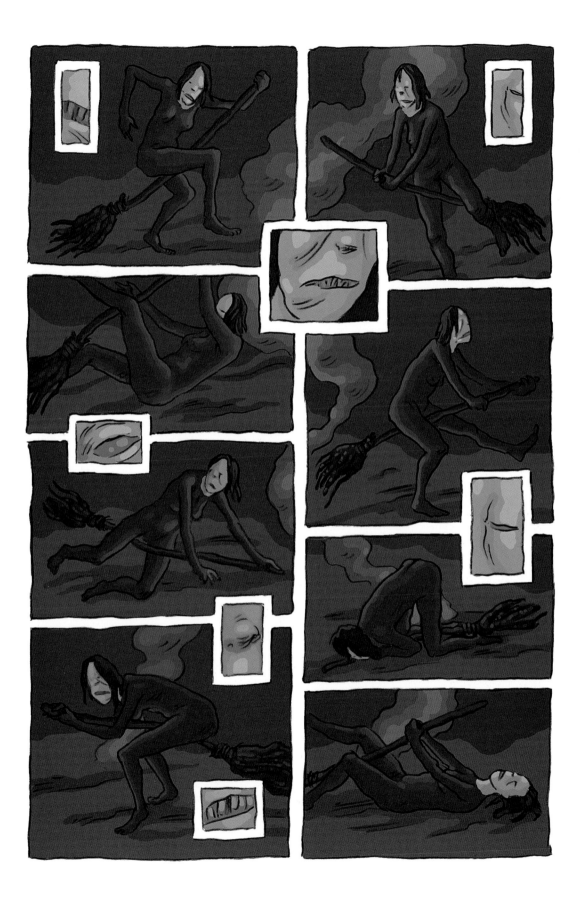

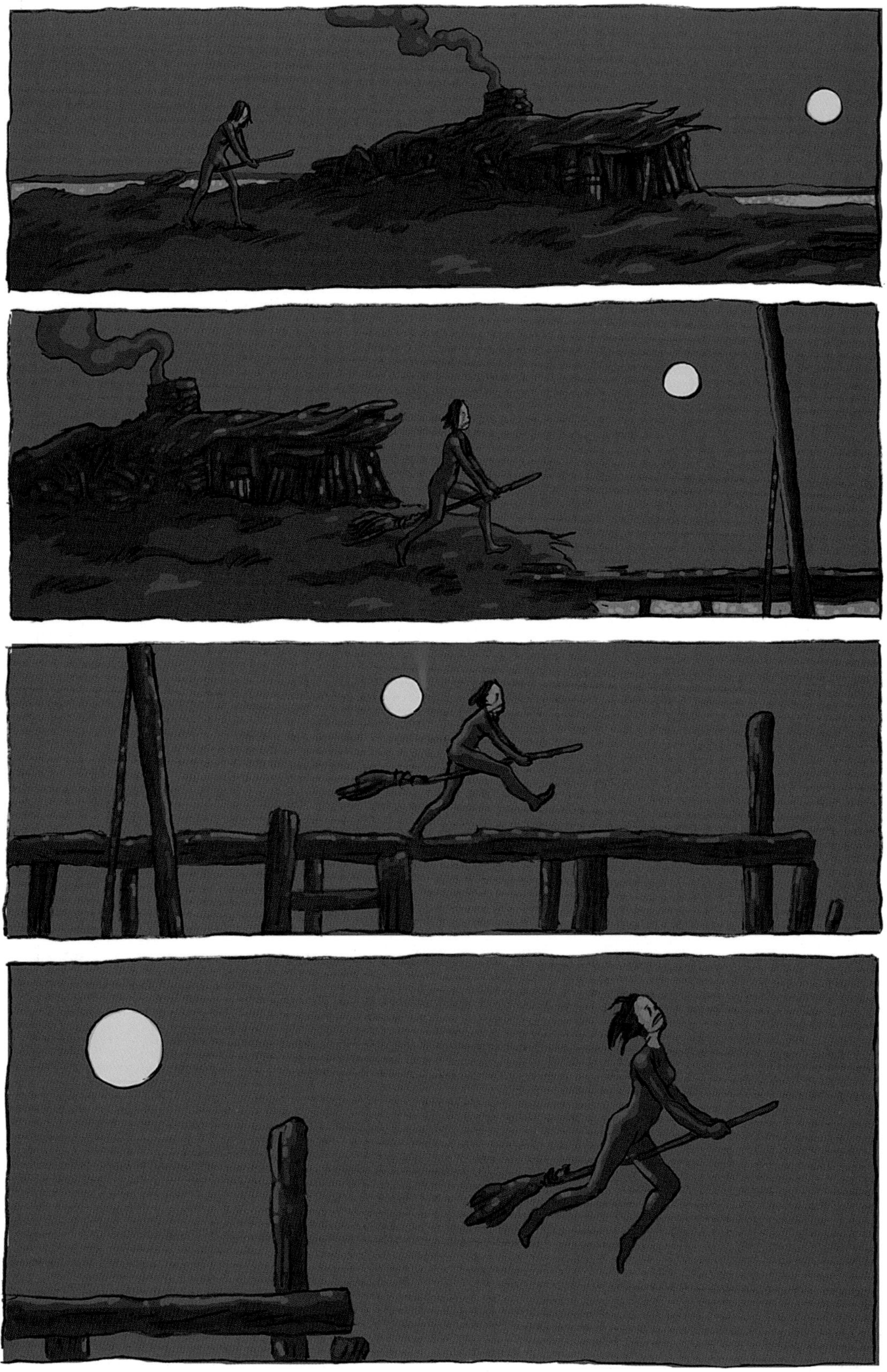

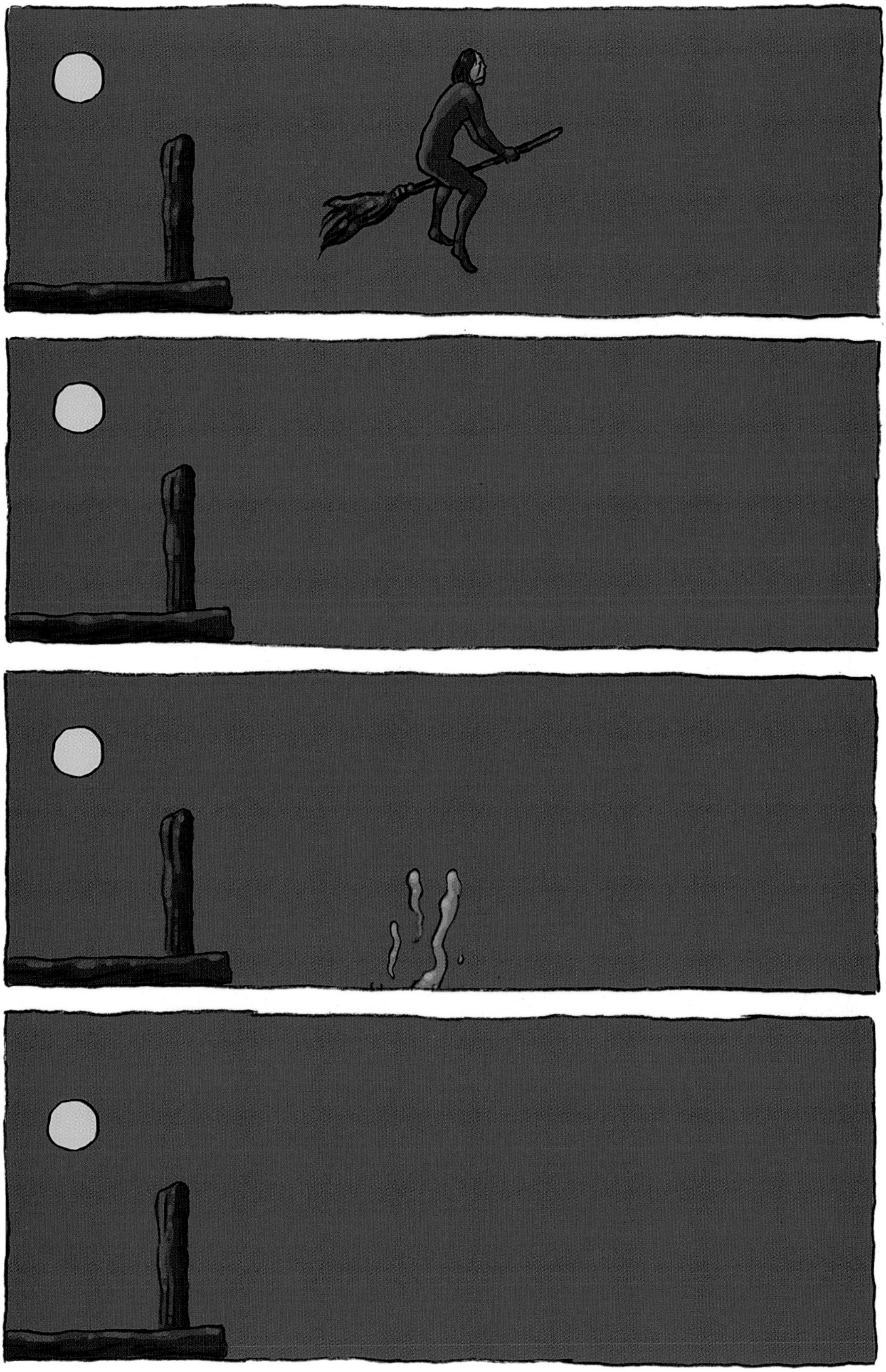

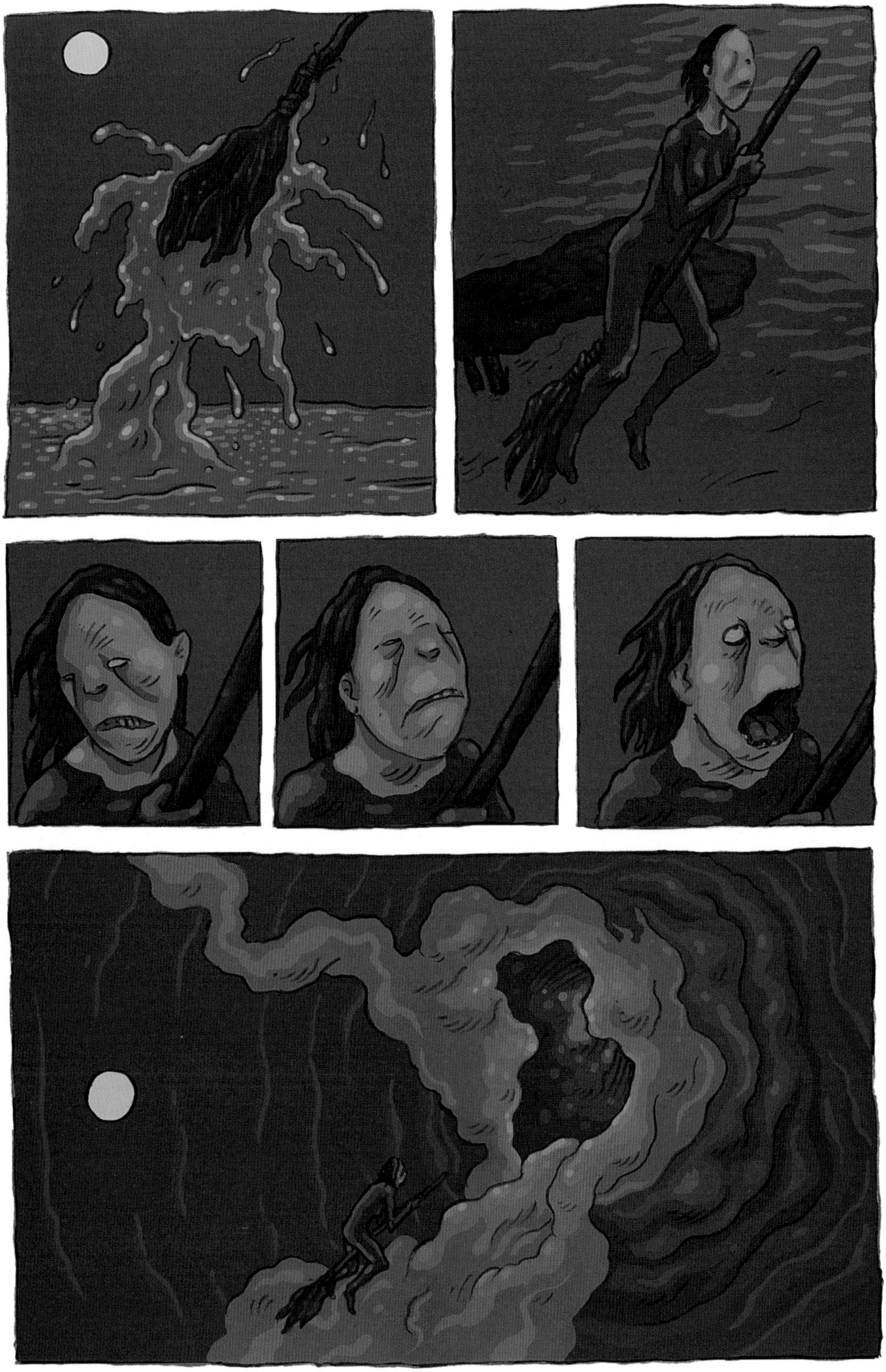

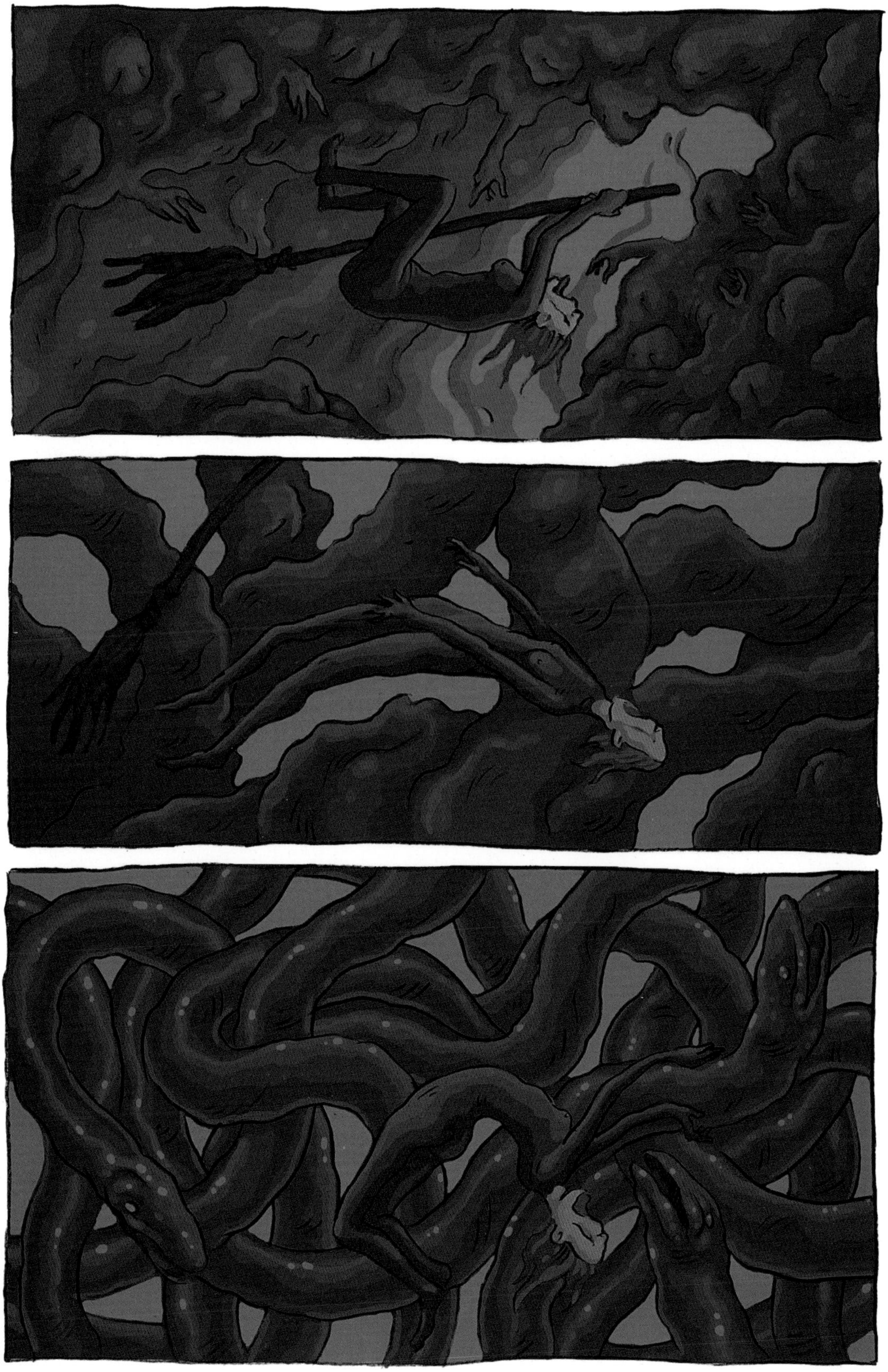

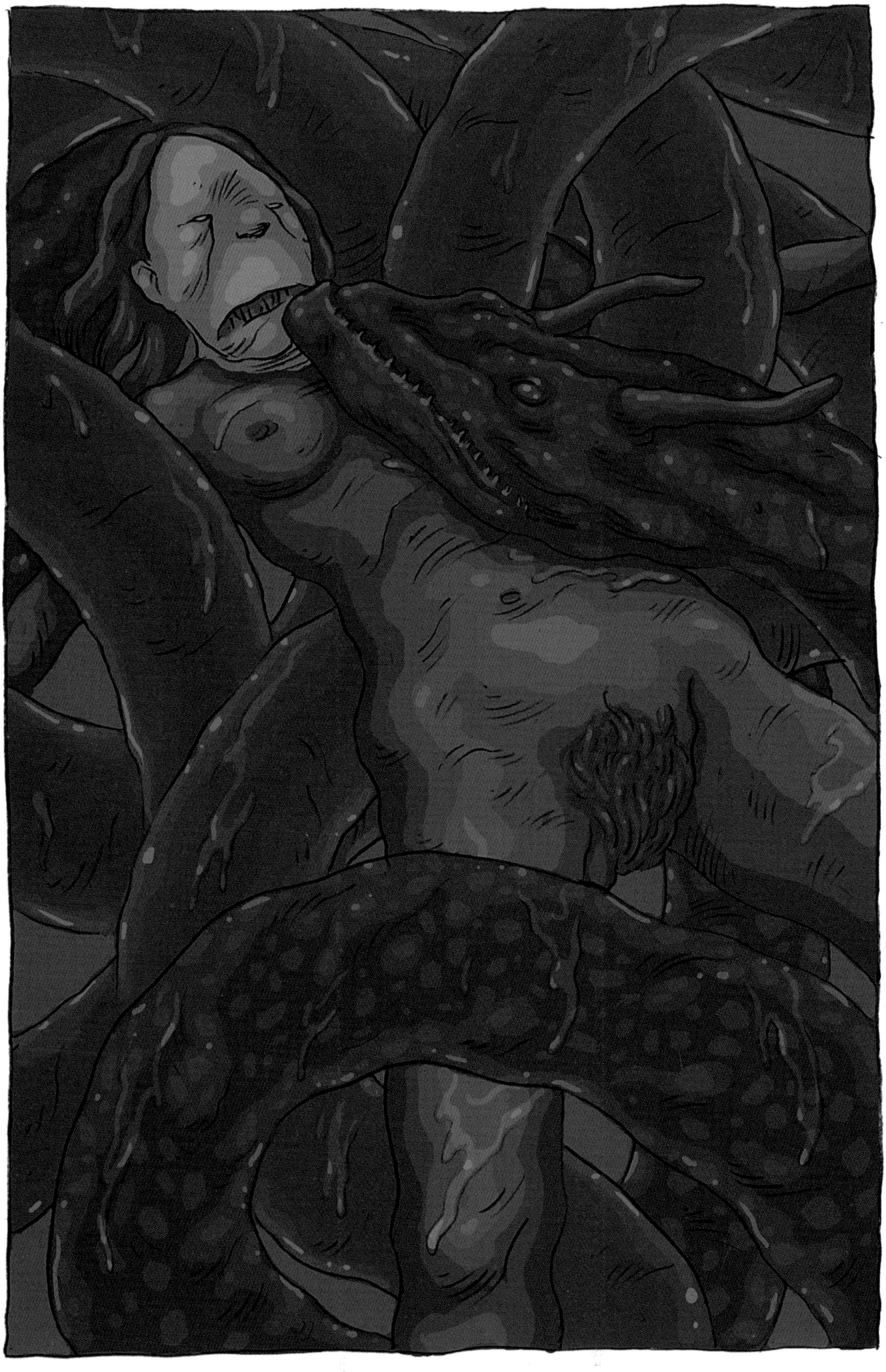

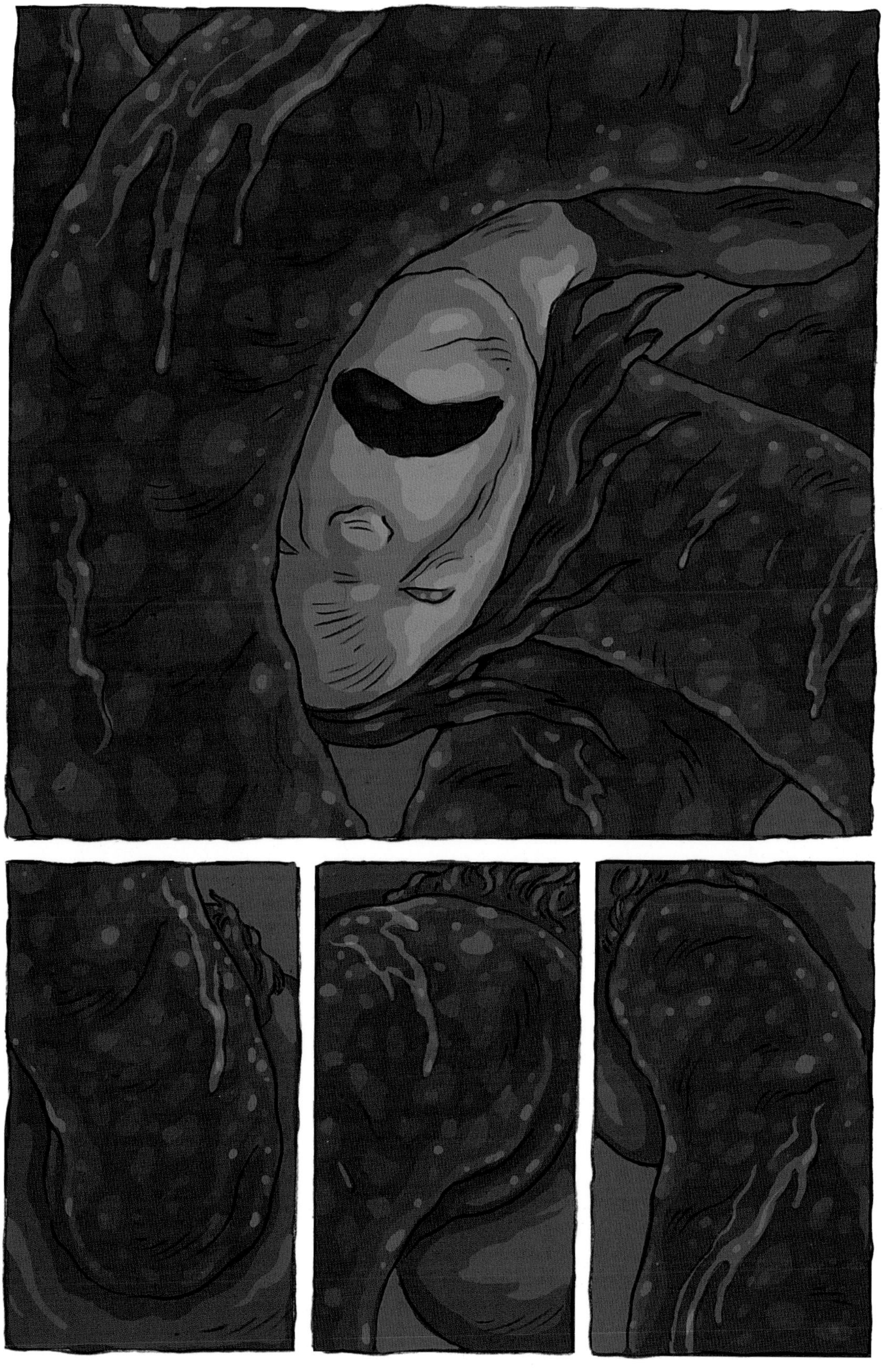

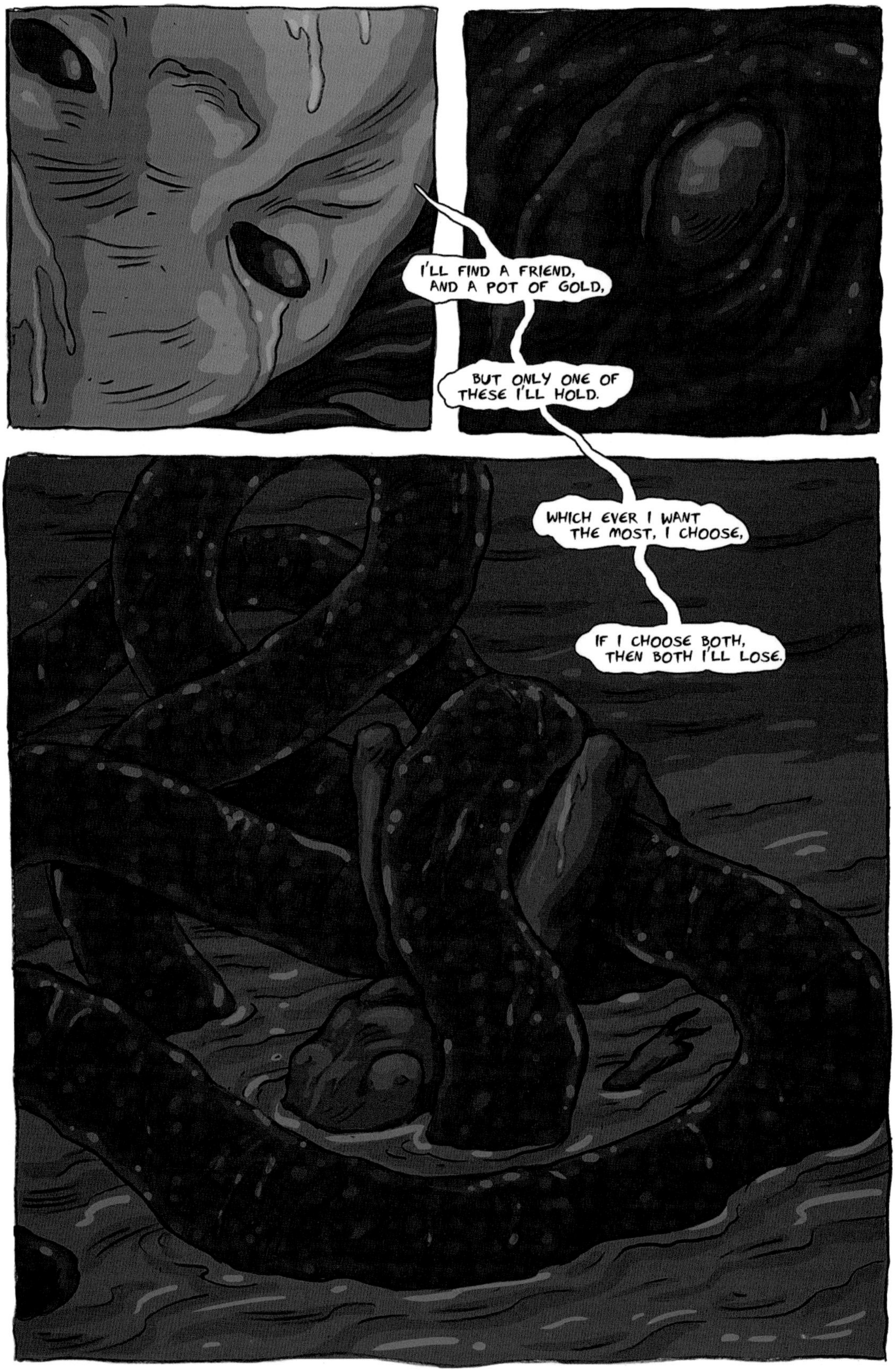
I'LL FIND A FRIEND, AND A POT OF GOLD,
BUT ONLY ONE OF THESE I'LL HOLD.
WHICH EVER I WANT THE MOST, I CHOOSE,
IF I CHOOSE BOTH, THEN BOTH I'LL LOSE.

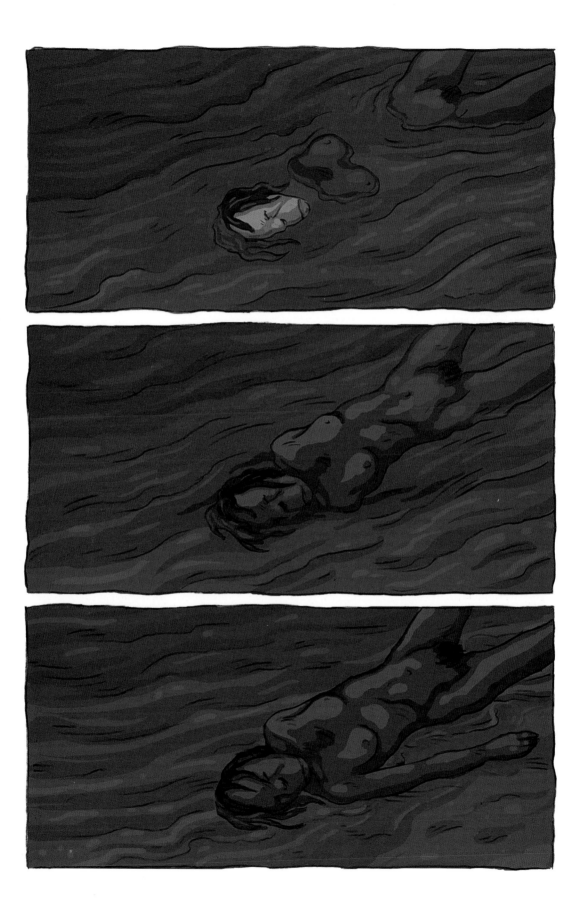

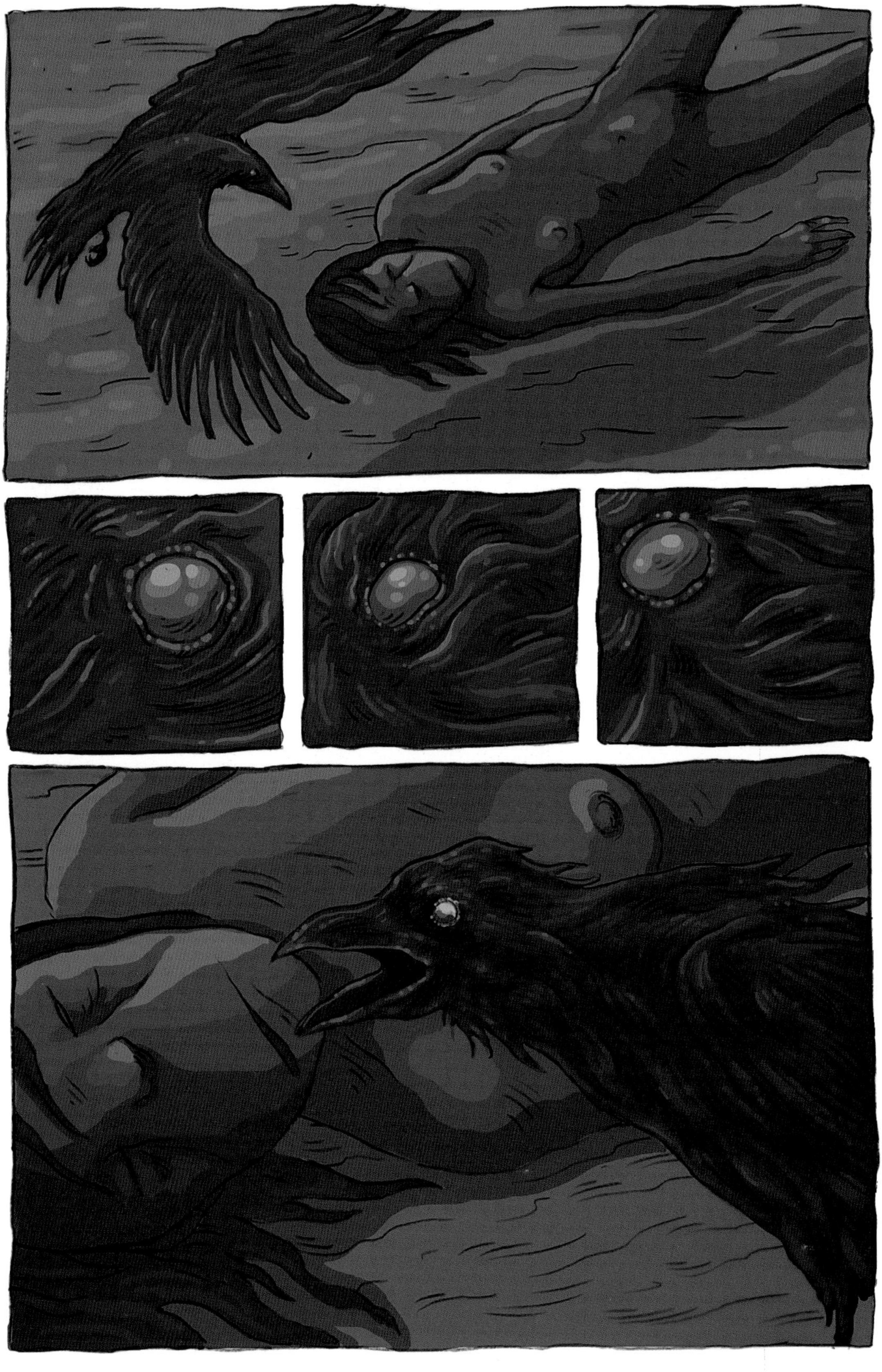

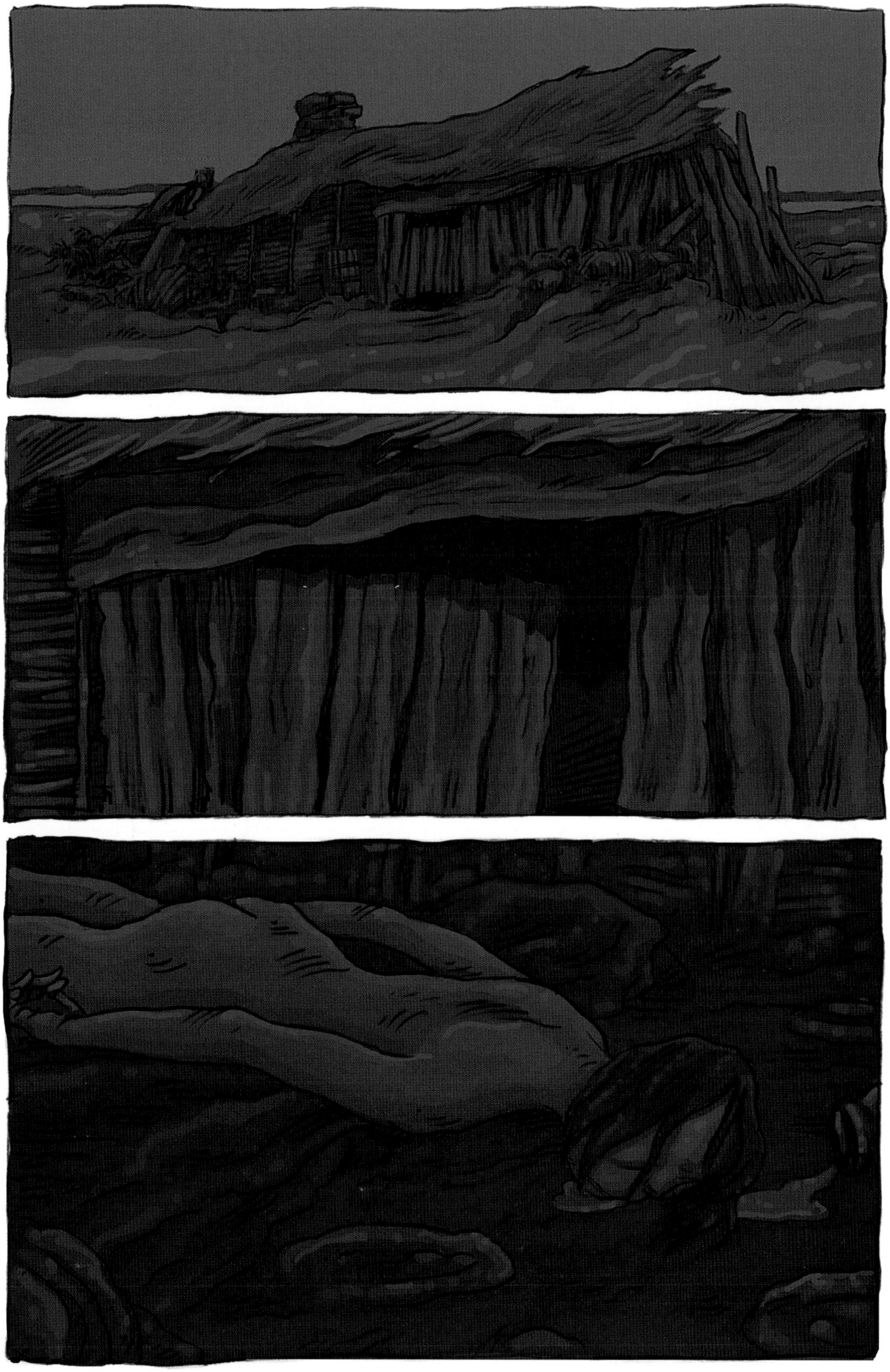

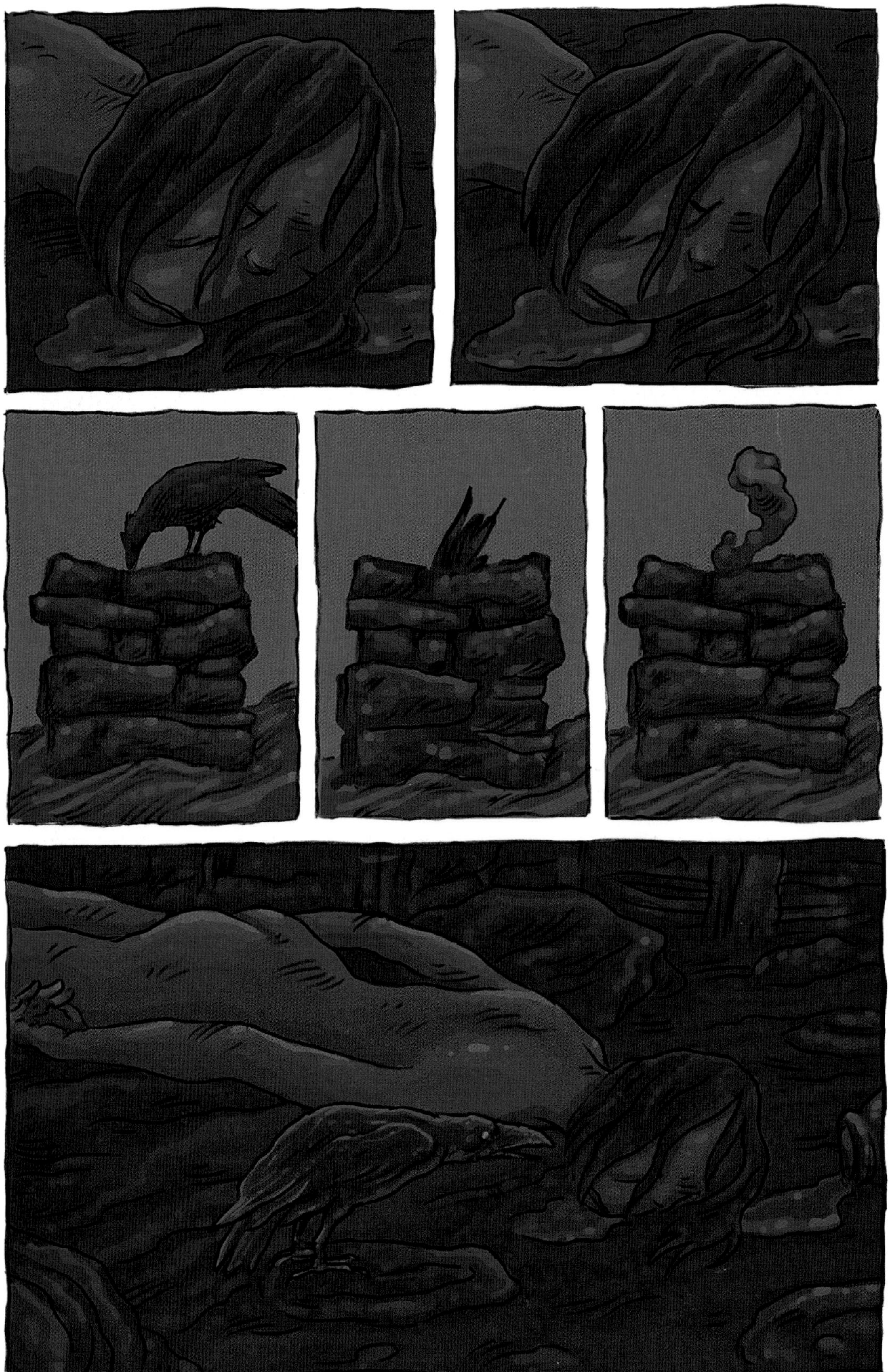

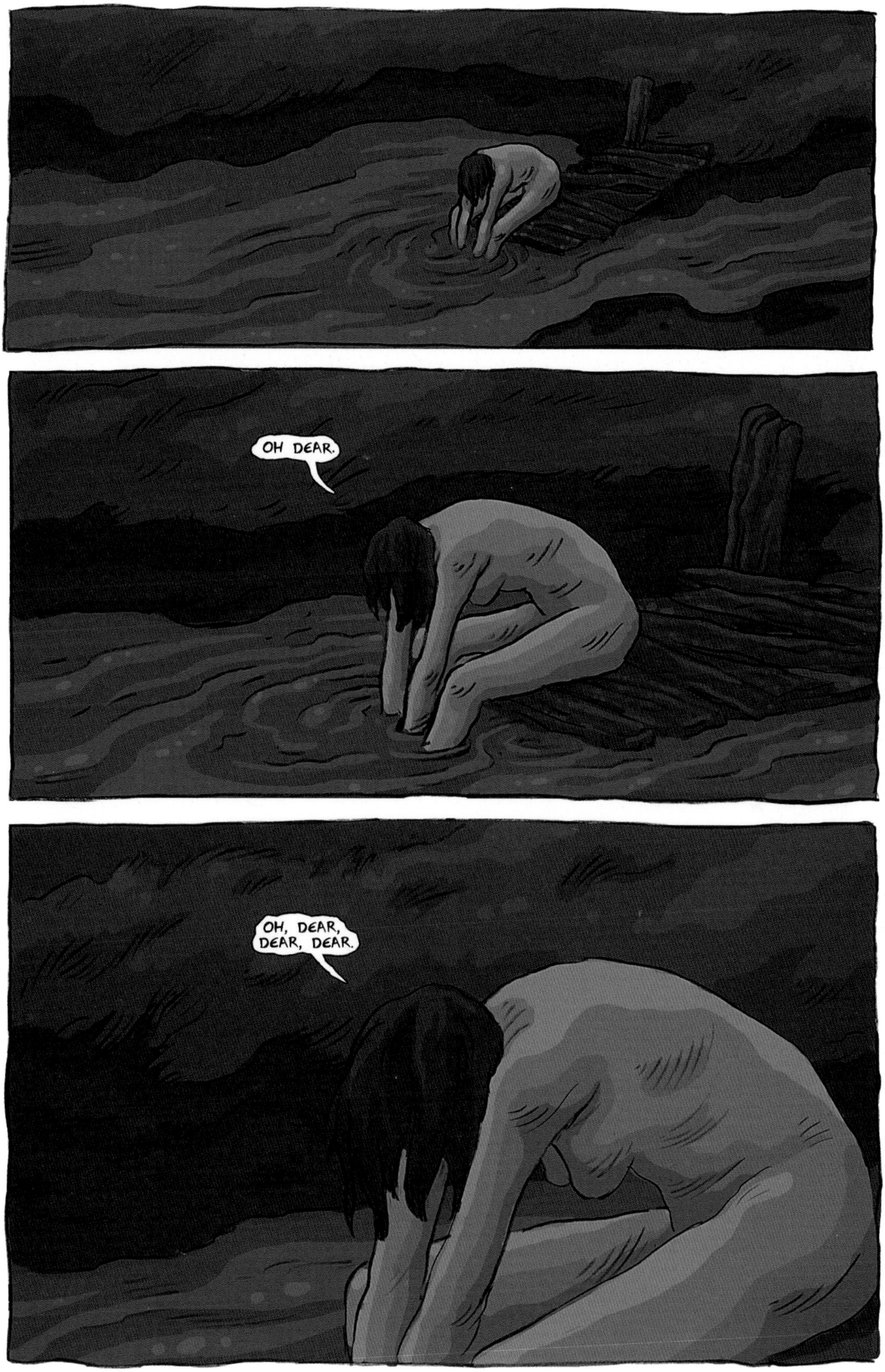
OH DEAR.
OH, DEAR, DEAR, DEAR.

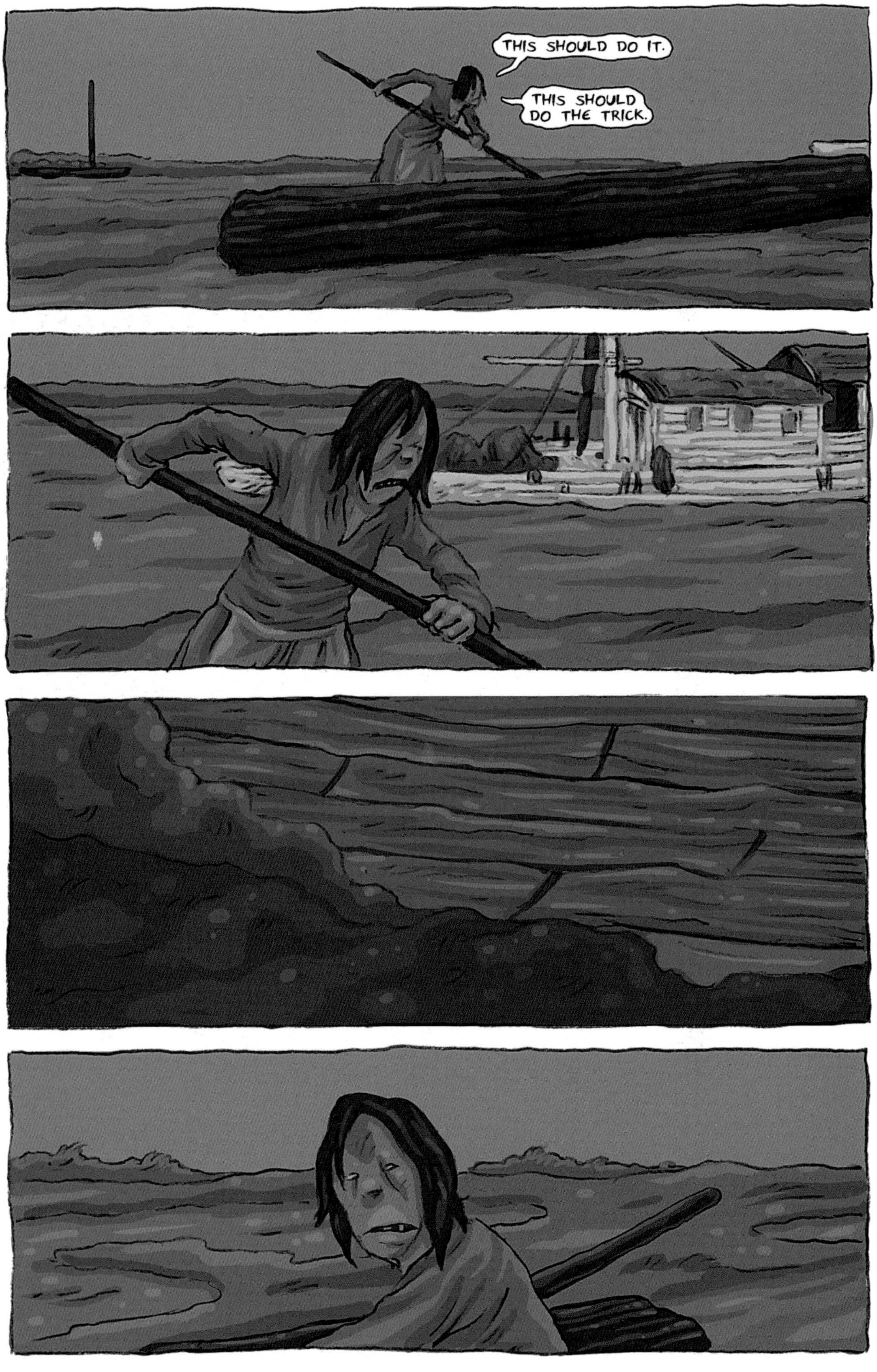
THIS SHOULD DO IT.
THIS SHOULD DO THE TRICK.

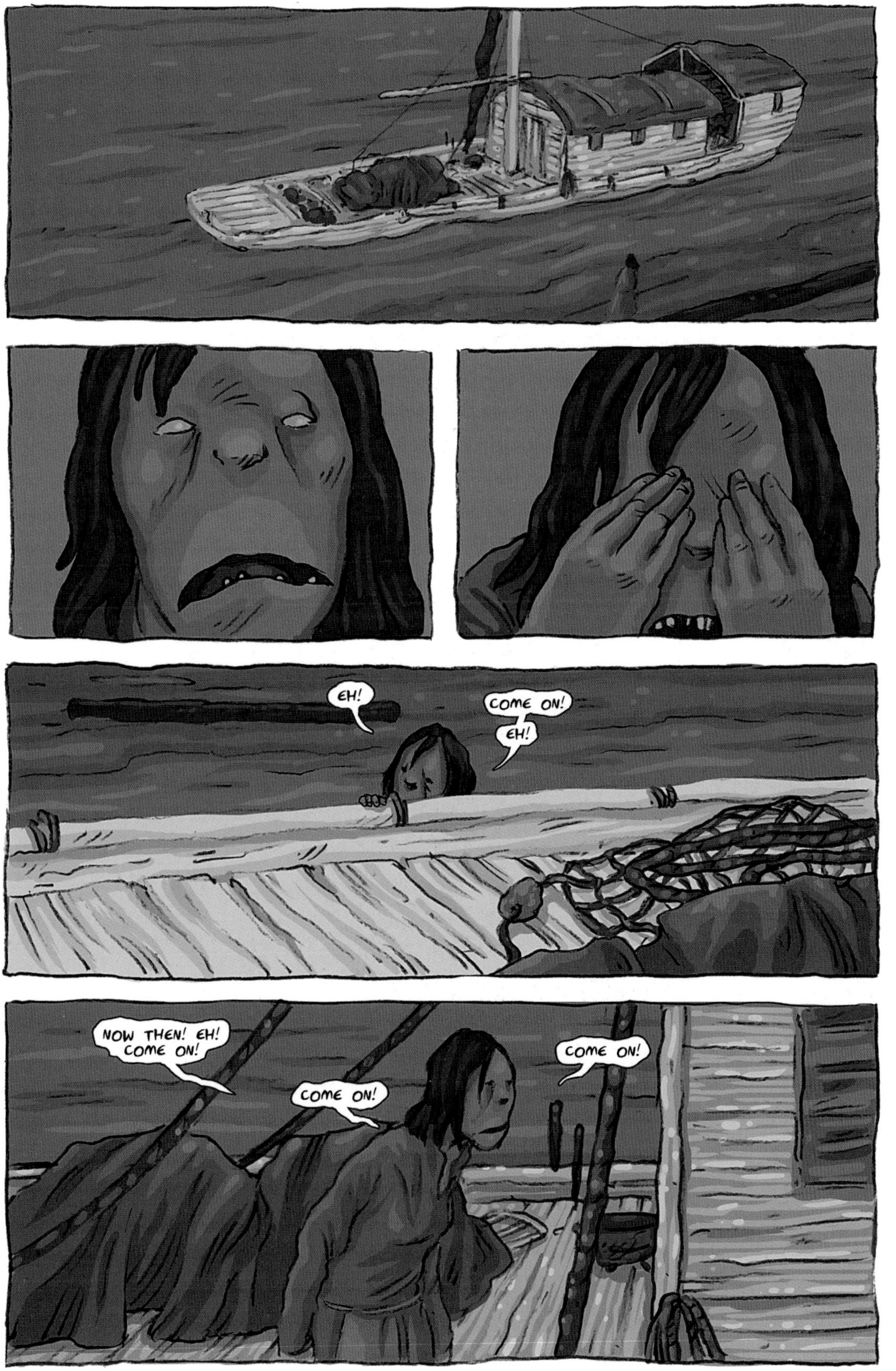
EH!
COME ON! EH!
NOW THEN! EH! COME ON!
COME ON!
COME ON!

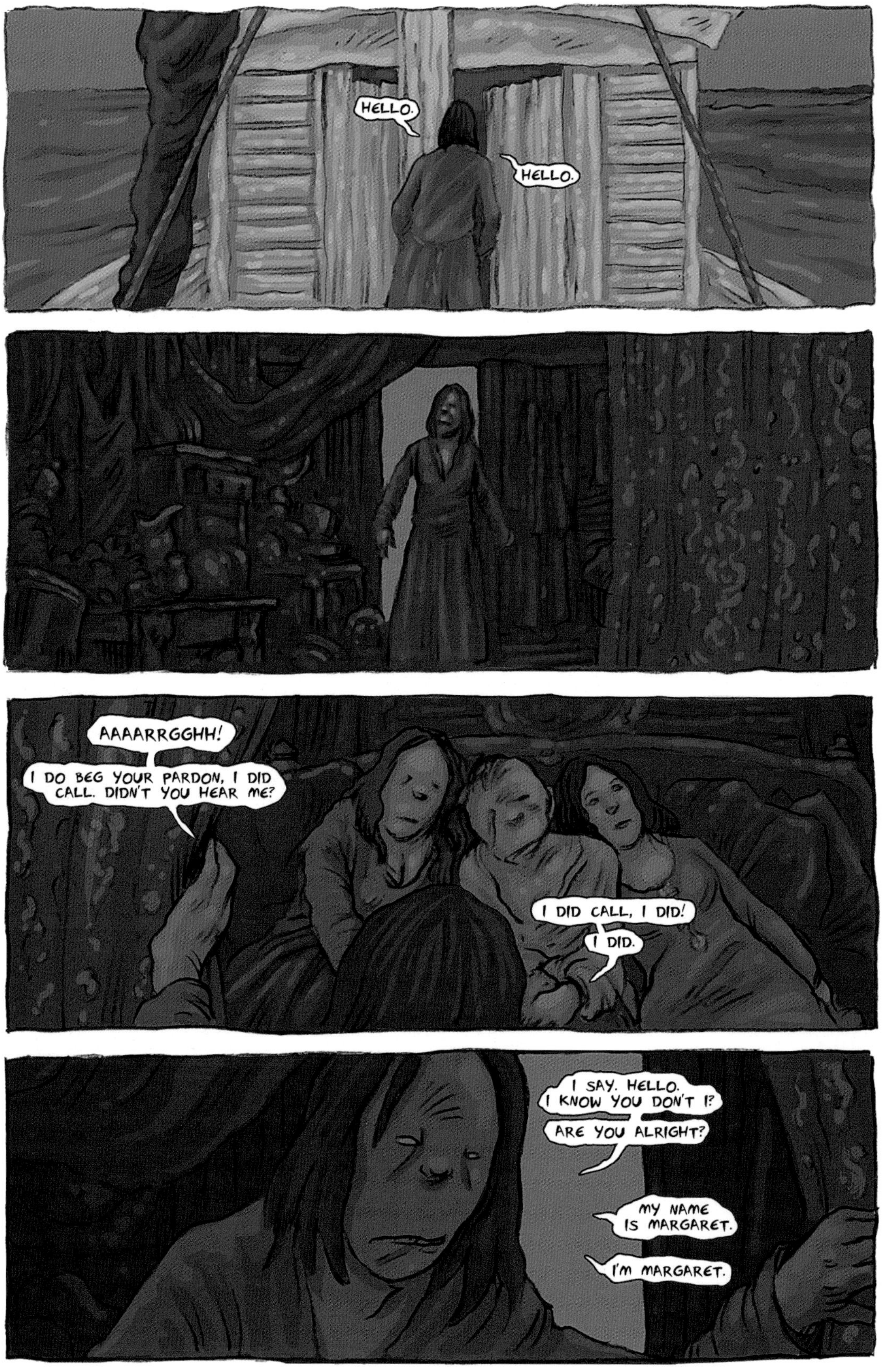
HELLO.
HELLO.
AAAARRGGHH!
I DO BEG YOUR PARDON, I DID CALL. DIDN'T YOU HEAR ME?
I DID CALL, I DID!
I DID.
I SAY. HELLO. I KNOW YOU DON'T I?
ARE YOU ALRIGHT?
MY NAME IS MARGARET.
I'M MARGARET.

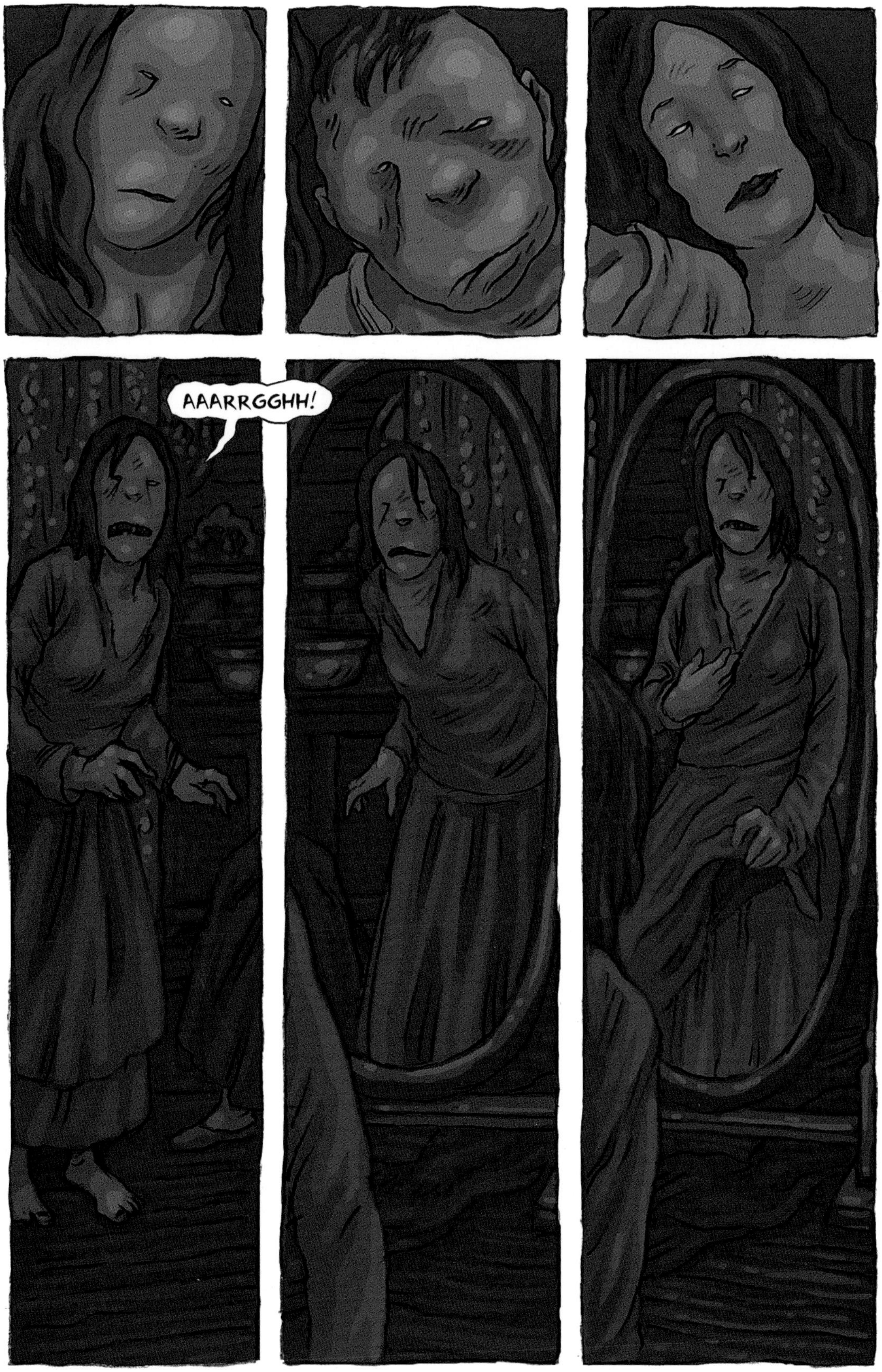
AAARRGGHH!

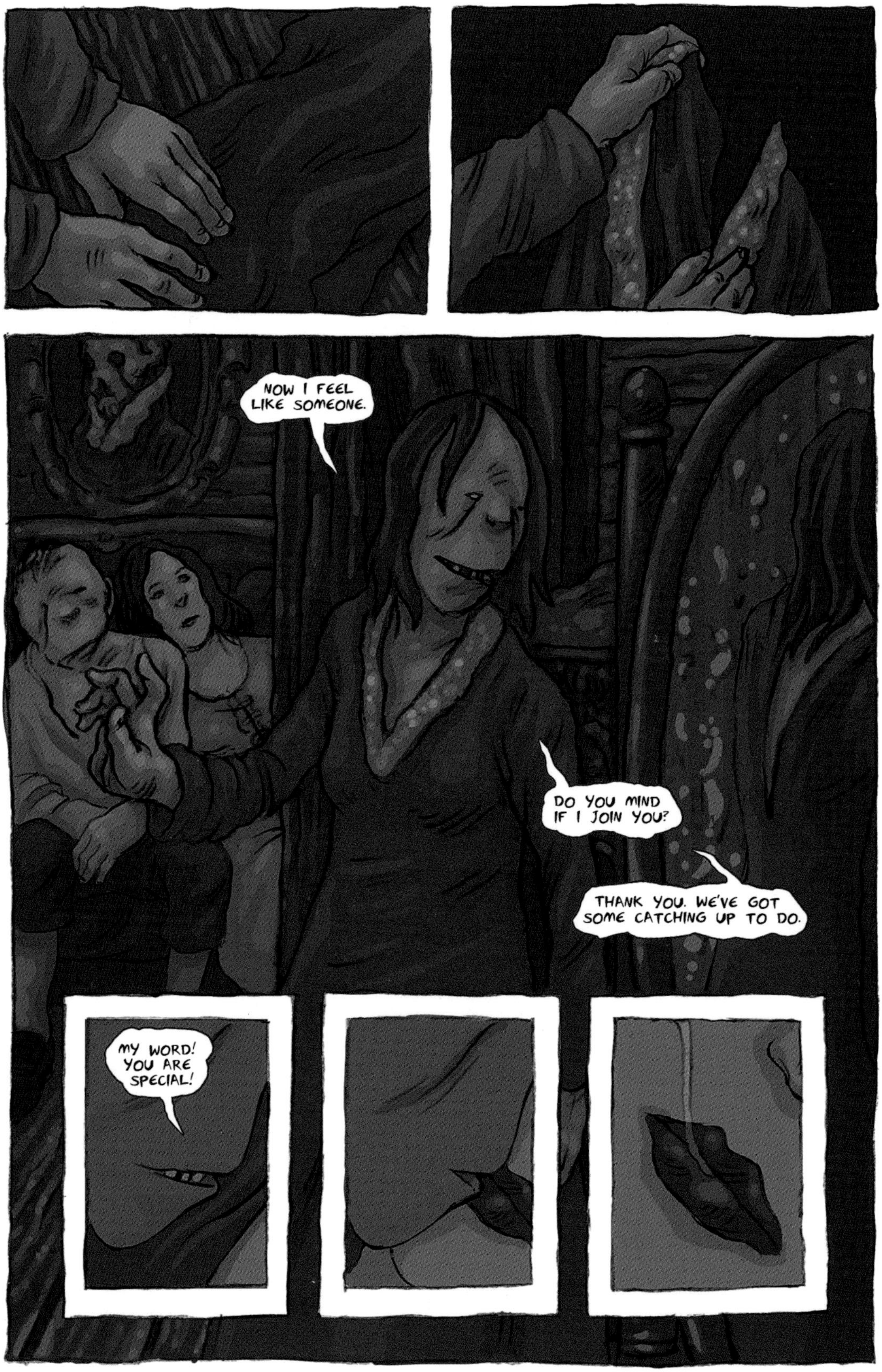
NOW I FEEL LIKE SOMEONE.
DO YOU MIND IF I JOIN YOU?
THANK YOU. WE'VE GOT SOME CATCHING UP TO DO.
MY WORD! YOU ARE SPECIAL!

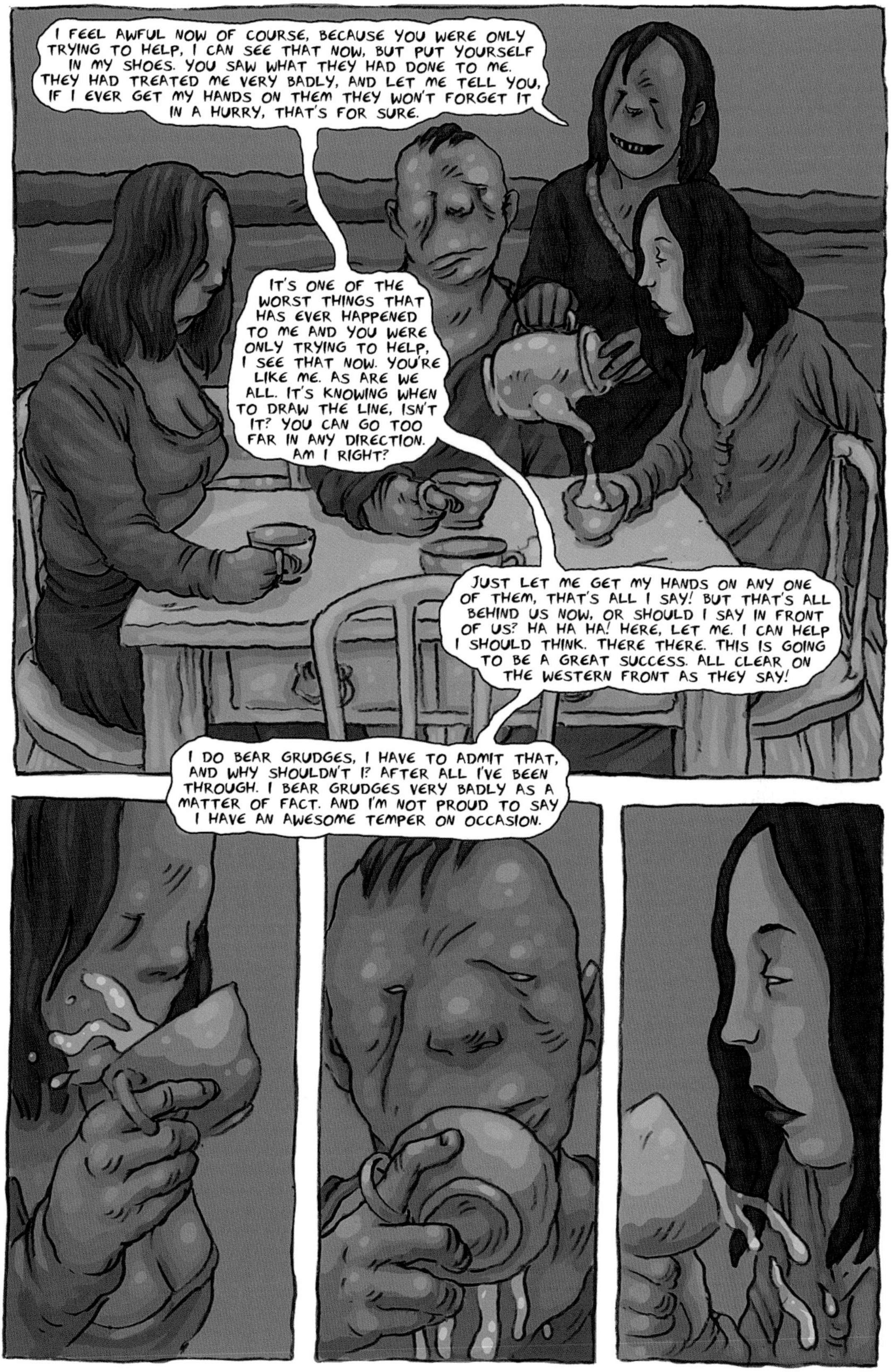
I FEEL AWFUL NOW OF COURSE, BECAUSE YOU WERE ONLY TRYING TO HELP, I CAN SEE THAT NOW, BUT PUT YOURSELF IN MY SHOES. YOU SAW WHAT THEY HAD DONE TO ME. THEY HAD TREATED ME VERY BADLY, AND LET ME TELL YOU, IF I EVER GET MY HANDS ON THEM THEY WON'T FORGET IT IN A HURRY, THAT'S FOR SURE.
IT'S ONE OF THE WORST THINGS THAT HAS EVER HAPPENED TO ME AND YOU WERE ONLY TRYING TO HELP, I SEE THAT NOW. YOU'RE LIKE ME. AS ARE WE ALL. IT'S KNOWING WHEN TO DRAW THE LINE, ISN'T IT? YOU CAN GO TOO FAR IN ANY DIRECTION. AM I RIGHT?
JUST LET ME GET MY HANDS ON ANY ONE OF THEM, THAT'S ALL I SAY! BUT THAT'S ALL BEHIND US NOW, OR SHOULD I SAY IN FRONT OF US? HA HA HA! HERE, LET ME. I CAN HELP I SHOULD THINK. THERE THERE. THIS IS GOING TO BE A GREAT SUCCESS. ALL CLEAR ON THE WESTERN FRONT AS THEY SAY!
I DO BEAR GRUDGES, I HAVE TO ADMIT THAT, AND WHY SHOULDN'T I? AFTER ALL I'VE BEEN THROUGH. I BEAR GRUDGES VERY BADLY AS A MATTER OF FACT. AND I'M NOT PROUD TO SAY I HAVE AN AWESOME TEMPER ON OCCASION.

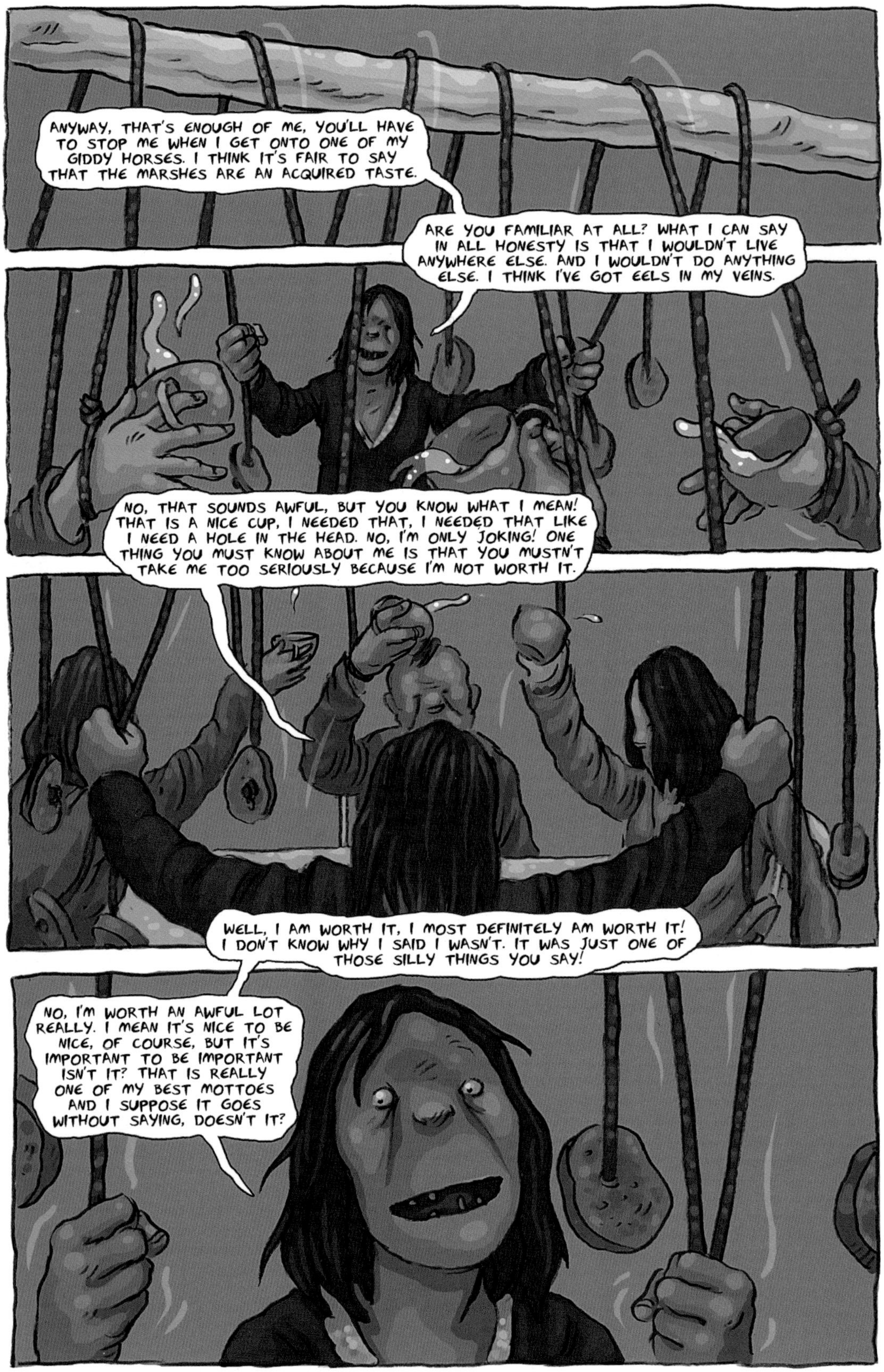
ANYWAY, THAT'S ENOUGH OF ME, YOU'LL HAVE TO STOP ME WHEN I GET ONTO ONE OF MY GIDDY HORSES. I THINK IT'S FAIR TO SAY THAT THE MARSHES ARE AN ACQUIRED TASTE.
ARE YOU FAMILIAR AT ALL? WHAT I CAN SAY IN ALL HONESTY IS THAT I WOULDN'T LIVE ANYWHERE ELSE. AND I WOULDN'T DO ANYTHING ELSE. I THINK I'VE GOT EELS IN MY VEINS.
NO, THAT SOUNDS AWFUL, BUT YOU KNOW WHAT I MEAN! THAT IS A NICE CUP, I NEEDED THAT, I NEEDED THAT LIKE I NEED A HOLE IN THE HEAD. NO, I'M ONLY JOKING! ONE THING YOU MUST KNOW ABOUT ME IS THAT YOU MUSTN'T TAKE ME TOO SERIOUSLY BECAUSE I'M NOT WORTH IT.
WELL, I AM WORTH IT, I MOST DEFINITELY AM WORTH IT! I DON'T KNOW WHY I SAID I WASN'T. IT WAS JUST ONE OF THOSE SILLY THINGS YOU SAY!
NO, I'M WORTH AN AWFUL LOT REALLY. I MEAN IT'S NICE TO BE NICE, OF COURSE, BUT IT'S IMPORTANT TO BE IMPORTANT ISN'T IT? THAT IS REALLY ONE OF MY BEST MOTTOES AND I SUPPOSE IT GOES WITHOUT SAYING, DOESN'T IT?

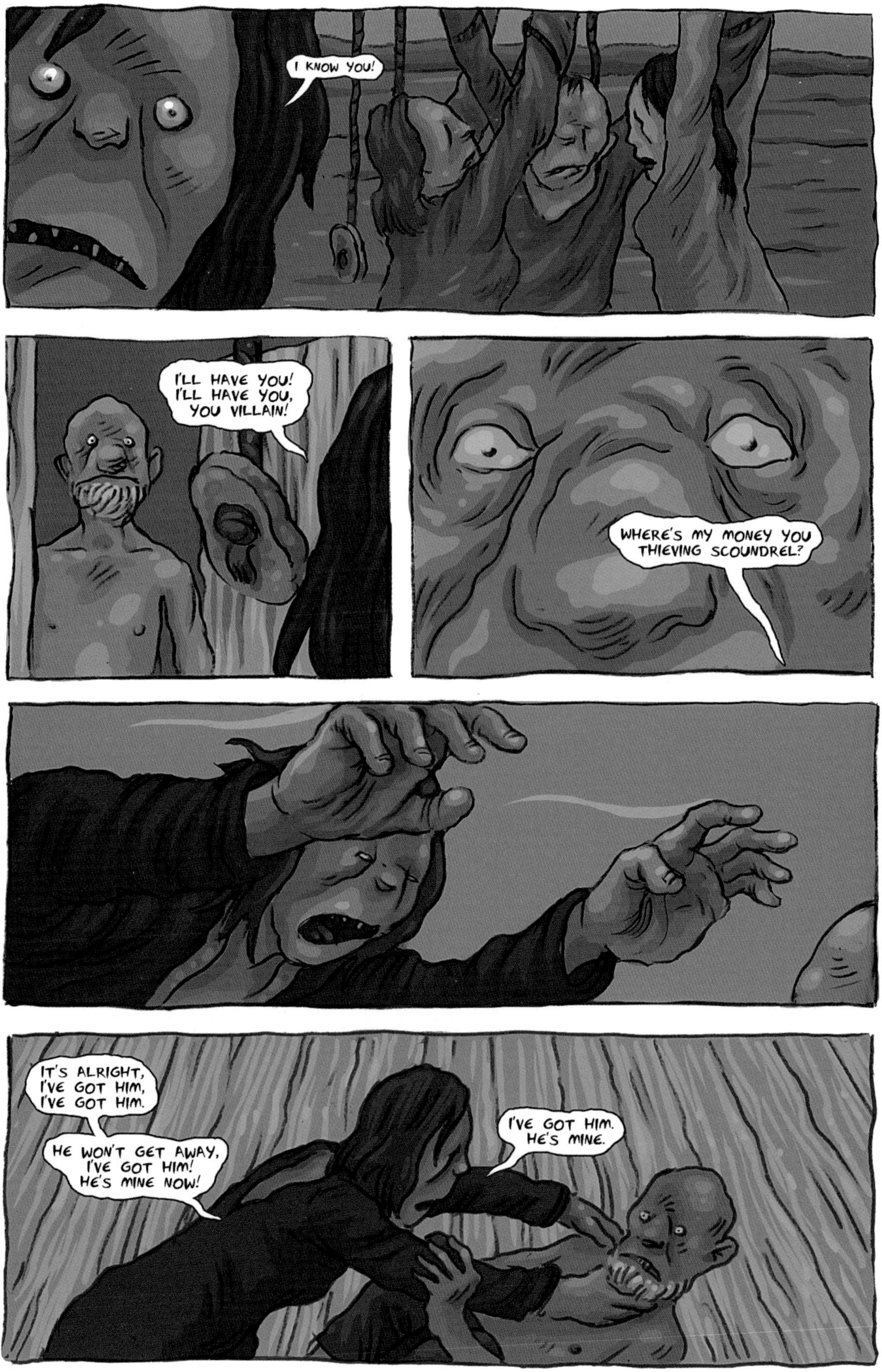
I KNOW YOU!
I'LL HAVE YOU! I'LL HAVE YOU, YOU VILLAIN!
WHERE'S MY MONEY YOU THIEVING SCOUNDREL?
IT'S ALRIGHT, I'VE GOT HIM, I'VE GOT HIM.
HE WON'T GET AWAY, I'VE GOT HIM! HE'S MINE NOW!
I'VE GOT HIM. HE'S MINE.

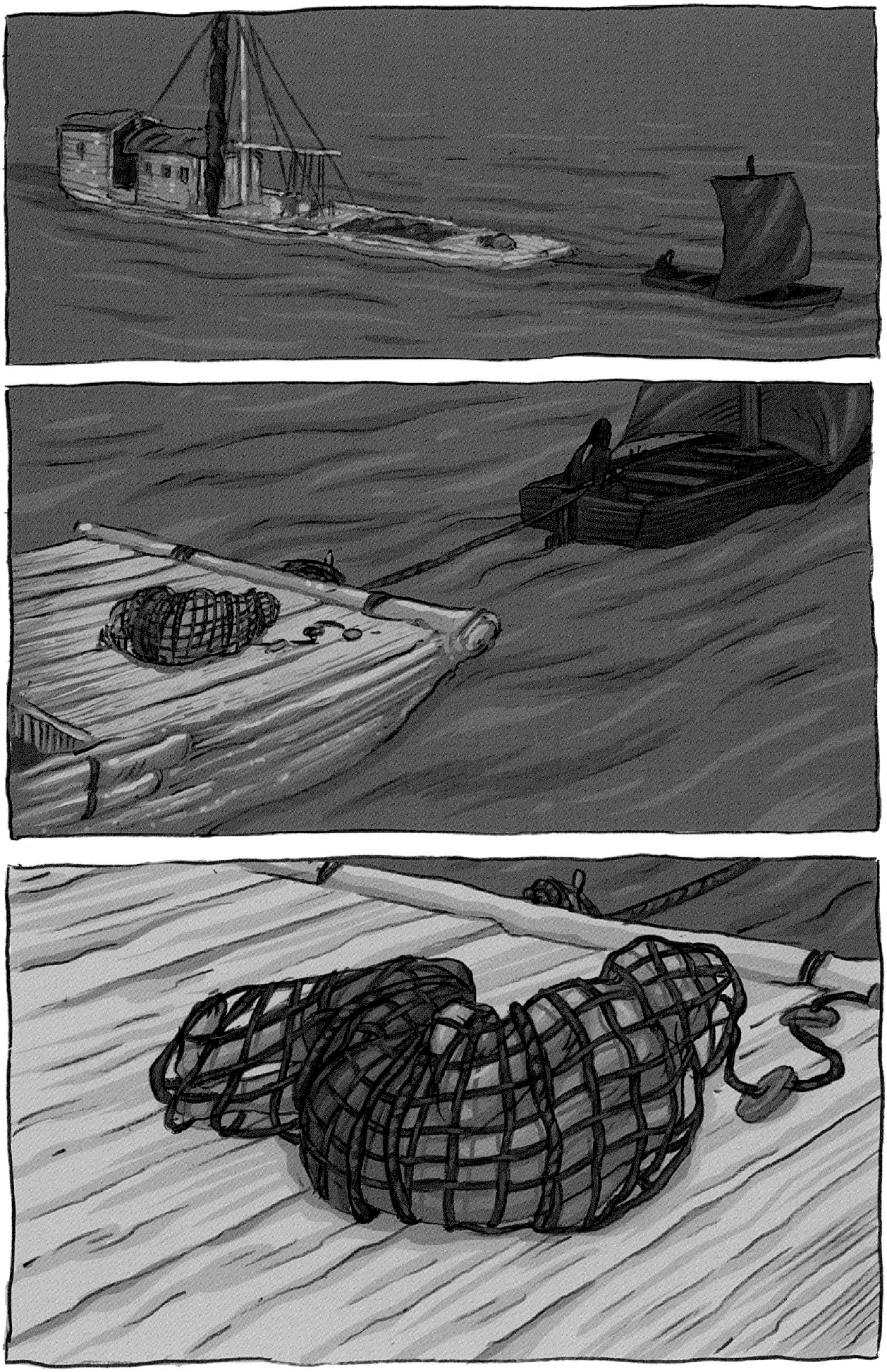

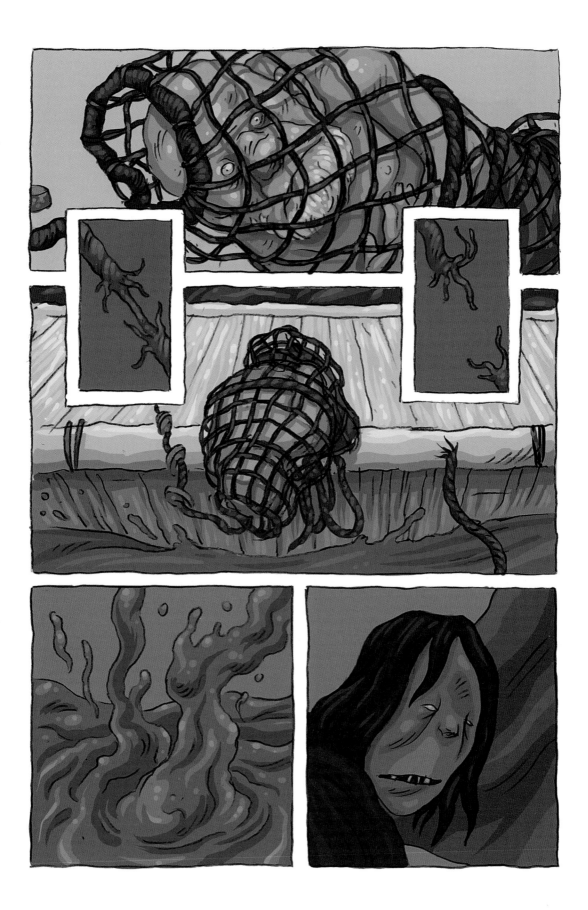

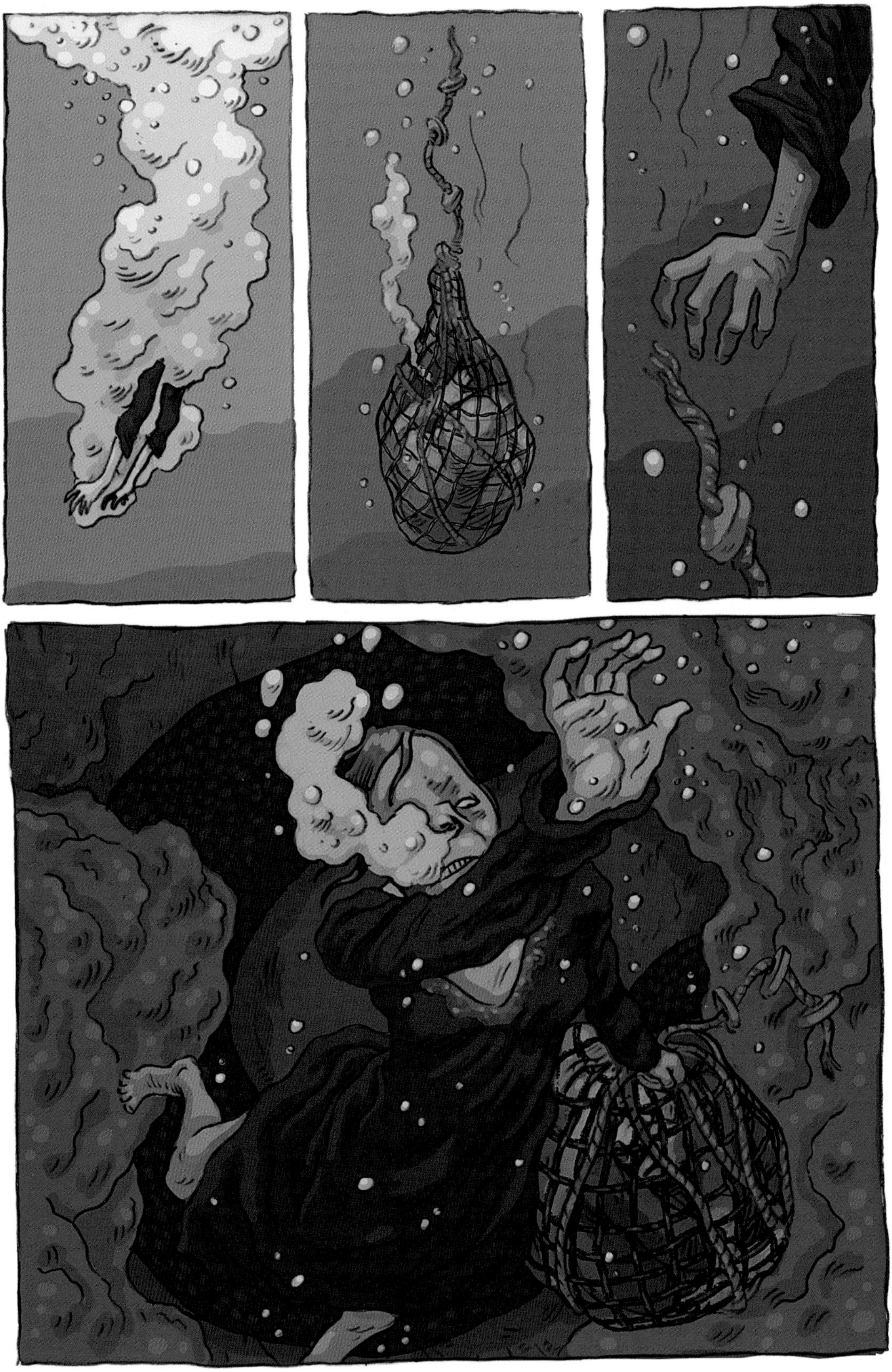

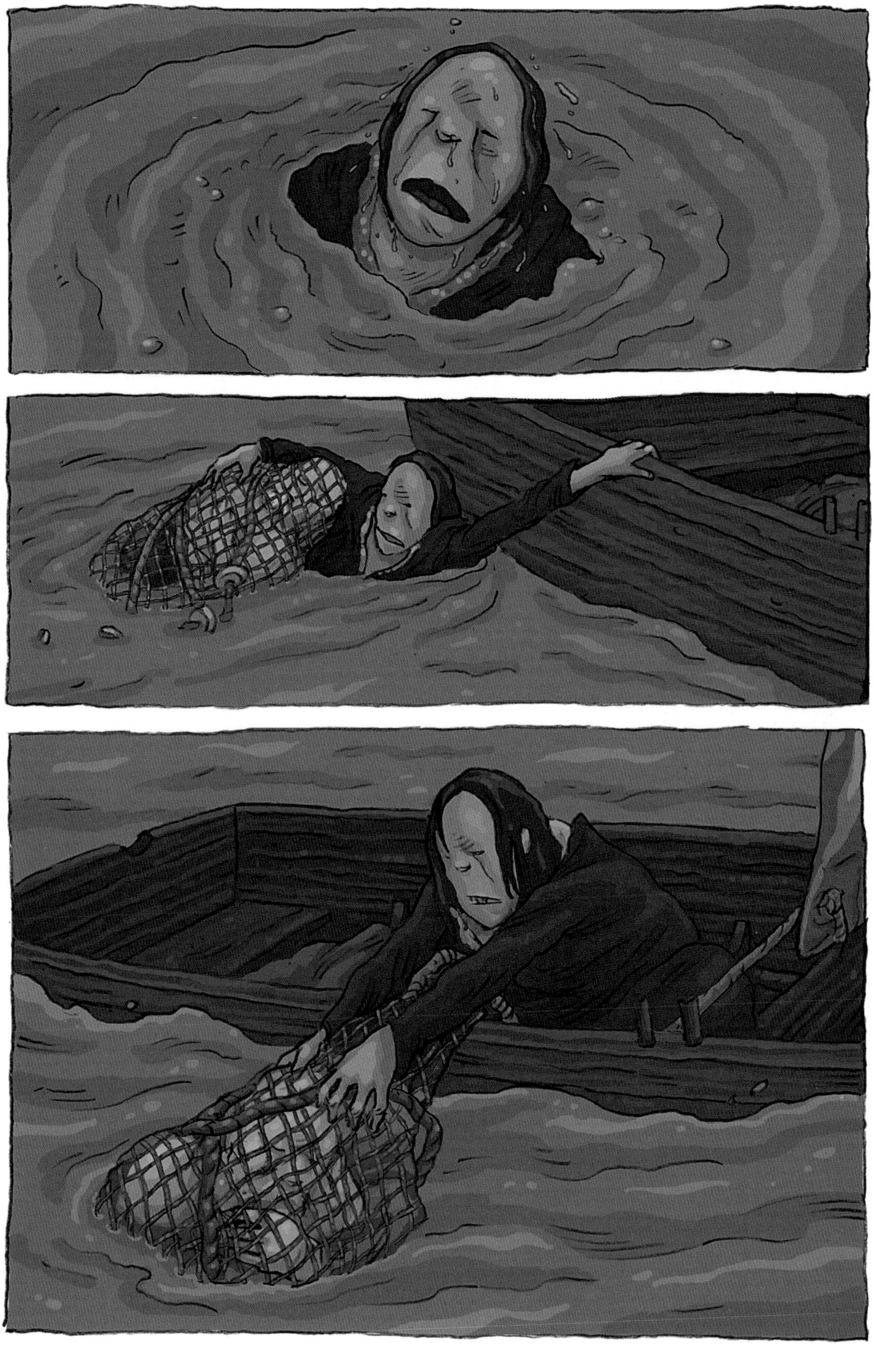

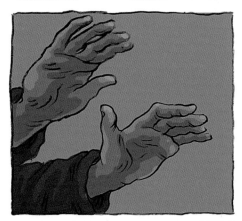

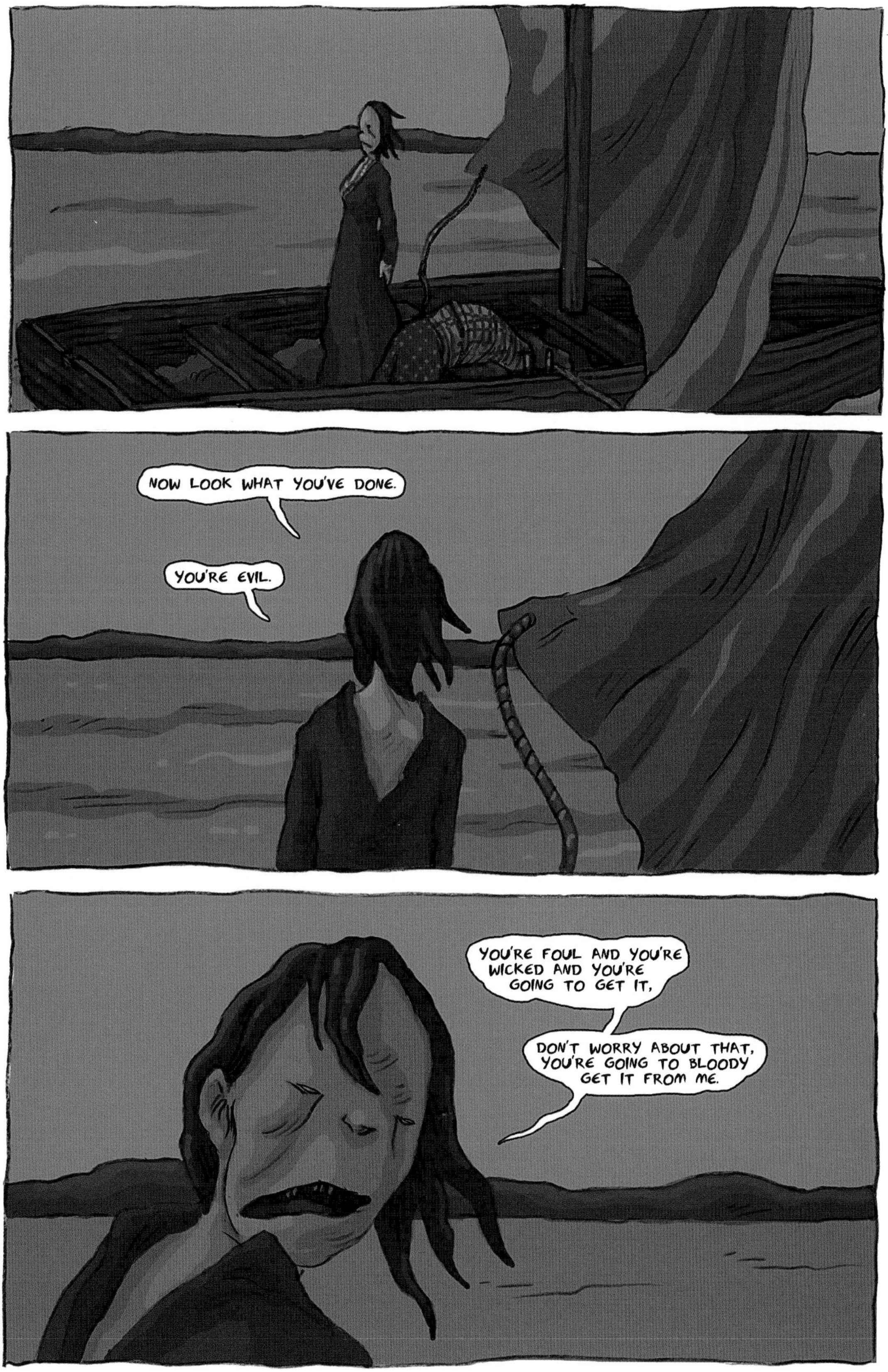
NOW LOOK WHAT YOU'VE DONE.
YOU'RE EVIL.
YOU'RE FOUL AND YOU'RE WICKED AND YOU'RE GOING TO GET IT,
DON'T WORRY ABOUT THAT, YOU'RE GOING TO BLOODY GET IT FROM ME.

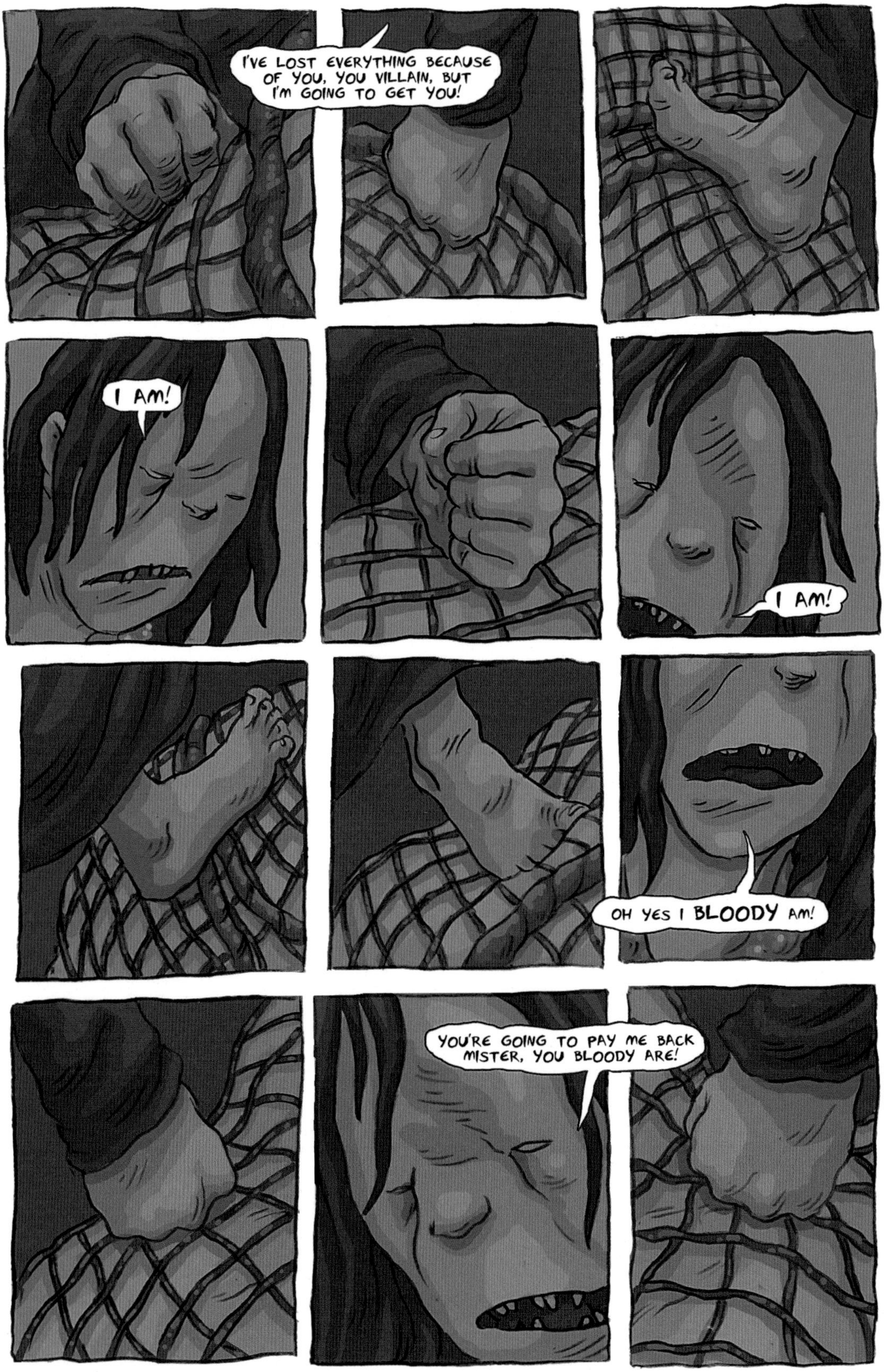
I'VE LOST EVERYTHING BECAUSE OF YOU, YOU VILLAIN, BUT I'M GOING TO GET YOU!
I AM!
I AM!
OH YES I BLOODY AM!
YOU'RE GOING TO PAY ME BACK MISTER, YOU BLOODY ARE!

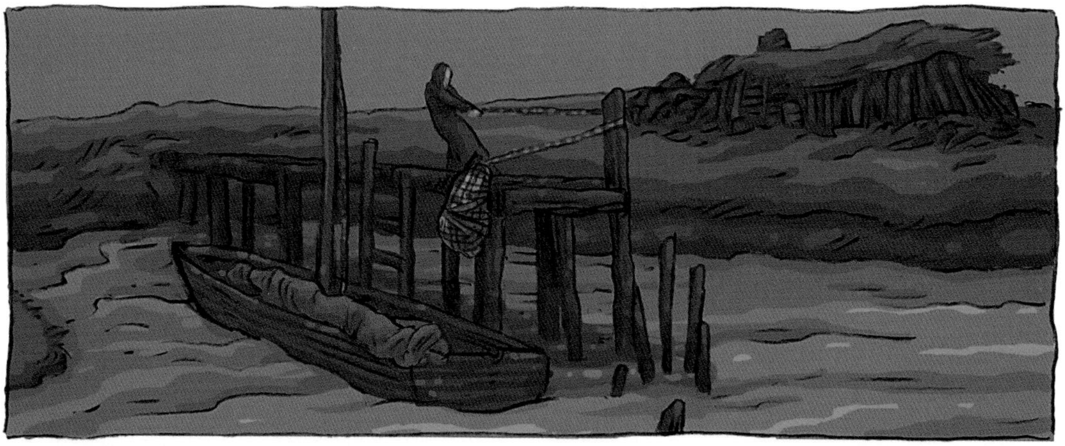

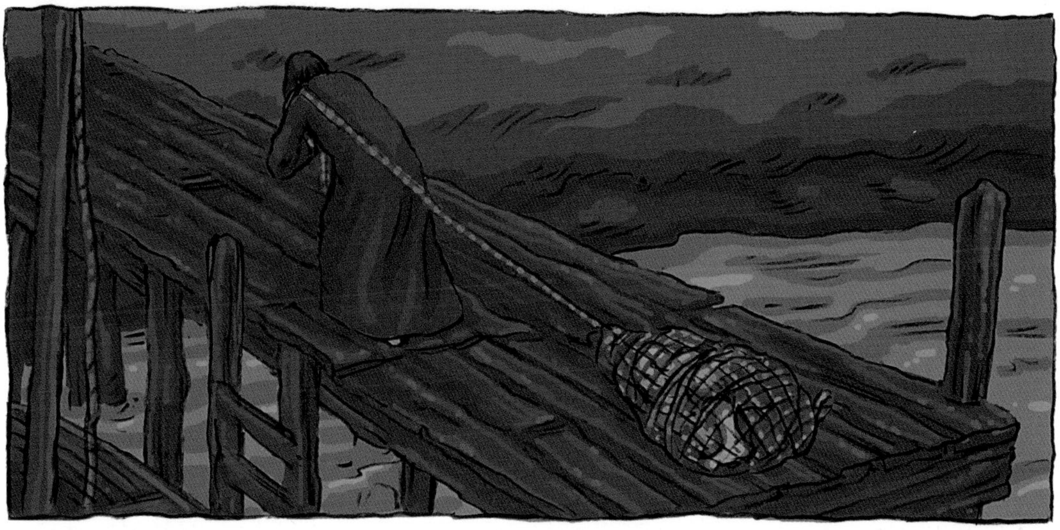

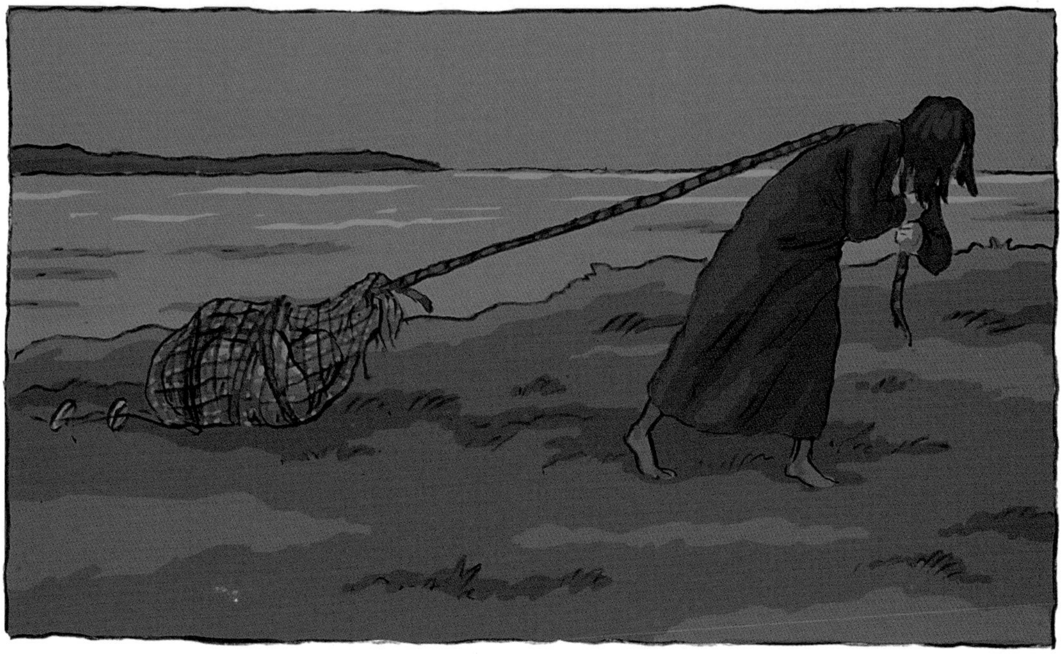

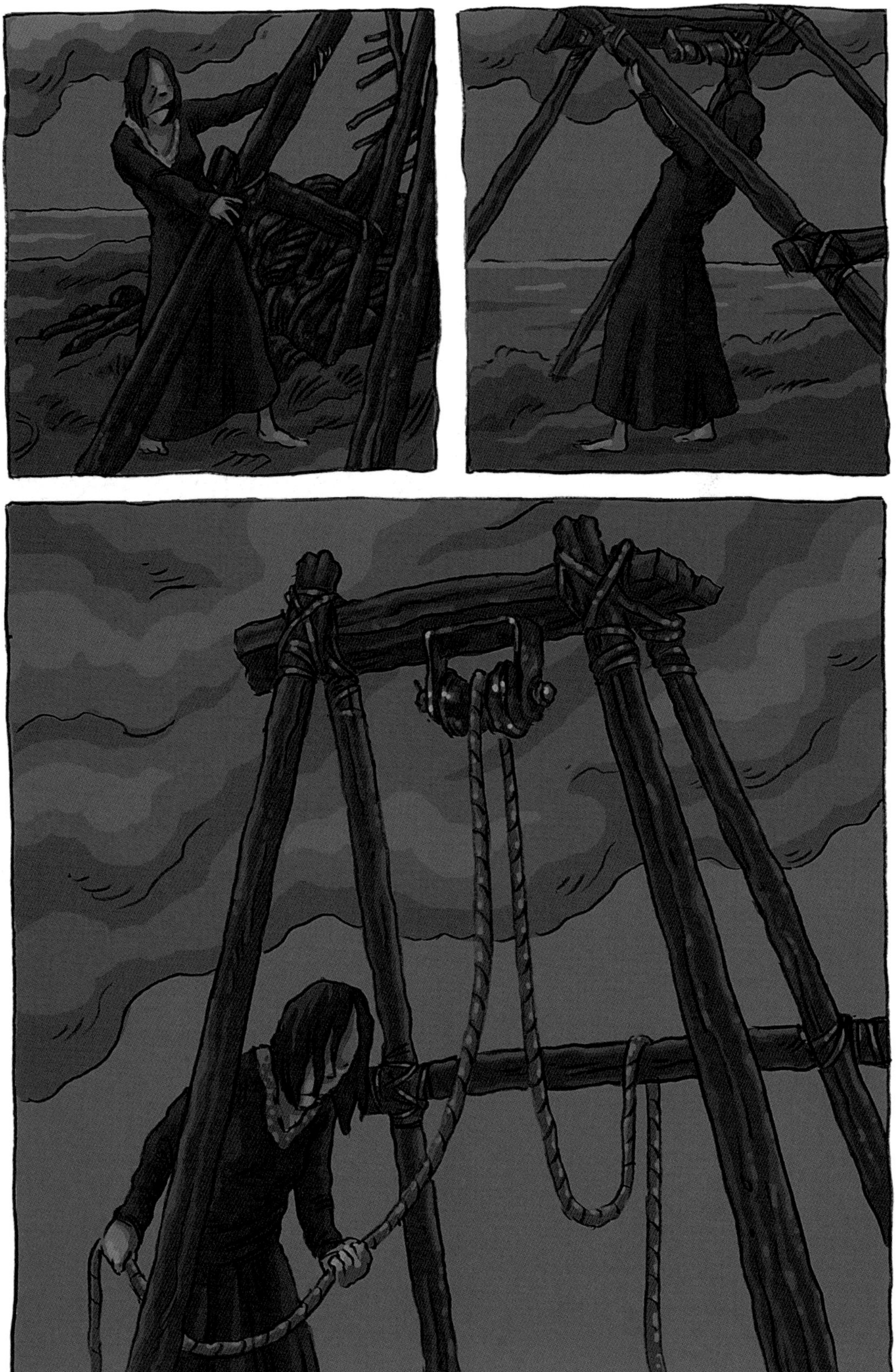

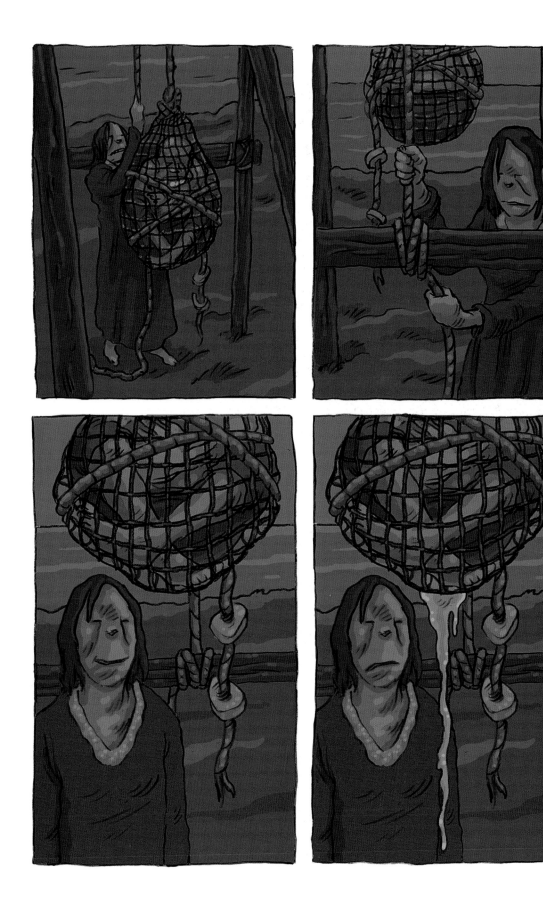

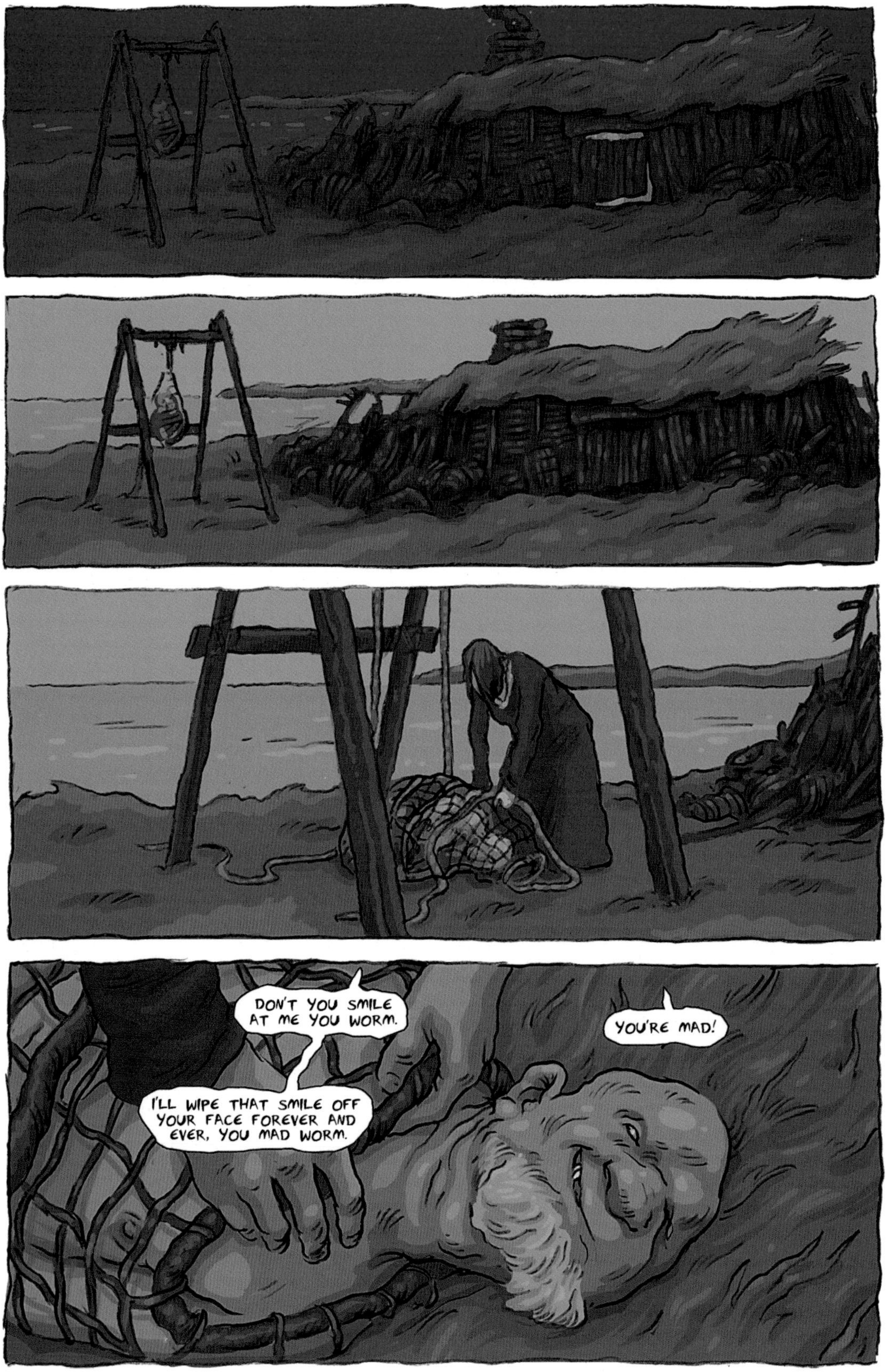
DON'T YOU SMILE AT ME YOU WORM.
YOU'RE MAD!
I'LL WIPE THAT SMILE OFF YOUR FACE FOREVER AND EVER, YOU MAD WORM.

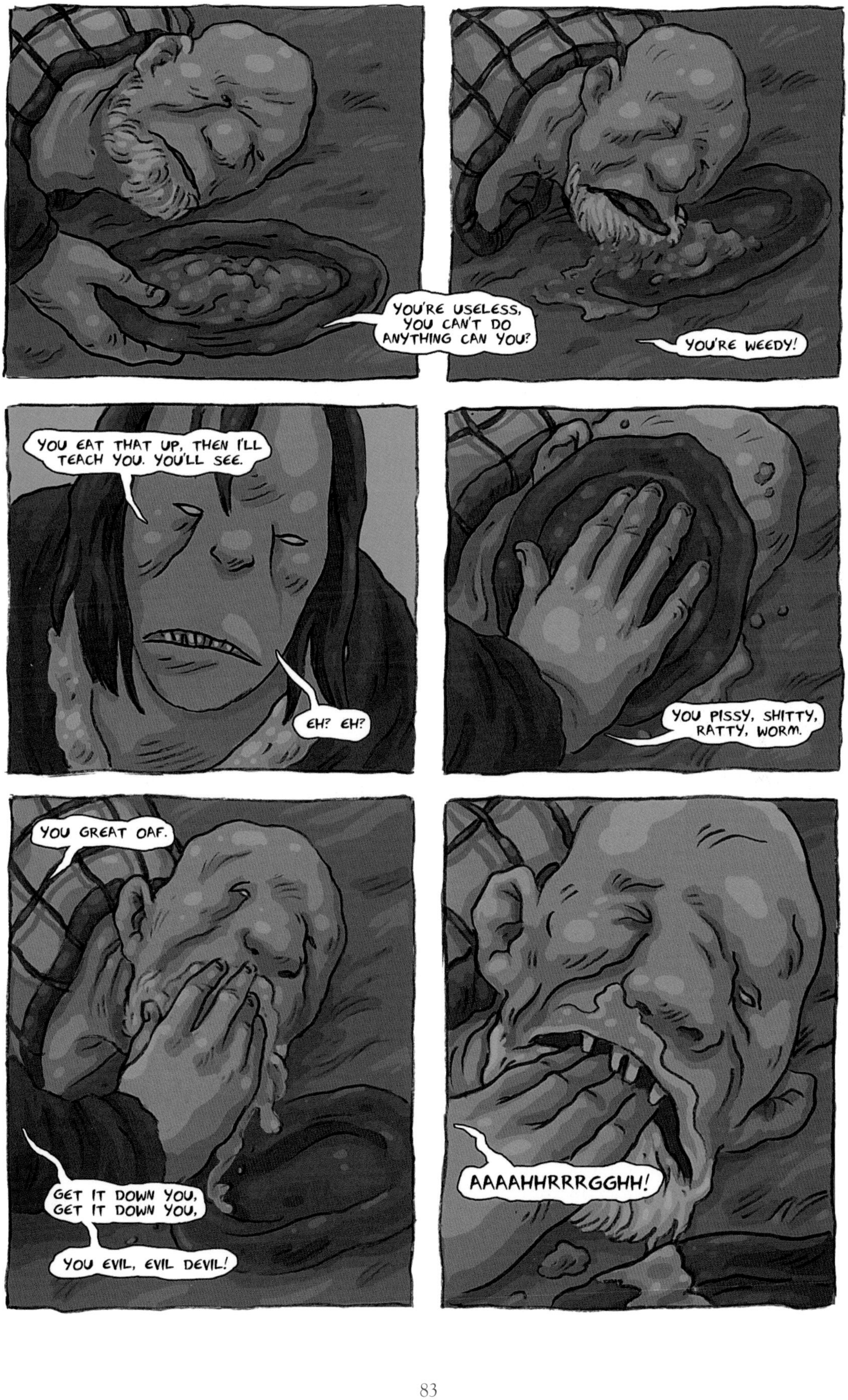
YOU'RE USELESS, YOU CAN'T DO ANYTHING CAN YOU?
YOU'RE WEEDY!
YOU EAT THAT UP, THEN I'LL TEACH YOU. YOU'LL SEE.
EH? EH?
YOU PISSY, SHITTY, RATTY, WORM.
YOU GREAT OAF.
GET IT DOWN YOU, GET IT DOWN YOU,
YOU EVIL, EVIL DEVIL!
AAAAHHRRRGGHH!

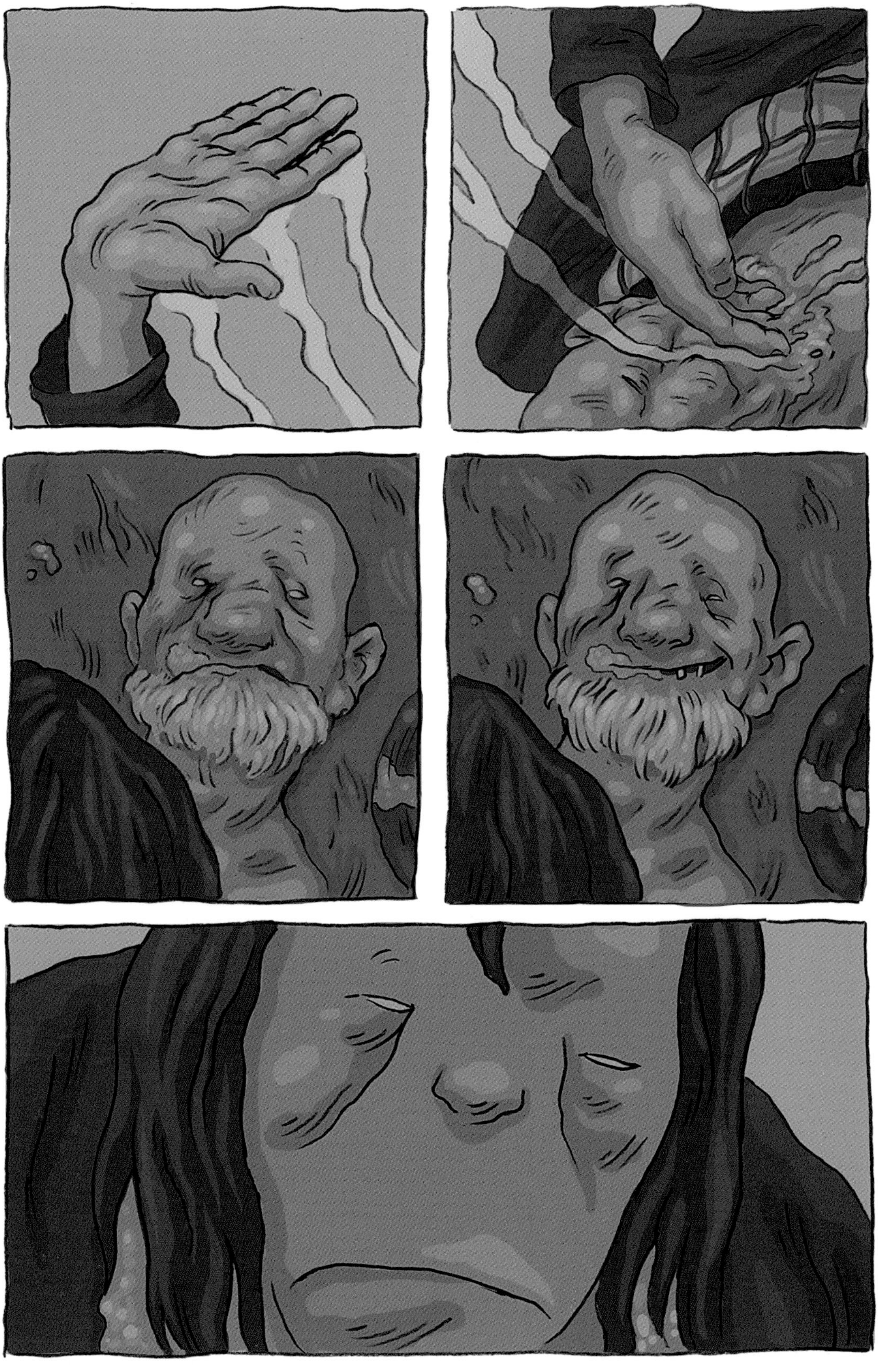

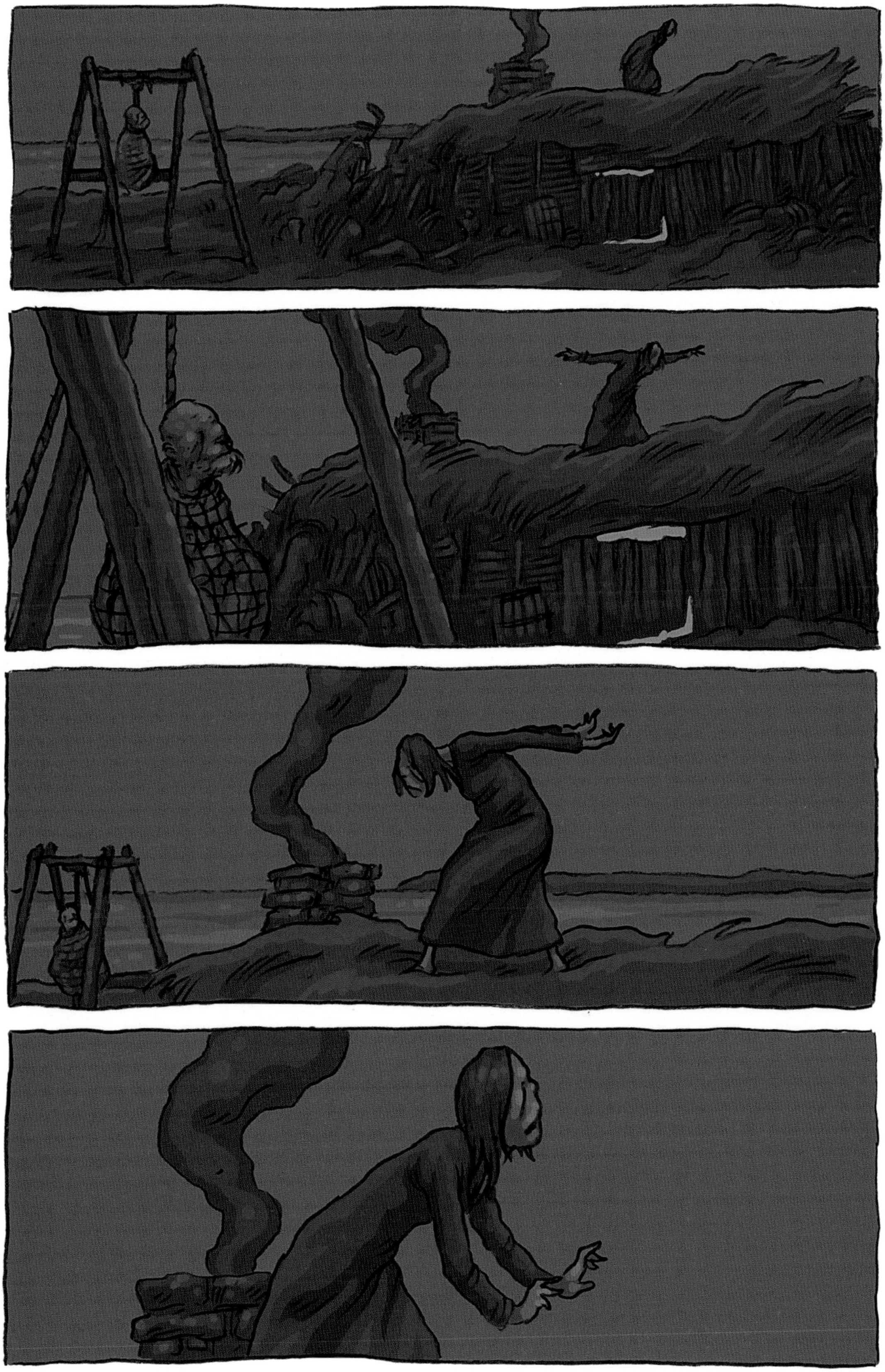

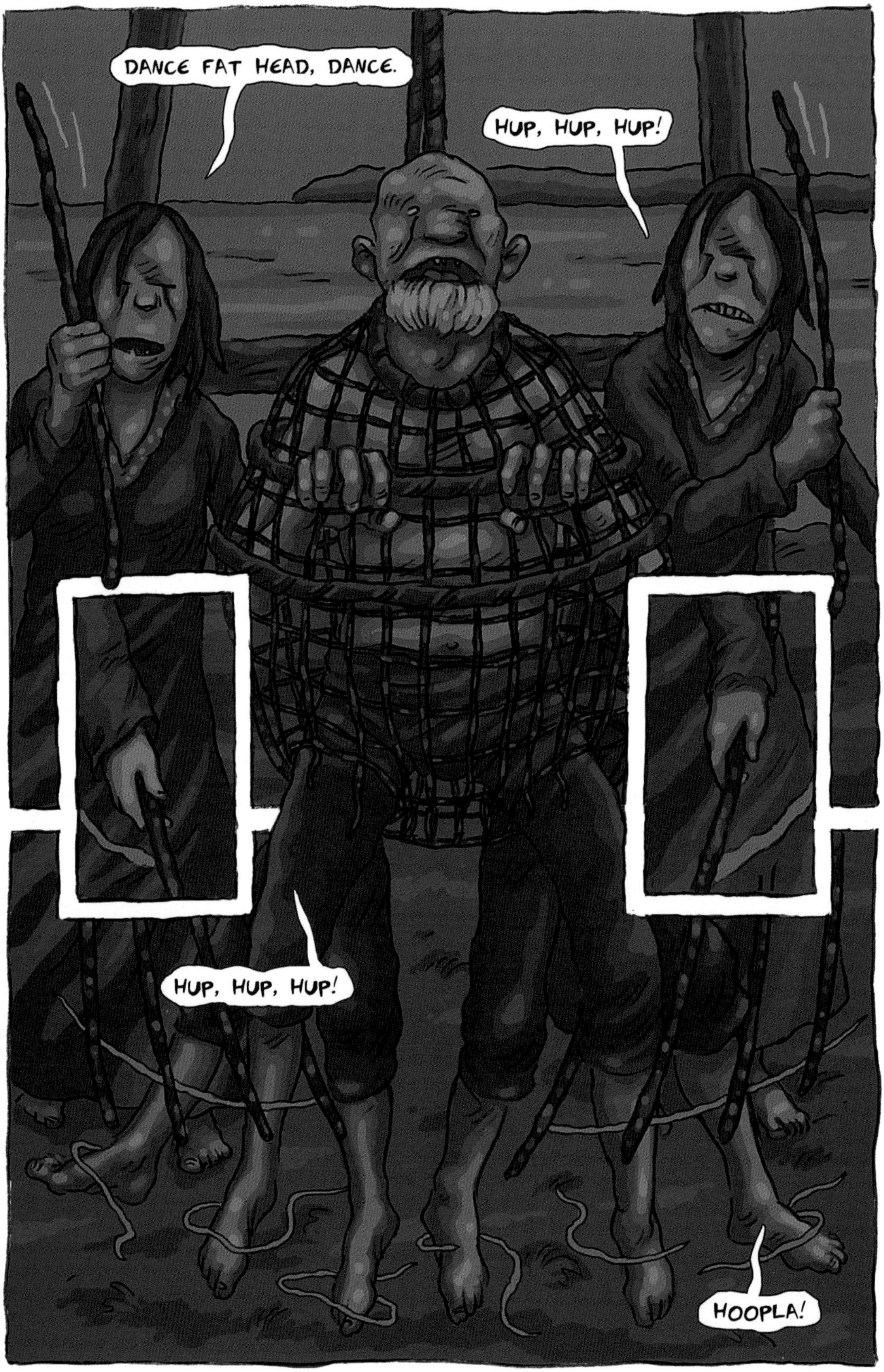
DANCE FAT HEAD, DANCE.
HUP, HUP, HUP!
HUP, HUP, HUP!
HOOPLA!

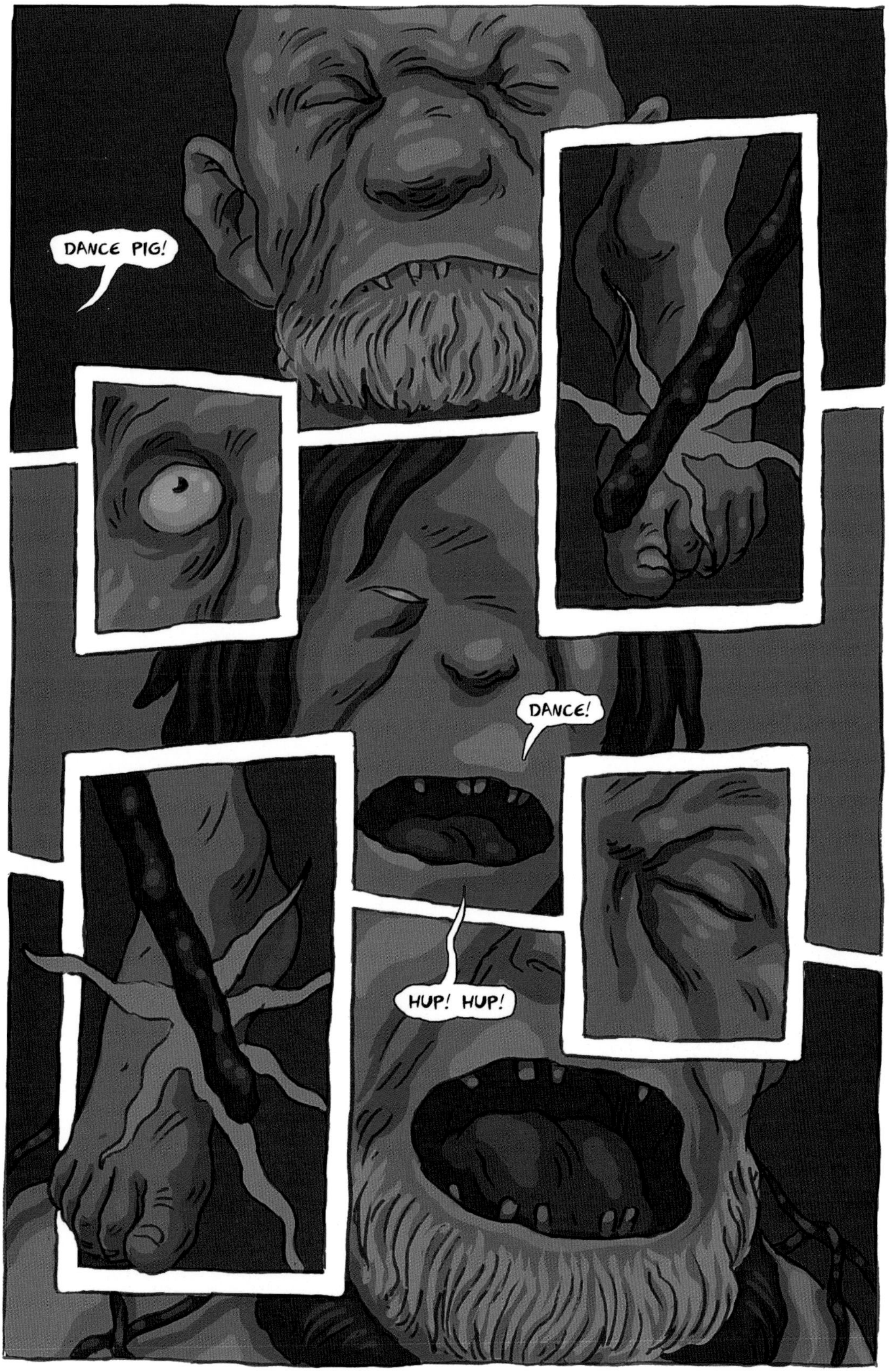
DANCE PIG!
DANCE!
HUP! HUP!

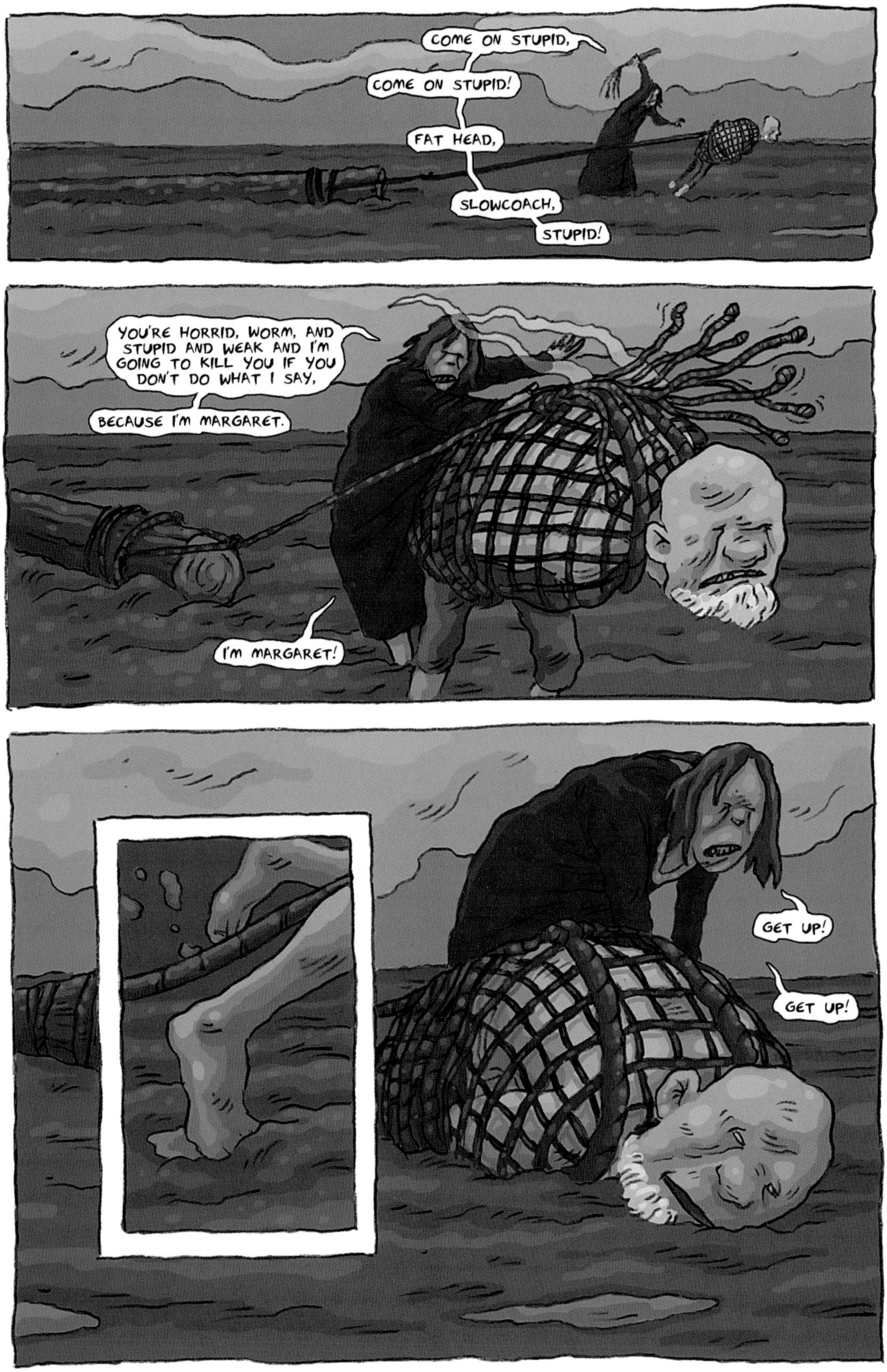
COME ON STUPID,
COME ON STUPID!
FAT HEAD,
SLOWCOACH,
STUPID!
YOU'RE HORRID, WORM, AND STUPID AND WEAK AND I'M GOING TO KILL YOU IF YOU DON'T DO WHAT I SAY,
BECAUSE I'M MARGARET.
I'M MARGARET!
GET UP!
GET UP!

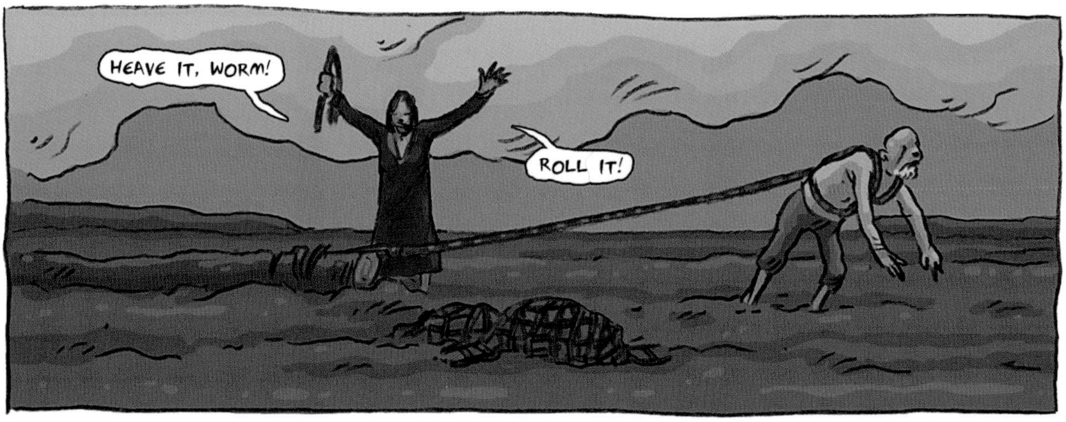
HEAVE IT, WORM!
ROLL IT!

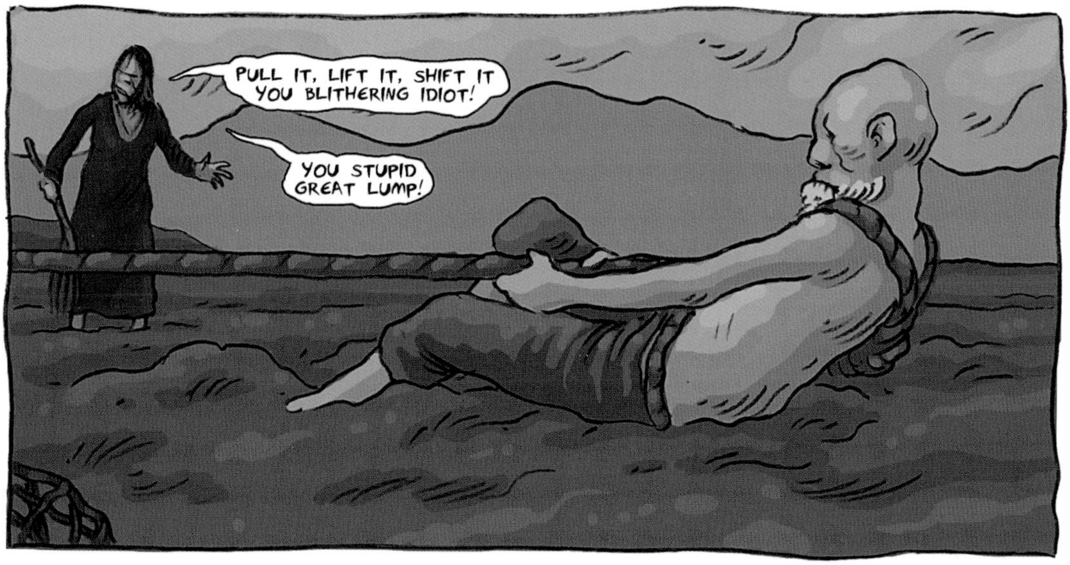
PULL IT, LIFT IT, SHIFT IT YOU BLITHERING IDIOT!
YOU STUPID GREAT LUMP!

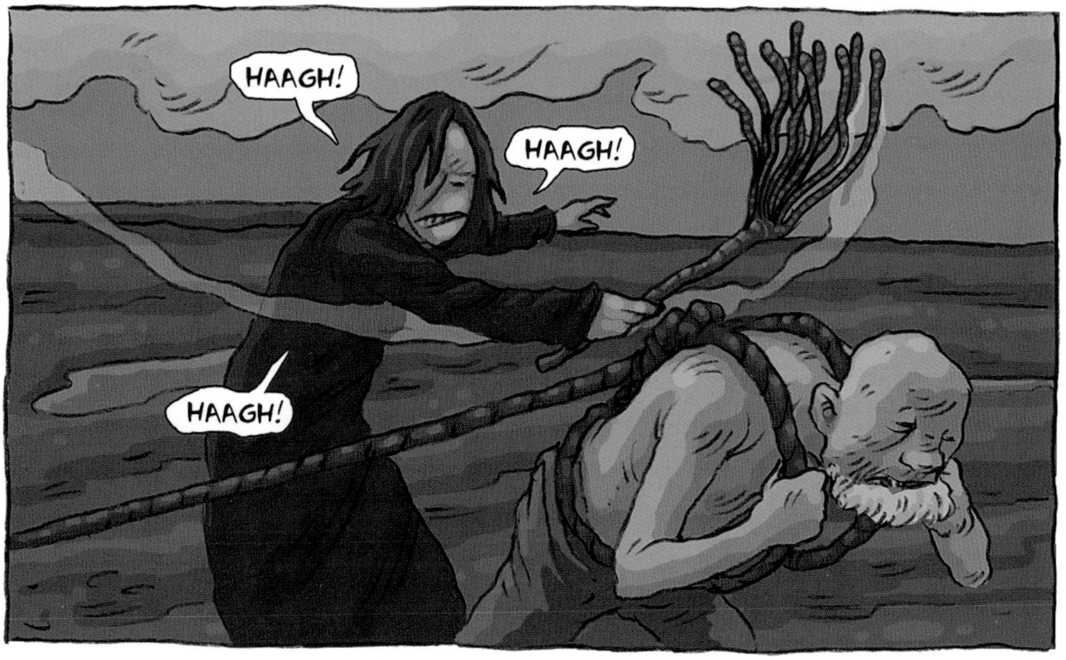
HAAGH!
HAAGH!
HAAGH!

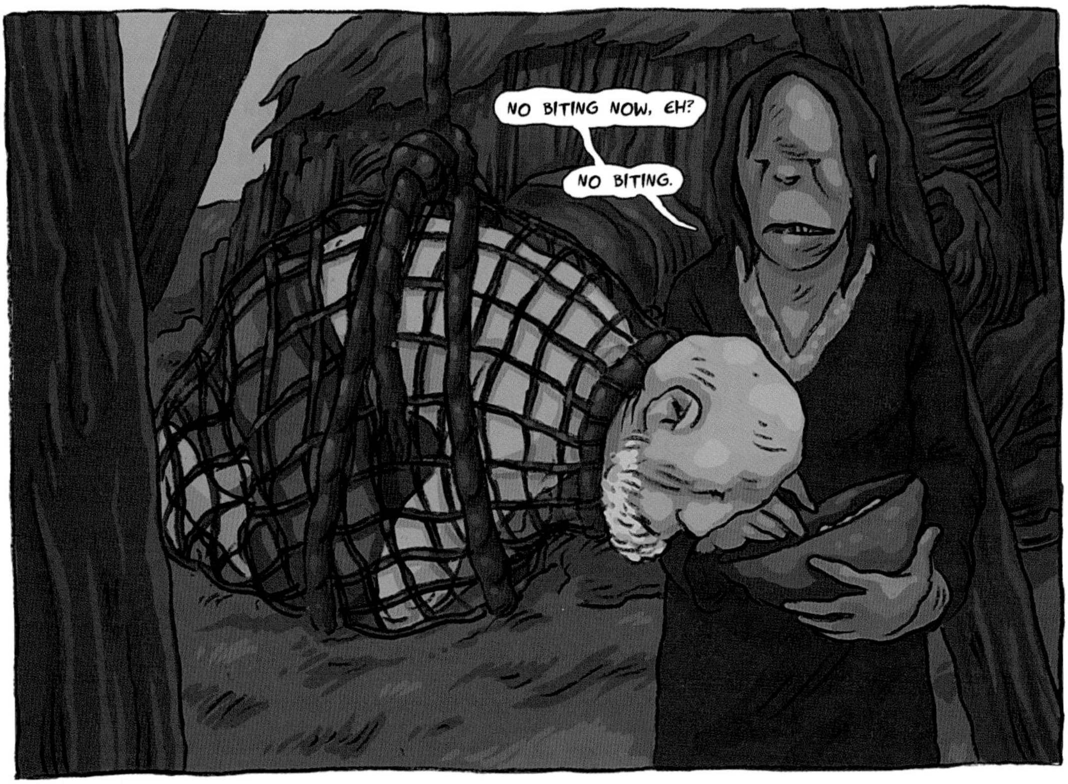
NO BITING NOW, EH?
NO BITING.

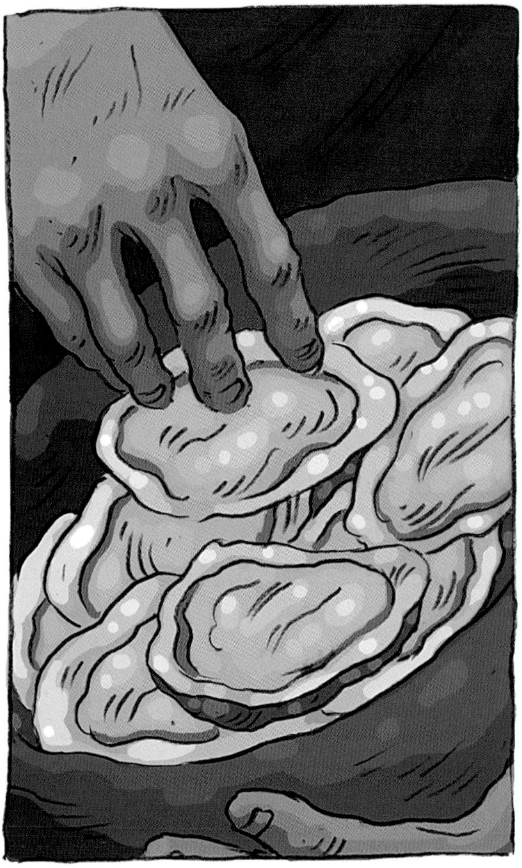

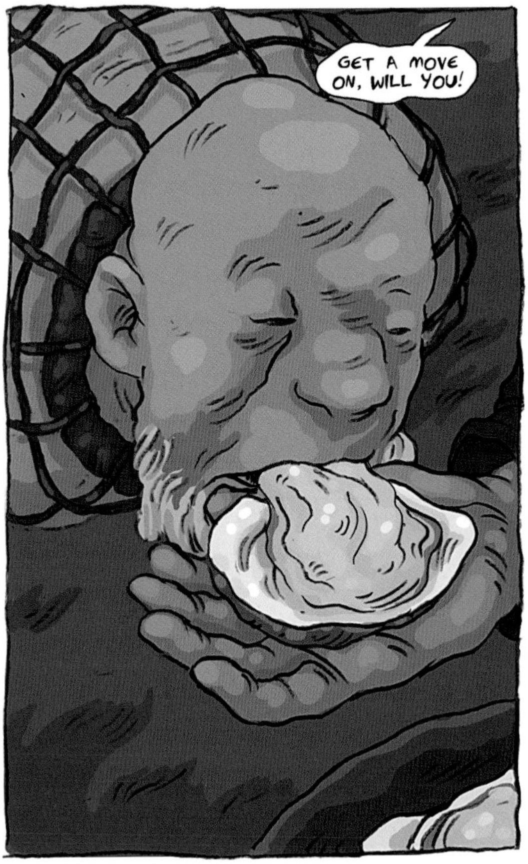
GET A MOVE ON, WILL YOU!

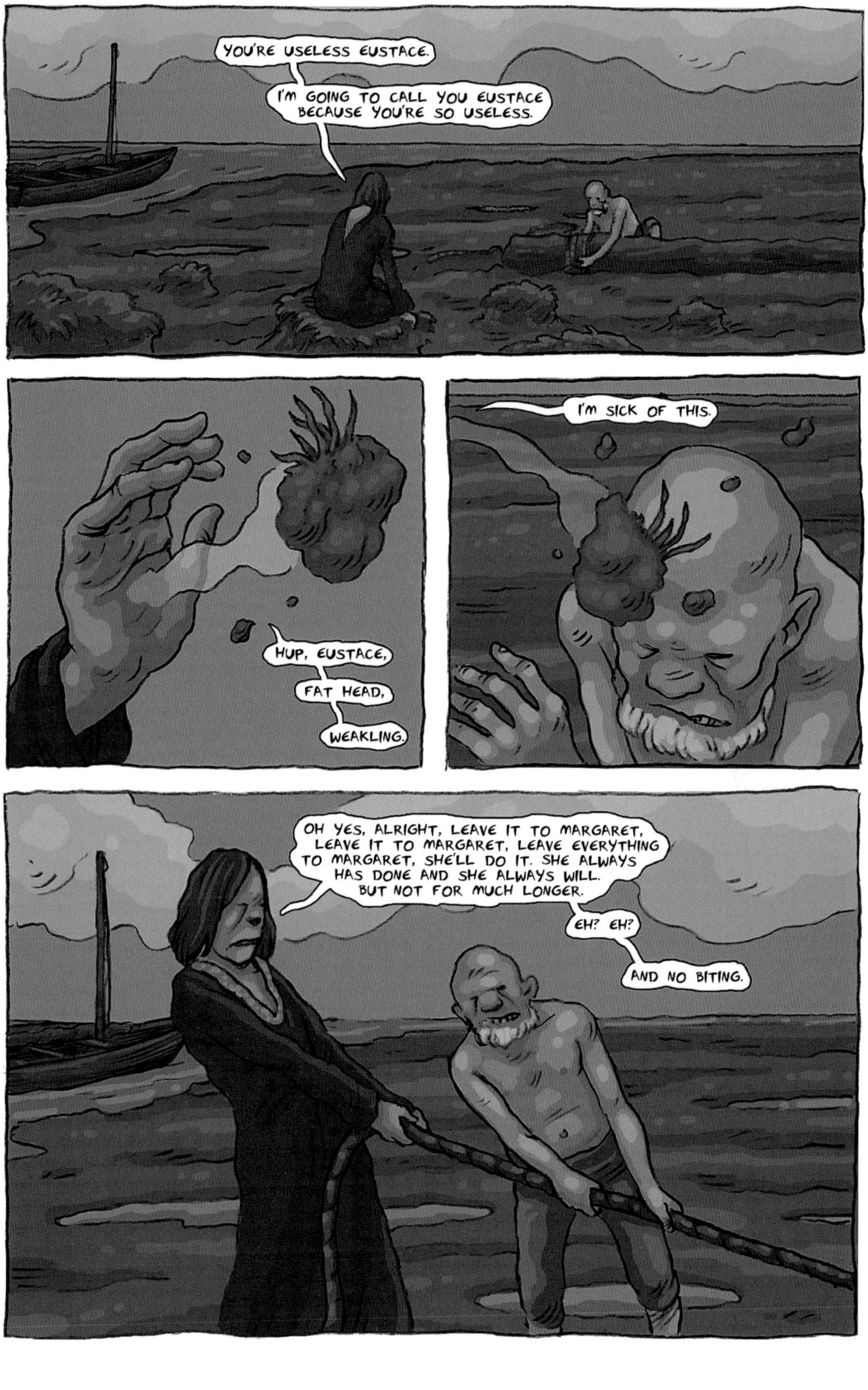
YOU'RE USELESS EUSTACE.
I'M GOING TO CALL YOU EUSTACE BECAUSE YOU'RE SO USELESS.
HUP, EUSTACE,
FAT HEAD,
WEAKLING.
I'M SICK OF THIS.
OH YES, ALRIGHT, LEAVE IT TO MARGARET, LEAVE IT TO MARGARET, LEAVE EVERYTHING TO MARGARET, SHE'LL DO IT. SHE ALWAYS HAS DONE AND SHE ALWAYS WILL. BUT NOT FOR MUCH LONGER.
EH? EH?
AND NO BITING.

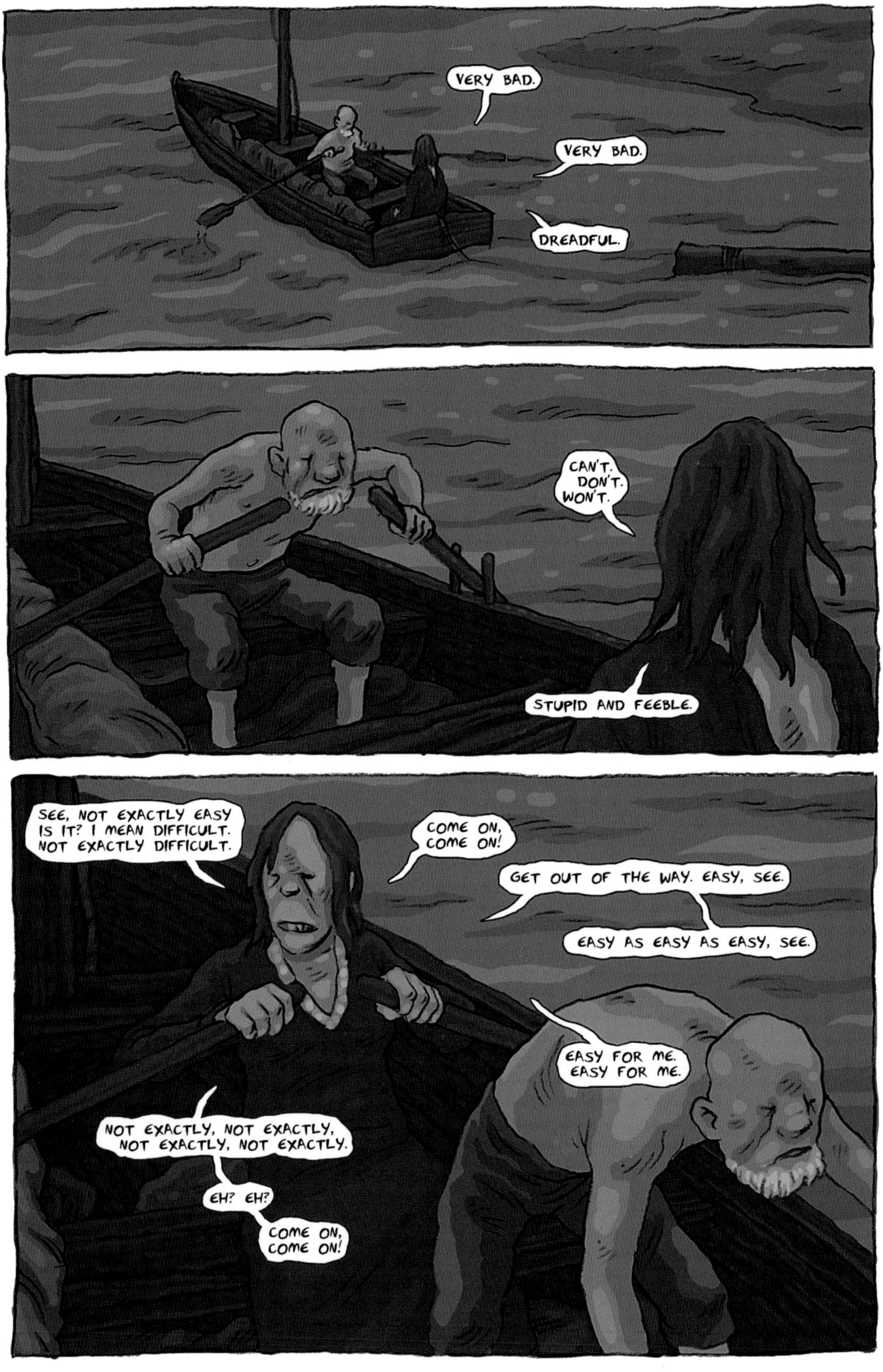
VERY BAD.
VERY BAD.
DREADFUL.
CAN'T. DON'T. WON'T.
STUPID AND FEEBLE.
SEE, NOT EXACTLY EASY IS IT? I MEAN DIFFICULT. NOT EXACTLY DIFFICULT.
COME ON, COME ON!
GET OUT OF THE WAY. EASY, SEE.
EASY AS EASY AS EASY, SEE.
EASY FOR ME. EASY FOR ME.
NOT EXACTLY, NOT EXACTLY, NOT EXACTLY, NOT EXACTLY.
EH? EH?
COME ON, COME ON!

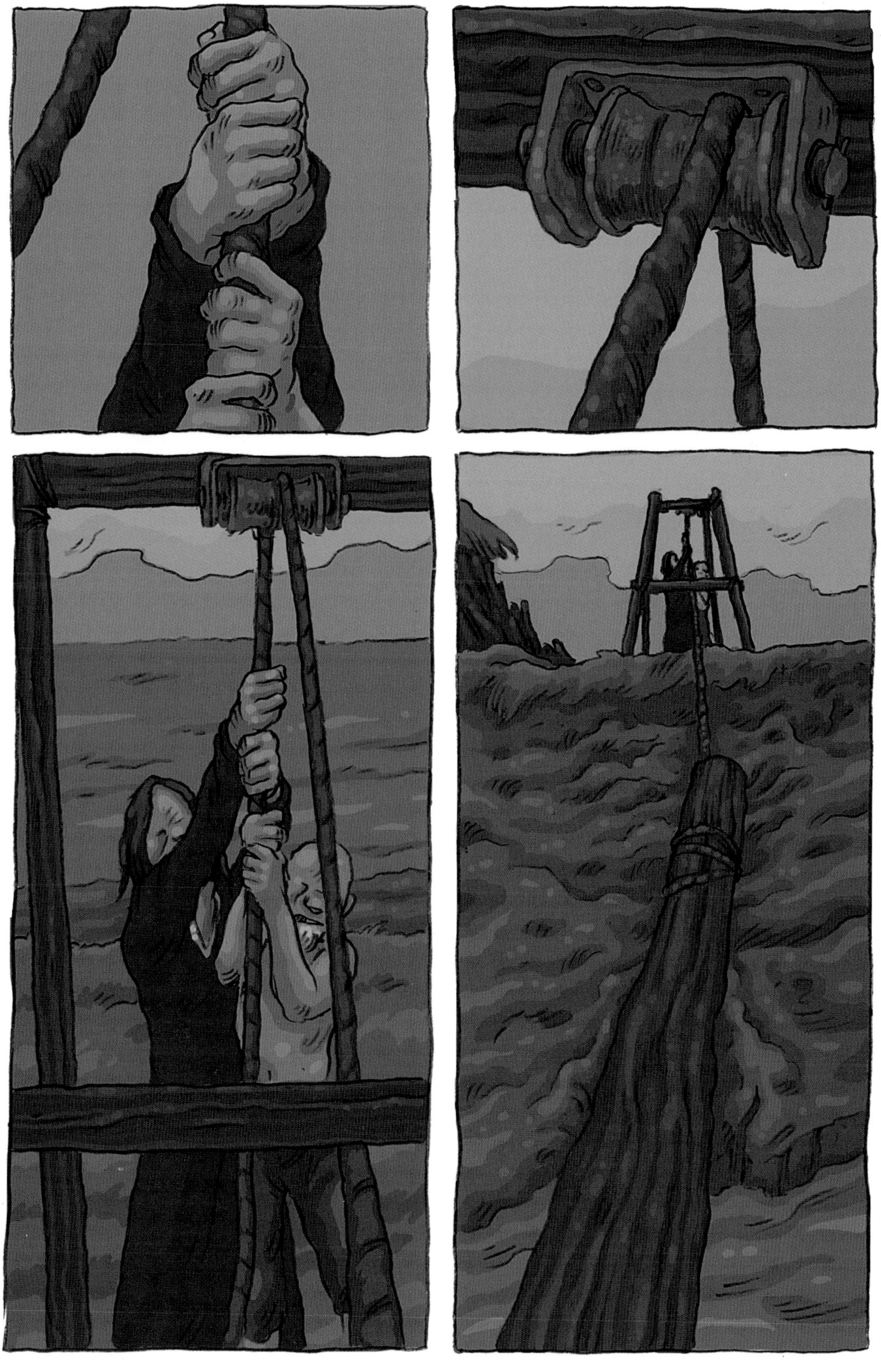

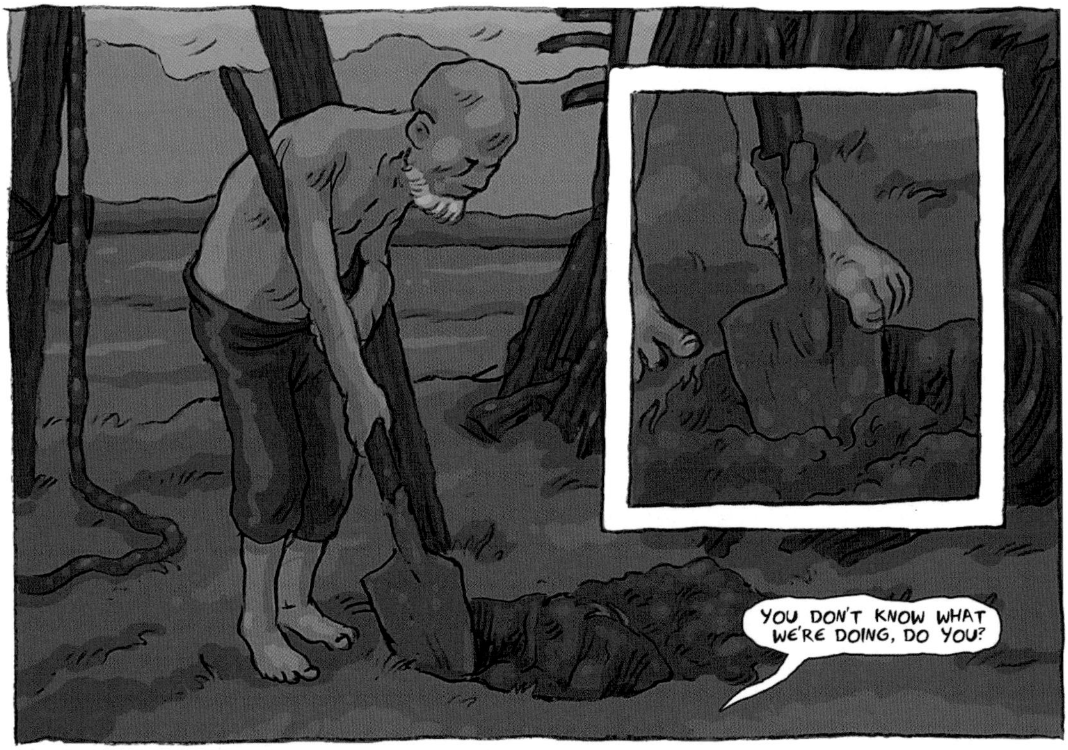
YOU DON'T KNOW WHAT WE'RE DOING, DO YOU?

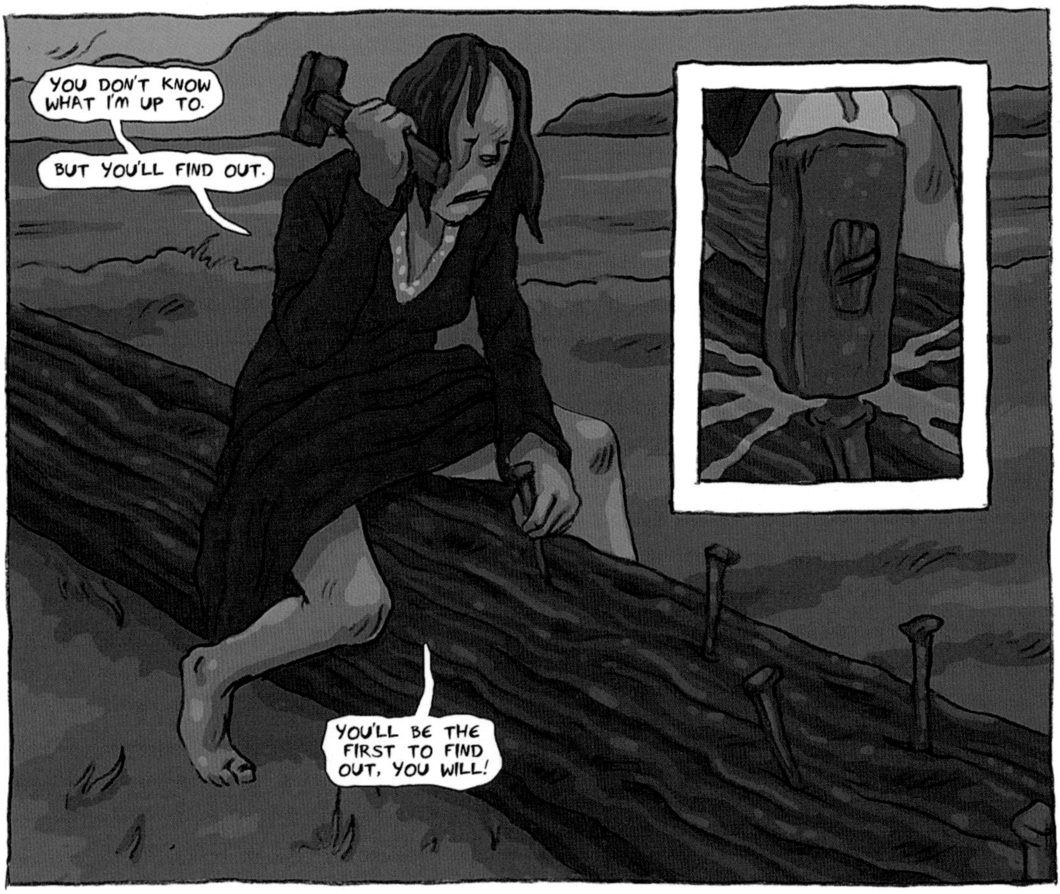
YOU DON'T KNOW WHAT I'M UP TO.
BUT YOU'LL FIND OUT.
YOU'LL BE THE FIRST TO FIND OUT, YOU WILL!

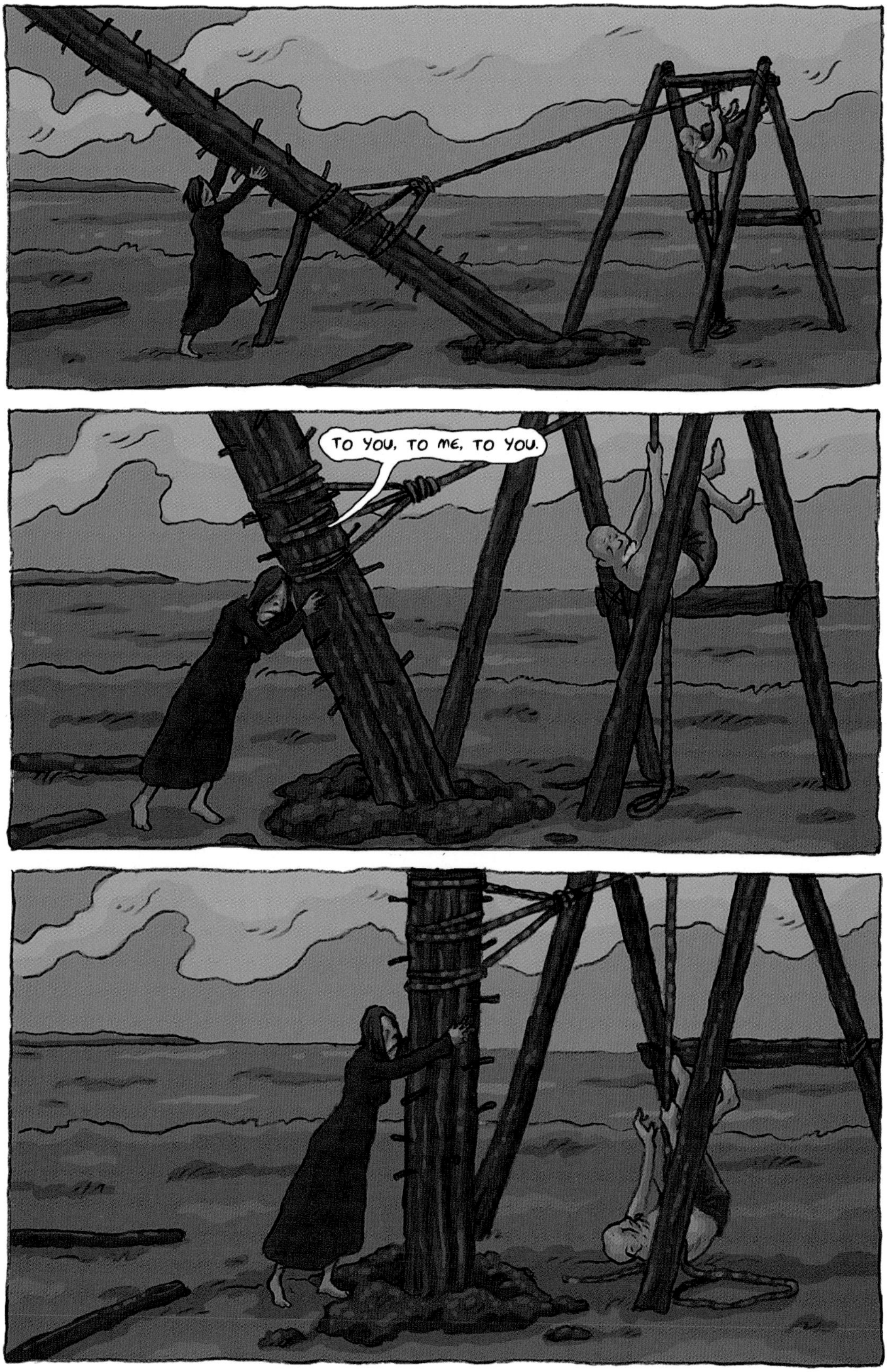
TO YOU, TO ME, TO YOU.

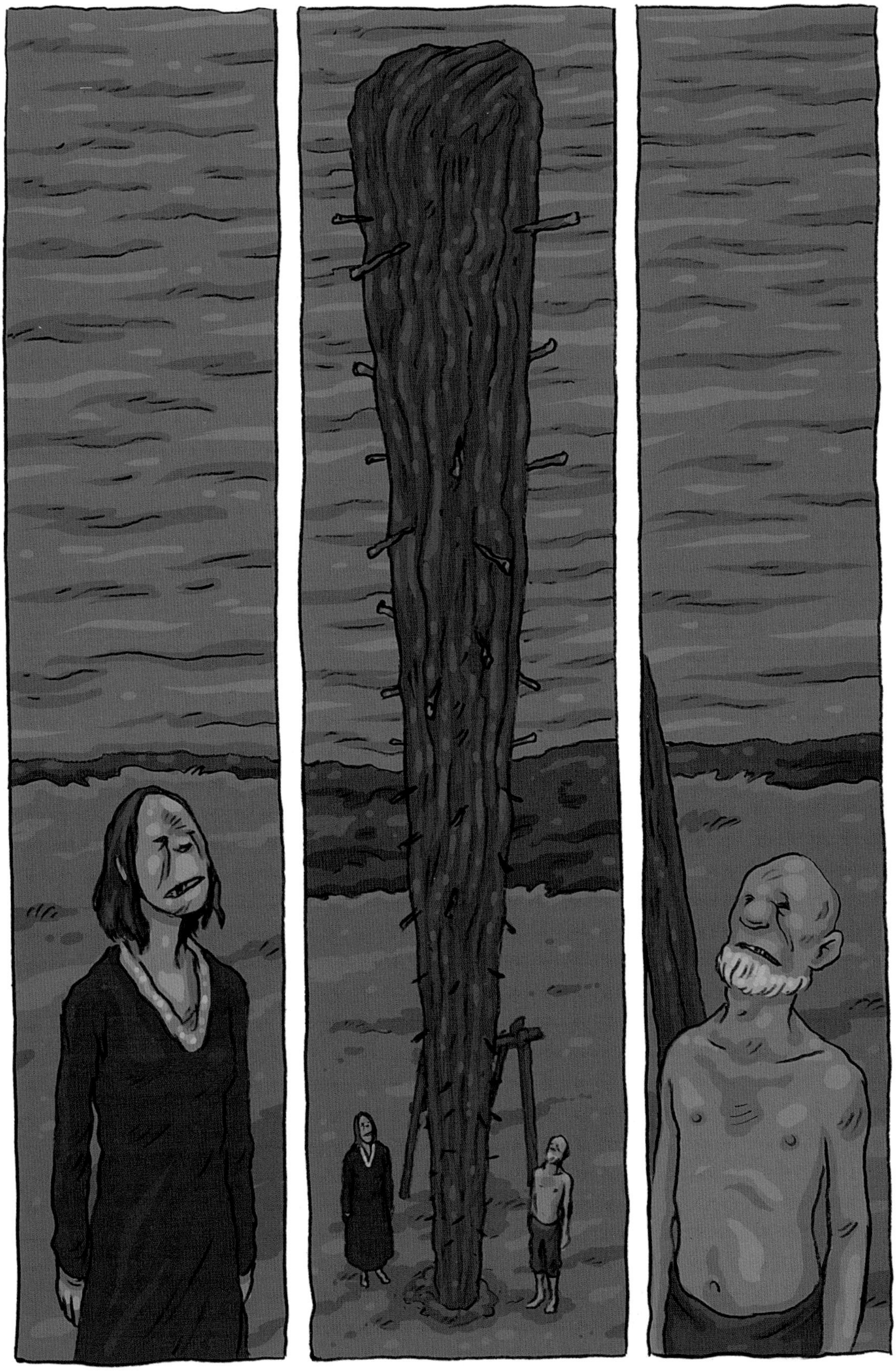

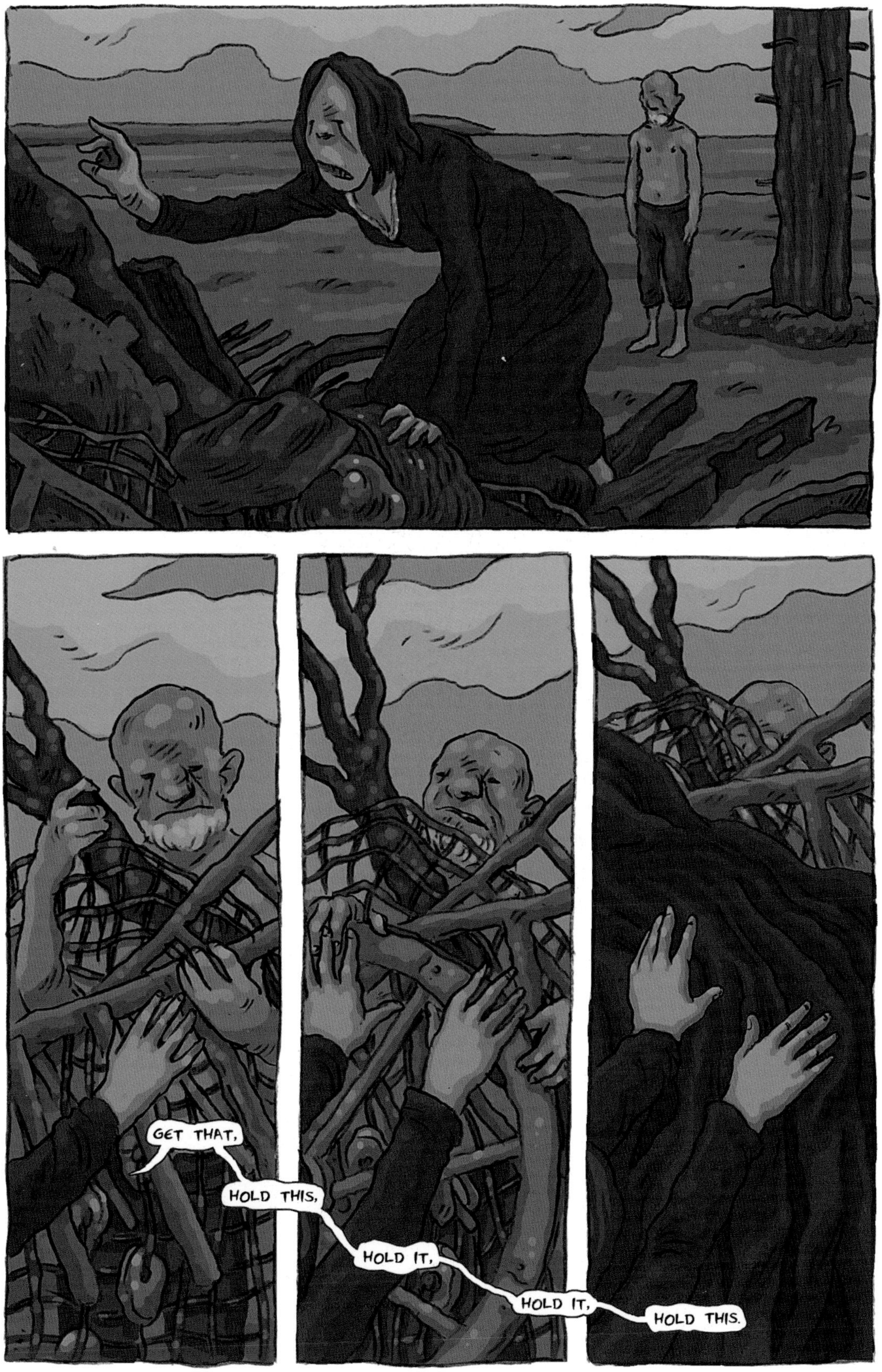
GET THAT,
HOLD THIS,
HOLD IT,
HOLD IT,
HOLD THIS.

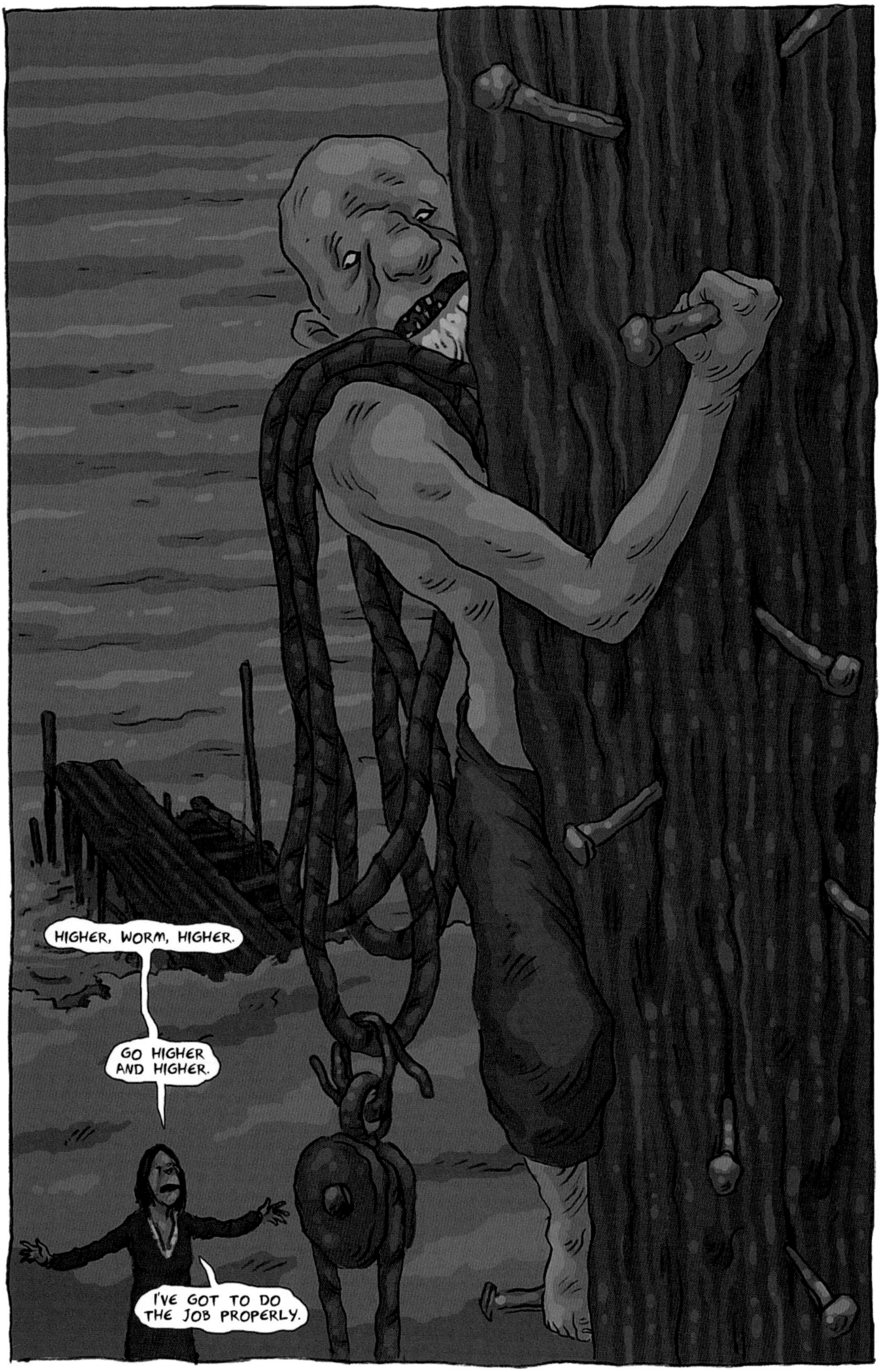
HIGHER, WORM, HIGHER.
GO HIGHER AND HIGHER.
I'VE GOT TO DO THE JOB PROPERLY.

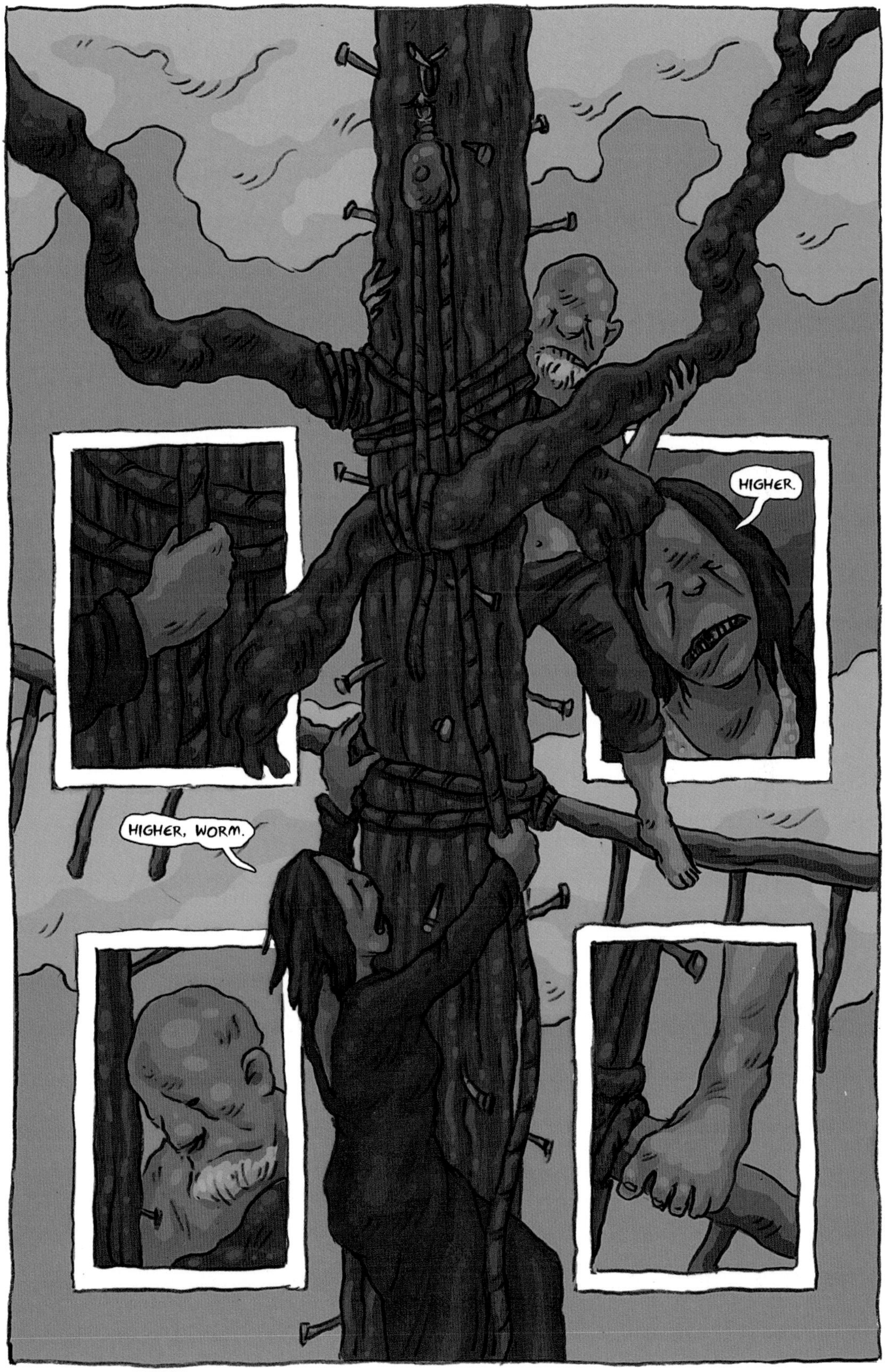
HIGHER.
HIGHER, WORM.

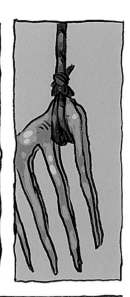

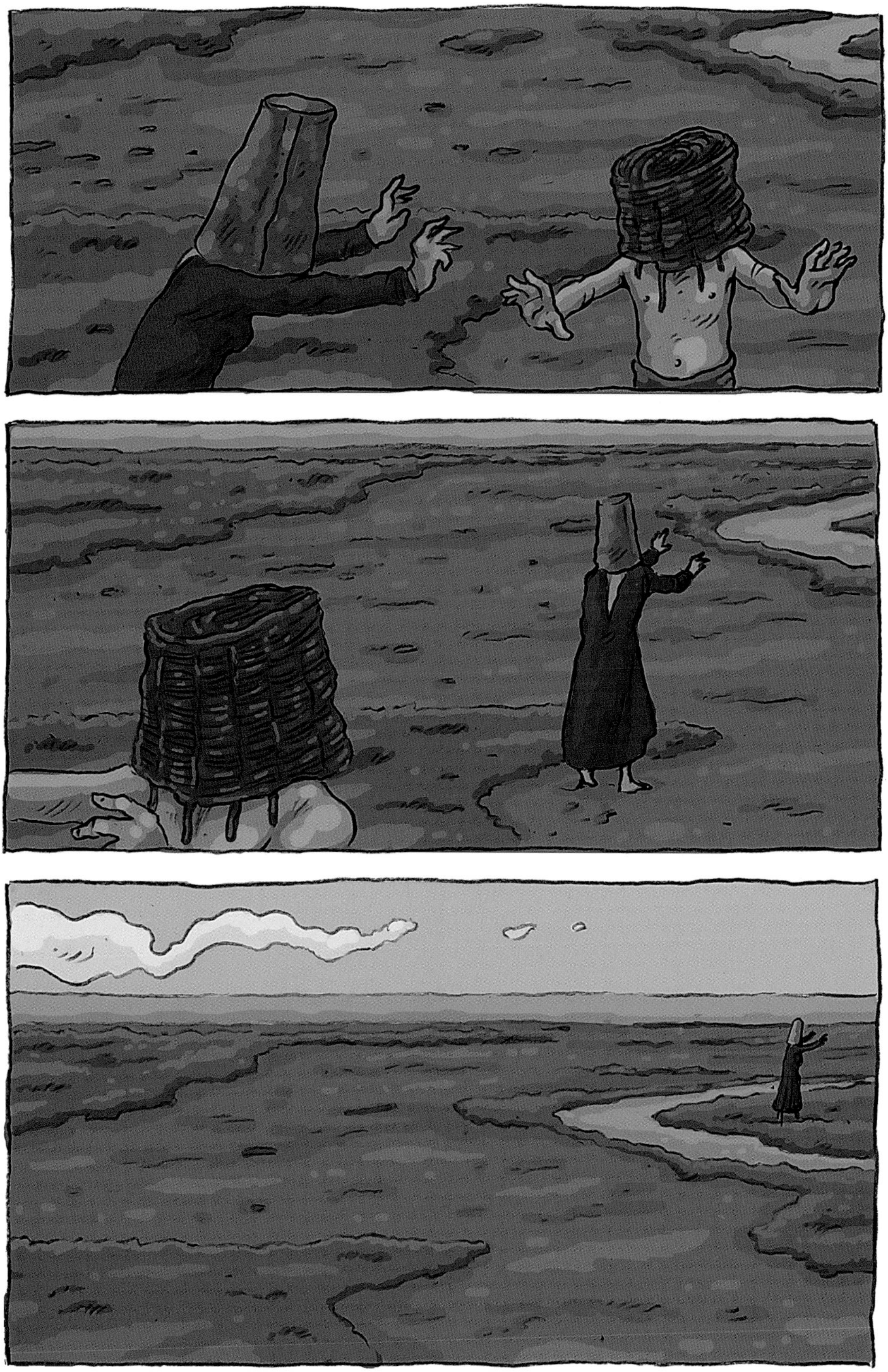

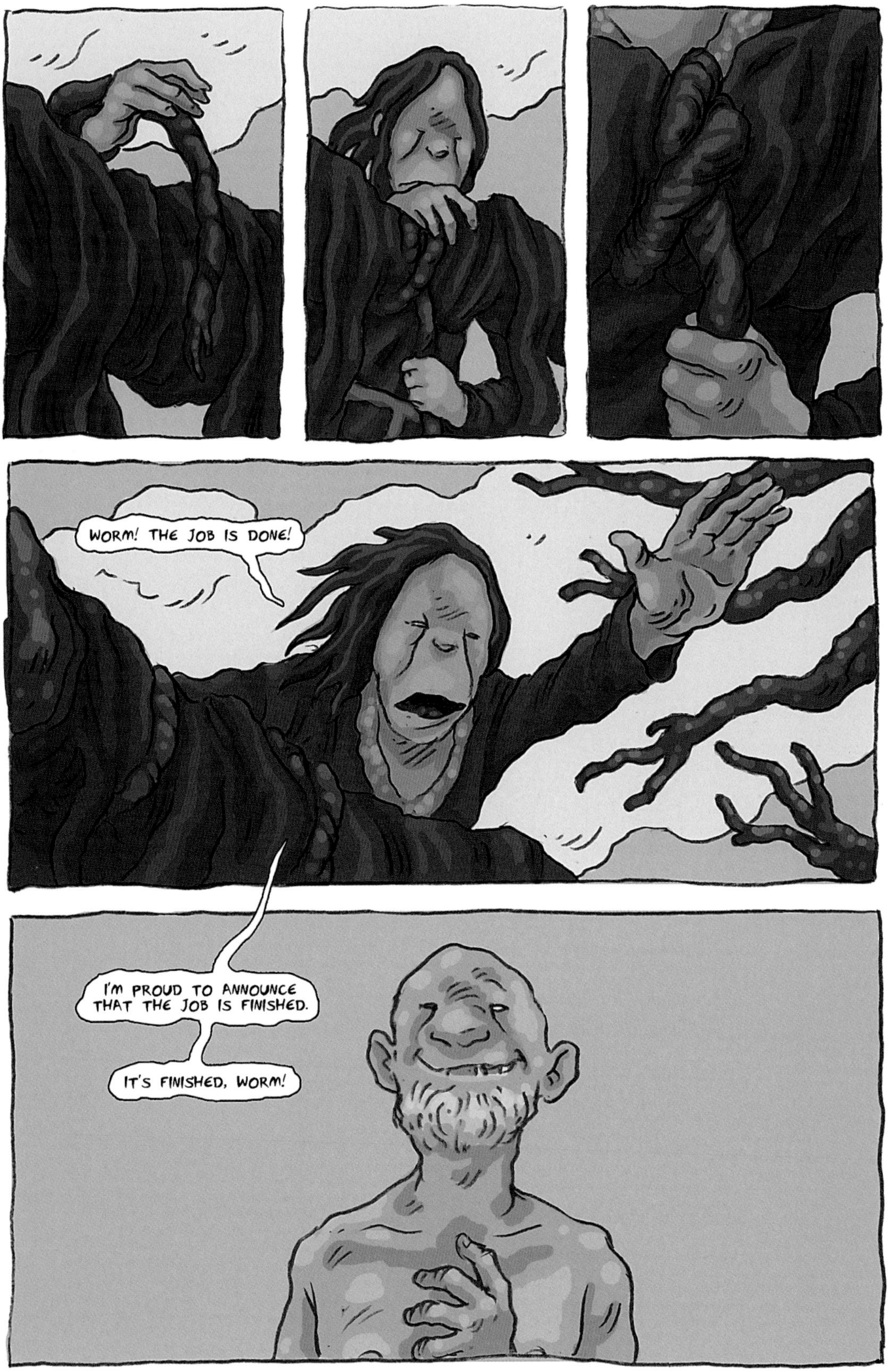
WORM! THE JOB IS DONE!
I'M PROUD TO ANNOUNCE THAT THE JOB IS FINISHED.
IT'S FINISHED, WORM!

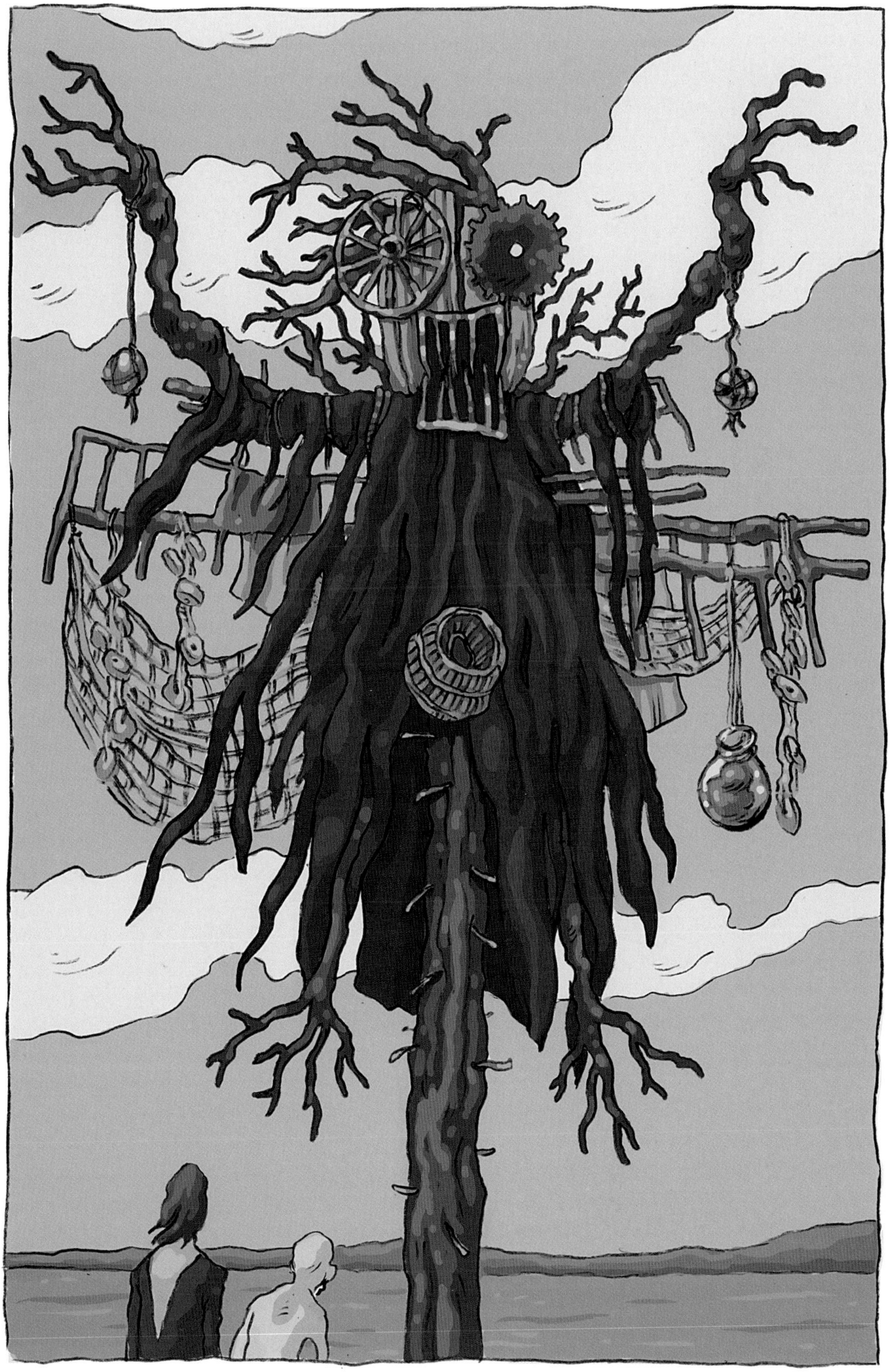

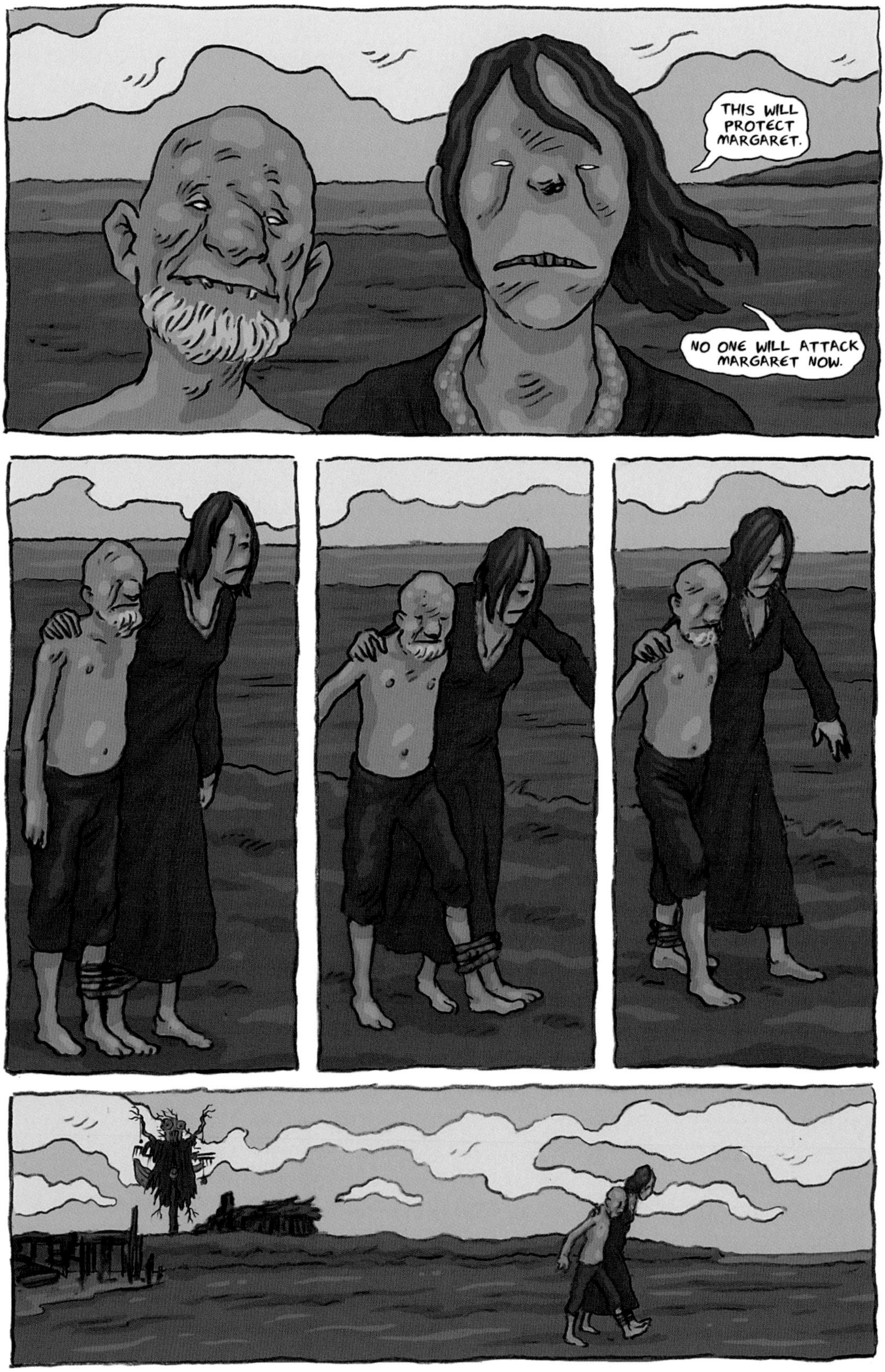
THIS WILL PROTECT MARGARET.
NO ONE WILL ATTACK MARGARET NOW.

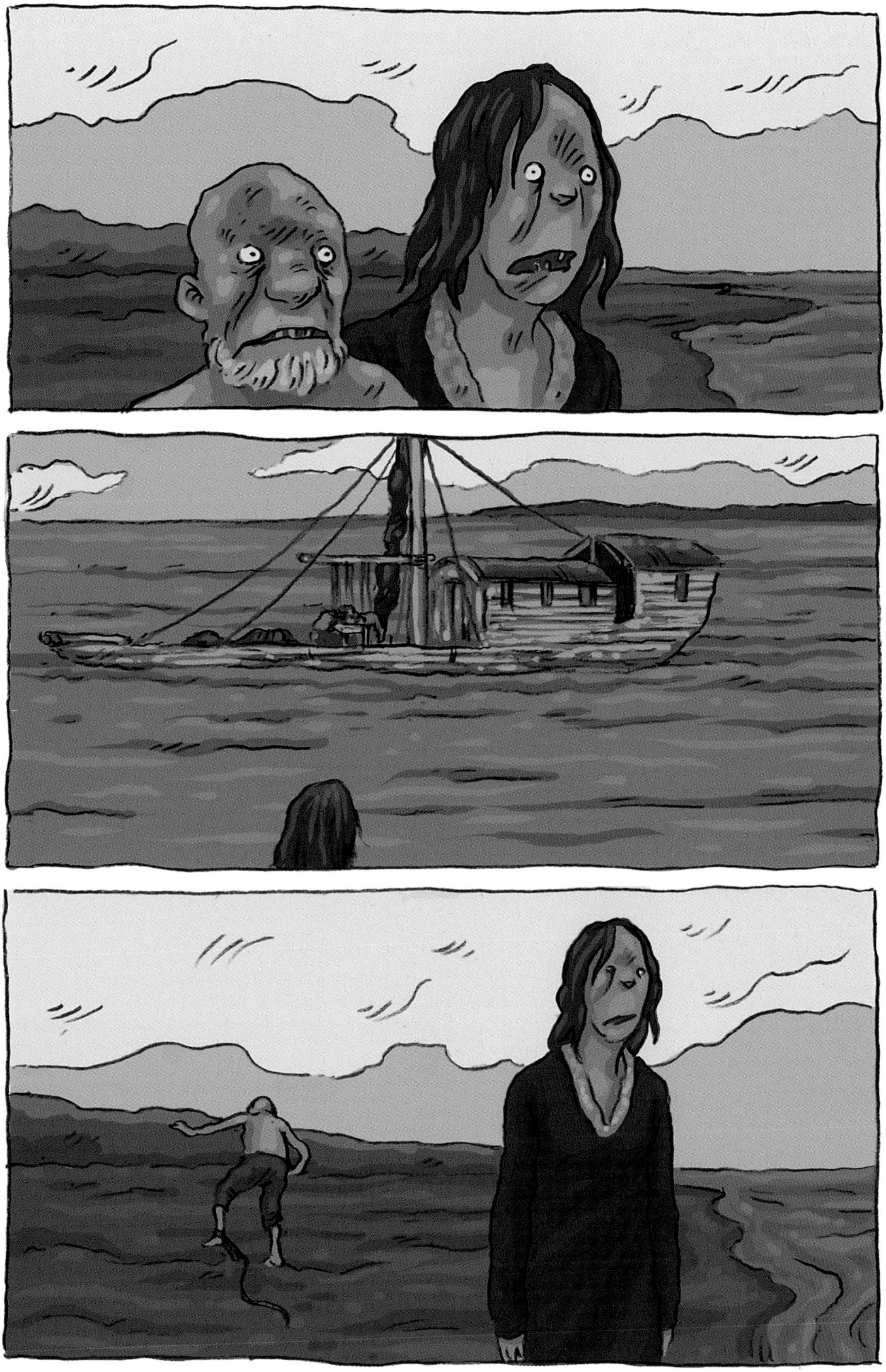

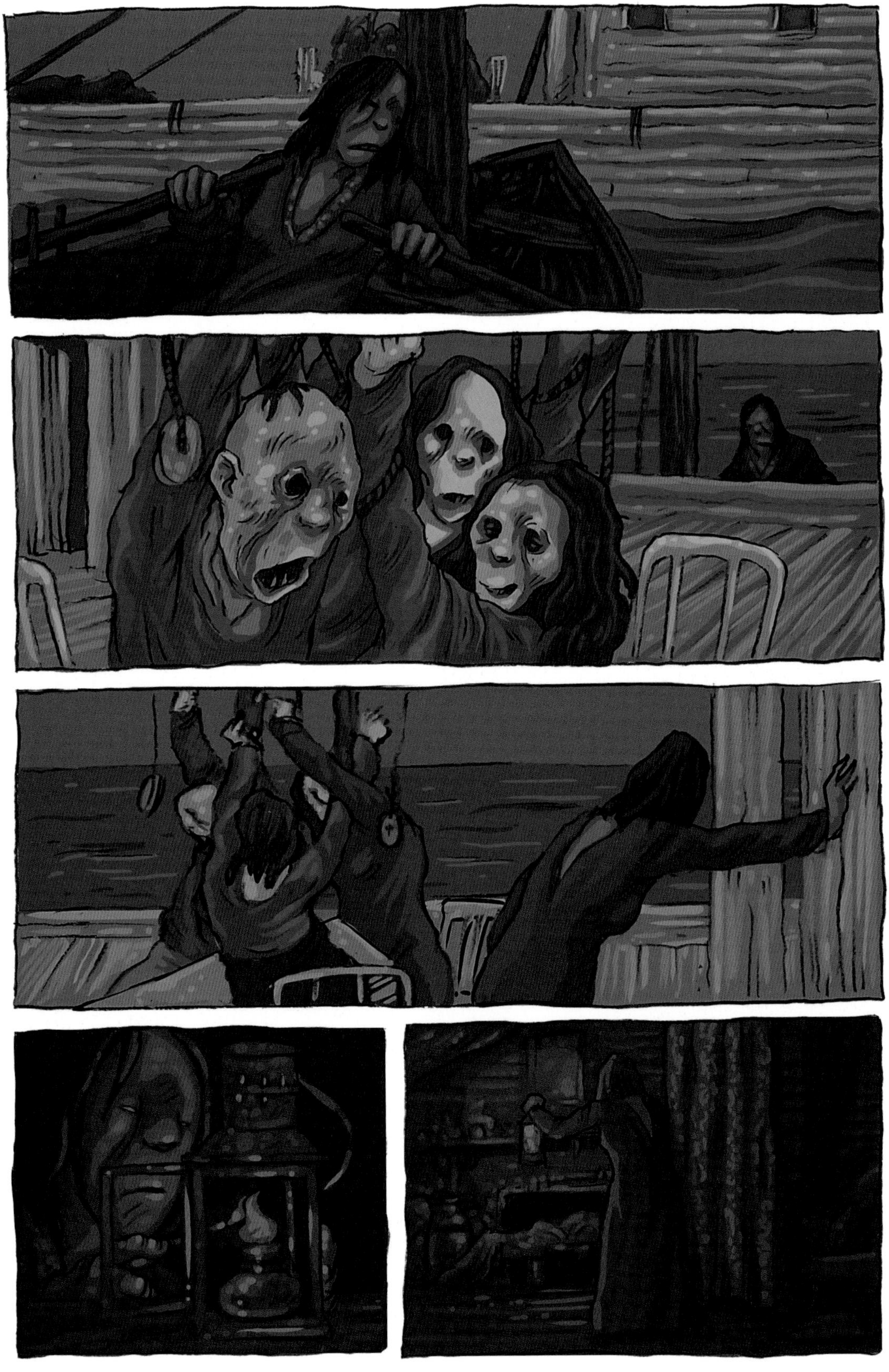

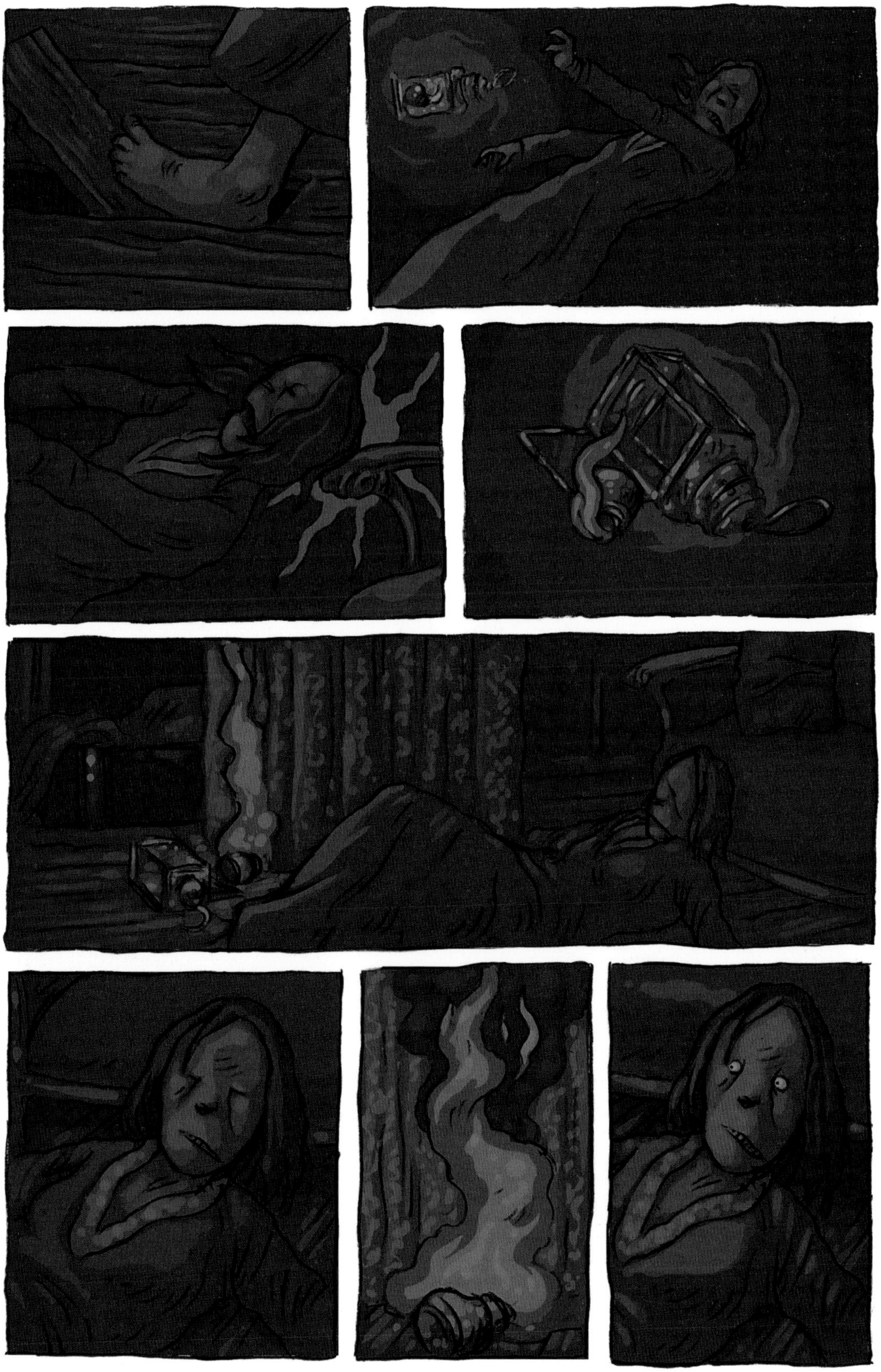

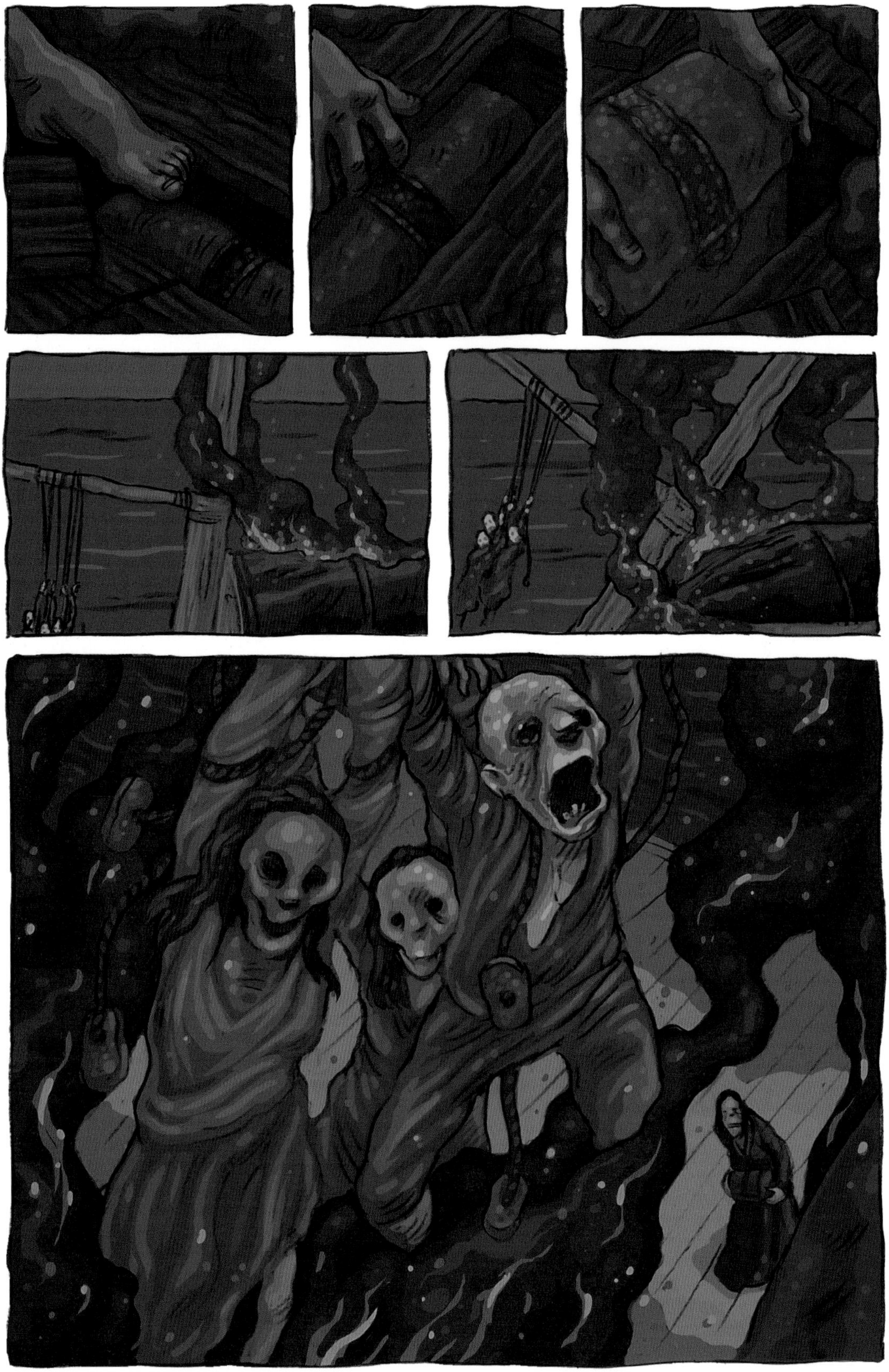

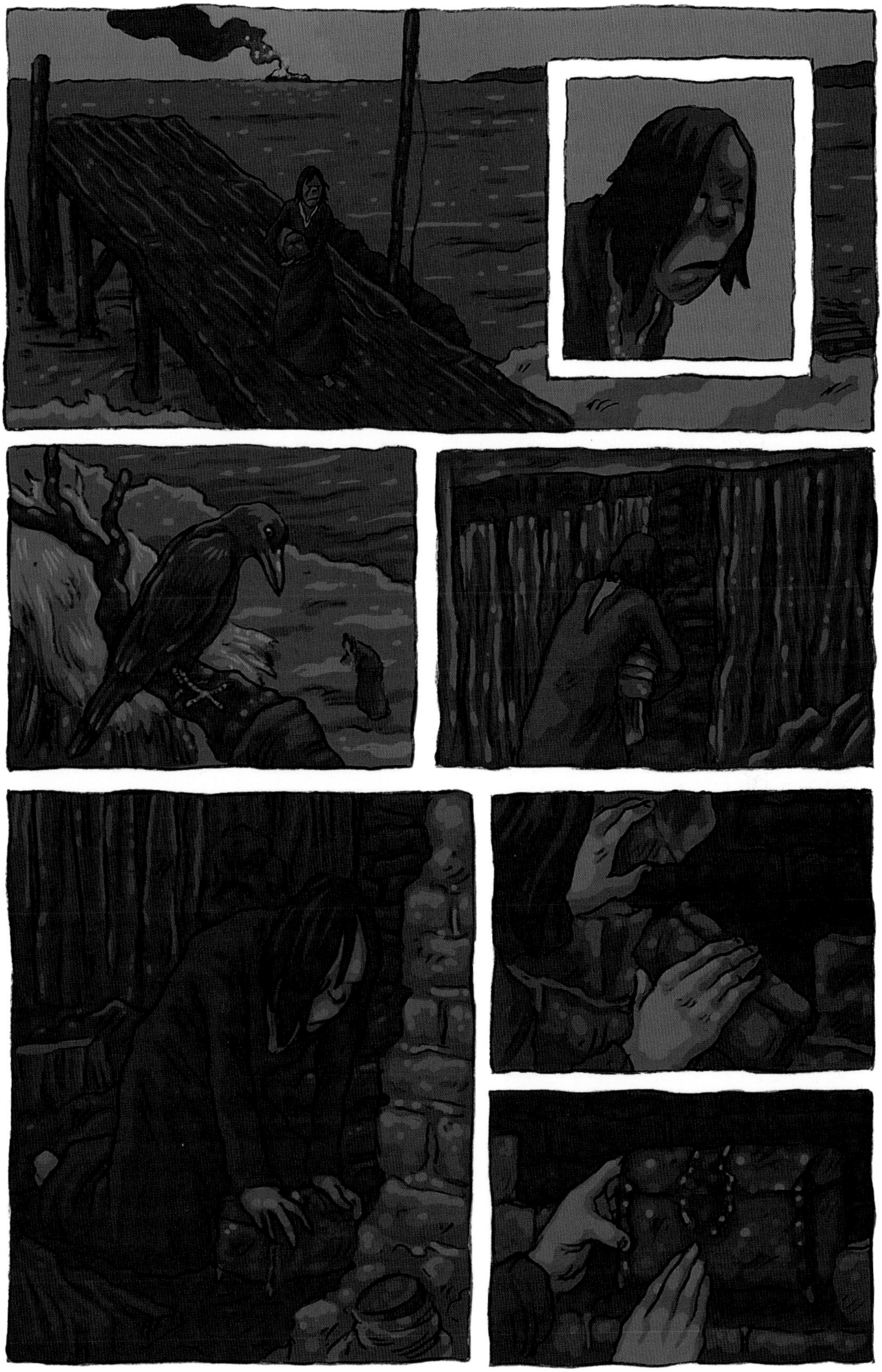

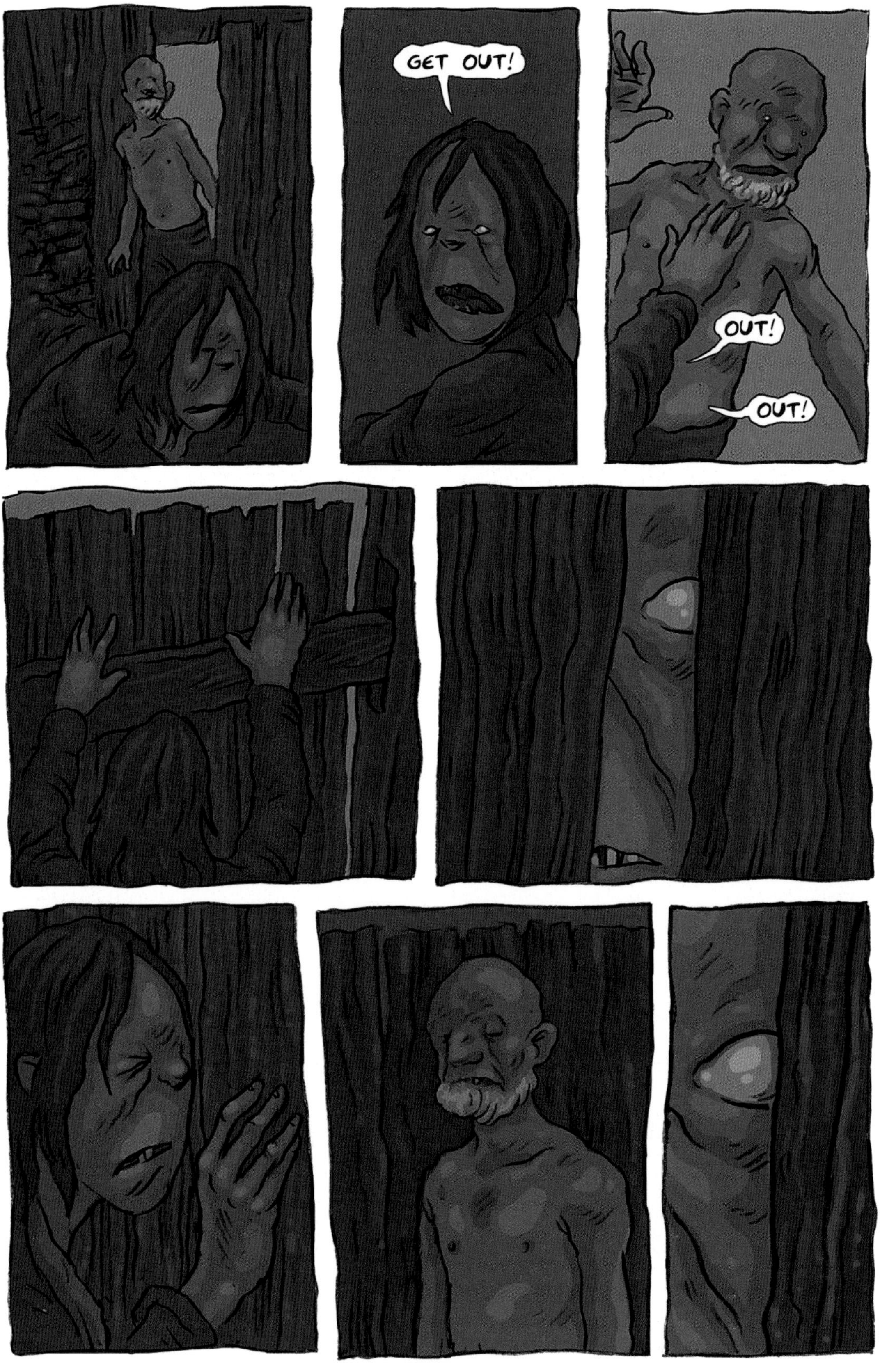
GET OUT!
OUT!
OUT!

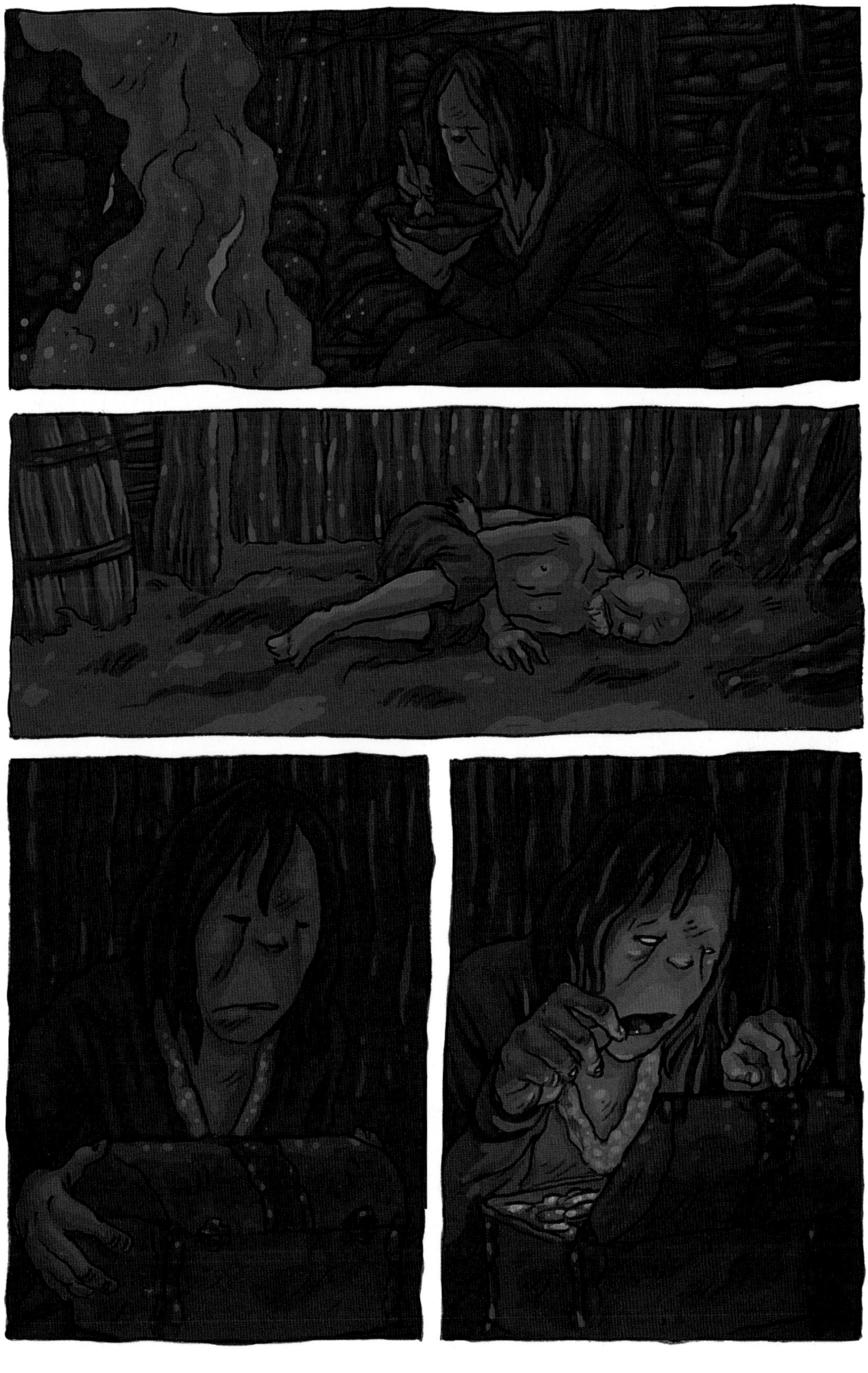

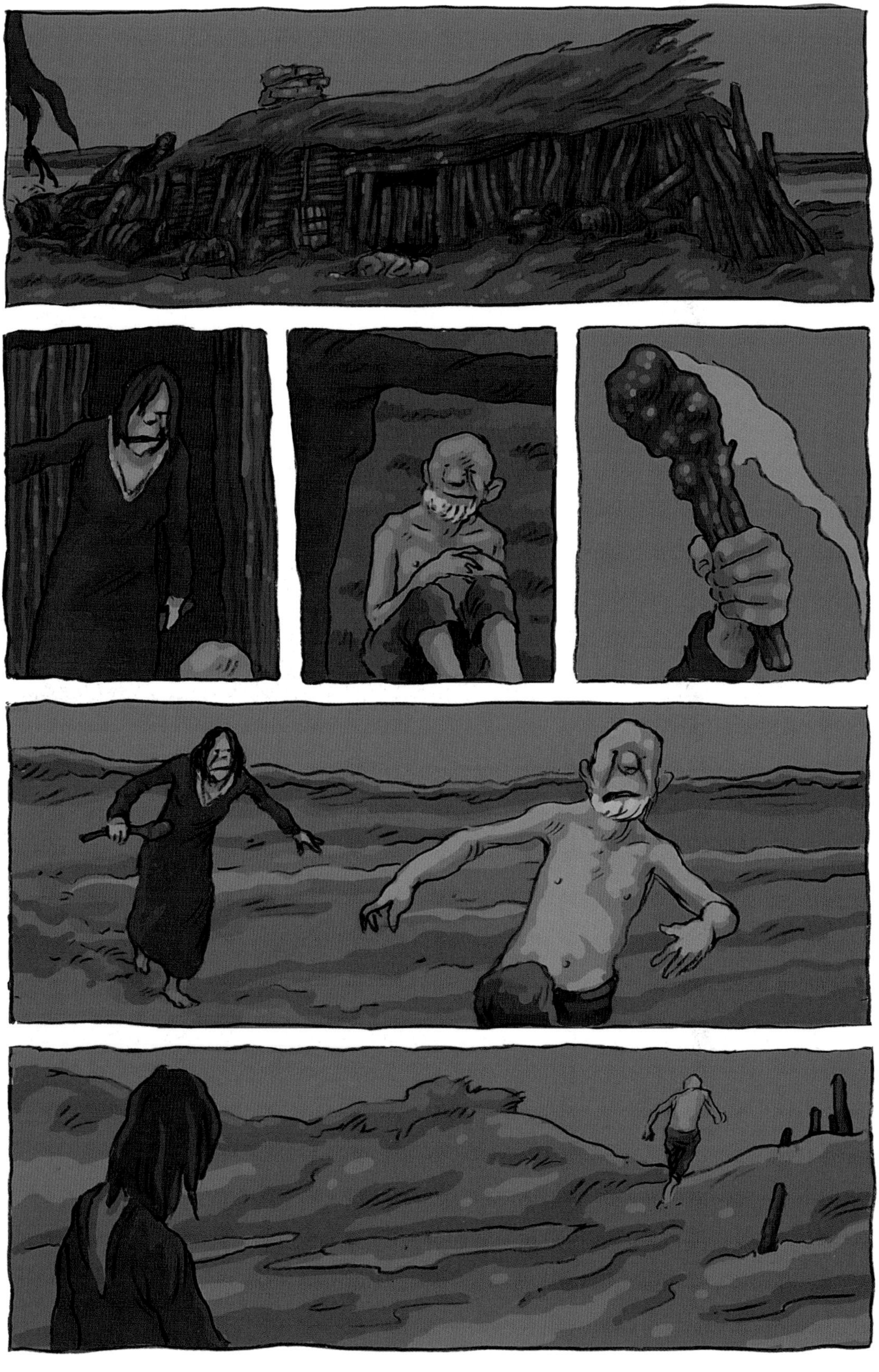

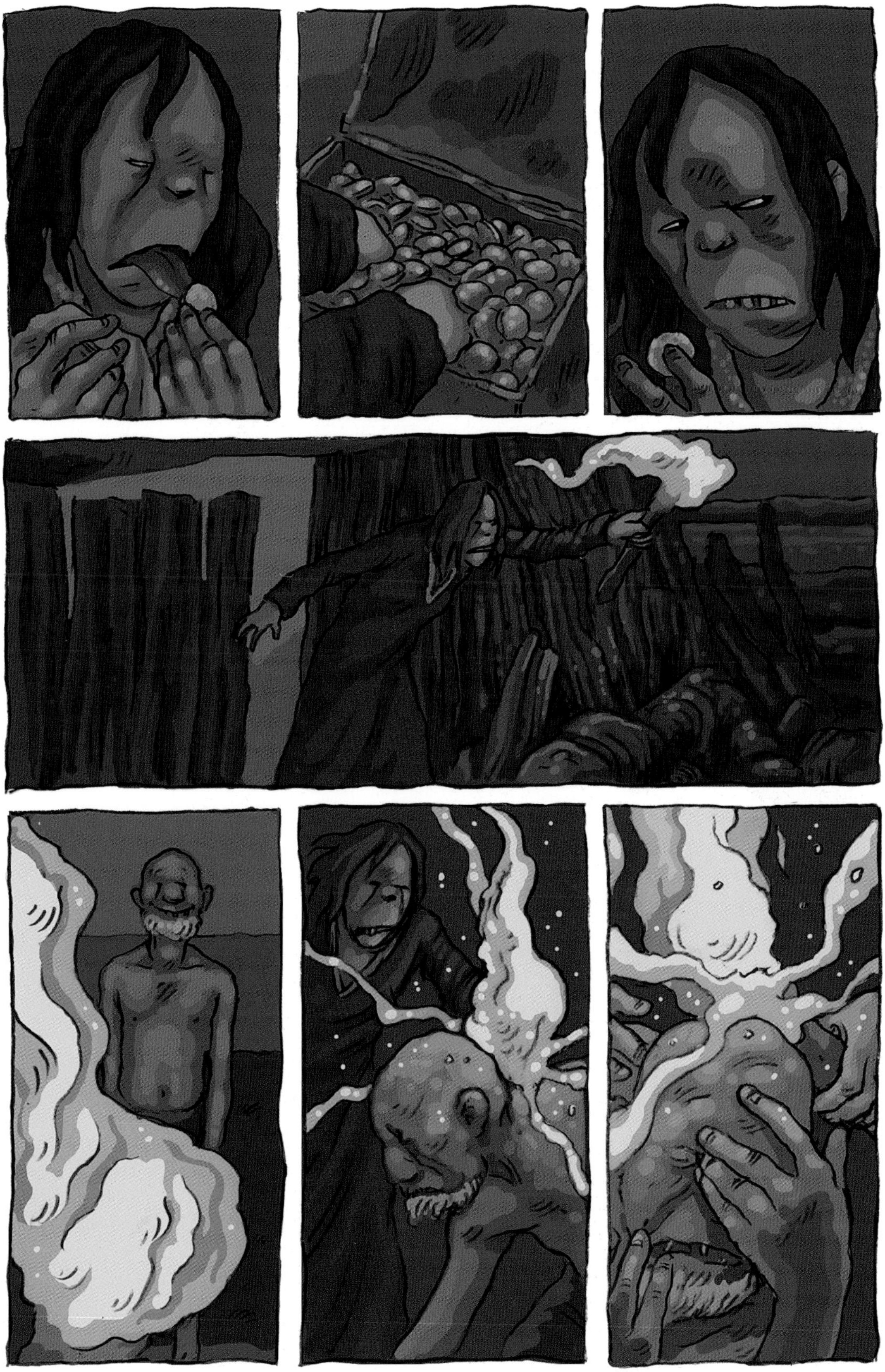

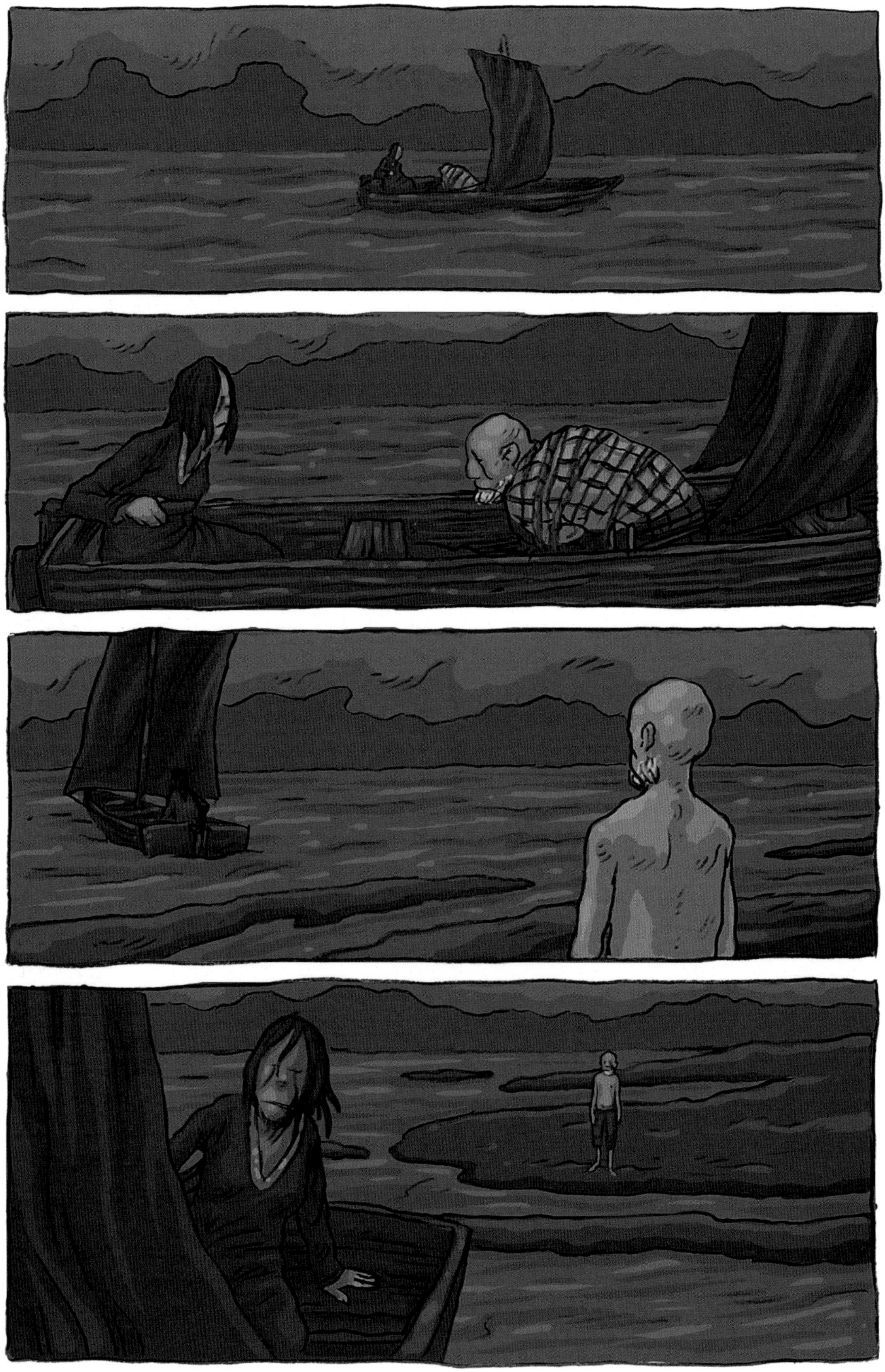

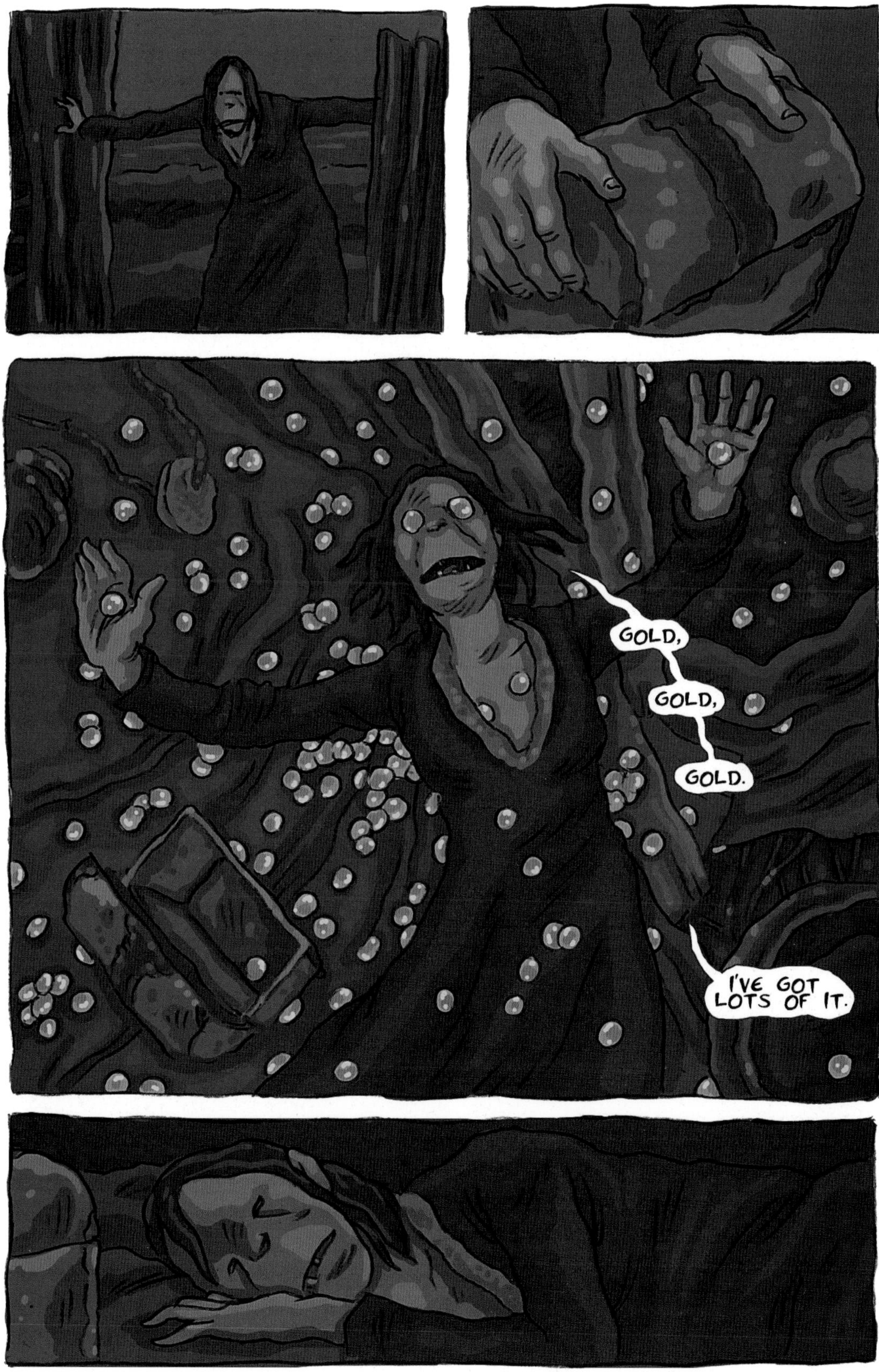
GOLD,
GOLD,
GOLD.
I'VE GOT LOTS OF IT.

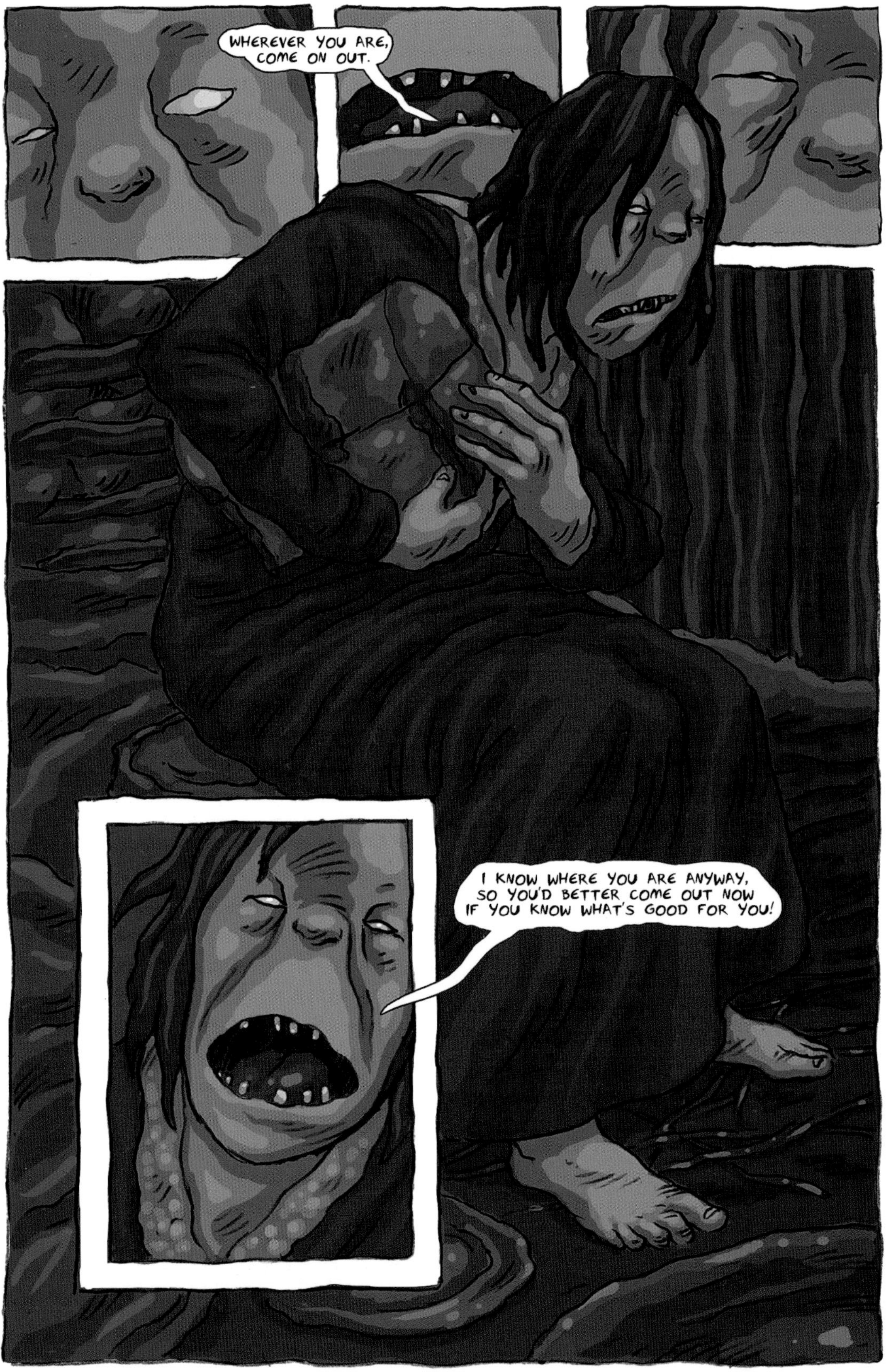
WHEREVER YOU ARE, COME ON OUT.
I KNOW WHERE YOU ARE ANYWAY, SO YOU'D BETTER COME OUT NOW IF YOU KNOW WHAT'S GOOD FOR YOU!

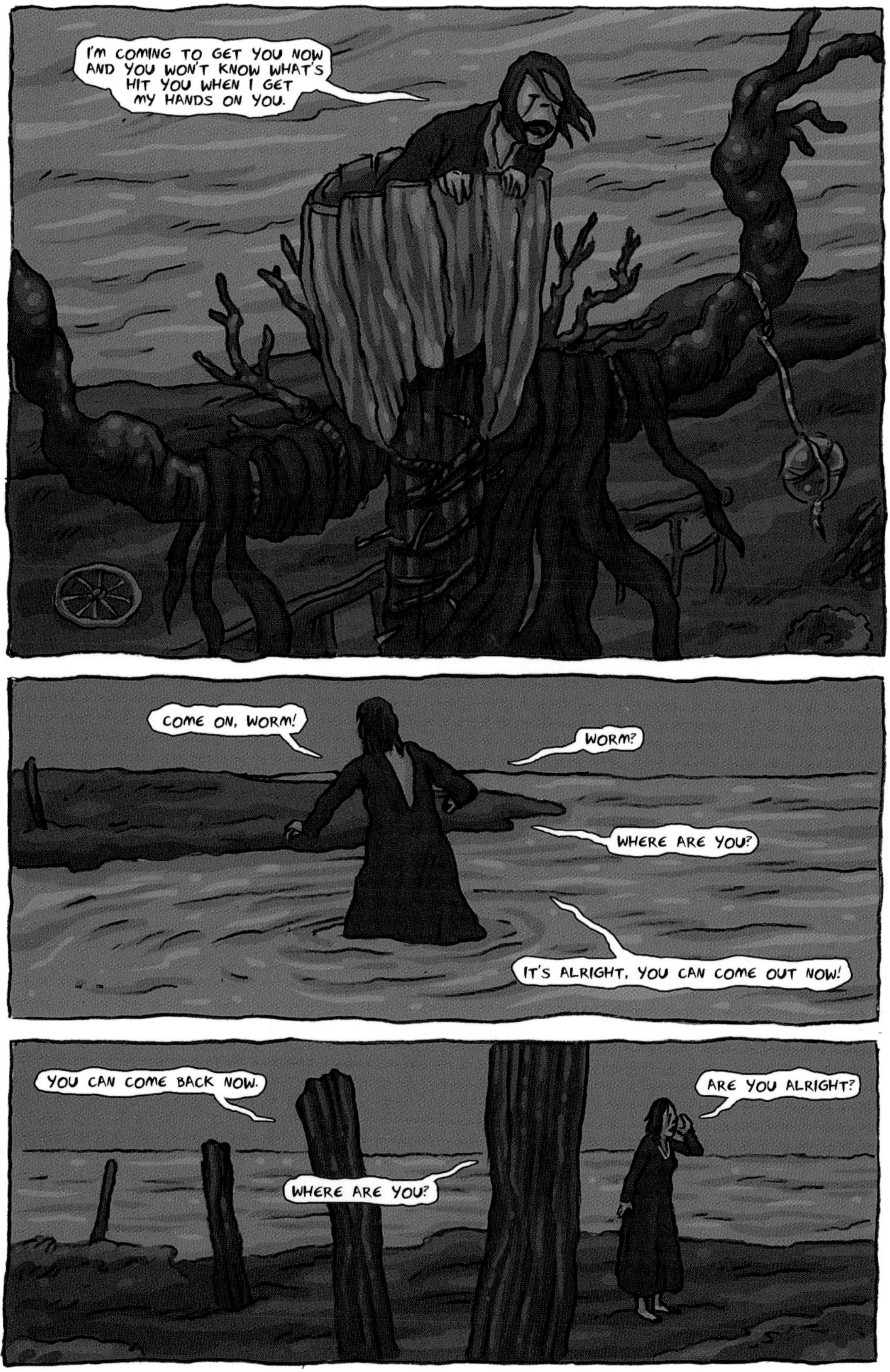
I'M COMING TO GET YOU NOW AND YOU WON'T KNOW WHAT'S HIT YOU WHEN I GET MY HANDS ON YOU.
COME ON, WORM!
WORM?
WHERE ARE YOU?
IT'S ALRIGHT, YOU CAN COME OUT NOW!
YOU CAN COME BACK NOW.
ARE YOU ALRIGHT?
WHERE ARE YOU?

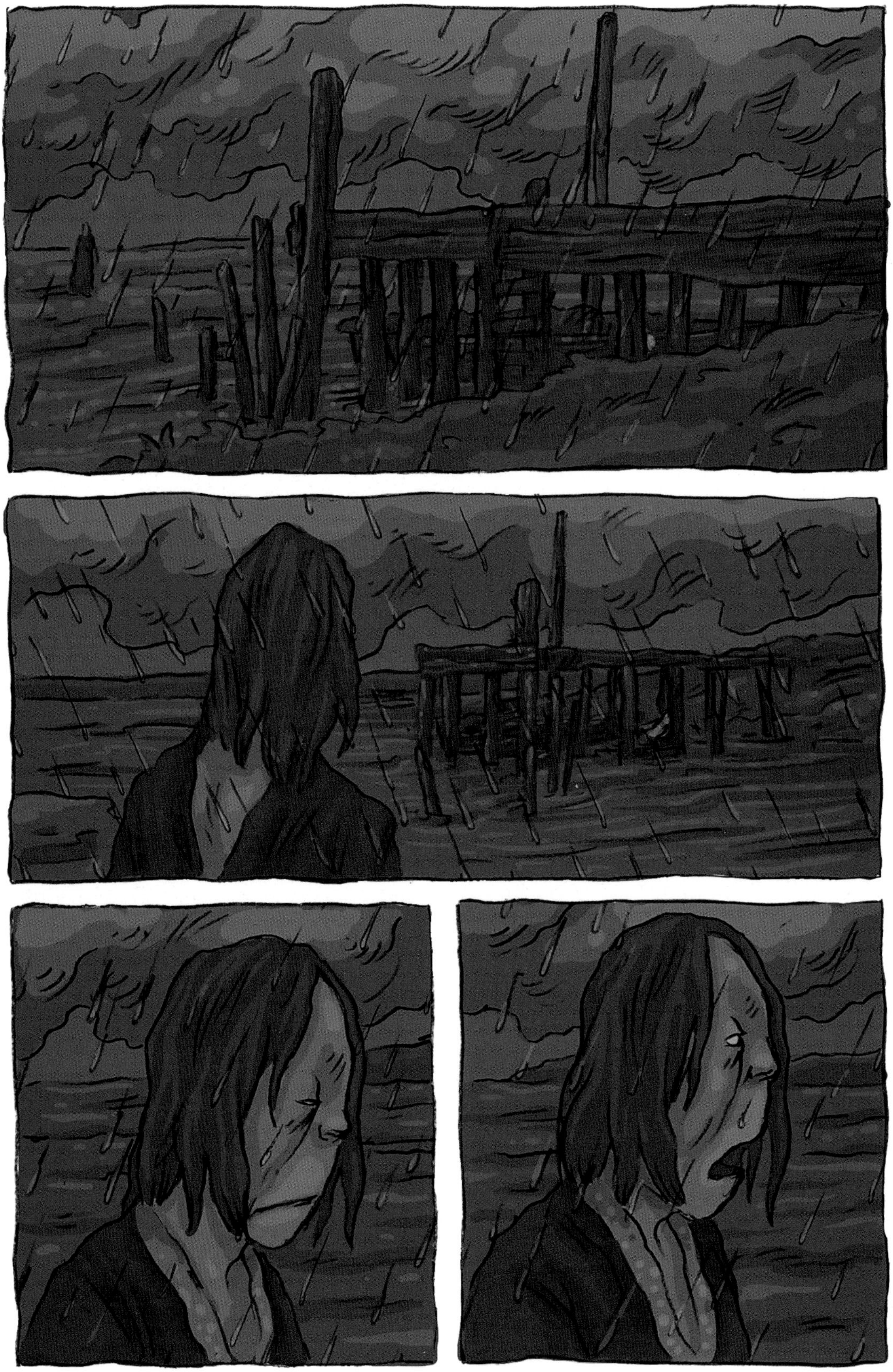

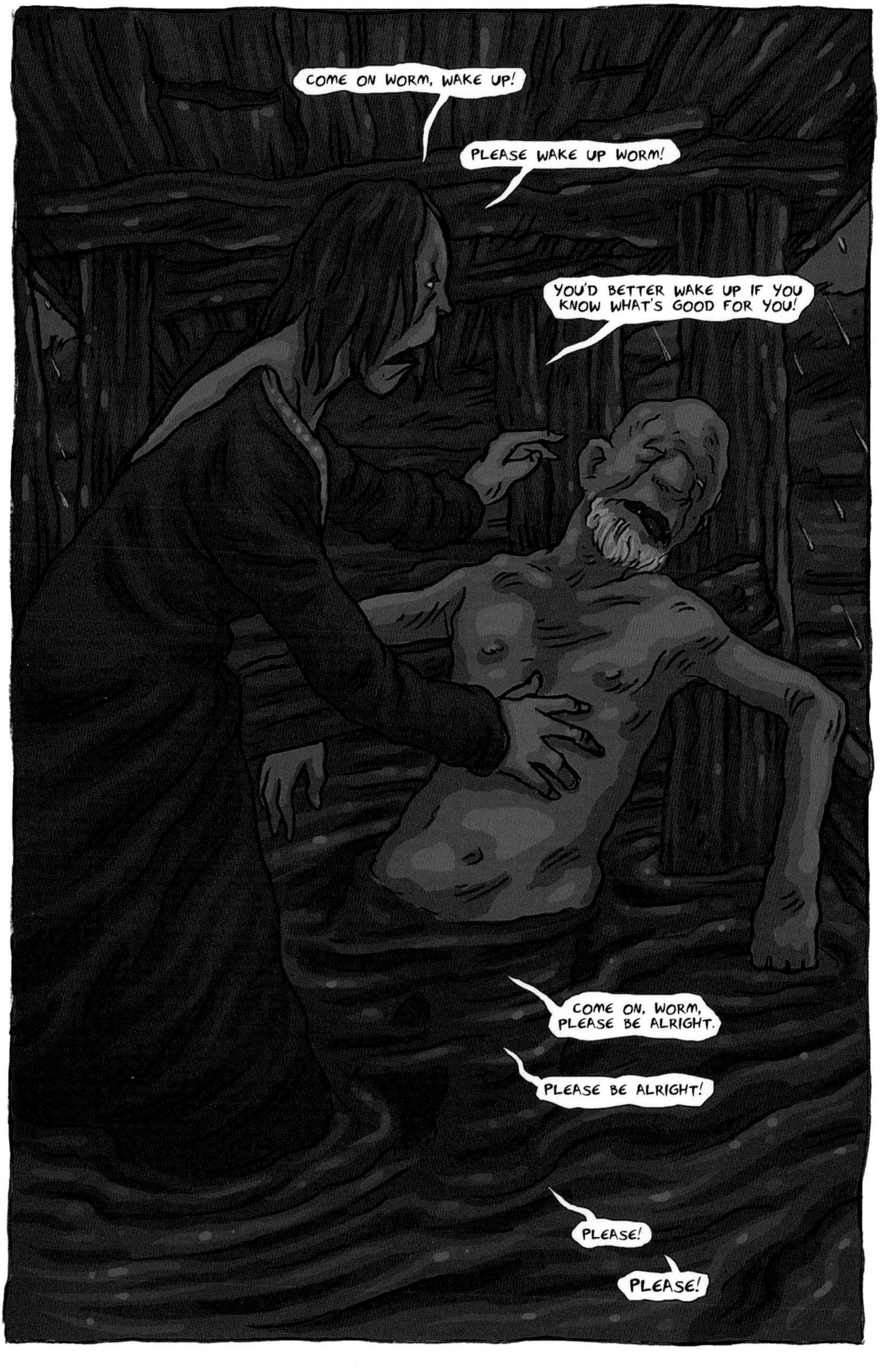
COME ON WORM, WAKE UP!
PLEASE WAKE UP WORM!
YOU'D BETTER WAKE UP IF YOU KNOW WHAT'S GOOD FOR YOU!
COME ON, WORM, PLEASE BE ALRIGHT.
PLEASE BE ALRIGHT!
PLEASE!
PLEASE!

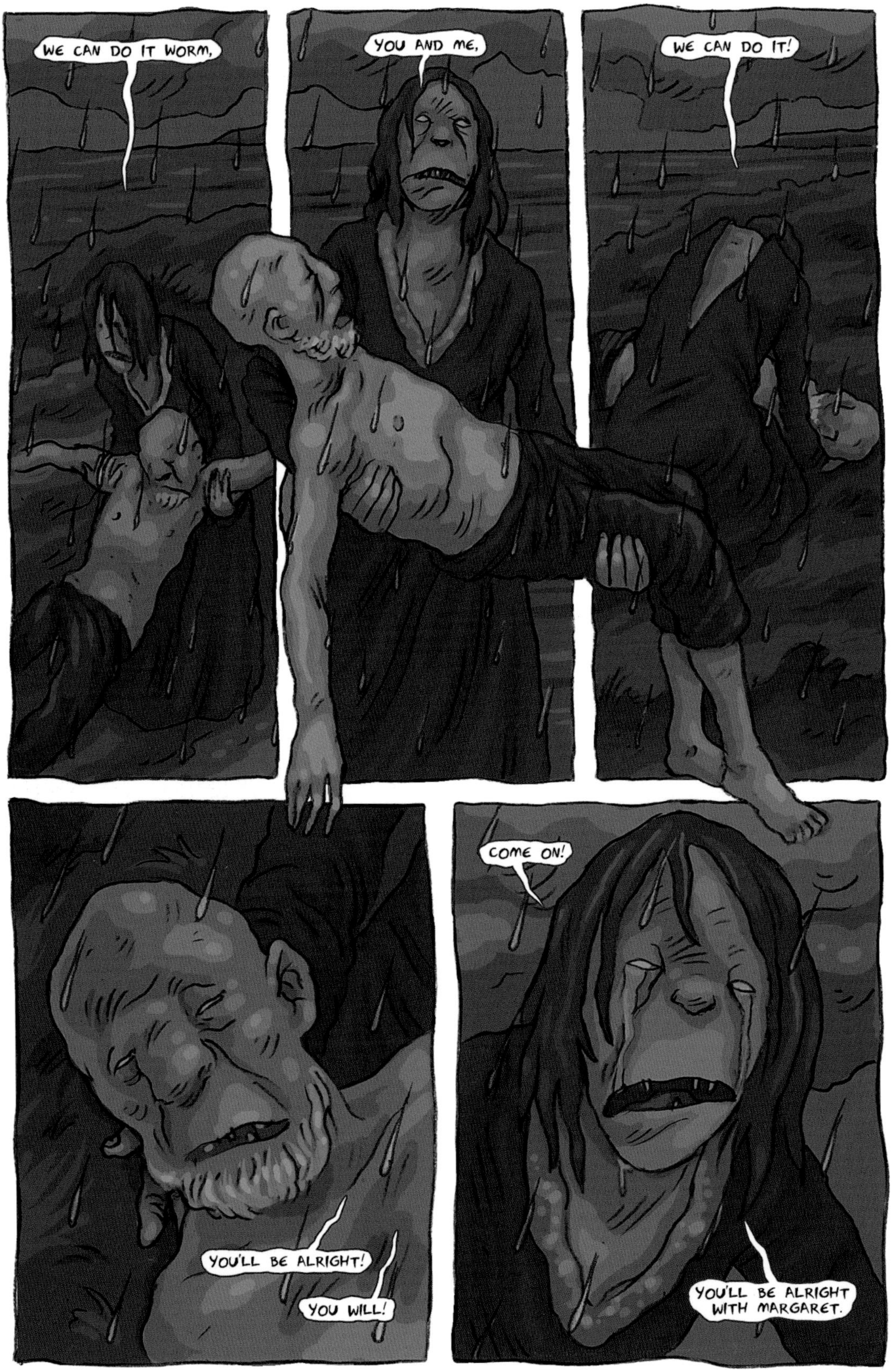
WE CAN DO IT WORM,
YOU AND ME,
WE CAN DO IT!
YOU'LL BE ALRIGHT!
YOU WILL!
COME ON!
YOU'LL BE ALRIGHT WITH MARGARET.

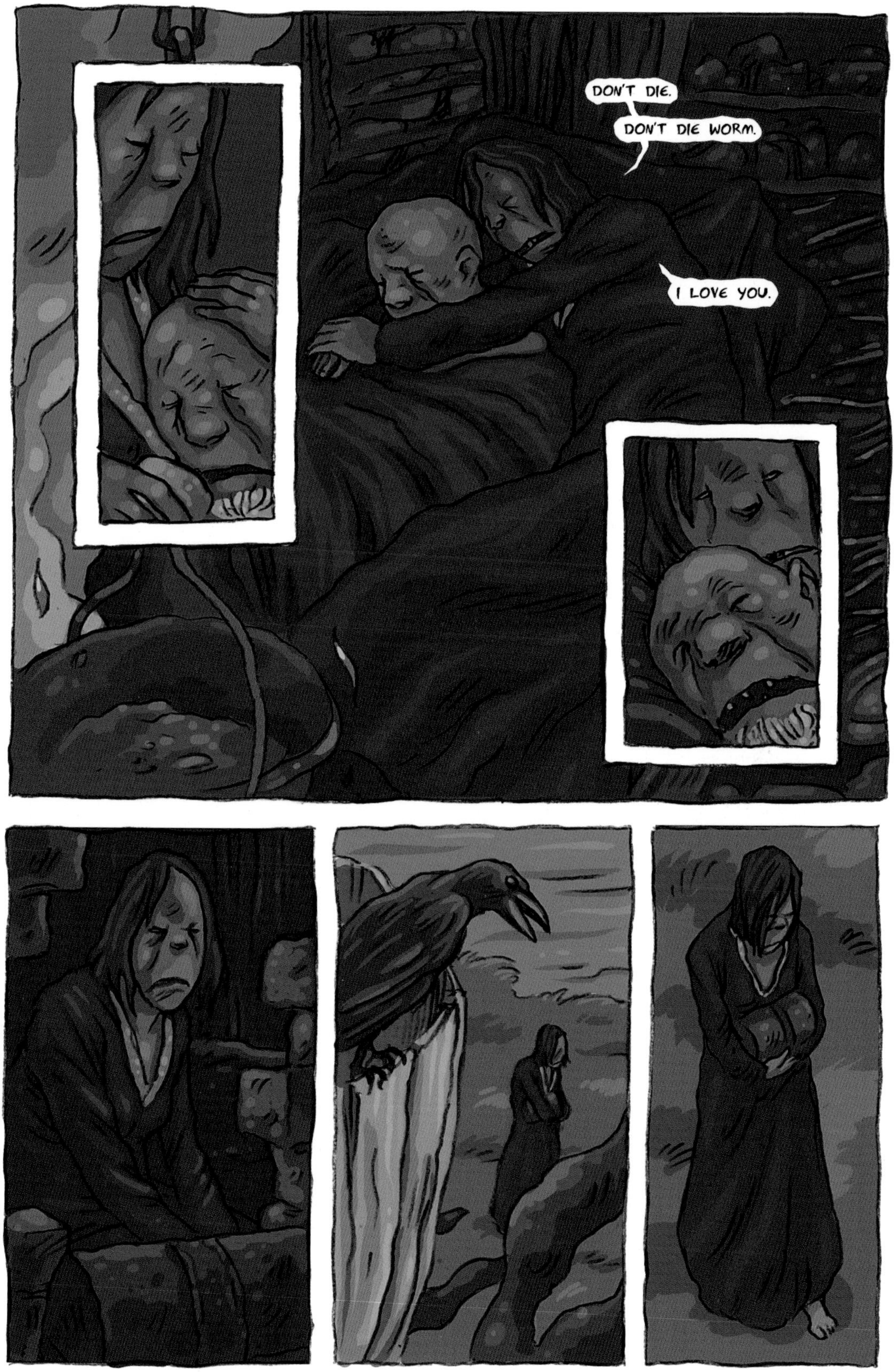
DON'T DIE.
DON'T DIE WORM.
I LOVE YOU.

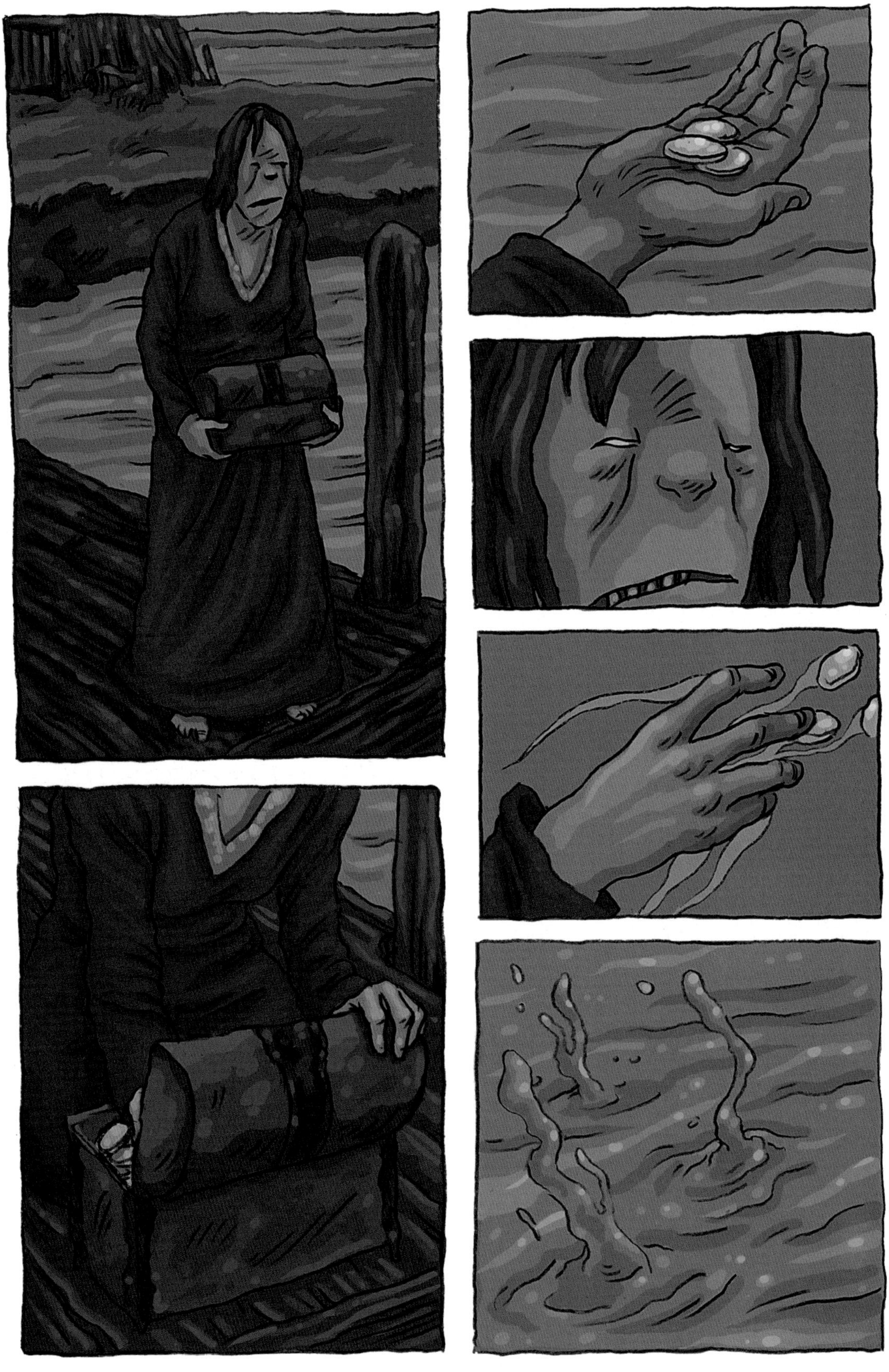

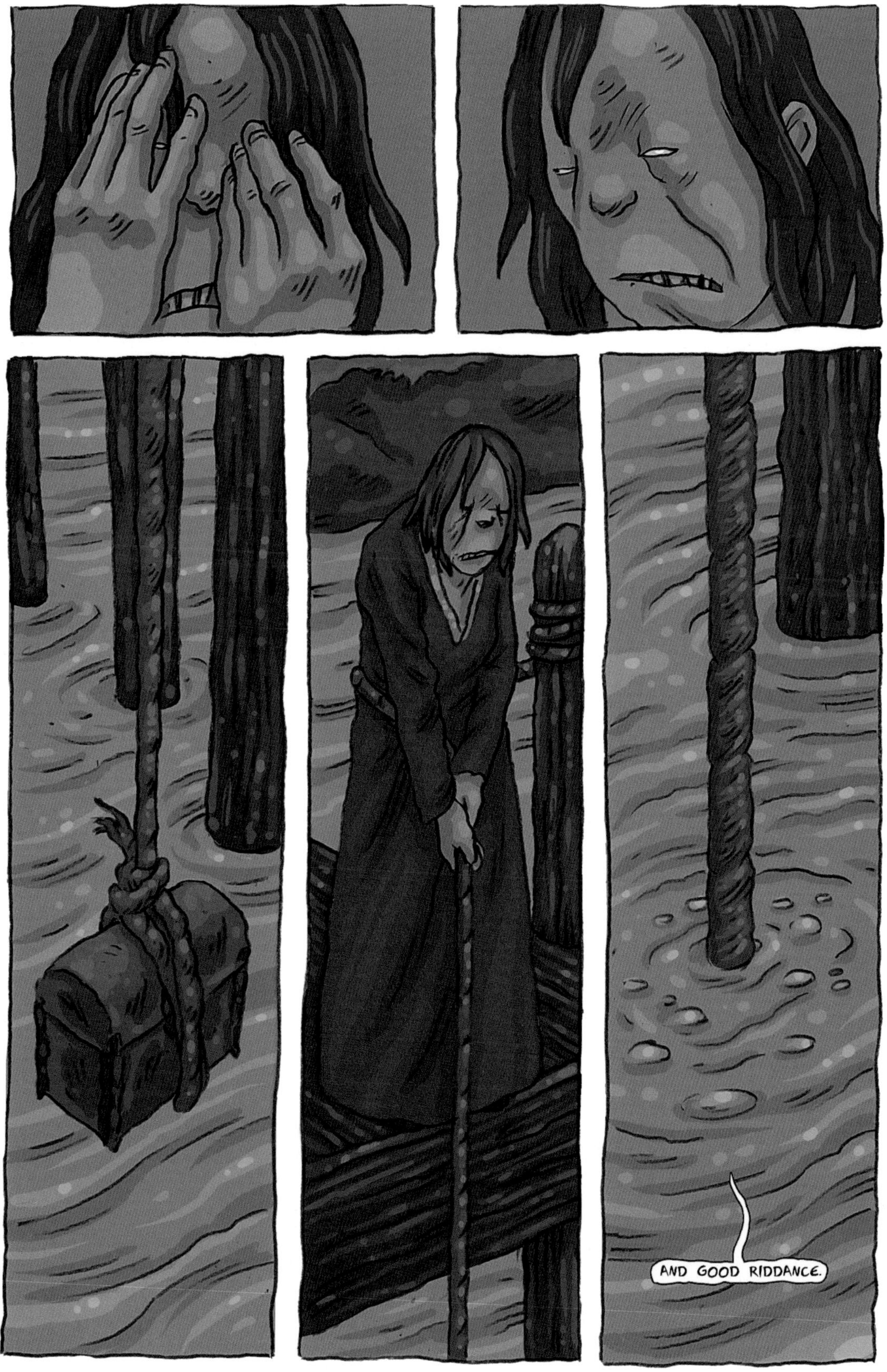
AND GOOD RIDDANCE.

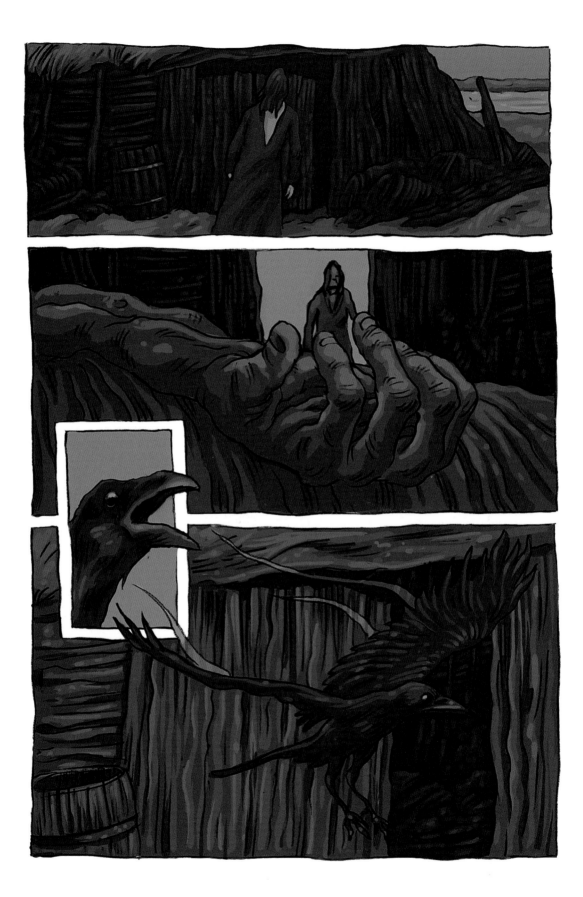

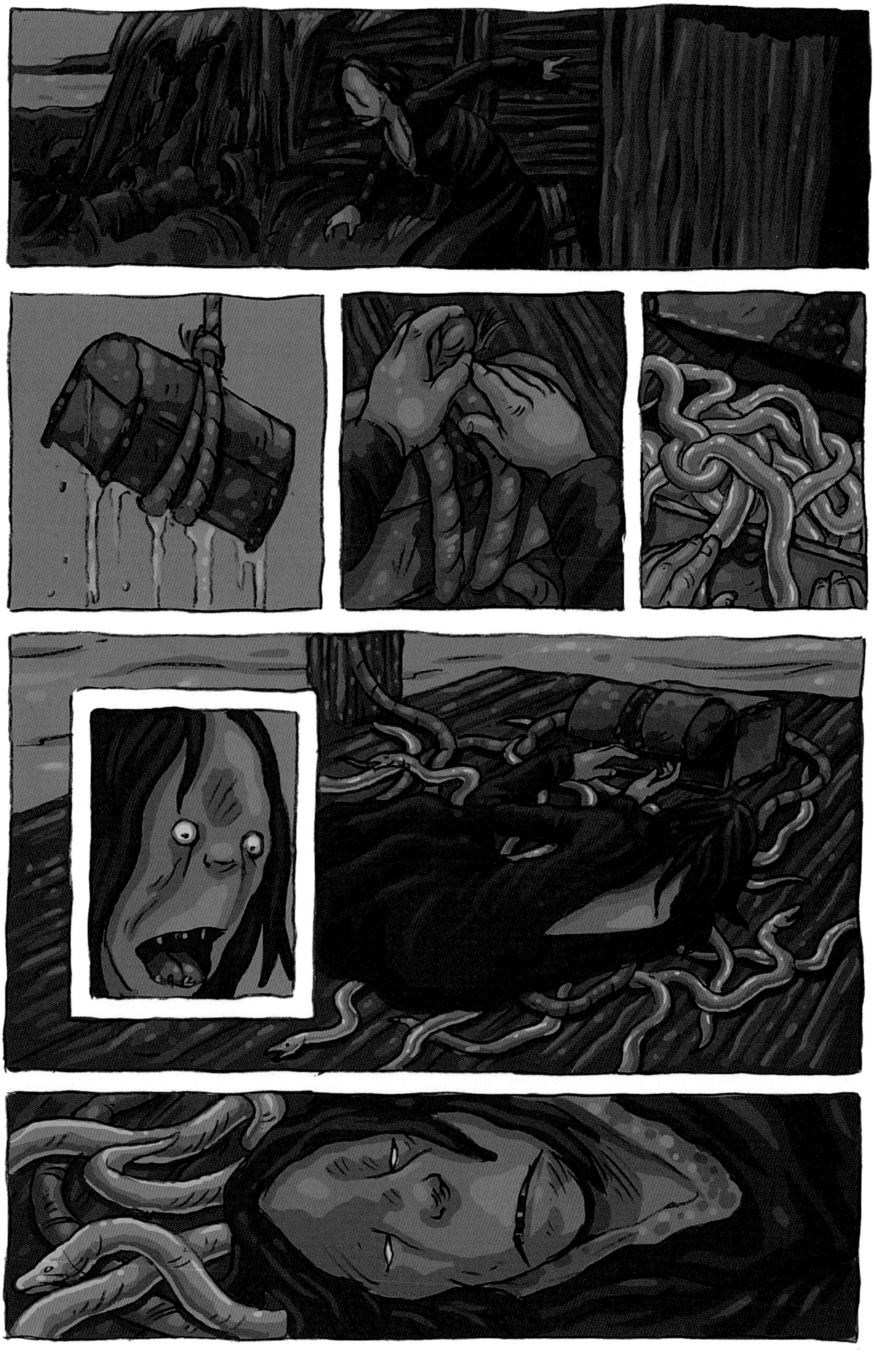

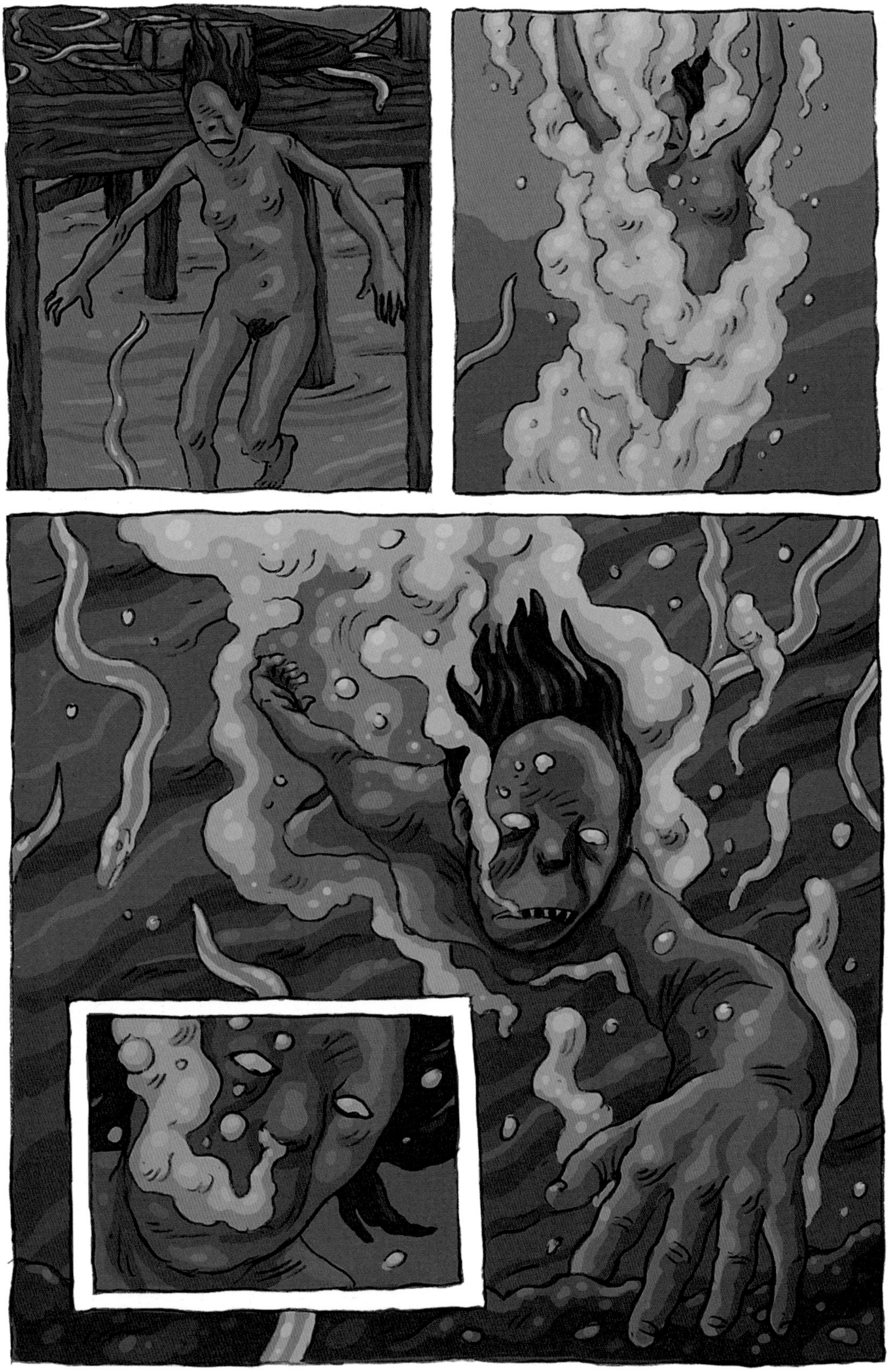

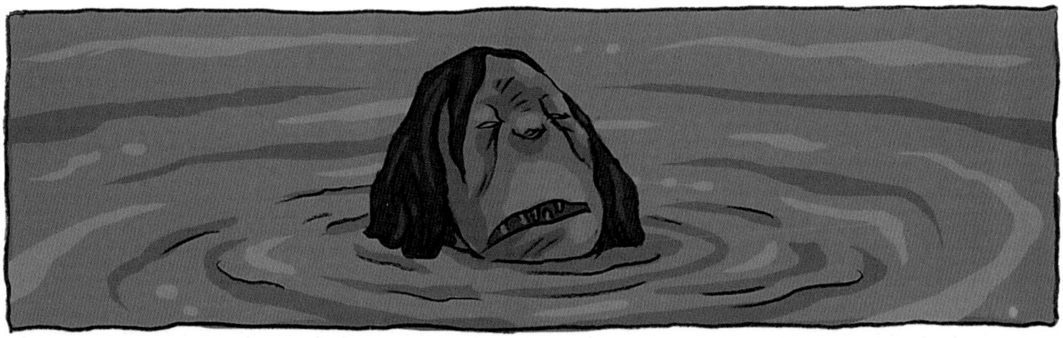

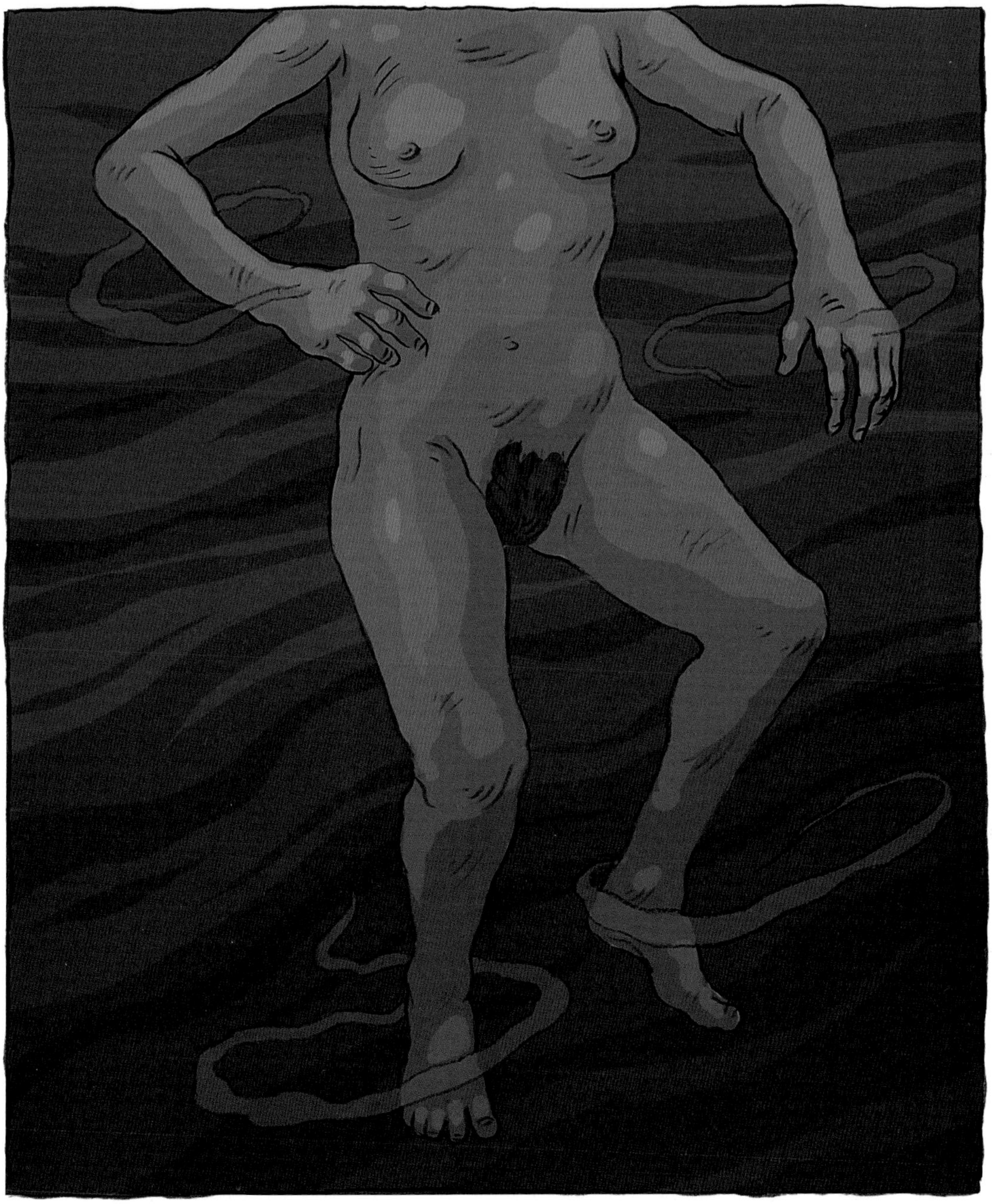

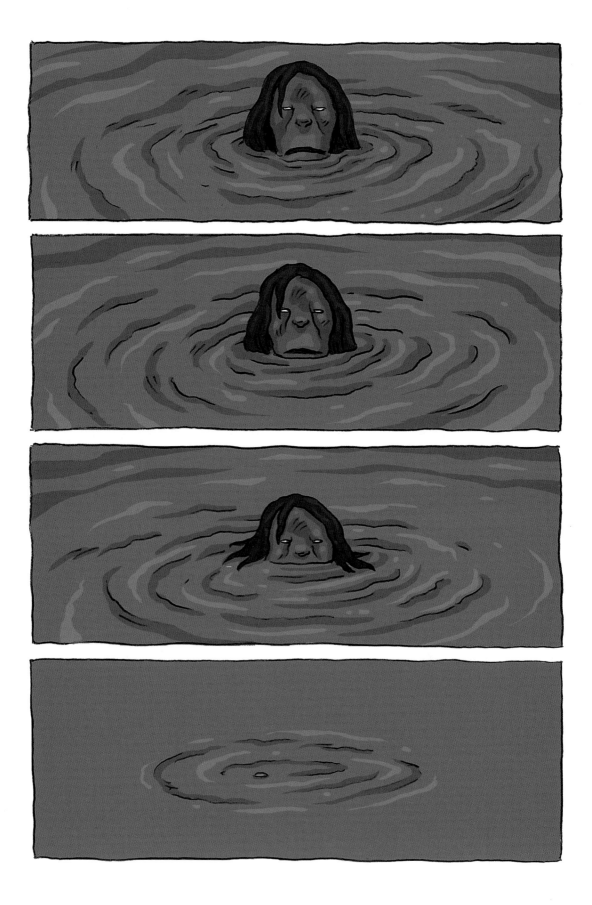